FIRE
STORM

Library of Congress Cataloging in Publication Data

Duncan, Robert Lipscomb (date)
    Fire storm.

    I. Title.
PZ4.D913Fi [PS3554.U465]   813'.5'4   78-6747
ISBN 0-688-03363-6

BOOK DESIGN   **CARL WEISS**

Printed in the United States of America.

First Edition

1 2 3 4 5 6 7 8 9 10

FIRE
STORM

Also by Robert L. Duncan

TEMPLE DOGS

DRAGONS AT THE GATE

THE DAY THE SUN FELL

Under the pseudonym of James Hall Roberts

THE FEBRUARY PLAN

THE BURNING SKY

THE Q DOCUMENT

FIRE STORM

ROBERT L. DUNCAN

WILLIAM MORROW AND COMPANY, INC.

NEW YORK   1978

Library of Congress Cataloging in Publication Data

Duncan, Robert Lipscomb (date)
    Fire storm.

    I. Title.
PZ4.D913Fi [PS3554.U465]   813'.5'4   78-6747
ISBN 0-688-03363-6

BOOK DESIGN   CARL WEISS

Printed in the United States of America.

First Edition

1   2   3   4   5   6   7   8   9   10

FIRE
STORM

PART

1

THE CALL FROM IVES MEANT TROUBLE, CORWIN WAS SURE OF that. His first thought was that the roof had finally caved in and that Ives wanted to discuss his plans for liquidating the company. As Corwin put on his jacket, he could see the symbol of Ives's failure through the office window, the partially constructed tanker on the ways, which blocked his view of the shipyard like a massive abstract sculpture. Corwin would like to have seen it finished because it had an extraordinary design, a computerized engine room, a triumph of automation in which a minimum crew would tend a gigantic machine that would run itself, beyond human decision and human error.

Human error, Corwin thought as he went down the hallway, that was what was sinking Ives, his inability to project the future with any great accuracy, the failure of the gut instinct to protect against the vagaries of a world market that demanded supertankers at a time when Ives had committed himself to the construction of small tankers, and almost perversely, a demand for small tankers when Ives had put everything he had into the Very Large Crude Carrier on the ways.

But as he opened the door to Ives's office, he could see that this was not going to be doomsday at all but instead the fighting of another peripheral skirmish. For Ives was on the telephone, a frown on his square face, and he signaled Corwin to come on in and then turned to glower out the window at the low swirling clouds. It was beginning to rain out on Tokyo Bay, sheets of water that would be engulfing the shipyard at any moment. Ives was a solid, muscular man, somewhere in his mid-fifties, Corwin supposed, and clearly out of place in the confines of an office where his physical energy could not be released.

He grunted into the telephone and slammed it down, leaning back in his chair. "Goddamn this weather," he said. "We're forty-five days behind schedule as it is and we've got a typhoon off Kyushu and the fucking Japanese welders are going to pull off the minute the rain hits. Do you know what they're demanding? They want the company to hire a full-time Shinto priest to guarantee good weather and protect them from lightning."

"Then hire one," Corwin said. "If it keeps them on the job."

"Fucking Orientals. My Japanese board of directors is always on my ass. I don't know why I got into the tanker business in the first place." He shuffled through a file of folders on the desk, drew one out, and placed it in front of Corwin. "And now there's this. Maybe you can make some sense of it. One of our captains killed a crew member."

Corwin examined the file folder. "Forsythe, William C.," he read aloud from the cover. "Captain of the *San Marin*."

"Do you know him?"

"Not personally, no. But I know his record and I know his ship. It's on the run from the Persian Gulf to Yokohama, right?"

Ives nodded. "He's been master of the *San Marin* for fifteen years. He's an old hand, one of the best."

Corwin sat down, thumbing through the file, giving it a cursory examination. "What happened?" he said. "Who did he kill?"

"His report is in the folder. Some engineer's assistant he hired out of the Persian Gulf. A Japanese national."

"What do you want from me? There will be a hearing and that should take care of the matter."

"I don't want a hearing," Ives said, thoughtfully. "I've got enough trouble with my directors as it is." He took the time to light a small cigar. "Do you know what a Japanese Maritime hearing would require in terms of time? I've scheduled the *San Marin* out of here in forty-eight hours. Talk to Forsythe. See how serious this is."

Ah, the dirty work, yes, and Corwin knew immediately why he was drawing the assignment. As president of the company, Ives was covering his ass: If Corwin approved the captain as fit and authorized his sailing and there was further trouble, Ives would not be held accountable. "I've been with the company long enough for you to level with me," Corwin said. "What do you want to come of all this?"

"I would like you to give me an in-house report full of extenuating circumstances," Ives said, with a sharp gleam in his eye. "Forsythe's account is brief, thank God, but it's vague and open to conjecture. I wouldn't be wounded if you discovered that the seaman was high on dope and threatening the safety of the *San Marin*. Something like that." A crack of thunder shook the room and the rain hit, streaming down the window. "Today goes down the drain," Ives said, peering out. "There go the welders." There was resignation in his voice. "I've alerted Forsythe that you'll be down."

Corwin put the report in his attaché case, clicked it shut. "Where's the *San Marin*?"

"Pier one seventy-six. Yokohama."

"I'll give you a call when I've talked to him."

"Do that," Ives said, but he had already picked up the telephone and in a moment began to convey a cold tone of disappointment in perfect Japanese to one of his shop stewards.

Corwin went back to his office where a secretary handed him the list of calls during his absence and then poured a cup of coffee for him, putting it on the desk before she left the room. He did not touch the coffee, instead he opened a fresh bottle of bourbon and poured himself a stiff one. The assignment facing him was going to be a tricky one. International maritime law was vague, national jurisdictions uncertain. An American captain had killed a Japanese national on a ship under Liberian registry in Malaysian waters. He would have to check to make certain, but he believed that the Japanese would claim jurisdiction here—their maritime unions were especially strong—and he would have to move around them if it became necessary.

He sipped the drink, knowing he should call Lisa and tell her he was going to be late because he had to go to Yokohama. He decided against it. Once he was through with this assignment, he would put in for vacation and take her back to the States for a month. At forty, he was still in good physical shape but he had been pushing too hard for the past year and could use the respite.

He opened the folder and sat back in his chair to read the captain's report, a little surprised to find it in the captain's handwriting, a slanting cursive, the letters shaky, as if the captain had been highly distraught when he put the words down. Corwin flipped back to the personnel file. Forsythe was only sixty-three years old, with impressive training and an exemplary record. He was a qualified pilot in a dozen major ports from Hong Kong to Tokyo, a veteran of the Second World War and naval action in the South Pacific where he had worked his way up from stoker on the black gangs in multiple boiler rooms to the master of his own ship. Under PHYSICAL CONDITION, Corwin saw the notation: "recurrent malaria." That could explain the shaky handwriting.

The report itself was brief and to the point:

On 28 July, in Dakar, an engineer's mate was signed

aboard the *San Marin* by Chief Engineer McCulloch. He was a Japanese male, twenty-seven years old, named Okata Abe.

On 17 August, with the breakdown of a condenser in the Straits of Malacca, I gave the order to anchor out of the sea-lane while repairs were effected. Strict watch standards were maintained against hazardous conditions existing in that unregulated passage.

At 2100 hours, on being informed that repairs had been completed, I proceeded into the channel, establishing a strict radar watch. At 2132, Okata ascended the ladder on the port side and came onto the bridgewing. In a belligerent manner, he informed me that he was a member of the Red Watch, a revolutionary organization, that he was taking over the *San Marin* and demanded that the course be changed to take the ship back through the Straits to a port on the east coast of Africa.

At this point, I went into the wheelhouse and returned with a pistol. I informed Okata he was under arrest. He attempted to seize the pistol, which discharged during the struggle, the bullet striking him, I believe, in the chest. He fell over the rail. I immediately threw a lighted flotation ring into the water and sounded the man overboard alarm. The body was not recovered. Search ended at 2436 hours, 17 August.

Corwin rubbed his forehead fretfully, glancing at the captain's scrawled signature. Jesus, the effrontery of the ship's masters, the gall of this particular captain to chronicle on paper an incomplete and self-serving account that could cause the company a great deal of trouble before it was finished. He rang his secretary, propped the document up in front of him.

"I am looking at Master's Report MR dash seventeen hyphen, signed William C. Forsythe. I want to know if there was any on-board investigation, if there were any de-positions taken from the crew concerning the incident. Find out if there were any Xeroxed copies circulated through the company and who has them."

"Yes, sir. Right away."

He called his assistant's office and Jordan came on the line, unhurried, relaxed. "You want to take a run down to Yokohama?" Corwin asked.

"Give me five minutes."

"I need some information first, Pete."

"Shoot."

"I want to know if there's an organization called the Japanese Red Watch."

"I can give you an affirmative on that. You want a break-down?"

"Yes. I also want to know if there's a man named Okata Abe connected with it."

"I'll check it out. How soon do you want to go to Yoko-hama?"

"Thirty minutes," he said and severed the connection.

Within fifteen minutes the secretary was in his office with the information typed on a sheet. She squinted at the paper. "First," she said, "the report was stamped in yesterday at three o'clock. It went immediately to Mr. Ives. There were no copies. Second, as far as anyone knows, there were no depositions from the crew members, no follow-up investiga-tion of any sort."

"All right," he said, "thank you."

On impulse, he put the report in his attaché case and de-cided to walk the block to Jordan's office. The rain was heavy now, great sheets of water spilling straight down with no force of wind behind them, and he unfurled his umbrella before he left the portico of the smaller building that served as executive offices and started up the walkway toward the taller concrete building sitting astride a slight rise. He was always amazed at the Japanese dock area, the cranes and gantries rising against the rainswept sky like trees in a sterile forest, the land scooped away here and filled with concrete there. A continual flow of trucks moved through the mass of buildings to dump loads of fill rock into the bay. When Corwin reached the headquarters building, he took the elevator to the third floor. Ives had insisted on erecting a new and more modern structure at dockside where he could physically overlook construction, but Corwin vastly preferred this older building that had been established by a Dutch shipping firm in the 1920s. It was shabby and the wide corridors were scabrous with multiple layers of green paint and there was always the smell of sweat and seawater here. He passed a lounge full of layover crewmen sitting around and drinking coffee and he felt a momentary envy that he was not one of them, concerned with no more than the next voyage and a repetition of duty they had done all their working lives, with nothing of consequence at stake.

Jordan was in his office, shirt-sleeved, his clothes a shambles, an easygoing man in his early forties, straw-colored hair and a perpetual good humor. He sat with his feet propped up on the desk, the telephone tucked into the angular hollow between head and shoulder. He looked up from the notes he was scribbling, said something in Japanese into the telephone, then grinned at Corwin and motioned him toward a chair. Corwin moved some papers from a wooden chair, sat down, realized that he had missed lunch and that the whiskey had dulled him. Jordan put down the telephone, made another note as if not to lose the information he had just gained. Then he lighted a pipe.

"Interesting," he said. "What's our connection with the Red Watch?"

"Then you're positive there is such an organization?"

"Oh, hell yes," Jordan said. "Absolutely the quintessence of the superkooks, the new terrorists." According to the

Tokyo Metropolitan Police, he went on, the Red Watch had a membership of close to a thousand, most of them in the Tokyo–Yokohama Metroplex and they were erratic and highly volatile young men. Six of them were currently in a Mexico City prison for an attempt on the life of the Mexican president that had failed only when their car, wired with explosives, broke down before it could ram into the presidential limousine.

Okata Abe was titular head of the Red Watch, a man of thirty who had made a fortune in the Japanese movies as an actor and had used both his charisma and his money to put together a following of supermilitants. Second-in-command was Okata's older brother who had taken the name of Hiroshige after the Japanese artist of the nineteenth century. "Okata's currently in Dakar where he went to blow up some oil refineries," Jordan said. "That's what my sources tell me. He's still there as far as anyone knows."

"No," Corwin said, shaking his head. "He's at the bottom of the Malacca Straits." He went on to tell Jordan of the captain's report. There was a bemused expression on Jordan's face as he listened as if he heard but could not quite believe.

"Well," Jordan said, "the captain's story stinks. Either he's lying or it's not the same Okata."

"How?"

"Okata Abe is a grandstanding bastard. He once sliced his own stomach with a razor in front of his group and then stood there exhorting his men with his guts exposed until he passed out." He relighted his pipe. "No, if Okata decided to hijack a tanker, he would have put half a dozen men on board, blown up the resistance, and cut off the captain's head with a sword."

"Suppose it was the same Okata who died on the *San Marin*. What could we expect from the Japanese?"

"A couple of reactions," Jordan said. "Officially, the Japanese government would be pleased because militant organizations such as the Red Watch are a pain in the ass to them, an embarrassment, but they won't express that publicly. They would have to pretend impartiality and hold a hearing before an official board, which would be a long and drawn-out affair, three months at the very least, while evidence was taken from the crew. In the end, of course, the captain would be acquitted because Okata was a notorious nuisance. But that's only the government reaction."

"And the other?"

"The Red Watch would have to react," Jordan said. "Their pride would demand that. If the San Marin were still in port, they'd have to blow it up. If not, any of our ships would be fair game."

Corwin glanced at his watch, time ticking away and the afternoon half gone. Another five hours minimum stretched ahead of him. Lisa was waiting in the apartment. That confrontation was still in front of him and he knew he was deliberately delaying it. "Shit," Corwin said. "Get the car and a Japanese driver. We're going to have to come up with something pretty damn fast."

He picked up the telephone, knowing he could delay it no longer. As he heard it ring on the other end, he began to believe that Lisa had gone out, but as he was about to hang up, she answered.

"It's me," he said.

"All right."

"I have to go to Yokohama. I won't be back until nine o'clock."

"That's par for the course, isn't it?" she said. "No sarcasm, darling, just a statement of fact."

"Will you be there when I get back?"

"Certainly," she said. "We need to talk. You do agree about that, don't you?"

"Yes," he said. "We do need to talk."

2

The rain was still falling when the company car reached Yokohama, and as they approached the docks, the Japanese driver sounded his horn and a uniformed guard emerged from a heavy door, wearing sidearms. He peered into the rear window of the car, examining Jordan and Corwin, and then nodded back toward a small window in the building, screened with mesh. The electrically controlled gate swung open and then closed again the moment the car was through. The driver parked beneath a portico at the dock superintendent's office and Corwin went inside, Jordan following.

The dock superintendent was a large Japanese named Watanabe who spoke perfect English and was so thoroughly Americanized that Corwin could not picture him leading a traditional Japanese life in a small apartment in Yokohama, sitting on a reed floor and eating rice. He shook Corwin's hand, then turned to answer a Japanese query on the base radio. "I'm glad to see you boys," he said when he was through. "The gloom around here is so thick you could cut it with a knife. What's going on?"

"A tempest in a teapot," Corwin said. "How many of the *San Marin*'s crew are still on board?"

"None," Watanabe said. "Except the captain. We have skeleton replacement. You going to relieve him of command?"

"I don't know. What are you loading?"

"High-octane aviation fuel. For Kobe."

"Departure?"

"Eleven-forty-three tomorrow, if the weather holds and the typhoon decides to veer off. Personally, I think she'll be lucky to get off in forty-eight hours."

Corwin turned to Jordan. "That doesn't give us much time. I want you to get a crew list and a steno. You'll probably have to hit all the bars in Yokohama, but track down the men you can and get whatever kind of statements you can. Call me when you get something."

"Will do," Jordan said.

Corwin looked through the window at the massive hull of the *San Marin* at a far dock, partially obscured by a giant cylindrical storage tank and the shroud of rain. "Get on the horn and let Forsythe know I'm coming aboard, officially."

"One more thing. His daughter's on board with him." Watanabe's face was curious but he did not press it.

Insanity, Corwin thought, as he walked across the concrete dock area, the rain drumming against the umbrella. Jordan had been entirely too sanguine about his estimate of the official government reaction to this incident. Japanese politics were currently unstable, the Diet itself a nest of feuds, and some political faction was bound to pick up this shooting and make a national incident out of it.

The *San Marin* loomed like a cliff in the rain, the Plimsoll line high above the edge of the dock, demonstrating that the loading had just begun, the pumps beating through the sound of the rain, the giant black pressure hoses trailing like snakes from the starboard side of the ship down to the recessed complex of lines lying along the dockway. A spume of water gushed from the engine room vents, the seawater that cooled the condensers, and he could see the radar crossarms revolving, the big scanner on top, the short range beneath.

He had always felt a special fondness for the *San Marin*, an affection that he could not explain. She was a great lumbering vessel almost six hundred feet long, fat in the beam, built more for utility than beauty, designed to carry in excess of two hundred thousand barrels of product, her superstructures bluff and square, her single stack only slightly raked, as if at the last minute her designer had decided to give her a touch of grace. Perhaps his admiration for her came from the fact that he knew her history and the number of times she had almost been lost to the sea, grounded at Narragansett, adrift and dead in heavy seas in the Indian Ocean, severely fractured by a massive storm in the North Atlantic, patched up, rewelded, tanks converted to carry light. She had endured, survived. He liked that.

From the look of the ship as Corwin climbed the steep cleated gangway, he could gauge something of the character of the man who commanded her, for in the glare of the work lights on the rain-splattered deck, he could not see the scaly patches of steel covered with preservative, the grays and reddish browns, no, the deck had been freshly painted, stark black, and the valves and fitting beneath the catwalk white. The immaculate condition of the ship was undoubtedly a projection of Forsythe himself.

He climbed to the catwalk and went forward to the bridge section, expecting to find the captain in his quarters, but instead he was stopped by a Japanese mess steward in a white coat who directed him to the deserted lounge room, properly decorated with teak paneling and comfortable chairs.

"A drink, sir?" the steward said. Corwin asked for bourbon and water and when it was served stood studying a map of the world that covered half a wall, multicolored lines connecting most of the major ports of the world, so solidly interlaced they formed a dense web.

"It's one of my affectations," a voice said behind him and he turned to see Captain Forsythe coming into the room, fully uniformed. Corwin was shocked by the stark frailty of the man. He was a tall, gaunt man with a grayish pallor to his face, hollowed dull eyes, and a deceptive openness that was really not open at all but rather the captain's way of dealing with a remoteness that could never be bridged. He looked at the map instead of Corwin. "The *San Marin* has logged over a million miles," he said. "I bring new officers here to im-

press them with a very solid history and to remind them
that they will leave this ship as sound as when they came
aboard." He turned to take a glass the steward offered him,
tasting it thoughtfully, nodding his approval before the
steward disappeared. "But I realize you aren't interested
either in the ship's history or my approach to discipline."

"We have a problem," Corwin said, sitting down in a
leather chair. "I'm interested in solutions."

Forsythe smiled thinly. "You will have my complete cooperation." He sat down across from him. "It's the Okata
business, I suppose."

"That's correct," Corwin said. He removed the Master's
Report from his attaché case. "I'll be frank with you, Captain. This is a poor report, incomplete. If a maritime court
got hold of this, they would not only certify you as incom-
petent, they would make mincemeat out of you. You don't
have any accompanying documents, no depositions from
your officers."

There was a slight tremor in Forsythe's fingers on the
glass, an almost imperceptible vagueness to his eyes. "It's
not a good report, I'll admit that," he said. "Frankly, Mr.
Corwin, I don't expect the matter to go as far as a hearing.
A man threatened the safety of my ship and I dealt with
him. That was what I was trying to convey in the report,
nothing more."

"In the old days that might have worked," Corwin said,
unrelenting. "But not anymore. You killed a Japanese and
it turns out that he wasn't an itinerant seaman looking for
a berth but an important political personality. There's no
way his death is going to go unnoticed. Now, even if we
decided to sit on this report, your crew will talk about it.
The word may already be out. So we're going to have to
come up with a better account. We'll begin at the beginning
and go through the whole thing." He checked the report.

"McCulloch signed him on. Were you informed?"

"I may have been informed as a matter of routine. I don't even think I saw the man before our run-in, but we were having trouble with a pump and I can't swear to that. I can't see that it makes any difference."

"I want to deal with Okata's final demands, his assertion that he intended to take over the ship. Who can corroborate that?"

"We were alone, on the port bridgewing."

"Who was at the conn?"

"I would have to check the log. The first officer, I would think. Adams."

"But you're not sure."

"Reasonably so. Yes, I remember. Adams was in the bridge house."

"But he did not see Okata talking to you?"

"No. He had his hands full. He was monitoring radar. We were in a precarious position, Mr. Corwin. Too, it was dark."

"And Okata approached you and said what?"

"That he was taking over the ship."

"What was his manner?"

"What do you suppose it would be?" Forsythe said. "Aggressive, belligerent."

"And he was armed?"

"I assumed so."

"Did he threaten you with a weapon? Did he tell you he would shoot you if you didn't cooperate?"

"He implied as much."

"But he didn't use the words, 'I will shoot you' or anything similar."

"He could have. I don't remember."

"Then it's possible he wasn't armed at all."

"I assumed he was armed. I stand by that statement."

Corwin shook his head. "He allowed you time to go into

the wheelhouse and get a pistol. If he was armed, he would have made some attempt to stop you."

Forsythe said nothing, concentrating on the drink. He shrugged slightly.

"And this presumably armed radical, risking his life to try to commandeer your ship, allowed you the freedom to go into the wheelhouse where you could either summon help or arm yourself, and yet he made no effort either to follow you or to stop you. Do you still hold to that?"

"As I say, it's a poor report."

"Then amend it," Corwin said, flatly. "Jesus Christ, Captain, I'm not here to prosecute you. I'm here to help you clarify this thing."

Forsythe pursed his lips. "I have been with the *San Marin* for fifteen years, Mr. Corwin." He shrugged slightly, grimacing as if his thoughts were not pleasant. "I'm not used to having my judgment questioned nor my word. But I can see that the report is not logical. Nevertheless, to the best of my recollection, that was the way it happened. I was under the influence of medication at the time. So I can amend only by simplifying. Okata did come onto the bridgewing and make his demands. I did come into possession of the pistol. There was a struggle and he was shot and fell overboard."

Corwin decided to take another tack. "When you went into the wheelhouse, did you say anything to Adams? Did you tell him what was happening?"

"He was behind the radar, on the other side of the bridge. I may have spoken to him, I don't know."

"He did come out onto the bridgewing when he heard the shot."

"Yes."

"Then he can confirm that much."

"If you can find him," Forsythe said. "He left the ship when we arrived. He has his master's papers now and I think he received a command of his own, somewhere in the Middle East, I believe. You could probably get a forwarding address through personnel."

"Your log entry contains an account of the shooting, correct?"

"Only of the man overboard. The name, the time, rescue attempts." Vague, yes, the captain's voice was trailing off and he was turning the glass in his hands, absently, no great force behind his words.

"No mention of his demands or the shooting?"

"He was a radical," Forsythe said. "A son of a bitch who was jeopardizing my ship. I would not have shot him if he had not forced me to, but I have no regrets." He finished the drink, placed the empty glass on the table. "I don't like any of this, but that goes without saying. Now, if you decide to take this to a hearing, I'll tell them the same thing I told you."

Corwin stood up, tired. The trip to Yokohama had not been fruitless after all and Ives had been right not to involve the legal department in this, the batteries of lawyers who would eventually discover what he now felt to be true, that the old man indeed could supply no more information than he had given in the report. If there was no supporting evidence from the crew to characterize Okata as either a menace or a potential threat, the killing would be interpreted as the irrational act of a sincere man whose judgment had been severely impaired by medication.

Corwin closed the attaché case, the lock clicking shut with a note of finality. "Frankly, Captain, what you did has put the company in a hell of a predicament and I haven't the slightest idea how it's going to be resolved. I'll get back to you as soon as possible."

Forsythe stood up with some effort, as if he were fatigued. His eyes were watery. He extended his hand and Corwin found the fingers bony, the flesh cold. "I would invite you to stay for dinner but the galley is on a standby basis."

As Corwin left the salon, he raised his umbrella against the rain. The sky had darkened; he was startled to find it as late as it was. As he moved down the gangway he was aware of the woman standing next to it, bareheaded, dark hair plastered across her forehead, the whitest skin he had ever seen, a lean angular woman in jeans, late twenties perhaps, dripping wet. Under the right circumstances, she would be considered beautiful, with that wide dramatic mouth of hers, but at the moment she was belligerent and obviously chilled.

"I'm Faye Forsythe, Mr. Corwin," she said, flatly.

The daughter, yes, there was a certain resemblance in the high cheekbones, the rather piercing blue eyes. "What can I do for you?"

"I need to talk to you."

"If it's about your father, I don't see much point to it."

"I think there is. There's a bar outside the gate. I only want five minutes of your time."

"All right. Take the umbrella. You look drowned."

She shook her head, dismissing the offer and he followed her across the dock to the office, very much aware of the time, wondering if Lisa would still be there by the time he made it back to Tokyo. He saw the car waiting for him at the rear of the office, the live coal of the driver's cigarette glaring through the windshield. He paused long enough to tell Watanabe to send the car in fifteen minutes and then followed Forsythe's daughter through the gate.

The woman evidently knew the waterfront. She turned down a lane past a warehouse, then walked up an alley and there was the bar, no more than a hole in the wall with light spilling through a small window onto the pavement. Inside was a collection of tables and two semienclosed booths at the back. Sailors, a few dock workers, all Japanese, and he slid into the booth and propped the folded umbrella against the seat, lighting the candle on the table himself, tired, wanting nothing more than to have this over with and to be on his way.

Faye sat down across from him, brushing the wet hair from her face, fumbling for a cigarette, leaning forward to light it from the candle, her eyes never moving from Corwin's face.

"What kind of trouble is he in?" she said.

"I can't tell you that."

"I know all about the man he shot," she said impatiently, leaning back against the booth. "My God, I'm tired. I was at your office in Tokyo earlier. They said you were in conference."

"I'm afraid I'm going to have to hold you to the five minutes," he said. He looked up to the waitress, ordered a bourbon.

"What will you have?"

"Anything will do," she said. "Bourbon's fine."

She waited until the drinks were served. "What are you going to do to him?"

"I'm not going to do anything to him," he said. "If you're asking me what's going to happen, I don't know."

She fished in her purse, awkwardly, and placed a small pistol on the table. He sipped his drink, said nothing. "I was prepared to shoot somebody this afternoon if I could see that it would help my father in any way."

"It wouldn't have," he said, evenly. "I suggest you put the pistol back in your purse. The Japanese have very strict gun laws."

"It isn't loaded now," she said. She stared at it as if it were foreign to her. Finally she replaced it in her purse. "I'm twenty-eight years old," she said, almost absently. "I intend to protect my father and I don't have a damn thing to bargain with. You have no idea how frustrating that is. I don't think I could have shot anybody. I thought about sex, but that's too available here."

Now, for the first time he was in touch with the desperation beyond her anger. "How long have you been over here?" he said.

"Two months. I was supposed to get together with him before his last run."

"Two months?" he said. "Where have you been living? How have you been living?"

"I've enjoyed it actually," she said, momentarily distracted. "I got a job with the English edition of a Japanese newspaper as a copy editor." She removed a handkerchief from her purse and began to blot the water from her face. "How much do you know about my father?"

"I met him for the first time just now."

"What do you do for the company?"

"On paper I'm a VP," he said. "In reality, I'm a troubleshooter for Ives. There's always enough going wrong in this business to keep me occupied."

"So my father has become your problem."

"In a way, yes."

"And you conclude that he's another old-line quixotic ship's master who's exceeded his authority."

"Not exactly."

"That's what he wants you to think," she said. "I spent the day with him today." She tasted the drink, grimaced slightly. "Are you married?"

"No."

"Tell me, are you always bound by the book if there are extenuating circumstances?"

"Your father has put the company in a difficult position. It's my job to get the company out. That's all I'm doing. The book doesn't give me any easy answers."

"You won't get any answers from him," she said. "He really doesn't know what happened." She traced a pattern in the moisture on the tabletop with the tip of her index finger. "He's served your company for a hell of a long time and so you are going to give him a break now. You're going to let him make his final run to prove to everybody concerned that you have faith in him and then he's going back to the States and retire."

"I would like to do that," Corwin said. "But it isn't that simple."

"I think it is," she said, looking directly at him. "Otherwise it will come out that one of your line captains has been so heavily doped up over the last two months that he's been totally irresponsible and that your company has been derelict in its duty by not running routine medical inspections and allowing something like that to happen. I believe he acted in defense of his ship, but in any hearing, what he did will be interpreted as manslaughter. So it will cost your company a hell of a lot before it's done, if you let it go that far."

"You're saying that he's been heavily sedated for the last two months?" Corwin said. "Does he have a habit?"

"You can put it that way if you like," she said with a humorless smile. "He has one hell of a habit, Mr. Corwin. He takes morphine as casually as most people take aspirin, but only when the pain's too much for him." She paused, the smile gone. She wiped out the pattern on the table with the edge of her hand. "He doesn't have malaria. He's dying, that's the simple truth of it. He has a terminal goddamn cancer and within a month, at the most, I will be burying him. So I am going to see that he has some dignity to his last weeks, Mr. Corwin, and that's the way it is."

3

In his years with the company, he had trained himself to rest whenever he had the opportunity and now, during the ride back to Tokyo, he dozed fitfully, his mind never fully relaxed, vaguely haunted by Forsythe's impending death, not only from the complications it could bring to the investigation but on a deeper and more personal level as well. He had seen many dying men over the years, victims of maritime accidents, burned men, maimed men, bandaged and sedated, lying on hospital beds in a dozen different countries, and he had talked to them, gathered information about the disasters that had engulfed them. To a man, as long as there had been the faintest flicker of coherence about them there had been hope that as the terror that had befallen them had come from the outside, so the forces of medical staffs and modern technology could save them.

But it was not so with Forsythe, for he had been betrayed from within by some single aberrant cell that had run wild and there was no hope at all in those dull eyes, only a glazed numbness and a drug-induced freedom from pain. And in his state of semiwakefulness, Corwin was reminded of his own mortality and only through an exertion of will was he able to separate himself from what was happening to the captain and so maintain his objectivity about the matter.

By the time the car reached the hotel, the rain had stopped and he said good-night to the driver and went into the lobby, pausing briefly at the desk to pick up the messages he knew would be there, the omnipresent call from Ives, the three calls from Jordan, all requesting a return call. It was already ten o'clock and there was enough urgency in these calls to carry him another four hours minimum before he got to bed.

And paramount now was Lisa who might or might not be waiting in the apartment on the fourth floor, who might or might not be willing to talk. They had been living together for the past six months, but in the last couple of weeks the relationship had gone to hell, with Lisa moody and noncommunicative most of the time. He took the elevator up to the fourth floor, let himself in through the handsomely carved door into the long living room with the white carpet, the marble tables Lisa had ordered for the suite, shopping for the low divans herself. There was a marvelous sensuality in everything she touched.

He could hear the shower running, the stereo playing in the bedroom. He put his attaché case on one end of the wet bar, poured himself a cup of coffee, and when the telephone rang answered it on the first ring.

"Trouble," Ives said.

"When isn't there trouble?" Corwin said.

"This is particularly large scale," Ives went on. "It seems that a positive identification has been made of a badly decomposed body found floating in the Malaccan Straits, dredged up by a Japanese freighter and carried to the medical officials in Singapore. The remains have been kept refrigerated by the coroner's office only because the dental work contained large amounts of gold, a certain sign the deceased was someone of affluence and therefore important enough to warrant investigation. Okata's men have also come into possession of information that Okata boarded a tanker in Dakar and they have a flag description and stack markings that identified the tanker as one of ours."

"You're right, trouble on a large scale."

"The bastards move very quickly," Ives said in a flat voice. "They made an inquiry here and I had our PR inform them that we know nothing about it but that we would certainly check. I would think we might want to take this to a hearing after all."

"I don't think so," Corwin said. He told Ives of the meeting with the daughter, the captain's condition.

"Then I would say that the Okata plaintiffs would have grounds for a civil suit," Ives said. "If that's the case, I had better get legal on this right away."

"No," Corwin said. "Hold off until I hear from Jordan. I think we may have some possibilities."

"I would consider you a fucking miracle worker," Ives said.

"Okay, we'll sit on this until morning. I'll be sleeping here tonight, so if you get any hard information, call me."

Corwin put the telephone back on the cradle. The noise from the shower had stopped and Lisa came out of the bedroom, a towel around her shoulders. An incredibly beautiful woman, skin glistening with drops of water, her long blonde hair pinned atop her head to keep it dry. "I'm glad you're back," she said, unsmiling. "Has it stopped raining?"

"For the time being."

She proceeded to dry herself with great attention to her breasts and thighs, perfectly at home in her nakedness, in this white immaculate room she had created for herself. She was a soft and well-contoured woman, a living Renoir. She loosed her hair and let it fall around her shoulders, then she put on a white silk robe that seemed to drift around her. "I take it you don't want to go out for dinner," she said. "Or have you eaten already?"

"I haven't eaten. I haven't had time."

"That doesn't surprise me." Her voice had an edge to it. "Food's not all that important when you come right down to it. There are better ways to use your time."

"What are you trying to say to me?"

"That's one of your strengths, darling," she said, with a dry smile. "The ability to reduce any feelings to a rational question." She sat down on the divan, away from him. "Six months ago, when I moved in with you, I considered that a valuable trait."

"Which isn't so valuable anymore."

"Exactly right." One hand rested across the sheerly covered breasts, long white fingers tipped with intense red nails. "So let's say that I have lived in this dry land of rationality long enough to know it's not for me. I'm calling it a day, a semi-year, whatever. I'm flying to the States on the dawn flight tomorrow."

"Alone."

"Never alone."

"I see. Who's to be my replacement?"

"He's a broker in Japanese stocks, a real son of a bitch leading a highly precarious life."

The telephone rang and her eyes remained on him, knowingly, as if there were no doubt in her mind that he would pick it up. He let it ring four times and then answered it. It was Jordan.

"Can you call me back?" Corwin said.

"No," Jordan said. "I'm calling from a bar in Yokohama."

"All right. What do you have?"

"A damn peculiar situation," Jordan said. He had tracked down at least eight crew members, he went on, including some engineers from the boiler room as well as Erickson, the deck officer. What information he got from them was completely lacking in any detail that could corroborate Forsythe's story. Three or four Orientals had signed on at Dakar and they assumed that one of them was Okata (from later discussions), but the Orientals had been given nicknames and the engineers had difficulty telling them apart. One of the Orientals, the man they assumed was Okata, had never talked with them at all but simply did as he was told and stayed to himself. In the incident that had taken place in the Malaccan Straits, no one was even aware that Okata had gone up to meet the captain.

"The crew's willing to swear in any direction you want to go to protect the captain," Jordan said. "But they honestly don't know."

"Have you got a line on Adams, the first officer?"

"We can track him but he's not going to be of any help. There was a hell of a lot of discussion going on after the man overboard. There was never any mention of a fight or a pistol shot. And if Adams had witnessed anything, he would have passed it on." Jordan paused. "What do you want me to do?"

"I'll have to give it some thought. I'll see you in the morning." He put the telephone on the cradle, thoughtfully, aware that Lisa was still watching him. He could not interpret the continuing smile on her face.

"Now, who is the son of a bitch you were talking about?" he said.

"You don't know him."

"When did you meet him?"

"I can see why you're considered the best in your field, darling. You're going to amass all the evidence and then sort it out and make a good rational decision about what you're going to do. I met him three weeks ago, while you were in Hong Kong. I had a modeling assignment, went to a party afterward, and there he was."

"We've had a good six months."

"Corwin's semiannual report. I'm not making fun of you, darling, but living with you is like living with a beneficent computer. You're consistently good in bed and I never fail to come to orgasm. Paul's not that reliable. Last week he couldn't get it up and he got so raving mad he broke a very expensive lamp, smashed it all to pieces. But you would consider that whimsically destructive, wouldn't you?"

"Yes," he said. "You're equating irresponsibility with excitement. That's a damn poor reason to go. You don't have to."

"No," she said. "I don't have to do anything and that's the most damning thing about it. I would like to feel compelled for once, swept away. I would like to be engulfed by crisis."

"Then you've goddamned well created one," he said, sitting down, a drink in his hand. "What do you see in him?"

"Massive flaws."

"And what in the hell is that supposed to mean?"

"He has rages over everything, minor things that shouldn't upset him, but they do. He takes absolutely outrageous and impossible positions. He drives too fast, drinks too much. He scares the hell out of me sometimes, and he likes me."

"Likes," he said. "You're leaving because he likes you?"

"Can you say the same? Do you feel anything about me at all?"

Familiar ground, yes, an exploration of territory they had covered a hundred times before and even as they talked he felt betraying, for by morning she would be gone with another man for reasons he did not fully understand, and even at this moment a part of his mind was sorting through the Forsythe business, balancing the perceptions of the crew against those of the captain. He was under immense pressure now with telephone calls to complete, decisions to make. "I think you're a bored bitch who doesn't know a good thing when she has it."

"That's a hopeful noise," she said. "At least you have some feeling about it."

The telephone rang again. This time it was Ives. "I'm sorry to disturb you, Corwin, but things are deteriorating."

"What's happening?"

"I just heard from the Red Watch again. They have a definite connection between him and the *San Marin*. They have a letter from him saying that he was signing aboard the ship and witnesses in Dakar who saw him board." There was a slight pause on the line. "We need to discuss this tonight and take immediate action."

"I'd like to delay this until morning," Corwin said, looking at Lisa who was standing by the window, knowing his decision even before he made it.

"It can't be done," Ives said. "They're already making threats. Let's say the American Bar in Shinjuku, half an hour." The line went dead.

She did not turn from the window. "You don't need to explain. Another something has just come up."

"Yes," he said. "Do something for me. Think about this. In a couple of weeks, I'll take some time off and we'll go to San Francisco."

Her back was to him. "I don't think it would make a difference, darling, none at all. We've been together six months and you think you know me pretty well. Right?"

"I know you very well. And I don't want you to go."

"You're right about one thing. I am a foolish woman. So if you answer one question, a foolish question, I'll stay."

"What's the question?"

"Tell me the color of my eyes."

In that instant his eyes went blank, the obvious suddenly obscured, and all he could visualize was the piercing blue eyes of Forsythe's daughter. *I don't know.* Too tired, yes, and his hesitant silence was damning and eloquent. She turned toward him slowly, her eyes brimming with tears, but she would not cry.

"I guess that says it all," she said. "I'm sorry for you, Charles. You really have no idea what you missed." She went into the bedroom, closing the door behind her. Corwin sat silent, the glass cold against his hand, feeling empty as if he had lost something important without knowing exactly what it was.

Brown.

2

THE MOMENT CORWIN'S TAXI PULLED UP IN FRONT OF THE American Bar, Ives was already on the sidewalk, waiting to intercept him. He thrust a handful of hundred-yen notes at the driver. "I have a car waiting," he said, once the taxi pulled off. As they walked down the sidewalk toward the limousine, Corwin realized he had never seen Ives so agitated before, his steps hurried, a rattled expression on his face. "Fuck them all," Ives said, opening the limousine door, waving Corwin in and then joining him. He tapped on the glass, told the driver to move ahead. He sank back against the seat, fidgeting with a gold lighter, snapping the case open and shut.

"It's an insane fucking world," he said. "We should have dumped Forsythe last year." He clicked the lighter into flame, lighted a cigarette that he snuffed out almost immediately. "One of Okata's men came to the shipyard just as I was leaving. He nearly caused a riot."

"You talked to him?"

"Why in the hell should I talk to him?" Ives said. "These goddamned Orientals are totally unpredictable. This son of a bitch pulled a knife on the man at the gate." He began to calm himself, rubbing the golden side of the lighter with his thumb. "They'll screw us into the ground if they find out what really happened," he said. "The Japanese unions are after my ass anyway."

Logic, yes, a linear progression, and Corwin allowed his

mind to sort out the problem at hand into the smaller com-
ponent parts that could be dealt with. He did not understand
the Japanese mind and he had worked in the Orient long
enough to know he would never comprehend it, but he could
project with some accuracy what the Japanese would do. In
this case, Ives's fears were well grounded. The Japanese mili-
tants were in constant search of provocative incidents and
Okata's death at the hands of a doped-out American captain
would provide a perfect one. There would be no mitigating
circumstance.

He told Ives what he had found out about the captain and
Jordan's interviews with the crew.

"I don't see that any of that helps us," Ives said.

"There's nothing to indicate Okata ever threatened to take
over the ship," Corwin said, thinking it through. "Conversely,
there's no evidence to suggest that Forsythe shot Okata, unless
the body in Singapore has a bullet hole in it."

"Shit, the body was in pieces," Ives said, musingly.

"Then we'll take a different tack." He fished the captain's
report out of his attaché case. "Do you have a night stenog-
rapher on duty?"

"I'll get one." He picked up the telephone, spoke in
Japanese, and in a few minutes handed the telephone to
Corwin.

"Who am I talking to?" Corwin said, into the telephone.

"This is Elaine Smith, Mr. Corwin."

She was American, fine, he would not have to struggle with
the finer shadings that would have been required had she
been Japanese. "I am going to dictate a report to you, Elaine.
I want you to put this on a maritime accident form ten sixty-
four B, under the name of Forsythe, William C., dated seventeen August. You can verify name spellings and other data
by referring to Extraordinary Report four sixty-three, filed
under Forsythe. Do you have that?"

"Yes, sir. I understand."

As he began to dictate, he found himself falling into the rhythm of the captain's language, the combination of terse sentences and long discursive phrases, recasting what had happened aboard the *San Marin* into something that could be handled. He shaped the killing into an accident. A crew member named Okata had come onto the bridgewing at a time when the *San Marin* was about to get under way. The captain had been concentrating on avoiding the considerable hazard of the sea-lanes and was paying little attention to Okata when he lost his balance and fell over the rail. Immediately, the captain had thrown a lighted buoy into the darkness and ordered the ship brought around in a standard search-and-rescue pattern. Corwin paused.

"I want you to get the log entry and plug in the statement concerning the rescue efforts just as they appear in the log, Elaine," he said. "I want the statement typed within the hour, four copies. I'll pick them up."

When he had finished the dictation, he noticed that Ives was considerably more relaxed, the tension transformed into curiosity. "That's a goddamned ingenious approach," he said. "Will it hold up?"

"They can't prove otherwise."

"And we admit a limited culpability, right?" Ives said.

"Right. No more than the standard apology of an employer whose employee has suffered a fatal accident."

"Set up a cash payment," Ives said. "That's traditional."

"How high do you want to go?"

Ives shrugged, thoroughly relaxed now. "Whatever's necessary," he said. "And for God's sake, take Forsythe's fucking pistol away from him. And then let's see if we can keep this out of the papers."

"They won't want the publicity any more than we do," Corwin said. "Do you have a contact point with Okata's group?"

"Yes," Ives said. "The man who threatened the guard left

his business card. Incidentally, I apologize for dragging you out tonight."

"That's what I get paid for."

"I apologize anyway. Hell, once you get through with the Okata business, take some time off."

"I may do that," Corwin said. He fell silent, looking out into the dark streets, the city asleep, and Lisa would be dozing lightly as she always did when she was alone, the lamp still on beside the bed, the magazine still held limply in her hand. He had miscalculated there, blown the relationship, but he could not believe that his actions were irreversible. He would talk to her again and take his vacation and they would spend the time together and he would make it up to her.

Once they reached the shipyard and he had the new report in hand, he called the hotel and asked to be connected with his room, waiting for her to come onto the line, but it continued to ring, unanswered. He signaled the hotel operator.

"I don't get an answer," he said. "This is Mr. Corwin. Do you have a message for me?"

"One moment, sir," the Japanese said. "Yes, sir. Shall I read it to you?"

"Please."

"It says, 'To seem to have no flaws is the biggest flaw of all. I'll send for my things.' "

"That's all it says?"

"Yes, sir."

He turned his attention to the report.

2

The *San Marin* lay lower in the water, the pumps still working to fill the tanks. The sun as it came up created a blinding glare on the water and Corwin was fatigued to the point of numbness, slightly irritated by the ebullient Jordan who appeared to have an inexhaustible and boundless energy. The day was going to be a scorcher. The air was perfectly still, stagnant, heavy with the smell of sulfur.

The driver parked near the dock office and Corwin finished shaving, examining his lean face in the mirror as he ran the electric razor over his chin. Jordan was going over a sheaf of papers, scheduling, whistling to himself, a tuneless, contented sound. "There's a meeting of the Japanese Maritime Union tonight at eight," he said. "They're going to take a position on the divestiture movement in the United States and send a telegram to Senator Vetter." He paused thoughtfully. "What do you think's going to happen back in the States, Charlie? You think the government's going to bust up the oil companies?"

"If I had a massive conglomerate, I'd be climbing the walls every time Vetter comes around," Corwin said. "Hell, every time there's another scandal in the oil community, another hike in prices, he gains another group of supporters. And sooner or later he's going to get a foothold and he's going to force one oil company to divest a subsidiary, Texaco to give up its retail outlets or Exxon its refineries and the whole fucking business is going to come unraveled. It's the battle of the century."

"The Japanese money's on the senator," Jordan said. "They think he's a cross between Buddha and Ralph Nader."

Corwin clicked off the razor. "You're able to read the Japanese mind pretty well, aren't you, Pete?"

"You mean because I'm married to one?"

"Yes."

"Only Tamiko, I'm afraid," Jordan said. "To know one is not to know all. But I enjoy all things Japanese. They think in terms of black and white, very few shades of gray, and there's comfort in that. There's a rule for everything. I want you to meet Tamiko sometime."

"I'd like that."

Jordan put the papers away. "Something else has come up that I don't know how to handle. I've heard rumors that Ives is overextended, that he may go under. The boys at Sanko Steamship want a firm commitment that their leases on the three tankers will be extended."

"Give them the reassurance they want. But just between us, the company's in trouble. Maybe Ives can pull it out, I don't know." He used the mirror to straighten his tie, his mind moving to Forsythe. He wasn't sure what the captain's reaction was going to be to the revised report, but he wasn't going to give him any choice in the matter.

He slid out of the car, flipping a thumbs up to Jordan and then threaded his way across the dock area, aware that Faye was standing at the head of the companionway on the bridge superstructure, watching him. The captain's daughter would be running interference again today but he had no objection. Her father was going to be removed from an impossible situation. He mounted to the catwalk and moved forward, shading his eyes with his hand as he looked at her. She was not a beautiful woman, her features were too angular for that, but she had class that even the jeans and sweat shirt couldn't hide.

"Good morning," he said as he reached the companionway. "Where's the captain?"

"In his quarters," she said. She took out a pair of sunglasses and put them on. "What has the company decided?"

"He'll be off the hook."

She shrugged as if she were satisfied, then walked with him to her father's quarters, opening the door and allowing Corwin to precede her. Forsythe was having breakfast, sitting at a small table near the porthole that overlooked the foredeck. He was surrounded by mementos of his career, pictures of ships and crews and ports, a scrimshaw of elephants, a shelf of worn volumes on seamanship. He glanced up at Corwin and then continued to poke at his food. "May I offer you breakfast?" he said, clearing his throat, his voice strained.

"No, thank you," Corwin said.

"You've met my daughter?"

"Yes."

The hand carried a fragment of toast to the mouth. "I had enormous capabilities," Forsythe said, as if speaking to himself. "At one time I was a Rhodes scholar, Mr. Corwin, and it was my highest ambition to become a politician, someplace where I could have had an effect on the world. But when the war came, I enlisted in the merchant marine. And then time passed. My daughter says you know about my illness."

"Yes."

"I don't mind dying," Forsythe said, no self-pity in his voice. "I have come very close to death many times over the years, and under those circumstances, it would have been a waste. But now I feel that it's worthwhile at least to the extent that it can be for a greater good. Do you share my opinion that America is declining, Mr. Corwin, that something must be done?"

"We'll have to discuss politics some other time, Captain," Corwin said. He opened the attaché case and removed a copy of the new statement, which he placed before the captain. Forsythe did not look at it. He blotted his mouth with a napkin and then carefully folded the linen and placed it by his plate.

"If you have a pen, I'll sign it."

"Not without understanding what's in it."

"Then suppose you tell me."

"It's basically simple. You did not know Okata except by name. You witnessed his fall overboard and instituted search and rescue. You did not find the body." Forsythe's eyes were vague. Corwin was not certain he was listening. "It's important that you read the statement, Captain. It's highly likely you will be asked for details of the accident somewhere down the line. When that happens, it's imperative that you give no information that is not contained in this statement."

"You're being patronizing," Forsythe said, without force. "I know full well what I am supposed to do and how to go about it." He took the pen that Corwin offered him and laboriously signed at the bottom of the page. Corwin put the signed copy in the attaché case and gave Forsythe an extra copy.

"Now," Corwin said, "I want your pistol, Captain. Forsythe looked momentarily blank. "The pistol with which you say you shot Okata. Is it here or on the bridge?"

Forsythe stood up, opened a drawer, and removed the boxed pistol. Corwin broke the cylinder and examined the cartridges. One had been fired. He snapped it shut and replaced it in the case. "This will be cleaned and returned to you when you're back in the States."

"What provisions are you making for him?" Faye said from the inset couch.

"I can handle my own affairs," Forsythe said.

"I want to know what arrangements have been made."

Corwin gave the answer to Forsythe. "You'll take the *San Marin* to Kobe when the weather clears. You'll be relieved there and flown back to the States on retirement status."

Corwin put the box containing the pistol into his attaché case. He felt a vague dissatisfaction, as if something had happened here that he could not quite fathom, something stemming from Forsythe's attitude perhaps, as if the captain was functioning on a level totally apart from what was happening here. Forsythe was examining the remains of his breakfast, the food scarcely touched, the pieces of toast and ham. "You really have no idea what's happening in the world, do you?" he said to Corwin.

"The whole world is a powder keg, Mr. Corwin. I shan't be sorry to leave it."

Corwin closed his attaché case. "I'll have you booked on a

flight directly from Kobe," he said. "Good luck, Captain."

He walked back into the open air and Faye followed him out. "Are you going back into Tokyo?" he said.

"Yes."

"I'd appreciate a lift."

"Sure."

It was only after they were in the limousine that she appeared to relax somewhat, the tension draining out of her, leaving her reflective, her eyes obscured by the huge dark ovals of her glasses. "He's not really like that, you know," she said.

"Like what?"

"Bitter, vague, rambling. It's not easy for a man like that to face dying, despite everything he says to the contrary. He used to talk about death as if it were a Wagnerian rite, something really big and dramatic. I think he always pictured it happening at sea, suddenly, in an engagement with the enemy or straining to save the ship, not in an illness that was going to leave him addled." She shook her head. "Do you think he's competent to take the ship to Kobe?"

"Probably not," he said. "But I'm assigning him a new first officer named Jennings who will make things go all right. Jennings will be the new ship's master when your father leaves."

"I apologize to you," she said.

"For what?"

"For threatening you. I thought the company was doing something to my father. Did he really shoot that man?"

"I don't know."

"I don't think he shot anybody," she said. "May I have a cigarette?"

He offered her one and lighted it for her. "What makes you think that?"

"The way he rambled about it," she said, inhaling. "He was saying the Japanese deserved to be killed and that a lot of people deserved to be killed. But he thought it hadn't happened yet." She shrugged. "Anyway, all I wanted was to see that he got a fair shake out of all this. And that's done."

"Will you be going back to the States with him?"

"Not with him, no. I have some things to be finished here first."

Jordan buzzed from the front seat. "The driver needs a destination, Miss Forsythe. Where would you like to go?"

"Any station on the Yamate line," she said. "I have an appointment in Shinjuku. It's easier to get there by train than by car." She fell silent until the car drew to a stop in front of one of the electric line stations. She thanked Corwin and then climbed out of the car and went up the concrete steps to the platform, looking rather frail and small.

Jordan took her place in the backseat and tapped on the glass to instruct the driver to move on. "I've been on the phone with Ives," he said. "We have a meeting with Okata's brother, Hiroshige, if you want it."

"When?"

"Now."

"There's no sense delaying it," Corwin said, removing his briefing sheet on the Red Watch from his attaché case to check Hiroshige's background. He was considered to be an intellectual, almost monklike in his habits, a recluse who had built his brother's image as a leader while providing a direction to the movement's operations. "Have you had contact with this Hiroshige before?"

"No. Ives supplied the research and the contacts."

"Where are we meeting?"

"Chiba. An industrial district. An old meeting hall."

Very well then, Corwin thought, it was likely to be a long drawn-out affair that would occupy the better part of the day, a final resolution to be delayed for weeks with the negotiation back and forth toward a satisfactory cash settlement. He was not so certain now that the accident story would hold under close examination and he made a mental note to see that Forsythe was shielded from any but official interrogation until he left Japan.

"I want you to put a good Japanese PR man on this," Corwin said. "We're going to do nothing, but if they choose to report Okata's death to the press, then we have to be ready to handle it. We'll want to play his eccentricities, his irrationality. I'll want it played so that Okata's falling off a ship will seem entirely logical."

"I'll set it up."

The address in Chiba was an old manufacturing district, a small brick building that had somehow been spared the ravages of war and the razing that accompanied the rebuilding of the city. It was surrounded by a massive steelworks with batteries of giant smokestacks pluming into the sky. The air stank. The exterior of the building itself was undergoing repair; a latticework of bamboo scaffolding encompassed the front, swarming with Japanese workmen who seemed to be taking out the bricks one at a time, cleaning and resetting them. When the limousine stopped, Corwin got out and waited for Jordan to join him, looking up at the second floor of the building and a row of windows that had been covered with papers against the contamination of the workmen.

"We'll play this by ear," Corwin said. "I won't have any objections if we drag this out a week or two."

"Right," Jordan said.

The stairway was ancient, narrow, steep, the walls plastered with pictures of Okata in his dramatic roles, one of a wiry handsome young man in a Kamikaze uniform standing against the background of a massive rising-sun flag, a reflection of the Japanese militarism of the Second World War. And suddenly Corwin felt his stomach tighten reflexively and his skin crawled, for at the head of the stairs, on the dimly lighted landing, he saw two Japanese men, both in their late twenties, in uniforms, armed with automatic weapons. He had approached this whole thing too rationally, as a business conference, and he had the feeling that either of those Japanese could suddenly open up with their automatic weapons and cut them dead on the staircase without a flicker of feeling.

He glanced at Jordan who had a quizzical expression on his face. "We'll play this one very firmly," Corwin said. "They'll want the money more than they'll want two dead Americans. You explain to them that I will not negotiate with Hiroshige as long as there are any weapons in the room."

"Very good," Jordan said, quietly. "They'll respect that."

He walked ahead to carry out the preliminaries in a low and guttural Japanese while Corwin, as the principal, remained uninvolved. One of the Japanese went through a door, returned, grunted assent.

"Hiroshige agrees," Jordan said.

Corwin went through the door into a large meeting hall in the terminal stages of disrepair, the sunlight filtering in through the old newspapers covering the windows, a creaky wood floor, dusty, littered with trash. At the far end was a Western-style table against the backdrop of a massive portrait of Okata and there sat the man Corwin took to be Hiroshige, short, powerfully built, in his mid-thirties, dressed in a black turtleneck sweater, his hair hanging in strands around his thick neck. He peered at Corwin through heavy glasses, asked Corwin to sit down.

The intellectual in defiance, Corwin gathered, no observance of the traditional greetings and yet the language Hiroshige used was strictly formal, almost ceremonial. He paid no attention at all to Jordan who was clearly subordinate. Abruptly, he switched to English. "Perhaps you would prefer that we talk in English," Hiroshige said. "I am equally at home in both languages."

"It makes no difference to me."

Hiroshige looked off into the shadows of the room, blinking in the artificial twilight, scowling, and in a moment one of his men brought cups to the table and poured thick black coffee from a battered aluminum pot. Hiroshige picked up the cup and cradled it in both hands, his eyes peering at Corwin above the rims of his glasses. "You have news about my brother's death."

"Perhaps," Corwin said.

"We know that he's dead. We know that he was killed on the *San Marin*."

"That's not precisely correct," Corwin said. "A man named Okata was aboard the *San Marin*. Whether he was your brother or not remains to be proved."

"I would ask you not to be obscure with me," Hiroshige said. "It won't do either of us any good for you to be obscure. My brother was on your ship and he was killed."

"There was a man named Okata aboard the *San Marin* and he fell overboard. The ship's master did everything possible to find him."

"Fell."

"Yes." Corwin removed the accident report the captain had signed, slid it across the rough surface of the table, going through the formalities with the almost certain conviction now that Hiroshige had no feelings whatsoever concerning his brother's death. He put the coffee cup down and flicked one corner of the report with his thumb in a desultory way, not bothering to read it. "This doesn't prove anything."

"That's right," Corwin said. "There's no proof in either direction. You may be able to show that the Okata aboard our tanker was indeed your brother, but that's going to take you a hell of a long time. We're willing to admit the probability that it was and despite the fact that we have no liability for his death, we're prepared to pay seven and one-half million yen to his beneficiaries with an expression of sincere condolences."

"Approximately twenty-five thousand dollars."

"Yes."

Hiroshige pushed back from the table and stood up. He was even shorter than Corwin had first perceived, slightly bowed legs, and he stood in front of his brother's poster, lighting a cigarette, looking at the oversized image, his head hunched forward as if to bring it into focus. "Do you know what this accident can do to your company?" he said. "Do you have the slightest idea the kind of trouble this accident can generate?"

"None," Corwin said, firmly.

"None?" Hiroshige said with an incredulous smile, as if he could not believe what he was hearing. "You have no idea of the things we can do," Hiroshige said. And he stood with the cigarette dangling from the corner of his mouth and proceeded to launch into a harangue that was pure cant, a shrill panegyric that Corwin realized had been delivered many times before. The Japanese had a way of working themselves up to a fevered pitch and Hiroshige was following the route. The Red Watch was the new antidote for the corruption of worldwide big business that had polluted the Japanese ideal, and Corwin had but to look at the selfless patriots in Mexico City who had been ready to blow themselves up in order to bring down the president of Mexico to know what the Red Watch was willing to do.

Corwin picked up the coffee and tasted it, bitter, thick, and he saw Jordan standing patiently at the side of the room and he wondered if Jordan was picking up the pervasive undertones in Hiroshige's diatribe. For Hiroshige was falling back on a rehearsed invective, a political speech and vague threats, no personal feelings exhibited at all. The whole thing was designed to up the ante, to increase the condolence money.

Corwin was tempted to call his bluff just for the hell of it, to withdraw any offer of payment, but he knew that would be a self-indulgence. As much as he disliked the idea of the Red Watch in general and this strutting little man in particular, money was the cheapest solution to the problem. Hiroshige was winding down. At an appropriate moment, Corwin interrupted.

"How much?" he said, flatly.

"Do you think you can absolve your company by the payment of money?"

"Yes," Corwin said. "How much?"

"A hundred and fifty thousand dollars, American, and a full apology from your company for placing my brother in a position that resulted in his death."

"The figure is all right," Corwin said. "But we will make the payment in yen. And we will release no statement at all concerning the death of your brother. If you choose to make that public, we will deny it."

"There's no way you can deny it," Hiroshige said.

"It will cost you a hell of a lot of money to find that out. If it comes to a full power struggle between our company and your group, we will eventually win because we have the advantage of Japanese law on our side. On the other hand, you can cause a certain amount of physical harassment, which we would just as soon avoid. But it's up to you. I'm willing to play it either way."

Hiroshige sat down again, pinching the remnant of cigarette between thumb and forefinger. He dropped it to the floor, ground it out beneath the heel of his boot. His signal was clear; capitulation. "The money is to be paid in American dollars."

"That's not convenient."

"That's a firm condition."

"All right. I will agree to that."

"The payment is to be made to me personally, within

twenty-four hours, at a place that I will stipulate."

And now it fell into place, the whole thing, concluded, for Hiroshige would not only inherit his brother's place in the organization but take delivery of the money as well. He was amused, but he did not show it. "Done," he said.

Hiroshige wrote a telephone number on the corner of a newspaper, ripped off the piece, and handed it to him. "Call me at this number in exactly two hours."

Corwin stood up, put the accident report back in his briefcase. He went down the stairs, followed by Jordan, blinking as he emerged into the bright sunlight.

"Well?" he said to Jordan, once they were in the limousine and under way.

"There was something terribly wrong with that meeting," Jordan said, scratching his chin.

"In what way?"

"Hell, I don't know. It's just a feeling, but there's something that doesn't add up."

"Hiroshige is just another greedy son of a bitch in a long line of them," Corwin said. "But he'll honor the bargain." He said nothing more, relaxing against the seat, the sun warm through the tinted windows, the air semicold from the air-conditioning vents. Greed, venality, and nobody he knew was completely free of it. And Ives was playing the game on a high level, risking high millions in ships and computers, seeking to double or triple his stakes far past the amount of money he could spend in his lifetime. And Forsythe's daughter was ready to lay everything on the line to ensure her father's pension and there was no reason why this Japanese zealot would not play the game as well. Money was power and a secure base, a rescue net in case things went sour, and he himself was well caught up in the game. One tanker, yes, on an intercoastal run, and then perhaps two, steaming under his ownership, and a massive house in Santa Barbara, overlooking the sea . . .

He blinked, coming awake. He had dozed off. The limousine was pulling into the shipyard. It stopped at the main building. "I'll give you a call as soon as I talk to Ives," he said. "In the meantime, start putting a money package together."

"Right," Jordan said. Corwin watched him climbing the steps into the building before he signaled the driver to move on. Jordan was an exception, yes, perhaps the only man Corwin knew who was content to be exactly where he was, with no aspiration toward the big money or a high-level position, putting in his time on the job and then going home to his apartment in Shinanomachi and his Japanese wife. At times Corwin envied him.

Corwin found Ives on the dock, wearing a hard hat, surrounded by his staff assistants. He was confronting a Japanese in a business suit who apparently represented the Japanese maritime workers. Ives was pushing a fierce argument without raising his voice, a flood of protest that simply washed past the implacable Japanese who occasionally interjected a sentence or two.

As he joined Corwin, his face was flushed; his anger had not been pretense. He grimaced up at the structure of the ship then led the way up the stairs to his office, beginning to cool down by the time he closed the door behind him. The office was in its usual shambles, the piles of Telexes everywhere. The telephone was buzzing. He removed his hard hat and answered the call, sitting down in the engulfing leather chair behind his desk. "Yes?" he said, into the telephone. "All right, let me have it." He pinched the bridge of his nose. "Are you sure of the fucking facts? I don't want any goddamned perhaps or maybe." He listened, shook his head. "All right," he said. "Play it safe." He slammed the telephone back on the cradle, stood up, peered out the window at the sky, hands laced behind his back. "That goddamned fucking typhoon," he said with frustrated resignation. "It got hung up and now it's moving again. How in the hell can this happen to me? That goddamned steel plate is already overdue and it's stuck in Kobe." He went to the wet bar, poured himself a drink. "You want one?" he said to Corwin.

"No, thanks."

Ives downed the drink. It appeared to calm him. "I hope to hell you bring me good tidings of great joy."

"Everything's under control," Corwin said. He removed the pistol box from his attaché case, placed it on the desk. "This is the pistol you asked for. I don't think he shot anybody with it, by the way, but it really doesn't make any difference." He told Ives what he had found out about Forsythe's terminal illness, the voyage from the Persian Gulf. "I think the whole thing exists only in his mind. Nobody in the crew saw anything unusual about Okata."

Ives removed the pistol from the case, examining it gingerly, holding it by the barrel. "You don't believe the captain shot him?"

"No. There's nothing to confirm it anywhere down the line. But hold the pistol, just in case. And have it returned to Forsythe when he gets back to the States." He laid the accident report on the desk. "This is his amended statement. It's a peculiar goddamned situation because I think this fiction is probably very close to what really happened."

"You really want to give him command to Kobe?"

"It's a milk run and Jennings will back him. We'll fly Forsythe directly to the States from Kobe."

"You talk to Okata's brother? Did he agree to a cash settlement?"

"Yes. We're paying a hundred and fifty thousand, American."

"All right," Ives said, with a slight dismissing wave of his hand. "Take it from undesignated funds." He sank back in his chair. "Will that end it?"

"Yes," Corwin said.

"Thank God for that. I don't know how anybody does business in this fucking country," he said. "The climate's sour."

Corwin shrugged and took leave of Ives. Back in his office, he got ahold of Jordan on the phone.

"We have undesignated funds available," Jordan said. "What denominations?"

"Make them all hundreds," Corwin said. "Nonsequential serials. And put them in a case for me."

"Sure."

He put the digital clock on the corner of his desk and at precisely the agreed upon time, he dialed the number on the piece of newspaper. Hiroshige answered immediately. He was at a public telephone on a busy street. Corwin could hear the traffic noise in the background. His suspicions were confirmed. Hiroshige was taking the call in private and more than likely he would squirrel the money away and report back to the Red Watch that he had been unable to collect it.

"Are you ready to deliver?" he asked Corwin.

"Yes."

"These are my requirements. You will drive by yourself down to the village of Iwasa on the west side of Tokyo Bay. You will arrive there at five o'clock this evening. You will take the road south along the bluff and drive exactly five kilometers. At that point, you will get out of the car and walk into the trees overlooking the breakwater. You will wait for me there."

"I have another requirement," Corwin said.

"Ah?"

"I will expect you to sign a receipt for the money."

"No," Hiroshige said.

"I don't give a good goddamn where the money goes," Corwin said. "But your signature will be my insurance. If you release any information to the media, then I will release the receipt."

Hiroshige was silent on the line. Corwin could hear the roar of a diesel in the background, the bleat of an air horn. "All right," Hiroshige said. "A receipt. You have the directions."

"Yes."

"I will expect you at seventeen thirty hours."

3

He did not like driving through the Japanese traffic. He had never been able to adjust to a right-hand drive and the Japanese highway system was incomprehensible to him. On the expressway, he turned the radio dial until he found an English-language newscast. He only half listened to the report of storm damage in the Inland Sea, the swamping of a few fishing boats, a drowning off the north coast of Shikoku and the prediction that the Tokyo–Yokohama Metroplex area would receive heavy rains and wind gusts up to ninety miles an hour as the center of the storm slid off to the southeast and out to sea. Corwin could see a suggestion of heavy clouds back to the southwest, a perceptible darkening of the sky in an already thick atmosphere.

A horn blared at him from behind. He ignored it, keeping a steady speed, staying in his lane. There was no place else for him to go. He was boxed in, completely, in a mass of automobiles from which he could not extricate himself and he had no choice but to keep pace. To his right he saw the long line of plastic police mannequins, realistic from this distance. The Japanese used illusion as a control and the plastic police were everywhere, grouped along city streets as well as highways, and sometimes there would be a single live policeman among the replications, spotting speeders and radioing ahead to a patrol car. Simple, yes, and a driver was supposed to slow down at the sight of these blue uniforms, to be conditioned to obeying. But here on the expressway, there was no slackening of the pace, for the mass of cars was too great and there were insufficient police in the whole of Japan to stop them all.

In many ways, his life was like that, the pattern of his career determined by the accumulated pressures behind him and the competitive urge to pass those who were ahead of him. He was now making sixty thousand a year with all the fringe benefits, the use of any machine he could imagine, all of the comforts he wanted, plenty of sex in a country where a piece of ass was easily had. He had entered the relationship with Lisa as he had all others, as an exciting convenience, and he had known that sooner or later she would move out and he had not expected to be particularly troubled at her leaving. But she had unsettled him, that was the truth.

He saw his turn approaching, the exit ramp, and he closed the space between his car and the red Toyota ahead of him, gaining a few critical feet before he whipped the wheel to the left, slapping the horn with his right hand as he crowded into the lane of cars. His car dropped into the exit slot and went down the ramp. He thought too much, that was his trouble. She had accused him of being too rational and perhaps what she said was true, but that was his profession, the only edge he had on anybody else.

The traffic fell off below Yokohama and he picked a small road immediately west of the industrial complexes that fringed Tokyo Bay, the American military traffic picking up as he skirted the naval base at Yokosuka. The wind was up now, coming in gusts from the southwest; over the pine-covered ridges to the south he could see the cloud bank, so dark it was almost black, a ragged blue squall line running ahead of it. The small car trembled slightly in the open spaces, steadied again in the lee side of a ridge. He passed through the small town, an electric line train station and new houses clustered on the ridges, a new bedroom community for the megalopolis sprawling to the north, and once he passed it he was in the countryside again, the stands of fir trees clustered in the rocky upheavals.

He checked the speedometer, watched the kilometers crawl by. At five kilometers there was a clearing sufficiently wide to his right that he was able to pull his car off and into the trees. He got out, checked his watch. He was three minutes early. Below him, on the bay, the water was beginning to roil into whitecaps and the last of the Japanese fishing boats were pulling into the breakwater of a small fishing settlement, the inlet already filled with boats tied up along the pier and anchored in open water.

He had never seen the open water of the bay so deserted. Where generally there existed two lines of staggered traffic, inbound and outbound, there now existed a single containerized freighter steaming into the shelter of the bay, up toward Yokohama. More incredibly, a medium-sized tanker was coming down the bay and heading toward the open sea, a plume of black smoke rising from the single stack. Something about the tanker made him think she was in trouble, no specific details, for he could see nothing at this distance but the erratic track she was following. She was not in the regular sea-lane but instead she was dangerously close to the rocky western shore, and she was suffering a spill of considerable proportions. In her wake she left an almost invisible sheen on the surface of the water.

At this rate she would never make it through the narrows and into the open waters of the Pacific. Out of the clearly marked channel, it was possible she had ruptured a tank against one of the sharp volcanic rocks that shoaled on the west side of the bay. He could not believe there was a ship's master in service who would risk his vessel in such a manner, facing heavy weather with a fractured hull when by making a broad turn he could run before the wind back to Yokohama.

His stomach tightened. The ship was closer now and he recognized the *San Marin* veering seaward at the last possible moment to avoid the end of the rock-pile breakwater stretching like a snake into the choppy water, the head marked by a piling with a light on it. She was sitting low in the water, fully loaded, leaking like a sieve and his first thought was that Forsythe had gone around the bend, making the run on his own, not waiting for Jennings. To hell with Hiroshige, he thought, that deal could wait until later and he considered driving back into the village and finding a phone to call Ives. He decided against it.

Ives would already know. Forsythe could not have left Yokohama unobserved. Too, there was no time, for the *San Marin* had reached the sea-lane now, running at full speed. And the spill, caught in the landward current, was drifting inside the breakwater, an opalescent sheen. Jesus, high-test gasoline, a spill of major proportions and the real danger did not occur to him until he saw one last straggling fishing boat wallowing its way through the swells into the breakwater. There was a sudden flash and the water was ablaze, a low wall of flame reaching inward, a goddamned field of it, flashing around the hulls of the anchored boats. One boat exploded, sending a shower of burning timbers onto the shore, a low shed aflame now, another gigantic explosion as the flames engulfed a marina fueling station.

Madness, the whole village afire in a matter of minutes, smoke whipping out over the bay, driven by an increasing wind while the *San Marin* receded into the distance, the spill cut off, nothing issuing from that ship except the aft release of seawater. He saw but he could not comprehend and then he felt the first spatterings of rain and barely made it into the car before the deluge broke, the torrents of water driven by a gale force wind that ripped a limb from a tree overhead and sent it sailing over the bluff. The meeting with Hiroshige faded into insignificance. He backed the car around, afraid that the wind would push it over the side. It rocked violently, threatened to overturn, the rain so heavy that the wipers could not clear the windshield, the engine sputtering as if it were swamped and close to dying. He edged out onto the pavement, blindly, keeping the car in first gear, moving slowly, certain that at any moment the tires would lose traction and the car would begin to roll.

He was angry now and his first concern was not for his own safety as such, not for the saving of his own skin but to make certain that Forsythe was stopped, the *San Marin* turned around. Forsythe had incinerated the people of that fishing settlement, directly or indirectly, and Corwin felt responsible. If he had followed his first inclination and stopped the son of a bitch, removed him from his command despite his empathy for the old man's predicament, this insanity would never have occurred.

The car trembled, moved transversely across the pavement and onto the rough gravel of the shoulder. The engine died. He was aware of the roar of the storm, the high-pitched shriek of the wind and the pounding of the rain against the body of the car, the windows so streaming he could not get his bearings.

He turned the key, his fingers trembling. The noise of the storm was so loud he could not hear the engine when it started and only the blinking of the warning lights on the dash let him know that it was running. He inched ahead, slowly, almost by feel sensing the moment when it was on the smooth pavement again. He leaned forward, trying to see through the windshield. He could see nothing except a vague outline of the terrain ahead of him, masses of gray and black, fitful glimpses of the center line. Cautiously, he released the clutch. The car inched forward.

It took him the better part of an hour to drive the five miles to the village and he knew he was close when he saw flashing red lights ahead of him and recognized the sharp curve of road that led into the village. A truck lay on its side, sprawled down the incline of a hill, and there was a police car and a wrecker on the shoulder. A large group of men stood braced against the wind, all of them bare to the waist, pulling on a rope. He inched past them and into the village, remembering a small Japanese inn that lay in the trees off to the right. He made the turn onto the side road and saw the shape of the low building through the downpour ahead of him. When he stopped the car he was trembling from the strain of the drive, exhausted.

He picked up the attaché case containing the money and bracing himself, opened the door, his breath taken away by the sudden onslaught of the wind and water. He staggered erratically against the force of the wind, gained the temporary respite of a masonry wall, pushed on again until he won the shelter of the entryway where he sat down on the low wooden step. He looked up again as a woman in a kimono came out of the door, bowing politely, going through the formal ritual of greeting even as the inn was shaking and threatening to blow away. He waved his hand vaguely as if the effort of talking was too much and then asked for a room with a telephone. He took off his shoes and put on the straw slippers that she provided him and he followed her down a hallway on a polished wooden floor.

The room was sparsely furnished—a low table with an overhanging lamp, an alcove with a traditional scroll, and a single fresh flower in a vase. The woman had a voice that sounded like a happy chirp and she remarked on the severity of the storm with a pleasant smile. It was only when she asked if she could dry his clothes for him that he realized he was soaked through. He took out his pack of cigarettes, found them wet and useless.

"I would also like some cigarettes," he said. "And dinner."

She bowed and retreated. He emptied his pockets and undressed down to his shorts, laying them out for the maid, then he sought out the adjoining toilet, toweling himself dry. There was a severe creaking in the beams above him and he felt as if the inn would disintegrate at any minute, but he was too tired to care. He found the telephone on a small corner shelf and dialed the operator. His command of Japanese escaped him temporarily. He asked for an English-speaking operator and told her he wanted to call Tokyo.

"I'm sorry, sir," the operator said. "But due to the storm, I can place no calls that are not of an urgent nature."

"This is very urgent," he said. He gave her the number of Ives's office at the shipyard and found himself on hold, the cold telephone tucked between his chin and shoulder. He glanced up at the maid as she came in with a tray, putting it on the small table. He gestured to her for a cigarette, accepted the light, listening to the static on the telephone line. The tobacco was stale, brackish, a Japanese brand.

In a few moments, the line rang through to the office and a Japanese night operator was on the line. She could only tell him that Ives's office was closed for the day and that Mr. Ives was not on the premises. When Corwin asked to be connected with some of his subordinates he knew had to be on duty, the operator rang various offices and then informed him that none of them were there.

"It is storming very heavily here," she said in excuse and he hung up.

He allowed the maid to hold the happi coat for him, a lightweight cloth robe with a design stenciled on the back, and he put it on and went through the formality of signing a registry card. He dismissed the maid after observing the proprieties and then pulled the table over to the telephone and began the tedious process of trying to call Jordan's apartment. He had no success. The operator reiterated the severity of the storm, the emergency use of the lines, and finally he gave up. He ate the rice and fish and delicately fried pieces of chicken on the tray, ravenously hungry. He ate without tasting and then sat at the table, cradling a cup in his hands, the ceiling groaning above him, the rain beating obliquely against the outside wooden screens. Hell, no more for today. He was chilled, exhausted. Rather than call the maid, he found the *futon* in a closet and unrolled the bedding on the floor himself. He turned off the lights, his mind numb with fatigue.

In the darkness, the sounds of the storm were accentuated and the whole wooden structure of the inn seemed to vibrate like a reed. He could not put the destruction of the fishing settlement out of his mind, the scene of the ship riding through the choppy waters and the contradiction of water and fire, the flash of flames and even now, in this rain, the fires would still be alive, the chain of explosions from fuel tanks on dozens of fishing boats.

He sat up, lighted another cigarette. He turned on the lights and tried the telephone again, a different operator. He insisted on the urgency of his call and finally she rang through for him and he heard Jordan's wife on the line. It was a poor connection, heavy with static, but he asked in Japanese to speak to Jordan.

"Corwin, is that you?"

"Yes," Corwin said. "I'm down below Yokohama. Have you heard what happened?"

"Jesus," Jordan said. "Was it really the *San Marin*? Did you see it?"

"It was the *San Marin*," Corwin said. He told Jordan what he had seen, but he was not sure how much Jordan heard. The line continued to crackle. "Have you talked to Ives?"

"I can't get him," Jordan said. "There's some confusion about the identity of the ship here."

"It was Forsythe's," Corwin repeated. "Goddamn him."

"Hiroshige didn't show up, did he?" Jordan said.

"How did you know that?"

"We need to talk, Charlie," Jordan said. "The whole thing's crazy as hell. Absolute insanity."

"What are you talking about?"

"I can't tell you on the telephone. I'm not sure yet anyway."

"I'm going to come on in. I'll meet you at your place in a couple of hours."

"That's not a good idea. I think somebody's watching me."

"Watching you?"

"Look, there's a tea pavilion on the grounds of the apartment complex. It'll be deserted. I'll meet you there."

"What's going on?" Corwin insisted. He could not be sure, but it sounded as if there were a sharp edge of fear in Jordan's voice. "Are you all right?"

"No, nothing's all right," Jordan said. "Everything's come unglued, I think. Especially me." There was heavy static on the line. The words were garbled. "I'll tell you about it when I see you."

"If I run into trouble on the way that holds me up, I'll call you." He severed the connection and dialed the maid. She protested that his clothes were not yet dry, but he told her it made no difference. He had to move on, and in the short journey from inn to car, he would be drenched again.

4

He made slower time than he had anticipated. The wind slackened somewhat as he passed Yokosuka, but the torrent of rain continued unabated and at places the road was covered by a running current, hubcap deep, and he had the feeling he was driving across a shallow lake without boundaries. Only by following the reference points of highway signs and the reflector poles set along the shoulder of the road was he able to stay on the pavement.

By the time he reached the expressway, he was too tired to care whether he made it or not. He hoped that the engine would quit, the matter taken out of his hands, forcing him to stop. The engine worked perfectly. A policeman in a slicker stood in the slow lane, a wreck, smashed metal, glass strewn everywhere, emergency lights blinking; the policeman motioned Corwin ahead, holding up a sign that said "Caution" in Japanese. He drove slowly, keeping the car in first gear, finally shifting into second as he edged into the slow lane. The Japanese drivers were crazy. Zero visibility, a screen of water so thick that other vehicles were little more than abstract lights if they could be seen at all, and still his car shuddered in the wake of trucks roaring blindly past him.

Frequent red lights, multiple wrecks, long lines of vehicles struggling past collisions only to speed up again when the casualties were past. He fought to stay awake. He clicked on the radio and turned it off again when he found more static than music. He smoked one cigarette after another until the small ashtray was overflowing. The initial shock of the burning village had been muted into a residual outrage and then into a sorting of the aspects of the practical problems it had raised.

For if Ives had been in financial trouble before, this incident would sink him. The Japanese were becoming more stringent all the time in their enforcement of penalties for oil spills, and with an accident of these proportions, the penalties could wipe him out. Ives might not only find himself bankrupt but imprisoned as well. Jesus, the rampant idiocy of it all, errors compounded, mistakes in judgment piling up until a couple of hundred people were dead and millions of dollars' worth of property destroyed, and even now the *San Marin* would be wallowing in the heavy seas off the coast of Honshu, a spaced-out captain at the helm. Ah, to hell with him; to hell with them all, at least for the present. Corwin would make the meeting with Jordan and then go back to the hotel and have another look at the confusion after he had slept.

By the time he reached Shinanomachi, there was no traffic whatsoever. The rain continued to pour straight down. The curbed streets were rivers. Jordan lived in an apartment complex that formed a three-sided square encompassing a Japanese sand garden and an open pavilion in the center, sheltered by trees. He parked the car at the curb next to a wall, letting himself through a heavy gate into the courtyard, drenched, chilled, not caring. From here the pavilion was a low-curved roof, partially obscured by trees. The apartments were all shuttered against the storm, no signs of life.

The sand garden was filled with rocks protruding from it to suggest islands and now the abstract had become real. It was flooded. He waded across it, his shoes full of water. He bumped his skin against one of the decorative rocks, fell sprawling, picked himself up, and slogged on. He reached the steps to the pavilion. It was empty, no sign of Jordan. He sank down onto a bench, shaking his lighter dry to coax a flame from it and check his watch. Almost two in the morning and he had missed Jordan by an hour. And even Jordan at his most patient would have waited no more than an hour before deciding that Corwin had broken down somewhere along the line without access to a telephone. Jordan would be in bed. He found his cigarettes wet again, but there were a couple he considered possible and he lighted one of them and studied the low shape of the apartment buildings. He could always stumble into those buildings in search of Jordan's apartment (he had been there once; he seemed to recall it was on the second floor), but the Japanese were heavily security conscious and he doubted he could enter one of those buildings without tangling with security personnel. To hell with it. He would call Jordan in the morning.

He sat there long enough to finish the cigarette, overcome by inertia. It would take him forty-five minutes to reach his hotel, but he could manage that. Perhaps he would call down for a bowl of hot noodles before he went to bed. He stood up, flipping the cigarette into the curtain of water, watching the spark go dark before it hit the ground. His legs were stiff. He set out across the garden again, lost his direction in the rain, and finally stumbled into the solid barrier of the fence. He followed it until he reached the gate and let himself out.

The moment he opened the car door, he froze. Jordan was sitting in the front passenger's seat, his head lolled back, straggling hair plastered against his thinning scalp, hands folded in the lap of his soaked suit, eyes half open as if he were looking straight ahead. His mouth hung slack as if he had been running and now gasping for breath. But there was no breath. Blood, a shirt stained red with it, almost black where the bullet had hit him, lightening to a pinkish stain where the blood had spread over the area of the wet shirt.

Dead, yes, my God, dead, the realization so sharp that Corwin closed the door without entering and the interior light went out and he stood leaning against the side of the car, suddenly sick to his stomach, racked with dry heaves and the taste of bile in his throat. And then it struck him. The man who had killed Jordan and put him in the car could still be here, somewhere in the surrounding darkness. He raised his head from the cold, wet surface of the car, peering into the black rain. He could see nothing.

He opened the car door and bracing himself slipped inside. He reached for Jordan's wrist, the flesh still slightly warm, the joint pliable. Jordan might not be dead at all. A small chance, against reason. He inserted the key in the ignition and ground the engine into life, clicking on the lights. He pulled away from the curb and floored the accelerator, the car raising a wake of spray as it leaped forward. He would find a hospital, an emergency call box, anything.

As he reached the corner, he saw two Japanese police patrol

cars moving slowly in the direction of the apartments and he drove into the middle of the intersection, leaving his lights on to illuminate him as he jumped out and stood in the glare, waving his arms to attract their attention. One of the cars stopped, the second driving past to stop behind his car. Half blinded by the lights, he moved forward, stopping only when he saw that the doors of the car were open and the Japanese officers behind them, guns drawn and pointed at him.

"I need help, goddamnit," he shouted at them. "I have an injured man in my car."

He turned. The light in his car went on as the officers from the second car reached it. He saw one of them leaning over Jordan. From his attitude, his lack of urgency, Corwin knew that Jordan was indeed dead. No mistake. No hope. He sagged slightly. One of the officers came out from behind the door and approached him through the rain. The polished surface of the rain cape over his shoulders gave him the appearance of a wet seal. He said something in Japanese and Corwin shook his head unable to comprehend anything.

The officer stopped a few feet in front of him, his face featureless. The light glinted on the barrel of his pistol. "Nothing sudden," he said, almost politely. "You are under arrest."

3

"YOU ARE AN INTELLIGENT MAN AND I ADMIRE INTELLIGENCE," the inspector was saying, leading the way down a tiled corridor. "Intelligence recognizes boundaries to what a reasonable man can accept and does not push past those boundaries." He came to a steel door with an inset window, allowed Corwin to enter, and then followed into a pleasant if efficient room, comfortable armchairs around a low table, an oversized map of the Kanto plain covering one wall, Tokyo and environs.

"I want to know the charges against me," Corwin said.

The inspector smiled, a facial reflex. Whatever appeared on the surface, Corwin knew that there was a solid, cold, unchangeable core to the man. Ito was oversized for a Japanese, an athlete with close-cropped hair, his body totally at ease in a navy-blue business suit. "Have a seat, Mr. Corwin," the inspector said.

"The charges."

"No charges as yet."

"Then I want to use the telephone."

"Soon." The inspector opened a drawer in the low table, removed a pack of American cigarettes and a small box of an English brand. He opened the American pack and Corwin took one, inhaling, leaning back in his chair. But he was here and Jordan was dead. The inspector opened the box of English cigarettes. "Suppose you tell me what happened?"

"I told your deputy. He recorded it."

"He doesn't speak English very well." The inspector lighted one of the English cigarettes, holding it as a prop to demonstrate his sense of easy congeniality. "Suppose you tell me. You drove up from Yokohama. What were you doing in Yokohama?"

"A business meeting."

"With whom?"

"A man named Stevenson."

"He can verify this?"

"He didn't show up because of the storm." A lie, yes, stupidity, but he needed time to think, to sort out.

"And you called Mr. Jordan from there."

"Yes. I arranged to meet him in the pavilion at his apartment."

"And?"

"He didn't meet me. When I returned to the car, I found him."

"Dead."

"Yes."

"How did he get there?"

"I don't know."

Inspector Ito waved the cigarette slightly as if trying to dispel the smoke. "How do you suppose he got there?"

"I don't know," Corwin said. "He was my friend. I had no reason to shoot him."

"Murder is often not reasonable, Mr. Corwin. I investigate dozens of murders a year and few of them are reasonable." He tapped a buzzer on the intercom and spoke into it. The door opened immediately and a uniformed officer brought in the attaché case and placed it on the table unopened. The inspector waited until he was gone. "Would you like a cup of coffee?"

"No," Corwin said. "I need to sleep."

"Certainly. Very soon." He put the cigarette in the groove of a brass ashtray and then he tapped the brass clasp of the attaché case with the immaculate nail of his index finger. "Strange," he said. "You have to admit that."

"What?"

"The money. Such a large amount in American currency."

"As far as I know, that's not illegal."

"That depends on what you were doing with it."

"I was making a payment."

"To whom?"

Corwin said nothing for a moment, inhaling the cigarette, trying to slow the pace of the questioning, the momentum. He tapped the ashes over the ashtray but they showered onto the floor. "Let me make a telephone call and I'll answer that for you."

"Soon," the inspector said, pleasantly. He pressed the buzzer again and the policeman came in with a box. It was placed on the table in front of the inspector who looked to Corwin. "Do you recognize this?"

"It looks familiar."

The inspector took his time opening the case and Corwin frowned, puzzled. It was Forsythe's pistol.

"Yes," Corwin said. "Where did you get it?"

"From the backseat of your car."

"Impossible."

"Nevertheless," the inspector said and left the word dangling. He took the pistol out of the case, handling it expertly, clicking open the cylinder. "A fine and efficient piece of lethal machinery," he said, sighting through the empty chambers. He placed it back in the presentation case, closed the lid. "Why do you say it's impossible?"

The hell with it, Corwin thought, for the inspector was making implications now, moving toward a predictable point that would see him dead-ended. There was no need to protect the company, to shelter Ives. For the inspector would not have that pistol now except for Ives's carelessness in not securing the pistol.

"Very well," he said with a sense of tired relief. "I will make a full statement."

"You wish to change your testimony."

"Yes."

The inspector leaned forward and pressed another button. "For your information, our conversation is being recorded now. I will have your statement transcribed and you can sign it."

"Good enough," Corwin said, and he told the inspector everything that had happened, the death of Okata on the *San Marin*, the subsequent drawing up of an accident report, the involvement of the Red Watch, and the company's decision to pay them off. He brought him up to the point where he had found Jordan in the car and then stopped. The inspector said nothing for a long moment. "And who did you deal with in the Red Watch?"

"Okata's brother. He calls himself Hiroshige."

"Hiroshige?"

"Yes."

"I know him." The inspector squinted at his watch. He was nearsighted. "You saw the fire at Futtsu?"

"Yes."

"And you here and now identify the responsible ship as the *San Marin*?" He was speaking to the concealed recorder now, laying in the key elements of the statement.

"Of course. Yes, it was the *San Marin*." Corwin's throat was dry. "Did that pistol kill Jordan?"

The inspector nodded. Silent assent. Nothing going onto the tape. "Your fingerprints are on the pistol. Who would want to place you in this predicament, Mr. Corwin?"

"I don't know."

"Our Japanese system of justice depends on possibilities,"

the inspector said, pressing his fingertips together. "The circumstances say that you killed Jordan because appearances lead to that conclusion. But I am a good judge of character, Mr. Corwin, and I would judge you to be a man of good sense, not easily carried away. I believe if you had shot Mr. Jordan in your vehicle, you would not have carried him away with you."

The inspector frowned thoughtfully, asked if for any reason, no matter how farfetched, somebody could be trying to implicate him, discredit him, frame him, put him out of commission. Corwin could not. But something nagged him, stuck in his memory.

"There's one thing," he said. "When I talked to Jordan on the telephone, he knew that the money had not been paid to Hiroshige, that Hiroshige had not shown up."

"Oh?" The inspector's interest heightened. "How?"

"I don't know. He said, 'The whole thing's crazy as hell, absolute insanity.' That was the reason he wanted to meet."

"I don't mean to inconvenience you, Mr. Corwin, I know you've been without sleep for a long time, but I think we can clear some of these matters up. If you don't feel up to it now, you can rest first."

"No," Corwin said. "I want it over with."

The inspector picked up the telephone, spoke in a staccato and imperative language, summoning the car. He put the telephone down and stood thoughtful, his right hand in his jacket pocket, looking at Corwin. "I'm sorry I can't offer you a change of clothing," he said. "You must be terribly uncomfortable."

Instantly, the door opened and a uniformed policeman came in, carrying a slicker for Corwin who put it on. It was slightly undersized but Corwin welcomed it. He followed the inspector outside, momentarily confused, having no idea where he was, what part of the city, for the rain was still coming down and there was a slight graying in the night sky to the east. He was startled. Dawn again. He had gone around the clock.

The inspector sat in the rear seat with him, chatting about the storm, the dumping of the rain, the canals that had become torrents, the drainage problems of the metropolis, the storm center that had already shifted far to the east, into the Pacific, so that Tokyo was now under the remote outer edge of the turbulent pinwheel. The forecasters were calling for clearing by midday. Corwin thought of the *San Marin*, somewhere at sea. Would Forsythe steam for Kobe now?

"What will you do about the *San Marin*?" he said.

"That's not my decision. The Transport Ministry will alert the Self-Defense Forces, I imagine. When the storm passes, the ship will be forced to turn back to Yokohama."

So be it, Corwin thought, and Forsythe would be spending the rest of his truncated life here, defending himself against charges of criminal negligence. The heavy morning traffic was slower than usual in the rain. Finally, he oriented himself. Chiba, and he could see the smokestacks against the sky.

"Can you direct us to the meeting place?"

"Turn right at the next intersection," Corwin said.

The car made the turn. "We have a procedure that I will ask you to follow, Mr. Corwin. Unless I ask you a question, you will remain quiet. The law requires it."

Corwin saw the building ahead, the web of bamboo scaffolding hung across the front. Even in the dawn rain a clot of workmen were gathered around a small fire sheltered by a canvas lean-to, squatting over a pile of bricks, patiently cleaning them. They did not look up at the police car parked in front of the building.

"You're sure this is the building, Mr. Corwin?" the inspector said.

"Yes, I'm sure."

He moved across the sidewalk in the rain, preceded by the uniformed officer, but from the minute Corwin entered the hallway and began to climb the stairs, he was dismayed. There were no Red Watch posters on the walls, no photographs of Okata, nothing but an official notice on a Japanese document, Xeroxed calligraphy and a bright red seal at the bottom. The officer went up the stairs two at a time and by the time Corwin reached the room he saw him standing in the center of deserted space. Some of the paper-covered windows had been blown in and there were water stains where the rain had collected.

Corwin shook his head, incredulous. Trash littered the floor, crumpled newspapers, tin cans, the stink of disuse all pervasive. Trickles of water dripped down from holes in the ceiling. He moved to the place where the table had been. Nothing to mark its existence. The inspector strolled casually around the large room, his hands clasped behind his back. "Could you have picked the wrong place?"

"No," Corwin said. "This is it. They were here."

The inspector shrugged, said something to the policeman who left the room. He looked around at the litter. "It's obvious that they moved in here for the meeting with you and then vacated. These radical groups never stay in one place."

The officer reappeared, bringing with him an old and toothless man wearing a workman's jacket with the company symbol stamped on the back. He carried his hat in his gnarled hands and he gave Corwin a perfunctory bow and then bowed to the inspector, hissing salutations. The inspector began to ask him questions and Corwin picked up the drift of his answers. The old man had been here all day yesterday and the building looked then just as it did now. There had been nobody in it, no posters on the wall. And finally Corwin could tolerate it no longer.

"What hours were you here?" he said in Japanese to the workman.

"All day." A wide and respectful smile.

"Where do you go to the toilet? Where do you eat your

lunch? You can't persuade me you were out there every minute."

"*Hai*," the workman said, taking no offense. He went to the toilet at the side of the building and ate his meals from a *bento* that he carried with him. "It is my obligation," he said to Corwin.

"Then if that's true, you saw me here, yesterday. I came in a black limousine and there was a group of Japanese already here."

The old man looked genuinely puzzled. "*Wakarimasen*," he said. A stream of words, phrases, caught between the desire to please and an obvious blankness and Corwin had the desire to force him to remember, to bring this one point straight, but the inspector dismissed him, glancing up toward the leaking ceiling, the streams of water pouring onto the hardwood floor.

"I apologize to you for putting you through all this," the inspector said. "I believe your story, Mr. Corwin, and I can guarantee you a successful resolution."

Once they reached the car, he told the uniformed officer to put out a call for Hiroshige, then he turned to Corwin with a calming smile. "We will have no difficulty now," he said. The inspector's voice was pacifying, conversational while the police car crept through the waterlogged streets. Corwin's mind drifted toward sleep, but the radio crackled and he came awake.

"You see?" the inspector said. "One of my men has already located Hiroshige. So I wouldn't worry if I were you."

"I want to make a telephone call. Then I want a shower, shave, breakfast, and a chance to sleep."

"I know this has been hard on you."

"I appreciate your sympathy," Corwin said, the irritation flaring again. "But I'm tired of your indirection. Make a formal charge if that's what you're going to do. Then I can at least handle this through my own legal channels."

"You don't have any rights," the inspector said, matter-of-factly. "And I don't think you want due process, Mr. Corwin. I can handle this case at my own discretion, within certain boundaries. You are far better off with my discretion, believe me, than you would be in the courts. I believe you. They might not."

"Do I get my telephone call?"

"Not yet."

"The shower, the shave, the breakfast?"

"Certainly. If you like, I will send a man to your apartment to bring you fresh clothing."

"I want an hour's rest."

"Of course. Time permitting."

They reached the station, a long low gray concrete building; he could not tell whether this was the place where he had been brought during the night. The car went down a ramp into a basement garage. "We have to take precautions," the inspector said. "There was a terrible row in the media this morning over the destruction of the fishing settlement. The rumor has gone out that we have a suspect. We have made no comment, of course, and your name certainly has not been mentioned. When you leave here, there won't be anything to connect you with this in any way."

The basement was damp, chilly, but Corwin did not care. He would not fight the process. The elevator carried them to the third floor, narrow corridors, the pervasive smell of raw concrete. "I can offer you private use of one of the large shower rooms," the inspector said, apologetically. "It's unfortunate that we don't have adequate facilities here."

The shower room was a long, open, tiled room with multiple shower heads protruding from one wall. The inspector left him there in the company of a younger Japanese officer who sat on a three-legged stool beyond the spray, a clipboard propped on one knee, asking questions while Corwin undressed and surrendered himself to the hot water. The Japanese did things backward. Only now were they filling in background information.

He put on the rough robe that the officer gave him and went into another room where the officer took an electric razor out of a case and plugged it into the wall, flipping it on before he gave it to Corwin. Corwin was amused. An electric razor. Certainly. They would have no sharp instruments, not in a culture where the supreme remedy was a self-imposed slash across the abdomen. He shaved without the benefit of a mirror, running his fingers over his jawbone to make certain he had missed nothing.

He was provided a bowl of rice, slices of raw fish, and he ate with relish. By the time he finished, his clothing had arrived and he put on the fresh suit. He was not refreshed. There was a slight muscular tick in his left hand. He was not as resilient as he once had been. In his early thirties, he had often gone forty-eight hours without sleep, following up on a maritime accident, with sufficient reserve at the end to dictate the reports; but now he had no such reserve. He was depleted.

He was taken back to the office where Ito was sorting through the stacks of hundred-dollar bills on the table, occasionally studying one, writing serial numbers on a legal pad. "We have a peculiar situation here, Mr. Corwin. Where did this money come from?"

"I've been over that. You know damn well where it came from."

"From your comptroller's office."

"Yes."

"From what account?"

"It's an undesignated account."

"That's the problem," Ito said, drumming the pencil against the table. "Unfortunately, the comptroller of your company flew back to the States this morning on his annual vacation," Ito said. "And no one in his office can find a record of it. They made a preliminary audit and they can't find any shortage of cash funds."

Impossible, Corwin thought, and yet it was happening. Of course, there would be no record of the money. It was a part of Ives's slush fund, money to be dispensed whenever there was a need for it. Extra legal. "Goddamnit, call Ives himself," Corwin said. "The son of a bitch authorized the money. It wouldn't have been paid without his authorization."

"That's a problem," Ito said evenly, standing up, adjusting his suit jacket, folding his reading glasses and inserting them into a case. "He's not available, but we have another lead on the money." Japanese requirements were quite stringent concerning foreign currencies, he went on, and whenever Japanese yen were converted into American dollars through a foreign exchange bank, records were kept.

"We have such a record from the foreign exchange branch in Shinjuku," Ito said. "This money has no connection with the Ives Company. The exchange was made by a Japanese trading company in behalf of an individual Japanese citizen."

"You're being naïve, Inspector," Corwin said. "That's exactly the procedure Ives would use to launder the money in the first place." He went momentarily blank, forgetting what line of thought he was following. To remain sharp, focused, yes, that was the problem, for he felt that in some way he was being trapped and should take steps to prevent it, but his mind was drifting.

He was aware of a slot window in the room, a long rectangle of light spilling across the neutral carpet, a sure indication that the clouds were breaking away. Was Ito talking? Yes. He was standing on the balls of his feet, rocking back and forth, almost imperceptibly, the goddamned box of English cigarettes in his hand and he was talking about money, about the Japanese who had received it.

Corwin shook his head. "We're going to have to call this off for now," he said.

"Beg your pardon?"

"I haven't slept in forty-eight hours."

"I'm sure you need your rest," Ito said. The telephone rang and he picked it up with a smooth sweep of his hand and Corwin could see him as a baseball player, that hand of his sweeping up a grounder in the stadium at Yoyogi. Ito said something, put the telephone down. "I will have to ask you to do one more thing," he said. "An hour at the most and the matter will be resolved and you can rest as long as you wish."

"An hour."

"Yes. First, I want you to look at the list of names on the table. Do you recognize any of them?"

Corwin picked up the paper, shook his head. There was a list of twenty-seven Japanese names. "No," he said.

He found himself walking to the car with Ito who glanced up at the breaking clouds and began to talk about his golf game, the difficulty of playing the courses around Tokyo, the mobs of people. Diversionary conversation, yes, and Corwin suddenly knew what he was doing. *Haragei*, the Japanese concept of stomach art, a gut game. He had run into it before, the putting on of a front, to conceal the true intentions. At no point had Ito considered him innocent and all of this talk was designed to keep him cooperative while Ito drove the car through narrow alleys, slipping into boulevards and congested lanes. Corwin said nothing. His head was hurting. He found his sunglasses in his suit pocket and slipped them on against the reflected glare of the streets. "Where are we going?" he said, finally.

"We located Hiroshige," Ito said. "He's a little reluctant to talk, but that's not surprising, considering the political stance he's taken. He shares the paranoia of the revisionists. Since he has returned to the militarism of the late 1930s, he views the police as they were then."

"Jordan's widow," Corwin said.

"What?"

"I need to talk to her. Jordan loved her a great deal. I want to know when the funeral is scheduled." Foolishness, he thought, to be worrying about Jordan's funeral.

They were approaching a building on a slight rise, surrounded by an economical expanse of lawn and trees spotted here and there for shade. It was a hospital. He turned a questioning face to the inspector. "What's Hiroshige doing in a hospital?"

"Diagnostic tests," Ito said. "Something to do with leg muscles, I believe. That's the reason I didn't insist on his coming to the station."

Inside, the hospital was antiseptic but cheerful, an institution run by Japanese Catholics, and he was struck by the incongruity of Oriental nuns and a crucifix hanging on a white wall, an Oriental Christ.

The elevator opened onto the fourth floor and Ito led the way into the sunroom, rather old-fashioned, a wall of small-paned windows opened to the south, overlooking a residential district. A nun was watering plants. She smiled and nodded to Ito as he asked her a question, then pointed out the red box of the pay telephone on a window table next to a wicker chair.

Corwin looked to Ito. "You're going to permit me to make a telephone call?"

"Of course. I asked that Hiroshige be brought here for our interview."

Corwin nodded, fumbled in his pocket for change, inserted the aluminum coins in the slot on the telephone, pausing a moment to recall Ives's number. Why did so many Tokyo numbers begin with zero? Did they regard it as an integer?

He got the wrong number. His dialing had been in error. This was not the time to make mistakes. He took out his pen, wrote the numbers on a slip of paper, dialed them exactly. He was openly relieved when he got past the switchboard and the secretary and Ives himself came onto the line, strangely subdued.

"I've been expecting your call," Ives said. "What's happening?"

Where to approach the confusion, where to begin, that was the problem when it was difficult to keep anything in clear focus. He cleared his throat. "I need a hell of a lot of answers, Ives. You know about the village. Who gave Forsythe clearance to sail?"

"He didn't need clearance, you know that," Ives said. "He's a fully licensed pilot for Tokyo Bay. He just made a call for tugs and put out on his own. What happened to you, Charlie?"

"I'm in police custody, that's what happened to me. I want a number of things out of the company. First, I want a statement from you concerning the payoff of the Japanese radicals. There's some confusion about where that money came from. Then I want a full disclosure concerning Forsythe and the death of Okata. When the *San Marin*'s located, I want a statement from Forsythe." The nun was watering a plant with variegated leaves, chatting with Ito who sat in a wicker chair, legs crossed, the creases of his trousers perfectly straight, the tips of his fingers pressed together.

"You haven't heard?" Ives said. "There's no way you could have. I just got the report."

"Heard what?"

"The *San Marin*'s missing, presumed sunk," Ives said. The Japanese Self-Defense Forces had just contacted him. They had received a mayday distress during the height of the storm and one of their planes had spotted a small oil slick and debris approximately one hundred miles southeast of the Futtsu

Straits. An aerial photograph confirmed the lettering on one shredded lifeboat as coming from the *San Marin*. The Japanese authorities concluded that the *San Marin* had run into winds in excess of a hundred miles an hour and a sea with seventy-five-foot waves. Helicopters had made a grid search and found no survivors. "So that's done," Ives said. "Now I don't know what in the hell got into you, Charlie, but I'm sure you have good reasons. I'm in touch with my board of directors and even if they won't back you, I will."

The line went dead. The goddamned Japanese telephones, and there was a time limit on a toll call and when it was up the line went dead. No recourse. He fumbled in his pocket. No more coins. A fat Japanese man was being wheeled into the room by a nurse. Irrelevant. What was Ives saying? What in the hell was he talking about? He put down the telephone. Through the window he saw a large block of blackbirds wheeling in the sunlight, their wings iridescent. The inspector had not changed position. He was talking to the man in the wheelchair. Corwin stood up, stretching the stiffness out of his legs, walking across the room to where the inspector sat. The man in the wheelchair glanced up at him and then went on with the lighting of his cigarette, his hands trembling slightly.

Ito had a curious expression on his face. "You don't know this gentleman?" Ito said, nodding toward the man in the wheelchair.

"No," Corwin said. "Should I?"

Ito spoke to the man in the wheelchair, in Japanese, asking him if he knew Corwin and the man responded in a vague negative, his hand bringing the cigarette to his face in a jerky, stabbing motion, and Corwin knew that this tableau had been arranged, the physical positioning, the results known in advance.

"This is the man known as Hiroshige, Mr. Corwin," Ito said, evenly.

"Impossible," Corwin said. "It's not the same man."

"I didn't believe it was," Ito said. "But I had to be sure. It seems that Hiroshige has been in this hospital for the last month. In addition to his leg problems, he also has a nervous disorder."

Neatly trapped, yes, snared, hooked, and surprisingly, Corwin felt no panic, no alarm, as if he had already absorbed too much for that. Could it be that Ives was at the center of what was happening? Possible, yes. No reason. Corwin had to keep his mind free. He was an expert at sorting out, at disentangling. By unraveling one thread at a time, he could eventually free himself. He sat down, facing Hiroshige whose eyes were dulled as if he were preoccupied with his own thoughts.

"He's quite impossible," Ito said, as if Hiroshige was not really there at all. "The prognosis is not a hopeful one, I'm afraid." He nodded to the nurse who wheeled Hiroshige away abruptly and almost immediately the nun appeared with a silver tray and proceeded to pour coffee.

Corwin sipped the coffee. It was hot, bitter. "Suppose you level with me," he said evenly. "No more pretense."

"Perhaps you're right," Ito said. He was cool, unruffled. He rubbed his manicured fingers along the sleeve of his jacket. "We will assume that the young men of the Red Watch are erratic terrorists and they are able to get a lot of action out of Okata. He was crazy, of course, but very imaginative. He kept his men active, drilling them all the time, sending them all over the world." He ran a finger around the rim of the coffee cup. "We have no idea why he was trying to steal the *San Marin*. Maybe he was going to sell the cargo, but he was killed in the process. Do you wish more coffee?"

"No. Go on."

"His men would have to take some action to avenge his death. They could make an attack on the ship in the harbor, of course, cause trouble for the company. But instead, I believe that they actually stole the ship from the dock, to carry through what their leader had failed to accomplish."

"So that's what you think?"

"Yes."

"Impossible." Corwin finished the coffee, the bitter taste lingering in his mouth. "They couldn't have stolen the ship without alerting security forces all over the harbor. They couldn't have known that Forsythe was remaining on board. It couldn't have happened, none of it. Watanabe runs tight security."

"There is a way," Ito said, with no change of expression. "I could build a good case if I didn't believe to the contrary. You could have provided them with everything they needed. All of the evidence points to you."

Corwin blinked silently.

"Just consider," Ito said, shifting in his chair away from a direct shaft of sunlight. "You were contacted by the Red Watch who arranged a meeting and offered you a proposition. If you would arrange to put them on board the *San Marin* they would pay you the sum of a hundred and fifty thousand dollars. But they couldn't be certain you would follow through without betraying them as soon as they steamed out of Yokohama. Also, they could not be certain of the cargo. If it was, say, asphaltic tar, for instance, it would be useless to them. So they arranged for the payment to be made near the Futtsu Strait, at an isolated place where they could test that cargo by spilling and igniting. You would be far enough from a telephone that you couldn't spread any alarm at all before they made the open water and the cover of the storm."

Corwin laughed slightly. "Ingenious," he said. "God-damned clever."

"The crew put aboard the *San Marin*," Ito said. "They were all Red Watch, all authorized by you."

"You can prove that?"

"No," Ito said. "It's customary here for an employer to stand by his employees. Ives refuses to say anything. But take the matter of the money exchange. We have traced that far enough to know it did not go to the Ives Company. It went to somebody connected with the Red Watch."

Loopholes, yes, large holes that could be exploited by a clever lawyer, they were bound to be there, but at the moment he could not see them. "So the money is delivered to me."

"Yes. And the storm hits before you can get away, so there is a wealth of witnesses to your progress back to Tokyo. You passed a wreck; you registered at an inn; there are telephone records; you were observed by an officer of the NRP on the expressway. And finally you went to see your colleague. His wife will testify, has testified, that he left the apartment to meet you and that he was highly agitated. He came down and met you." Ito paused as the nun refilled his coffee cup. Two more families entered the sunroom. A small girl sat silently in the corner making a cat's cradle of string on her fingers.

"You argued," Ito said. "Perhaps a progression of the discovery, outrage, leading to your shooting him. Or perhaps he was in on it and wanted a larger share. Nevertheless, you still had the pistol that you took from Captain Forsythe. Perhaps you didn't mean to kill him. The prosecutor would have to concede that because you have no criminal record of any sort, but the pistol was there and it became a convenience. You panicked when the deed was done, began to drive away, and when you saw the pair of metro patrol cars, you immediately surrendered."

Corwin watched the fingers of the moon-faced little girl as she continued to manipulate the string, now a triangle, now a complex web that became a Gordian knot and dissolved. Ah, shit, he had been set up. The pattern of events was too coordinated to be coincidental. It was carefully constructed.

"What do you want out of me?" he said.

"A demonstration of the truth," Ito said. He lighted a cigarette, smoked without inhaling. "If I had believed you guilty, I would have handled this differently. I would have placed you in a detention cell, interrogated, brought to trial."

"I don't believe you," Corwin said. "I've been around fraud all my life. You think I'm guilty as hell. How could you think otherwise? Someone's gone to a great deal of trouble to set this up."

"Who?"

"Ives, probably."

"For what reason?"

"I don't have the slightest idea. But you didn't put me in a cell because you want a hell of a lot more out of this than me. Am I right?"

"I don't believe you're guilty," Ito said, unruffled. "But even if you were guilty, we would consider your crime of lesser importance. The Red Watch is a continuing menace, an embarrassment to every decent Japanese citizen. If you had conspired with them and offered testimony to that effect, we would be very pleased to put them away."

"And what would I be offered in return?"

"I can't say."

"You have some idea."

"I can give you the range of possibilities. At one extreme, you might be offered immunity. At the other, you might have to plead guilty to self-defense in a struggle with Mr. Jordan. I can't say what the penalty would be in that case."

A bell rang somewhere in the hospital, a single clear peal. Corwin could not tell whether it was a call to mass or a doctor's signal. Ito had made his position quite clear, the logic of insanity, and if he was willing to plead guilty to something he had not done and testify against a political group, he would receive a lighter penalty than if he stood mute and allowed the circumstances to engulf him. They most certainly would; he could not escape them. He could not count on a logical unraveling of the truth to save him. If Ives had gone to this much trouble, then the countless minor details would be covered as well.

He was aware that Ito was waiting for an answer, sitting perfectly still, the smoke curling up from his cigarette. "I had nothing to do with it," Corwin said. He was aware that the words did not register. "I want you to call Ives at this number." He searched in his pocket for the scrap of paper, handed it to Ito. "It may not do any good, but I want to confront him. Tell him we will be there in thirty minutes. He is to have the cash records available from the seven three four special account. That will list all the Japanese trading companies he uses."

If Ito was disappointed, he did not show it. He carefully snuffed the cigarette in the ashtray full of sand. "I think you should know the risk, Mr. Corwin."

"What risk?"

"If you entered into a cooperative agreement with us, then we could shelter this whole affair until its conclusion, so to speak, keep it quiet. We will do our best to maintain security in any event, but if your name becomes publicly connected, you run the great risk of personal harm. A lot of people are very incensed about the deaths in the fishing settlement."

"I'll take the risk," Corwin said. He knew what he was going to do now. Ito stood up, glancing toward the telephone at the far side of the room. A maintenance man in a blue uniform was making a call.

"Special account seven three four," Ito said.

"That's correct."

"I'll arrange a meeting with him," Ito said. "I ask you not to worry if nothing comes of the meeting. Our system is very complex, difficult for Westerners to understand, but we have a high batting average." The maintenance man finished his conversation, made a perfunctory bow to the telephone, and put it back on the cradle. Ito made his way through a family cluster sitting next to a row of potted bamboo plants and in that instant Corwin stood up and went out the door into the hallway, walking quickly, half-dazed. He passed the elevator in favor of the stairwell and ran down it, slowing to a walk before he entered the lobby, crossing it to the sidewalk and the taxi stand. He expected to be stopped at any moment, to see Ito running from the building, or for a phalanx of police to emerge from the hazy sunshine. Too simple, yes, and a taxi door hissed open automatically and he climbed in and instructed the driver to take him to the nearest station on the loop line. Too easy and he knew it, for Ito had made no attempt to stop him. He could not congratulate himself on his ingenuity or his timing. It was highly possible Ito had planned this escape, encouraged it in the sure knowledge that Corwin could not escape from this tightly interlaced society and that he would in some way further his own incrimination.

It was only as he reached the station and climbed the concrete steps to the platform that he realized he had no plan, no goal, that he was simply fleeing from a sense of helplessness. He could count on staying free only until Ito could see that he was going nowhere, at which time he would be picked up again. He looked up at the sign swinging in the summer wind. Yoyogi, the name of the station, the *kitagana* characters spelling it out phonetically beneath the English letters. Three women in baggy *mompeis* were sweeping off a corner of the platform with straw brooms, piling twigs and branches from the storm into a single pile in the center of a cloth sling.

Changing, yes, he felt it. He knew nothing about the psychology of sleeplessness, but he was rising from a sluggish inertia into a heightened awareness, a kind of euphoria that would sustain him for a while. He was attracted by the papers on a newsstand, the photographs on a Japanese tabloid, pictures of the fishing settlement, other photographs of the oil slick and wreckage at sea. He bought the tabloid and asked the vendor for a copy of the English edition of *Asahi*, a newspaper noted for its accuracy and depth of reporting.

He boarded the next train, ticketed for Tokyo station. The car was partially filled; he found a seat near the door, saving the newspapers until he had decided on a course of action. His own apartment was out; likewise any contact with anyone at the company would be picked up immediately. He was determined now to disappear for a while, to give himself a chance to think. Hotels were beyond him; the registration cards were examined regularly by the police.

It would have to be someplace where he was not known and would not attract attention. He examined every alternative, came up with nothing. He checked the contents of his pockets. Everything had been transferred into the fresh suit. They had taken nothing from him at the station. He unfolded *Asahi* first, looking for the report of Jordan's death, found a small item on the tenth page, vaguely written, a notice of a homicide. He turned back to the first page, which for the most part was filled with news of the typhoon, damages in Shikoku and along the south coast of Honshu.

The report of the damage at the fishing settlement was most curious, for *Asahi* had concluded that the *San Marin* was damaged by the storm, causing a spill of aviation gasoline that had ignited and caused damage inside the breakwater and a fire along the waterfront. The International Red Cross was devoting special effort to the inhabitants of the settlement. The *San Marin* itself had become a victim of the storm, sinking with all hands some ninety-six miles off the Japanese coast.

He picked up the tabloid, studying the pictures, realizing that there was something wrong here without knowing exactly what disturbed him. The photographs were dramatic pictures of an official Japanese helicopter hovering over an oil slick that appeared as dark black patches against the choppy waters of the ocean and there was a litter of trash, boxes, barrels, wooden debris, and a lifeboat awash and wallowing almost immediately below the helicopter. It was tidy, self-contained, a perfect assemblage of wreckage, perhaps too much so, for in his career he had investigated hundreds of marine casualties connected with tankers and there was a crazy inconsistency to them as if the anomaly was the rule rather than the exception. Once, after an explosion had split a ship in half, the bow had sunk with all hands while the stern remained afloat, the men unharmed. After an explosion in the Persian Gulf, he had found a live house cat on a box full of glassware, none of the pieces chipped, after the ship had gone down.

This one disturbed him. If the *San Marin* had indeed been sunk by the storm, the wind and the heavy seas would have dispersed that wreckage, stringing it out for miles, and if there had really been an oil slick it would have been considerably larger than the one he saw in the photograph. He could not be certain of anything because he knew the sea too well to exclude any possibilities. But he wondered if the *San Marin* was at the bottom of the sea at all.

He examined the photographs in the tabloid and they tended to confirm his suspicions. If the spill had been gasoline, there would have been a dull sheen to the surface of the water, not the deep tarry black so apparent in the pictures. He turned back to the *Asahi* text to see if there was any mention of a laser analysis that could have confirmed the type of oil slick, but there was none. He could prove nothing at this point, of course, for maritime hearings were insistent on hard fact, not appearances, and the sinking of the *San Marin* could be demonstrated by the evidence.

Shit, what difference did it make anyway? Whatever the reasons for the *San Marin*'s survival or destruction, it would not affect his present predicament. His only hope lay in disappearing, in finding a way to leave the country. And then he remembered Forsythe's daughter and the fact that she worked for one of the newspapers in Tokyo. He was certain she spoke no Japanese, so that limited the field to three, the *Japan Times, The Mainichi Daily News,* and the *Asahi Evening News.* On a hunch, he decided on *Mainichi* and got off the train at Yuracucho, in the heart of the downtown district, making his way to a telephone booth where he asked for an English-speaking operator who gave him the *Mainichi* number. He managed to reach the switchboard and confirm that an American woman named Forsythe did indeed work there, before the three minutes was up and the line went dead abruptly. He put in another coin, dialed again, cursing beneath his breath. He told the switchboard operator to put him straight through to Miss Forsythe. Faye's voice came on the line.

"This is Corwin," he said. "I want to talk to you."

"You son of a bitch," she said and hung up on him.

He used his last coin to dial again. "Don't hang up," he said. "I believe your father is still alive."

There was silence on the line and he knew she was thinking it over. "What more do you want from me, Mr. Corwin?"

"I want you to meet me someplace, just to talk."

"About my father."

"Yes."

Another pause. "I'll meet you at the main gate of the Imperial Plaza in fifteen minutes." The line went dead again.

He walked down the street, through a heavy concentration of Japanese businessmen in Western-style suits, the ubiquitous white shirts and ties, as rigorously required now as uniforms had been in the old days. And seventy-two hours ago he had been in this district on business, and now he could no longer remember the name of the man across the table from him then, and this innocent street had become enemy territory.

The woman had become terribly important to him now. It was essential that she help him. Ito's plan, whatever it was, would only proceed to a certain point before he decided to have Corwin picked up, and even now Corwin imagined that he could feel the eyes of the men watching him, unseen, for they had surely tracked him from the hospital, passing him from hand to hand, from one observer to the next. Where was the surveillance now? On one of the upper floors of an adjacent building, a man with a pair of binoculars? The businessman across the street, heavyset, who seemed to be stopping to examine a piece of paper from his pocket before he went into the building?

The trick now was to escape a man he could not see, to out-guess the pattern Ito was using and then try to move against it, to become unpredictable. He could not lead them to the woman because she represented his last link to freedom. He stood at a corner, waiting for the light to change, then set off in a crowd of people, reversing himself in the middle of the street as he saw a taxi with an unoccupied sign flagging red in the window, the sign black calligraphy on a greenish-yellow background signifying an owner driver. He ran up to it, flashing three fingers, indicating that he would pay triple rate and he was inside the cab in what seemed like a fraction of a second. The light changed and the taxi moved on.

He told the driver to continue straight ahead and watched through the rear window with a feeling of futility, running from watchdogs he could not see, not knowing whether he was really being followed or not. The taxi reached a corner and Corwin directed the driver into a hard left and then, in the middle of the block, thrust the triple fare at the driver and got out. He walked up a narrow lane lined with noodle vendors and small shops, with strings of brightly colored paper lanterns overhead. He had his bearings now; the Im-perial Palace lay north and west and he set out at a steady pace, checking his watch. Ten minutes had elapsed since he had talked to her. If she arrived at the Imperial Plaza and he was not there, she would not wait for him. He continued to walk, picking up his pace, staying to the narrow streets, and when he came out onto the broad avenue flanking the palace moat, he saw her standing at a low balustrade, watching the swans. She was totally different from the way he had seen her aboard the *San Marin*, wearing a soft dress, her hair shining in the sunlight. She glanced at him as he approached and then turned her attention back to the swans.

"I'm a very skeptical woman, Mr. Corwin," she said. "My professors at Radcliffe said I was the most skeptical woman they had ever had."

"I don't doubt it." He felt very exposed in this open area.

"Why in the hell did you dispatch the *San Marin* into that storm?"

"I didn't dispatch it."

"Somebody ordered my father to go. He wouldn't have done it on his own."

He would have to risk it, he could not wait. To stay here would ensure ensnarement. "I don't intend to take the time to try and convince you. I can't stay here. The police are after me."

"Oh?" she said, looking at him directly.

"I gave you five minutes, remember? I think you owe me that much. But we can't talk here."

She considered a moment, shrugged. "Where, then? What do they want you for?"

"They think I killed a man."

He began to walk along the sidewalk fronting the plaza, the schoolbuses pumping children out, mobs of orderly little girls in powder-blue uniforms and round straw hats. Faye kept up with him, her large leather purse flopping at her side, her face curious. He led her across the boulevard and toward the Ginza, entering the first noodle shop he found, seating himself so that a translucent plastic screen sheltered him from the street. She sat at the narrow table across from him, waiting while he ordered tea.

"Whom did you kill?" she said.

"Nobody. I'm accused of killing Jordan, the man in the limousine. What do you do at *Mainichi*?"

"Rewrite," she said. "You're using up your five minutes, you know. What's this business about my father?"

"I think he's alive."

"Then you don't believe he went down with the *San Marin*?"

"I don't believe the *San Marin* went down at all," he said. He sat on the stool and quite suddenly he felt himself tipping, as if his balance had suddenly been snatched away from him. He caught himself with his two hands flat on the tabletop. He could feel the cold sweat popping out on his forehead. Dizzy.

"Are you all right?" she said, alarmed.

"Hell, no, I'm not all right," he said, irritated. "I'm about to drop in my tracks. Where's your apartment?"

"I'm not going to take you there."

"No, you're going back to work," he said. He stayed upright with effort, aware of the comfortable darkness of the corner of his mind, wanting to surrender to it. "I want you to bring me every scrap of information the newspaper has about the accident at the fishing settlement, the sinking of the *San Marin*. I want all the background you can get about Ives and his company and his finances."

"God, you look awful," she said. "You'd never make it to my apartment."

"Jesus," he said. "Don't argue with me and don't commiserate with me. You'll either go along with me or you won't and I'm not sure it matters either way."

She opened a purse, took out a key, and handed it to him. "My apartment is number five," she said. "I'll get a taxi and give him my address card."

"No," he said. "Give me the card and I'll show it to him."

She nodded, handed him the card, then paid the bill and

went out onto the street to hail a taxi. She returned momentarily. "Can you walk?" she said. "Do you need help?"

"We have to do nothing to attract attention, nothing to make anybody remember we were here." He forced himself to stand erect, walking a tightrope, blinking as he came into the bright sunlight, everything swimming around him, colors blurring. But he could make out the shape of the taxi, the door back, the yawning shadow of the backseat awaiting him.

"What time will you be there?" he said.

"About seven," she said. "You'd better understand me, Mr. Corwin. I'm still not sure whether I believe you, but I'll give you a chance."

"Seven o'clock," he said, and with great effort, entered the cab.

4

IVES SORTED THROUGH HIS WARDROBE AND PULLED OUT THE Italian suit, a very fine weave, navy blue, conservative. As he dressed, he was aware that he had the beginnings of a head-ache somewhere at the base of his skull and he knew it was tension because all of his nerves were tight and they seemed to stay that way all the time these days. He did not like the things he was going to have to do today, but he had long since learned that the only time you could have things exactly the way you wanted them was when you were at the top and that sure as hell didn't describe his position. He was on the downhill slope now, and if he didn't save his own ass, no one else would.

He paid scrupulous attention to his image in the mirror, wishing to hell Meg were here to pick the tie for him be-cause she had an absolute gift when it came to clothes. But she was in San Francisco, "playing" as she called it, and he decided as he picked a tie with a small pattern to it that he did not really want her here now, not at this point of crisis, for she had no understanding of what was about to happen to him and he did not want her to know.

Things were in motion, every step critical, but he could not afford to show any of the strain. The telephone rang as he finished knotting his tie and he picked it up. His secre-tary was on the line, asking if he was ready for the overseas call and he told her to put it through and then flipped the switch to put it on scrambler.

Campbell was on the line, his voice slightly imperious, yet eternally tentative. Ives hated to have to deal with him because Campbell was forever nitpicking, seizing on one small detail after another and worrying it to death. Perhaps that was the reason why the group had picked Campbell in the first place, why they trusted him, for in the end, unless everything was perfect, Campbell would call it off and know that they would support him and Ives would be the one to blame.

"I take it I caught you before the conference," Campbell said.

"They're due here in half an hour."

"We have the official photos taken by the Japan Self-Defense Forces," Campbell said. "They will undoubtedly have them too. We don't think you'll have any difficulty with anything except the northeast quadrant sequence and some of the close-ups of the lifeboat. I've talked to our Asian people and they say the Japanese will seize on the smaller details."

"This is only a preliminary meeting, for God's sake. We won't get into detail."

"It doesn't hurt to be prepared. The London insurance people seem to have an unusual interest in what's happening. Lord Swann himself is going to be representing the underwriting companies."

Shit, Ives thought, and immediately he could see Swann in his mind's eye, one of the old boys of the world of international business, an Englishman of immense wealth and diverse interests (oil, shipping, marine insurance, banking), and a predilection for exercising his power in every direction. Ives found him acerbic and perverse. Ives was able to read most men, predict at least the general course they would follow, but Swann was enigmatic. The headache had suddenly become intense and Ives paused a moment, opening the drawer to his desk for the vial of pills the company doctor had given him.

"Do you hear me?" Campbell said. "Do we still have a connection?"

"I hear you but I fucking well don't believe you," Ives said. He took two of the pills and washed them down with a mouthful of water. "He owns the goddamned marine insurance company and he wouldn't sit in on a claim like this unless he suspects something is going on. I think it's about time you filled me in on the whole project."

"No," Campbell said, firmly. "That's none of your business. And you don't need to worry about Swann. Our analysts here inform me that he intends to take a high-level post in London in the next month or two. So we think he's sitting in because this offers him a chance to please the Japanese government and reinforce his contacts there before he goes back to London. We just wanted you to be aware."

The pain was beginning to lessen. "All right, I'm aware."

"He shouldn't give you any trouble. They will undoubtedly want to go to a full-scale maritime hearing and your attitude should be cooperative, mystified, of course, because you don't know what happened any more than they do. We'll want a month's delay, at least, but you won't have any trouble getting that."

Ives could hear the rustle of paper on the other end of the line. The son of a bitch was using a written agenda. "Now we should discuss the other matter," he said. "When do you plan to take care of that?"

"This afternoon."

"We have to give you a red flag on that. You really don't have any experience in that area. We're not sure you can bring it off."

"Fuck your red flags," Ives said, losing his patience. "Do you think I want to do it? I will do it because there's no one else I can trust to do it. Everything has been examined to death. I'm holding my end up here and if anything goes wrong, it's my ass. So I'll take care of it. All you have to do is keep the schedule moving."

"The schedule is firm," Campbell said. "And I know how you feel about suggestions of any sort, but the red flags are important. Exercise extreme caution. When you've taken care of the termination, let me know."

Ives severed the connection. That other matter, Campbell and his goddamn euphemisms. "Killing" was the word, not "termination." Shit, it did no good to berate Campbell because he was on solid ground and had an infinite capacity to absorb and discount and continue on his original track without being diverted. And at this point, Ives realized that he himself was the only man vulnerable, for there was nothing to connect Campbell with any of this and Ives did not even know who the rest of them were.

He would have to calm himself. He relaxed in his chair a moment, allowing the pills time to work, remembering the doctor and his goddamned lectures about Type A and stress delivered in an offhanded man-to-man style, advising Ives to take it easy if he wanted a long and happy life and to try to think pleasant thoughts and relax more. He had to work now to keep his anger from flaring toward the doctor who was fit and tanned and had things made, no stress for him, just consultations and tennis courts. To hell with them all. His company would go down the drain, but the deal with Campbell would give him enough money to see him through for the rest of his life.

He picked up the telephone, called Dunn to make certain that exact protocol was being observed in the meeting. "And then I want my Cessna ready at five," Ives said. "I'm going to log a couple of hours."

He met his accountants in a small chamber outside the conference room and then led the way inside to meet the Japanese adjusters. He would be expected to do nothing

more at this meeting than to set a friendly tone, to demonstrate a spirit of cooperation, and then he could turn it over
to his subordinates who would begin the actual sorting out,
the value of the cargo and the tanker itself, the various
indemnity policies on members of the crew, and finally the
very knotty problem of the gasoline spill and the fire in the
fishing village.

The meeting was a short one, ceremonial, the Japanese
sketching in the parameters of negotiation, agreeing to hold
off any final determination until after the full investigation.
Swann said nothing. The Japanese adjusters agreed to meet
with Ives's lawyers during the afternoon. Ives went through
the ritual of seeing the Japanese bulldog to his limousine,
then turned his attention to Swann who was waiting for him
in the reception room. "Would you care to join me for a
drink, Lord Swann?"

"Coffee, perhaps," Swann said, following him to an informal sitting room next to his office. "The Japanese have
ruined me for tea. Abysmal."

Would it be too obvious if he took another couple of
pills? He decided against it. He could not take the risk. "I
was a little surprised to hear that you were sitting in today,"
Ives said.

"Oh?"

"I understand you're going back to London soon, on a
permanent basis. I'm glad to have you here, understand, but
this is such a routine matter."

"I would hardly call it that," Swann said. "There's such
a thin line in marine underwriting between fact and fabri-
cation and I have yet to be involved in a single instance
where it was possible to separate the two with absolute
conviction."

Ives's interest quickened. He did not show it. "You include the *San Marin* then."

"Of course," Swann said. "Especially the *San Marin*. Intriguing possibilities. A great many discrepancies here."

"In what way?"

"That your captain should decide to steam out in such heavy weather."

"Obviously he believed he was in no danger."

"The dumping of such quantities of gasoline in the lower bay."

"A terrible bit of business," Ives said.

"And no accident, I think. I know something about your Captain Forsythe. I met him on a number of occasions. He was an astute seaman, very conversant with the rules. If it was an accident, he would certainly have put around."

"I see your point."

Swann extinguished one cigarette, began another. "Are you familiar with the case of the *Malaysia Rose*? The *Belgian Conqueror*?"

"No."

"The *Malaysia Rose* signaled distress off the Florida keys in 1962. There was a heavy fog at the time and when it lifted the American Coast Guard found an oil slick, wreckage. On a tip from me, however, they instituted a grid search and found the *Malaysia Rose* three hundred miles out. The master of the vessel had simply stolen her. He could have sold the oil in South America. The *Belgian Conqueror* used the same scheme in 1971, only in that instance the first mate had actually killed the captain and taken over. He was apprehended in West Africa."

"Are you suggesting a parallel with the *San Marin*?"

"There is a rumor going around that the *San Marin* was taken over." Swann was peering out from beneath his eyebrows. "Is there any truth to that, Mr. Ives?"

Ives had to think fast, to hedge and yet leave the possibility open pending the right time. "I would like to answer you truthfully, Lord Swann," he said. "But my lawyers advise me that to discount an internal investigation we've got going here might prejudice the settlement of our claim."

"That's reasonable," Swann said. "There's one other item. I understand that one of your men witnessed the fire."

For a moment the breath caught in Ives's throat. He exhaled slowly and occupied himself with the coffee until he could formulate a reply. Swann could not be fishing; his information had to come from somewhere. Had the Japanese police released it? He doubted it. Was Corwin himself making calls? Impossible. "Are you speaking of Corwin?" he said, finally.

"I believe that's the name. Yes."

"Where did you get information about him?"

"I have friends in the Transport Ministry," Swann said. "They informed me that the metropolitan police had questioned one of your men who was in the area at the time of the fire. What information do you have?"

"Not much," Ives said. "I've had no report. But what jurisdiction would the metropolitan police have over a prefectural matter?"

"They're all connected," Swann said, making signs of leaving. He snubbed out his cigarette. "That's something I've learned from experience with the Japanese. You never tell a government official in one branch something you withheld from another. Information passes through the government by osmosis." He stood up. "I'll find out what I can about your man, Corwin. These other matters are food for thought. But as you say, if there's anything there, it will certainly surface."

"I appreciate your frankness," Ives said. But as soon as Swann had folded himself into the backseat of his limousine, Ives went back to his office and sank into his chair, taking two more pills. Campbell had been wrong. He had underestimated Swann. Corwin would now have to be silenced.

He buzzed his secretary and told her he was not to be disturbed. When the pills had calmed him, he removed the written schedule from the locked drawer in his desk and studied it as he leaned back in his chair. He checked off the conference he had just completed and then tapped the pencil against an incisor, thinking. There was no way anyone could have guessed that Swann would decide to intrude by taking the matter so seriously. But even that son of a bitch was not going to be able to move quickly enough.

His secretary buzzed him. "I have an urgent call for you, sir, but the caller won't identify himself."

"That's all right. Put him on."

He waited until he was sure the secretary was off the line. "What's going on?" he said.

"We have a problem. Corwin's no longer in custody."

"Hold on." He flipped the telephone onto the scrambler. "Now, what in the hell are you talking about?"

"There's nothing to worry about. He got away."

Grateful, yes, thankful for the anger that washed over him and that would make it possible for him to do what he was not certain he could do, and he knew instantly what was happening. "You fucking son of a bitch," he said. "You ought to know better than to try to pull this on me."

"I couldn't control it. But in some ways it could be for the better because we have complications at this end. Official inquiries. I couldn't have kept him isolated for very long."

"Where is he?"

"That's the problem. I don't know."

"Then you had better find out. You get on the ball and you root him out. Then you make sure he's permanently silenced."

There was a pause on the line. "That's a very complicated procedure."

I know what you're up to, you son of a bitch. But he forced himself to be deliberate, cool, for he could not afford to tip his hand now, to give any advance warning. "What will it take to have it done?"

"If I can locate him personally, it's no problem. But that may be very expensive. I can't talk to you anymore at the moment. Are we still meeting this afternoon?"

"Yes. Five-thirty." He put the telephone back on the cradle. The pills had left him slightly numb. He welcomed it. He did not want any feeling at the moment, no more anger, no sense of regret.

Perhaps he had made a mistake in going to Campbell in the first place, but his company was in serious trouble and Campbell had the contacts for discreet and intricate financing that had rescued many an ailing corporation. And perhaps when Campbell had first suggested the plan to him, coupling it with the prognosis that there was no way to salvage his company, he should have turned it down except that he saw within it the slimmest hope that somehow, given enough time, he could reverse his corporate fortunes himself. That had been a false hope.

He had the option to reverse things at this moment, to call Campbell and tell him to ram it up his ass, but there was nothing to be gained by it. Even if he could finish the tanker outside his window, it would never carry a drop of oil. Because even though there were only a few oil companies backing Campbell's plan, he did not doubt that the word had spread through a great many of them, for oil was not only a business but a fraternity as well, and if he backed out they would unite against him. To hell with it. He had given his word and he would honor it.

He spent the rest of the afternoon dealing with routine matters that had been set aside for the insurance inquiry, then he went downstairs to speak with McAdams, the head of security, a huge man in his early sixties who had spent most of his adult life in the Orient as a security adviser to foreign firms operating in Japan. For the past few years McAdams had been semimobile, plagued with back trouble, limiting himself to the security switchboard and the arms room, where Ives found him, at the locked rack of handguns, recording serial numbers on a Japanese government form.

"You need a better lighting system down here," Ives said.

"It'll do," McAdams said, glancing up only briefly, turning back to a pistol and entering a number on the form.

Ives was momentarily sickened by the sight of the pistols, remembering a dock worker who had been shot in the stomach in New Orleans, a black man who just lay there with the life running out of him, rolling back and forth threshing as if he could escape what had happened to him. It was the only time Ives had seen a man die and now he was within a hair's breadth of confiding the problem to McAdams, leveling with him. There would be no sense of judgment in the man and McAdams would probably find a competent professional for him. "Probably," that was the critical word here, the snag of a word that made it impossible. To pass the problem to McAdams would be to enlarge the circle of those who knew and the problem itself would branch out, for McAdams was known to drink too much and talk too much. No, this was something he had to do himself, and he would do it.

"I need the use of a pistol," he said to McAdams.

"For what purpose, sir?"

"Target shooting," Ives said. "I hate pistols myself, but I've been invited to participate in a Japanese pistol shoot and I can't very well back off."

"That's a problem," McAdams said, wetting his lips. "Our weapons are competent, but you couldn't say that we have anything of competition quality."

"I don't give a fuck how accurate I am."

"Well," McAdams said, scanning the rack of pistols with his eyes. "We should be able to work out something."

He picked up a pistol, checked the cylinder. "If you like I can check you out on it. It's a very simple mechanism after all, but it does take practice to use it efficiently. I would suggest that you fire a few rounds in the test room."

He allowed himself to be guided, learning to load, to remove the safety. He pointed the pistol into a barrel of sand and pulled the trigger, surprised at the kick of the butt against the palm of his hand, the jolt it delivered to his forearm, tremendous power unleashed. He fired until the cylinder was empty, then he reloaded and put the pistol into the pocket of his jacket and went back to his office. It wouldn't do; the weight of the pistol pulled down one side of his jacket. He found a leather envelope briefcase and placed the pistol into it. It formed a hard lump, but it would have to do.

He called for his car and relaxed during the short drive to the small airport in the suburbs, surprised to find that he was not overly nervous.

The small plane was rolled out of the hangar, a spotless piece of machinery tended by a single Japanese mechanic whose whole life was devoted to perfect maintenance. He bowed to Ives who returned his greeting and then climbed into the cockpit, placing the briefcase between the seat and the door. He put on his sunglasses, and after checking the instruments, revved up the engine, the soft roar filling his ears. He put on his soft leather gloves and then removed them, for he would need quick hands today. The gloves were an encumbrance.

Once he was in the air he felt an exhilarating sense of freedom, for he was beyond anyone's reach and he contented himself with the purr of the engine and the almost imperceptible vibration of the machine against the currents of air. He climbed to seven thousand feet, above the layer of smog that stratified like a yellow blanket along the surface. A filthy city, Tokyo, yet possessed of a certain charm from this perspective, the Sumida River snaking its way through the congestion of the plain, glittering in the sunlight, the bay a resplendent silver dotted with heavy freighter traffic and the swarms of smaller fishing boats, which looked like water insects from this height.

He was pleased to see that visibility was not unlimited. There was a persistent haze that obscured the symmetrical cone of Fujiyama to the southwest and any ground reference points were indistinct. He followed the bay until he left the land behind him and continued straight out to sea, leaving the shipping lanes that emptied into the great circle route to North America or into the Hawaiian pattern, and finally he could see no ships at all, only the broad and seemingly endless expanse of choppy water. There were heavier clouds out here; the sky would soon be overcast. The color of the sea was gradually changing from blue to pewter.

He banked back toward the coast and angled toward the Izu Peninsula, the resort area and a new landing strip that was part of a golf course development not yet opened. It loomed before him as a forest with strips of emerald-green grass and perfect greens with the paved strip a concrete rectangle, a wind sock limp. In a week or two the small deserted building to his left would house a crew to take care of corporation aircraft bringing executives here for an afternoon round of golf. But that would await the finishing touch—the goddamned Shinto priests to exorcise all malevolent spirits, the barrage of advertising, and the splash of opening ceremonies. He made a pass at twenty-five hundred feet. He saw no signs of life except for the small car sitting in its accustomed place in a grove of trees near the end of the runway.

The moment was close at hand and if he questioned it, it was only momentarily. He banked and came in for a perfect landing, smooth, no jarring of the wheels against the runway. He could feel the tension in his arms, a slight constricting of the muscles. He reached down with his left hand and opened the zippered top of the briefcase, making a dry run, making sure that the pistol was correctly positioned so he would not fumble it.

He taxied down the runway until he was opposite the car and then he turned the plane around, reaching over to open the door for the man who came across the open area at a slight run, pulling himself up and into the cabin.

Inspector Ito made himself comfortable as Ives revved the engine and maneuvered the plane off the ground, climbing sharply. Ito studied the ground intently. "If you don't mind," he said. "Follow the peninsula to the south. I bought some land there."

"All right." There was no hurry. The business was three-quarters done, proof of an old business axiom, Preparation is as important as execution, and he was certainly prepared. Ito was scanning the coastline.

"There," he said. "That's it. Come around to the right."

Ives saw a series of rock bluffs jutting out into the water. His hands were sweating slightly. He held the plane in a slow and circling bank, listening to Ito prattle on about what he intended to build on that bluff, a cantilevered villa, lots of glass, a combination of traditional Japanese building methods and contemporary Western architecture. He would have a narrow lane bulldozed to the site, sufficient to accommodate his sports car. He would keep his apartment in Tokyo as well, of course, until he came to mandatory retirement in his early fifties.

"You have it all planned then," Ives said with dry amusement. "And don't you suppose that some sharp-eyed son of a bitch in your department is going to wonder how you support a villa like that on a policeman's salary?"

"My wife will inherit some money," Ito said.

"You've broken our agreement," Ives said.

"Yes," Ito said. He placed his fingers against the instrument panel as if touching the power of the airplane.

"So," Ives said. "What makes you think I'm going to pay you one cent more than our agreement?"

"Logic," Ito said, with a smile. "I assumed when I went into this that it was a much smaller operation than it is. But now I can see that it's international and that makes it worth much, much more. He's loose in the city. I can find him and with some effort have him killed in an appropriate fashion. But you can't." He opened his omnipresent pack of English cigarettes. "In the long run, it's to your benefit as well."

"How?"

"At first my superiors were convinced that this was just a case in which one foreigner killed another and there was no more interest than that. But I established the case against him pretty well and now the whole government is interested in his connection with the Red Watch. Since he escaped, it is the same as if he admitted his guilt."

"How soon can you find Corwin again?"

"No problem," Ito said. "A day minimum, two days. But it can be arranged to fit any schedule you wish."

Far below, Ives saw a fishing trawler, the stern surrounded by a wheeling flock of birds; the trawler had become part of a natural process. Everything fed on something else and there was always a creature to scavenge the leavings, to tidy up. "How much more do you want?"

"A hundred thousand dollars," Ito said. He exhaled the smoke through his nostrils. Two dollars a pack for those English cigarettes of his, Ives thought. "You will be perfectly protected. I will arrange the killing as I did Jordan, through intermediaries. The assassin will have no idea when he kills Corwin who he is killing or why. He could never be traced to me and therefore there will be no connection with you."

The false security of the overconfident, Ives thought, and given enough time and effort anything could be traced because there was no overt action involving two people that did not leave a trail. "And what happens if I don't pay you the hundred thousand?" Ives said.

Ito laughed slightly, his lips pulled back from his teeth, as if he could not take the question seriously. "You are a very rich man and this is a very important item."

Ives sighed. There was no way around it, of course, and

he had known that instinctively from the beginning. It tapped into his frustration, the unfinished ship on the ways, the endless circle of complications in this fucking country that would strip him to nothing if he allowed it. Far below, he could see nothing except the slate gray of the ocean. How deep was it here? A thousand feet? Two thousand? It did not matter. He felt a numbness, a detachment.

"We will have to arrange a new landing strip," Ito was saying. "The golf course is going to be activated the first of next week. Perhaps we can arrange something simpler than this."

"Nothing is ever simple in this goddamned country," Ives said. His left arm was hanging limply at his side, the fingers brushing the butt of the pistol. He put the plane into a slow climb, easing back on the throttle, watching the airspeed indicator move downward.

"What are you doing?" Ito asked, more curious than concerned.

"This is a very versatile airplane," Ives said. "It's almost impossible to stall out." Floating now, drifting, and his fingers closed around the butt of the pistol and drew it up across his lap, the muzzle pointed directly at Ito who looked at it quizzically, as if he did not understand.

"What is it? What are you doing?"

"There's no room for betrayal in what I'm doing," Ives said. "Open the door."

Ito shook his head slowly from side to side as if he could not comprehend what was happening. His mouth remained fixed in a crazy smile. "You're kidding me," he said. "Look, forget the money."

"Open the door."

Ito sat transfixed, immobile, the cigarette still protruding from his fingers, but Ives knew he would not remain that way for long. He would progress from the frozen fear to some sort of action, delayed only by the realization that there was nothing he could do to keep the bullet from tearing through him. Perhaps he would open the door before he made his move, doing anything to delay, to gain him even a small reprieve.

"A terrible mistake," Ito said. "We can talk about this."

"Open the door," Ives said again.

Ito's fingers fumbled with the latch. There was a stricken look on his face but the eyes had changed, a quickening brightness. He pushed against the door. It opened slightly, closed with the force of the wind.

"All right," he said. "Since you can kill me anytime, there's no harm in talking first."

And in the instant before he moved, bracing himself to make one lunge at the pistol, Ives raised it and pulled the trigger, the concussion hurting his ears in the small cabin, the bullet catching Ito in the middle of the chest, pushing him back against the door. Ives rolled the plane to the right and Ito fell out the door, hanging on with a death grip, eyes wild, his hair feathered by the wind, his suit jacket whipping away, the stain spreading across his shirt. His mouth opened; he was yelling something, but the jacket had whipped around his face and Ives could not hear the words. He hung for an inordinate amount of time, but Ives did not fire again. He let him stay where he was, supporting his own weight against the void. He stopped yelling, made no attempt to pull himself back into the cabin and then he simply let go, falling backward, legs and arms outspread in an irregular X. Ives kept the plane in a slow and circling bank, watching the diminishing form until he lost it in a wisp of cloud.

He angled downward, rolling the plane to the left, securing the latch on the door. His cabin still smelled of sweetish smoke. He was slightly nauseated. At two hundred feet he began a series of passes over the water where he was certain Ito had gone down, but the face of the sea was blank, heavy swells, like hills in motion, the white froth of choppy water.

No one would ever find a trace of Ito's body. The fish would have him now; his flesh would be dissolved.

He raised the plane, increasing power, gaining altitude, back up to a comfortable ten thousand feet and then he took the time to examine the seat Ito had occupied. There was a fine layer of cigarette ash on the cushion, the crumpled butt of the cigarette on the floor. He brushed the ash away, reclaimed the cigarette butt and put it in his pocket, and then he saw the smear of blood on the back of the seat. He removed his handkerchief from his pocket and wiped it across the plastic leather surface, but there was a definite residual stain left behind, too obvious to be overlooked by the meticulous Japanese mechanic.

He rubbed his chin, looked toward the coastline, and then angled north so that if anybody took the trouble to observe, his aircraft would be spotted approaching Tokyo from the Chiba side. It had not been as difficult as he had imagined it would be, not at all, and in looking back it seemed as if it really had not happened to him at all, that it was purely an objective act, no feeling associated with it, something that was necessary and had been done. He turned his mind to Corwin, dealing with the change of status now that Ito was out of the picture. He would call Campbell and have him get in touch with the Red Watch and arrange for them to kill Corwin. That should not be too difficult. There were hundreds of them in Tokyo and Corwin would have to surface, sooner or later.

He crossed over the rocky ridge, the shallow side of Tokyo Bay; the air was filled with the crosscurrent of chatter from the Japanese controllers at the major airports to the south. He made a last-minute check of the cabin to make sure the blood was the only remaining item to be covered. Then he took out his pocketknife, opened one of the smaller blades, razor sharp, and with one swift and unequivocal motion drew the edge across the palm of his hand beneath the thumb.

The blood welled out and he allowed it to flow unchecked for a few moments, dripping onto the seat that Ito had occupied, none of it spilling onto his jacket. He could observe his own blood and feel totally objective, no pain, no discomfort. He wrapped his handkerchief tightly around his palm and then made his approach to the airport.

By the time he taxied to the hangar, the mechanic was waiting for him, opening the door when the engine stopped.

"Did you have a good flight?" the mechanic said, in Japanese.

"No," Ives said, displaying the bloodied hand. "I cut my hand. I'm afraid I've left you a mess to clean up." He looked back into the cabin. "Do you have something to take the blood out of the upholstery?"

The mechanic's attention had been successfully diverted; he was examining the cabin interior. What had been curiosity about the accident itself was now diverted to the solution of a technical problem. "I think so, yes," he said.

Ives picked up the envelope briefcase, walked to the other side of the plane, examining the fuselage near the door for any scratches Ito might have made, any signs of blood he might have left behind. There were none. The aluminum skin was unblemished, virginal, shining.

"How soon will you be requiring the aircraft again, sir?" the mechanic said.

"Not for a while," Ives said, vaguely. "But I want it cleaned up right away."

"It will be done," the mechanic said. "Within an hour, it will be spotless."

"Very good," Ives said. "That's what I want. Spotless."

5

It was dark when Corwin awakened and it took him a long moment to realize where he was, the apartment, the distant sounds of a radio, light leaking under the door. She was back, and she had not awakened him. He sat on the edge of the bed, slightly groggy, realizing that she had been in this room while he was asleep and had taken off his shoes. The bathroom, he remembered it off to his right and he found it, clicking on the light, startled at his own face in the mirror, gaunt, tired, his eyes hollowed and bloodshot.

He washed his face, felt more revived, opened the door to the living room, a small area colorfully decorated with Japanese banners and photographs. Faye was standing in the kitchen alcove, cooking something, wearing jeans and a T-shirt. She glanced at him.

"You look like you'll live," she said. "I'm cooking dinner but it will be awhile. Would you like a drink?"

"No," he said. "Did you bring the material?"

"On the coffee table," she said. "The stuff about you is on the top."

"About me?" he said, startled. He sat down on the low divan, contemplating the large stack of typewritten sheets, the glossy photos, and found himself looking at a picture of himself, carrying a briefcase, standing in front of the company headquarters, and he remembered the memorandum that had come down to all company officials, requesting co-operation with photographers for the publication of a brochure. "Where did this come from?" he said.

"From the police via your company," she said. She put the lid on the skillet, poured a cup of coffee, which she brought to him, setting it down on the coffee table in front of him before she sat down on the floor opposite him. "I think you should drink it," she said.

He picked up the cup. "When did I become news?"

"This afternoon," she said. It was one of those situations, she went on, not uncommon in Tokyo, in which a news story did not break so much as explode. An English underwriter named Swann had approached the paper ostensibly seeking information and in the process raised the possibility that the *San Marin* had not gone down at all. "He mentioned your name and one of the editors plugged into the Transport Ministry and the metro police. So the case they were building against you merged." The belief among the Japanese professionals was that Corwin had sold out the *San Marin* to members of the Red Watch.

"Jesus," Corwin said. "The police believe it. I'm sure of that."

"Is there anything to any of this?"

"No." He told her everything that had happened to him and as he talked about it he could see that Ives had him cold, for what reason he did not know. He could not believe that Ives would go to such elaborate lengths if he meant either to destroy his own vessel or to camouflage its theft.

"So you weren't involved."

"I was their goddamned pigeon. Nothing more."

"And what do you do now?"

"I'm not sure," he said. "I sure as hell can't be taken by the police."

"God, I hate ships and lines and management, the whole goddamned business," she said. She went back to the kitchen alcove and proceeded to put the contents of the skillet onto two plates. "You might as well have something to eat," she said, putting the plates on a small table.

He was considerably revived by the food, his hopes encouraged. After all, he was not without resources. He had been in this business a long time and he had been exposed to every deceptive practice in the industry, elaborate schemes to bilk companies, masters of vessels claiming losses at sea when they were directing a cargo percentage to lighters coming alongside outside of loading ports, scams, artifices, con games. All that remained was to find out which version of which scheme Ives was using, and why he had gone to the trouble to set him up.

"How well did you know my father?" she said.

"Quite well on paper," he said. "All of his performance statistics, everything about his career."

"And personally?"

"I didn't meet him until this run."

She pushed back from the table slightly, lighting her own cigarette. "He was a fine, dear man," she said. "An autocrat in the best sense of the word."

"Where's your mother?"

"She died when I was twelve. But he kept the house in San Pedro, right on the channel, and I took care of it while he was away. Not by myself, of course, because there was always a housekeeper, but I thought of it as my house. More coffee?"

"No," he said, openly curious. "If he knew he was dying, why didn't he quit immediately?"

"He was always a responsible man," she said. "He knew he didn't have long to live and yet he was still concerned about breaking in a new crew. He was fretting over names and qualifications, stewing because he was being saddled with a lot of Japanese. He never did like the Japanese. Maybe it was his war experience. I don't know."

"He knew about the Japanese crew? Are you sure?"

"Positive. What difference does it make?"

"A great deal. I think he knew what Ives was planning. I think he agreed to go along with it."

"He would never have gone along with anything he didn't believe in." She smiled sadly. "His main concern at the end, I think, was how he was going to take care of me. He was never able to see me as a grown woman capable of taking care of myself. He told me I would not have to worry about money after he was gone." She ground out her cigarette. "I think you're totally wrong, you know. I think the *San Marin* went down and he went with it. Finished. The end." She looked directly at him. "Tell me, are you all hung up on the company?"

"No."

"I don't believe that. Tell me about your women."

"That's none of your business."

She smiled slightly, stood up, began to clear the table. "You answered my question. You're about forty and there's no wife. You're not homosexual, or at least you don't put out those vibrations. So that means a series of women, tangential relationships, nothing permanent. I don't knock that, by the way. I've had a few of those myself." She put the dishes in the sink. "I think you should be aware of the odds," she said.

"What odds?"

"The odds against you. We have this gambling freak at work, down at the paper. He gives odds on anything, everything, political upheavals, anything in the news. The Japanese used to be heavy on astrologers. They treat him in the same way, the oracle of the newsroom."

"And he's put odds on me?"

"Of course. He's giving a hundred yen to fifty that the police will get you within twenty-four hours. He's giving even money that the Red Watch, if the rumors are true and they are involved, will eliminate you before the police get near you."

"And what are the odds that I'll get completely away?"

"A hundred to one against."

He flipped through the stack of papers and the more he read the more he was convinced that his hunch was correct, that Ives had arranged the whole business, the fake sinking, and at this moment the tanker was on a definite track, out of the regular shipping lanes, headed for God knew where. He found one news story that listed the possible connection between him and Jordan's death and the possession of the *San Marin* by members of the Red Watch. It was a Xerox copy of a story that had not yet been published and there were strings of Japanese characters penned in the margin. He handed it to her as she came back into the living room. "What's this?" he said.

"Interpretative reporting," she said, frowning at the Japanese characters. "One of the top reporters was asked to extrapolate and this is what he came up with. The notes along the side refer to the fill-in sources, I think. He's to talk to the maritime unions to see if any of the crew members on the run from the Persian Gulf filed reports. He's also got a follow-up with the inspector who's handling your case and he has an interview set with Swann."

Suddenly, he felt a sense of relief. He was on solid ground again. As long as the main charge against him was homicide, there was a strong chance the authorities could convict him, but now they had moved into areas that required considerable orchestration on Ives's part, considerable involvement of other people, the actors who had played the parts of the revolutionaries at the meeting hall in Chiba. And the money itself, the hundred and fifty thousand American dollars, the process by which it went through a trading company and back to Ives to be delivered to him required a record somewhere. Ives could not handle that transaction without leaving tracks. Somewhere in the complex of offices on the waterfront, somewhere in the maze of entries, there would be a discrepancy and he needed nothing more than the proper leverage to force an audit by the Japanese government.

"You could get into a great deal of trouble," he said. "Aiding and abetting a fugitive is pretty damned serious in Japan."

"Yes," she said. "They have a special prison for foreigners here in Tokyo."

"Then why take the risk?"

She shrugged slightly. "I have a sympathy for underdogs."

He looked at the picture of the oil slick again. "Can you get me Swann's home telephone number?"

"I think so, yes." She picked up the telephone and he was only half aware of the sequence of calls she went through, for his mind was already organizing the material he would present to Swann. He had seen Swann occasionally at the receptions, banquets, and cocktail parties that surrounded the oil business in the Far East and he had been in conversations with him at least twice. Swann had the reputation of being aloof but fair. How he would take this proposition, Corwin didn't know, but at the moment he represented a possibility of support.

Faye glanced at him from the telephone, scribbled something on a piece of paper, and then hung up. "I have a number but it may not be of any use to you." According to the men at the paper, Swann had a large house to the northwest of Shinjuku where he maintained a strict and guarded privacy. Night calls to the residence were invariably taken by an aide.

He took the paper from her and moved to the telephone. He dialed the number. It rang twice and then a male voice answered, repeating the last four digits of the number.

"My name is Corwin. It's urgent that I speak to Mr. Swann."

"He will be available at zero three-seven seven-three nine four three after nine in the morning."

"My name is Charles Corwin. Please tell Lord Swann it's now or not at all," Corwin said.

The line was vacated; he could not tell at first whether he had been cut off or put on hold, but in a few minutes Swann came on the line. If he was irritated by the intrusion, it was not apparent from his tone of voice. "Good evening, Mr. Corwin."

"You know who I am then?"

"Of course."

"We have to talk."

"About what?"

"The accident. The fire. The *San Marin*."

"We are talking, Mr. Corwin. But I fail to see what information you can provide me that I don't already have."

"I want a meeting with you. Tonight."

There was a pause on the line. "That places me in a rather difficult position, Mr. Corwin. My effectiveness here in Japan depends on my cooperation with the authorities. If I meet with you, I compromise my position in the eyes of the law."

Ah, he was a clever man, Corwin decided, leaving that slight crack of an opening, that suggestion that he would be willing to go contrary to the system if he had enough to gain by it. He was suggesting a quid pro quo and Corwin realized he had nothing to trade.

"Are you still there, Mr. Corwin?" Swann said.

"Yes," Corwin said. "I'm going to want a great deal out of you, Mr. Swann, and I'm in a poor bargaining position. I'm damn good at what I do and given enough room I think I can make a case that will benefit the both of us."

"I appreciate your position," Swann said, finally.

"Will you agree to a meeting?"

"I know your reputation," Swann said. "But I don't think you realize exactly what trouble you're in. My first duty is to my company, of course, and we would be pleased to discover that the *San Marin* did not go down at all, for whatever reason. But I doubt that you're going to have the opportunity to explore that subject."

"Oh?"

"My sources tell me that the Red Watch feels you were paid off to implicate them and that if the police don't get you, they certainly will. They claim they weren't involved in this. I wouldn't take their threat too lightly if I were you, Mr. Corwin. If you really think you have a lead to information that might clear you, I'll arrange a meeting with the authorities in which I would participate. In any event, you're going to need protective custody."

"I'll call you later tonight." He put the telephone on the cradle. His hands were sweating. He dialed the number of the dock, asked for the dockmaster, taking a chance. In a moment, Watanabe's voice came on the line.

"This is Corwin," he said.

"Goddamn," Watanabe said. "What's going on with you?"

"I need some help."

"A hell of a lot of it," Watanabe said. "Everybody's on your ass, friend."

"Including you?"

"Not me, no. I know you."

"I need some papers from you. If you don't want to get involved, say so and I'll back off."

Corwin told him what he wanted and then arranged a meeting in the dock area in an hour. He put the telephone down and then looked up as Faye approached him, carrying a glass, a skeptical expression on her face. "Bourbon and water," she said. He took the glass from her and she sat down across from him, shaking her head in amazement. "What is it with you, Corwin?" she said.

"I don't have any choice." He tasted the drink, the bourbon strong.

"Hell," she said. "You're not going to be able to make it across town by yourself. I'm going with you."

"There's no point to that."

"There's every point. If you disappear, I'll never know what happened."

"All right," he said. "Then call a taxi. Insist on their sending a driver who speaks and understands English."

"What do you have in mind?"

"Just make the call."

He went to the kitchen to find the bottle of bourbon and he was tempted to have another drink but he did not. He was at the right level now; he could still think clearly and he did not want to jeopardize that. He went through the drawers of the cupboards, listening to Faye on the telephone as she tried to communicate the absolute necessity of a driver who spoke perfect English to a dispatcher who spoke little English himself. He found a paper bag, much too large for the bottle, but it would have to do. He put the bottle inside, conformed the paper to its shape, left the top exposed. He poured a little in his hand, rubbed it on his sleeve. The smell was unmistakable.

"What are you doing?" she said as she put the telephone down.

"A small game of our own," he said. "Did you get the taxi?"

"With some effort. He should be here in twenty minutes."

"We're going to the bar near the dock in Yokohama," he said. "But not directly. Follow my lead and we'll be all right."

"What's supposed to be going on?"

"A family fight," he said. "We've been barhopping and I lost my wallet and I have to have it." He looked at her appraisingly. "Do you have a party dress?"

"No."

"The one you were wearing today. That will do nicely."

"Do you really think we can get away with this?"

"I don't know," he said. "If you don't want to come along, I'll go it alone."

"I wouldn't miss it. I'll only be a minute."

He had another drink while she changed. She came out of the bedroom, wearing the dress, beautiful. "Will this do?" she said.

"Perfect. Do you want a drink?"

"You're apparently having enough for both of us."

"Then I've created the right effect."

"Just so long as you're not too drunk to do what you have to do."

"I'm never that drunk. I lack the capacity." He took out his wallet, removed all the yen he had and gave them to her. "You'll pay the taxi," he said. "We're looking for my wallet, after all." She put the money in her purse. "I think we had better wait on the street. They never pay any attention to addresses."

He led the way into the cool night air, more aware of colors and sounds than he had been in a long time, the clicking of wooden *getas* on the sidewalk, the barking of a dog. The taxi was suddenly at the curb, the squeal of brakes, the hissing of the automatic door, and when he had put Faye in and had his first look at the face of the driver, he knew they were going to be all right. For they had drawn a young hip Japanese driver with a modified Afro haircut and the disdainful eyes of an instant categorizer.

"You speak English?" Corwin said directly to him, making certain that he could smell the whiskey. "If you don't speak English, then let me know goddamnit and we'll find another cab." The gauntlet was down, the immediate impression formed.

"Yes, I speak perfect English," the driver said.

"Then you're the first Japanese I've run across who does. Where did you learn it?"

"Tokyo University," the driver said. "Where can I take you?"

"That's the question," Corwin said. "That's the goddamned question of the night. You Japanese do business in the oddest fucking ways I've ever seen. Shit, it's no wonder you're all in financial trouble." He turned to Faye. "And you," he said. "The next time you insist we go barhopping with your goddamned Japanese friends, I'm going to ship your ass back to the States."

"I didn't know it would turn out like this," she said defiantly. "Besides, you lost your wallet. I didn't."

He turned to the driver again. "We went to a number of bars earlier. My wallet's in one of them. What do you say the odds are that it's still going to be there?"

"About the same as if you had left it in a bar where you come from." The voice was coldly polite. Good. Corwin could count on the driver's fixed memory of hauling a drunk *gaijin* and his browbeaten wife around the city.

"Hell, that's no good," Corwin said. "In St. Louis, a wallet with a couple of thousand in it would go like spit on a griddle. I thought you Japanese were known for your honesty. My name's Wellington and I'm going to make you a deal. If we find that wallet, I'm going to give you one hundred dollars."

"The fare is what you see on the meter," the driver said. "No more. No less. Now, where do you want to go?"

"We'll start in Yokohama. The waterfront district."

Only as the taxi pulled away did Corwin lean back against the seat.

"Wellington, for God's sake," she said, under her breath. "Don't you think that's a little heavy? Where did you get that name?"

"A girl I once knew," Corwin said. "Mary Ellen Wellington. I think she would have appreciated this situation."

"Did you do this often?"

"Never, as a matter of fact," he said. " 'Driven by sobriety,' that's my family motto. Grimness is the key. You can never be bitten in the back of the leg by a dog you take seriously. Would you like a drink?"

"Not unless you have some ice cubes squirreled away."

"You're frivolous, that's your trouble." He leaned forward, tapped the driver on the shoulder. "Are you ready for a drink? Fine American bourbon."

"I don't want one."

"Am I offending you? I understand that the Japanese are very sensitive."

"You're not offending me."

"Are there any strange goddamned hidden laws against my having a drink in a Tokyo taxi?"

"You can fall on the floor for all I care."

Excellent. He had broken the cool, brought out an insult, a minor victory considering the Japanese reserve. He unscrewed the lid on the bottle, drank a short one. He sat back again, enjoying the smell of the woman, the feel of her cramped close against him. He was well on the way to being drunk, but he did not care. He directed the driver to the expressway, pounded him with questions about Japanese business, all of them derogatory, interspersing the questions with berating Faye for a host of imaginary sins.

When they reached Yokohama, he picked two bars at random and left the driver and Faye in the running taxi while he went inside for a moment and came outside again, feigning anger that he had picked the wrong place, which was somehow the fault of the bars for all looking alike. He knew that he was stalling as well. For fixed in his mind was the possibility that Watanabe had reported the conversation and at this moment there were men gathered around that waterfront bar, waiting either to seize him or to kill him (either was possible; Jordan had been killed unawares, he himself had been arrested), and the paranoia within him now was so great that he trusted no one.

"Go straight ahead," he said to the driver. "It has to be on this goddamned street someplace."

They were less than a block from it now, the taxi careening down a narrow street. "There, that one," Corwin said, pointing ahead. The taxi stopped in front of it. "I may be a few minutes because I know this is the goddamned place where I lost it," he said, and there was more to say, he had not finished, yet he had run out of words. The night air was fresh, heavy with the smell of salt water. He saw a Japanese man down the lane, leaning against the wall, little more than a human shape in the darkness, and he wondered if this was the man who would be the one to kill him. To hell with it. It made no difference at the moment. He would have to do his best and let the rest of it go.

He went inside and Watanabe waved at him from a booth on the far side, but he stayed where he was for a moment until he saw that none of the other men were paying the slightest attention, not one head turned in his direction.

"How about a drink?" Watanabe said as Corwin sat down.

"No," Corwin said. "Any more at the moment and I couldn't navigate. Are you here alone?"

Watanabe looked confused. "What do you mean?"

"If you have set me up, tell me now. No deception, just the truth. I can accept it, but I don't want any more surprises."

"Hell, no," Watanabe said. "We're friends."

"I apologize," Corwin said. "It hasn't been the best of times for me. What do you have?"

"We've had investigators all over us," Watanabe said. "The metro police, the NRP, the Transport Ministry, the unions, insurance reps, a dozen assorted oil company representatives from all the majors. Nobody can come up with anything."

"Then they haven't known where to look. We'll start with the crew roster. Do you have it?"

Watanabe unfolded the sheets on the tabletop, smoothing them out with his fingers. Corwin glanced at it, the same list that Ito had shown him. "Who made this assignment?"

"You did," Watanabe said.

"How?"

"By memo from the head office."

"And my signature was on it?"

"Sure. There's a Xerox, second sheet."

It was there. His authorization, his name, perfectly dupli-
cated. He shook his head. "You didn't question this? An all-
Japanese crew?"

Watanabe smiled. "This is Japan, after all, Charlie."

"And the captain approved the roster?"

"He was so zonked-out it wouldn't have made any difference to him," Watanabe said, with a sigh.

"Were you there when they went on board?"

"Sure."

"And you didn't observe anything unusual?"

"I know what you're getting at," Watanabe said. "Could
they have been Red Watch? I can only tell you what I told
the police. There's nothing on the goddamned rosters to indicate political affiliation. And they could have been or they
couldn't have been. It was just a crew."

"Who signed on as first mate?"

Watanabe consulted the list. "A man named Suzuki. I
don't even remember him. I'm sorry about this, Charlie, but
I didn't question it anyplace along the line. The unions have
been pushing for all-Japanese crews for a long time so there's
nothing unusual there. It was an intercoastal run, Tokyo to
Kobe. I didn't even think about it."

"It's not your fault. Did you talk to Forsythe before he
sailed?"

"Yes," Watanabe said. "At least a dozen times. I'm the
dockmaster, after all."

"And you say he was zonked-out."

"Much of the time, sure. His medicine."

"Was he coherent when he sailed?"

"Yes," Watanabe said. "I discussed the weather with him. He thought he could run it out. He was anxious to go." As a matter of fact, he went on, that was the one thing that had disturbed him, which he only now remembered, not the captain's decision to undertake the voyage in the face of very rough weather, for that was Forsythe's prerogative and he was known for an occasional rashness. He was well aware of the storm; not only was he in constant touch with Harbor Weather, but he had his own radar going to keep abreast of conditions within twenty-five miles. But there had been an incongruity in his attitude, for there was something slightly awry with the calibration of the loran on the bridge and there had been some delay in getting the replacement parts from a Yokohama marine supply firm.

Ordinarily, there would have been no great push involved, for with the approach of heavy weather, the delay could have been absorbed in the waiting, but Forsythe had pushed every minute, first haranguing Watanabe until the repair crew was on board and then hanging over the repair crew as they worked, muttering about downtime and the inefficiency of Japanese workmen and generally making them miserable.

"The loran," Corwin said, thoughtfully. "And he was pushing to run under the storm."

"I don't know what was going through his mind," Watanabe said. "Hell, he's been strange ever since he hit port."

"How much bunkering fuel was he carrying?"

"Full."

"Where was the *San Marin* bound from Kobe?"

"Not scheduled. Probably back here. Intercoastal. I know what you're looking for, Charlie, some unusual procedure. But you're not going to find it."

"It has to be there," Corwin said. He was wasting his time and he knew it, trying to pull from Watanabe information that he did not have and a confirmation that Watanabe did not feel. "Did you get the papers for me?"

Watanabe produced the envelope and Corwin put it in the inside pocket of his jacket. "There's nothing there, Charlie," Watanabe said. "If I were you, I'd go back to the police. The Red Watch is a mean organization."

"I appreciate what you've done."

"What are friends for?" Watanabe said. "Anytime I can help, call." A moment of warmth from a friend and he was almost undone.

Outside, the darkness heavy, the taxi waiting, its engine a high-pitched whine and from far off he could hear the diesel horn of a freighter on the bay. Pulling himself together, he entered the taxi, uncapped the bottle, and took another strong pull before he nodded to the driver. "So much for the goddamned traditional Japanese honesty," he said. "I know I left it there but nobody would admit it. Take us back where you picked us up."

The taxi lurched forward and he put his arm around Faye and for a moment remembered all the women over the years, flashes of breasts and thighs, thickets of pubic hair, the abundance of sexuality all around him and it seemed as if all he had shared with these women was a sexual itch and a kind of dramatized relationship that had never been real. And he knew from the moment he entered the taxi that he would make love to this woman before the night was over. The spark was alive between them, that electricity that could become animosity or anger or a keenly sharp coming together.

"Did you find what you were looking for?" she said.

"I don't know," he said. "I haven't checked the figures but they should be there. Ah, the goddamned devious people of the world and they're bound to screw it up in the end because they can't cover all the bases. And I'm the best at ferreting out the truth. I have a reputation." His hand was resting on her leg, the warmth of her flesh rising to meet his palm. "To hell with it," he said. "I'm tired of their fucking puzzles."

When the taxi drew up in front of the apartment, he felt the need to effect a closure with this driver, to dissipate the tension he had so carefully built, but he did not. The impression must be left there. He counted out the exact fare on the meter, folded the bills, and handed them to the driver who drove off without a word.

Corwin carried the bottle back into the apartment. He opened the envelope, spread the papers on his lap, the typewritten figures slightly blurred. He ran his fingers down the columns. It was all here, but there was nothing that would stand up in court, nothing Ives could not explain away.

Faye went to the kitchen, poured bourbon into two glasses then added ice and came back to sit beside him on the low divan, handing him his drink and keeping separate from him, tucking her legs beneath her. "Wellington," she said, smiling. "That's a nice name."

He reached out gently and touched her hair, silk smooth, and she rested her head against his shoulder. Gentleness, yes, no urgency, not hurried, for he had had his fill of urgency. His hands explored her body, lightly, his fingertips finding her contours and hollows incredibly smooth, warm, secret, and her mouth came to his without prompting, open, receptive, tasting of bourbon, her eyes open, so close as to lose focus, but the expression within them was a wondering willingness. He found her breasts, the nipples expansive, erect, and slowly he undressed her and then himself. He was momentarily discomfited by his own nakedness, the whole expanse of flesh that belonged to him. He laughed aloud as he sat down beside her, cradling her again, the momentum of his desire temporarily suspended.

"What?" she said, with a half smile.

"Craziness," he said. "It just occurred to me that American boys should be born fully dressed."

"That would be inconvenient for the mothers," she said. "Painful."

"Maybe it's my generation or maybe it's just me," he said. "Startled at the sight of my own erection."

She reached out and touched it. "It's very handsome," she said. "You're a peculiar man."

"How so?"

"Most men take it so seriously, so dramatically." Her fingers closed on it, gently. "Most men are so desperate, somehow."

"You're making that more true by the moment." He eased himself onto the couch beside her and taking her head in his hands, kissed her, taking his time, feeling the warmth of her body against his. He brushed the back of his hand across her stomach and her legs opened to him and he moved above her, her hand restraining him for a moment, delaying entry, running him along the length of her vagina, around the opening until at the right moment she allowed him inside, as if she were giving him a gift. He extended himself fully into her and for a long moment did not move, filling her completely, and only then did he begin the rhythm, and any thinking was abandoned for the feeling, the slow rocking of their bodies together, the sound of her breathing, the instinctive responses of her body, locked to his. Abruptly, she stopped, her fingertips against his face.

"No, stop a minute," she said, her voice close to a whisper.

"Is something wrong?"

"I don't want it to end, not yet."

But he was buried within her, completely, and in that moment of looking into her face, her eyes half closed as if she were seeing beyond him, through him, her lips slightly parted, the pink of her tongue showing, he could see that she could not wait. A shudder passed through her, a trembling of pleasure.

He seized her, caught her up, her hands pressing against his lower back, urging him on until he was past the point of controlling, pushing into her while her body rose to meet his. And then he could feel the contractions, the moment of total surrender and he spent himself within her, only partially slowing the rhythm when he was through, drawing back slightly to bring her face into focus.

"My God," she said, her voice wondrous, contented.

"Yes, my God."

"That was special."

"There's more."

She laughed slightly. "You're not serious."

"Quite serious."

"It will have to wait until later."

"All right." He withdrew with a great feeling of peacefulness. "Would you like a cigarette?"

"No thanks."

He lighted one for himself. He felt her hand on the flat of his stomach, caressing, not insistent.

"I apologize," she said, quietly.

"For what?"

"When I first saw you, I think I said something about fucking you to get my father off the hook. Do you remember?"

"Yes."

"That wasn't true, not literally. I think I meant to shock you, to let you know that I would go to any lengths."

"You don't have to explain yourself to me."

"Oh, but I do. Because underneath all this exterior, I'm a romantic, darling. I know that's unfashionable now, because I'm supposed to be a goddamned pragmatist and to regard what just happened as if it were an intimate handshake, a roll in the hay, a pleasant way of discharging tension. Let me have a drag on your cigarette." She exhaled the smoke toward the ceiling, handed the cigarette back to him. "And if you come up with some complimentary remark at this moment about what a good lay I am, I'll kill you."

"That's not what I'm thinking."

"Then you don't think I'm a good lay," she said, smiling.

"Keep it up and I'll dump your ass on the floor."

"That might be nice," she said. "What are you thinking?"

"That I'd like to stay here with you under special circumstances, just the two of us, with nothing outside and plenty of time."

"That's pretty close to what I want to hear," she said. "How long a time?"

"Indeterminate." The ashes broke from the cigarette, showered onto his chest. She brushed them off with her fingertips.

"You don't have a great deal of chest hair," she said.

"Is that a criticism?"

"Just a comment." She sighed. "Hell."

"What does that mean?"

"I don't know what it means. Maybe it's just a general wariness because we're intimate now and you're making the appropriate sounds that I want to hear. But I don't even know you, not really, and yet here I am, trying to hang onto you in some way."

"You think too much."

"That's true," she said. She brushed the last of the ashes from his chest. "All right, time for realistic talk. We can't stay here forever. So what are you going to do?"

The future, the moment an hour from now, a day from now, and he had to consider it. He stood up, feeling sated and yet not satisfied, for there was always something hanging over him, something waiting to be done. The bourbon was beginning to wear off and he was not yet ready for that. He poured himself another drink. "It's a lousy situation and that's the truth," he said. He picked up his trousers, fumbled through the pocket until he found Swann's number. He dialed the telephone and when it was answered, asked to be connected with Swann.

"Swann here."

"This is Corwin. I want to talk to you, tonight."

There was a pause on the line while Swann considered it. "That can be arranged," he said. "I can come to meet you, if you like. Or I can send a car for you and we can talk here, at my place."

"Hold on." Corwin covered the mouthpiece and looked to Faye. "Where are we?"

"Yoyogi."

"Where's the Yoyogi station?"

"About a mile from here. Past the baseball stadium."

He uncovered the telephone. "There's a baseball stadium in Yoyogi. I'll be in front of it in half an hour."

"I would ask you to be very careful, Mr. Corwin. You're high on a number of lists."

"Half an hour," Corwin repeated and then severed the connection.

2

The baseball stadium was deserted, dark, no games tonight, with little traffic on the street, practically no pedestrians at all and he stood in the shadow of a low stone wall, not wanting to be here, thinking of Faye in the apartment waiting for him. A car passed, slowed, and for a moment he thought it was Swann's, but it had merely slowed to make a turn up a narrow street. The whiskey had worn off, and he was cold sober as he confronted the real situation in which he found himself. For he had been picked by a power much larger than himself to play a role that as yet he could not determine, and he was as expendable as an antiquated piece of machinery.

Two cars moved past him on an otherwise deserted street, one honking at the other, contention in a wide asphalt area for the sake of competition. Ah, he had bought into it, that was the difficulty, and he remembered Lisa who, even at this

short distance, tended to blur with the succession of women
he had slept with in the past few years, transitory, temporary
contacts on the way to someplace else, the mutual understanding sometimes tested but implicit. They were replaceable and he was replaceable and there was no commitment
beyond business schedules and whims and the more important goals down the line.

But as he stood here, restless, shifting from foot to foot,
he felt that things had changed (from circumstance or a
change in perspective, it did not matter), and in some sudden
and unexpected way he felt committed to Faye, not simply
chemically, the keen and fortuitous fucking, the appeal of
the body, but much more than that. There was more than
himself at stake now, and in his bargaining for the future,
she would be included.

Time passed, dragged. Perhaps Swann's car was not coming. Perhaps Swann had changed his mind, balancing potential against risk, deciding against a meeting. He put a
cigarette in his mouth, clicked his lighter into flame and at
that instant the stone wall exploded immediately to the right
of his face, chips stinging his skin. Reflexively he dropped
to the ground, the lighter clattering away from him, inex-
plicably continuing to burn, a guttering blue flame against
the darkness of the pavement. Jesus, a shot, a bullet, somebody firing at him and he scrambled away toward the deeper
shadows beyond the wall. Another bullet hit the wall behind
him and this time he heard the shot, not pronounced, like the
distant popping of a paper bag. He reached the cover of one
of the concrete columns of the stadium, darkness, his heart
pumping as if it would burst, gasping for breath. He leaned
against the rough concrete and waited.

Another shot, blind, they could not see him, firing along
the projected path they expected him to follow perhaps, the
whine of a ricochet, stone chips clattering. He peered out,
looking at the low business buildings across the street, dark-

ened at this time of night except for the faint glow of inner security lights. The rifleman was on the roof; he saw a brief stab of light from the weapon, heard the report, the whine of another bullet off the concrete. Incredible. The most populous city in the world, an overwhelming density of human beings, and yet for this moment he was occupying an isolated pocket of space in which only the two of them existed, himself and the man who was trying to kill him. Was the sniper alone or was there more than one, another moving in this same darkness that concealed him, the one to pin him down, the other taking his time to reach him in this concrete forest?

His ears strained. He heard the sound of a car, the headlights flashing briefly into the darkness as the car rounded a corner and came to a stop in front of the stadium. It was a limousine, long, black, Swann's car, certainly, a uniformed chauffeur climbing out from the driver's side, standing, looking at his watch and then down the street. The choice was here. Either Corwin could run for the car, exposing himself in the time it took to cross the thirty yards of open concrete, giving the rifleman a chance to take his time, to bring the running figure into the cross hairs of his sight, or Corwin could remain here, knowing that eventually the chauffeur would climb back in the car and drive off.

To hell with it. He would not be paralyzed. Neither would he run. He moved away from the shelter of the pilaster, into the open and he shouted out at the darkened roof across the street. "Do you understand English, you mother-fucking son of a bitch?" His voice echoed behind him. "Go ahead, shoot me, you bastard. We have a witness now. Take your best shot, you asshole." And he continued to walk toward the car, shouting imprecations while the Japanese chauffeur moved back to the car, nervously placing a hand on the opening latch. No movement from the roof. No gunfire. He reached the limousine.

"Mr. Corwin?" the chauffeur said, tentatively.

"Correct."

"I am from Mr. Swann." He opened the rear door, but Corwin continued to stand in the open for a long moment, a gesture of defiance before he allowed himself the luxury of entering the security of the limousine.

Swann's house sat in a grove of trees, obscured except for a pattern of lights through the foliage as the limousine paused at the high iron gates to be inspected by a guard before the gates opened electronically and the limousine pulled through. The drive looped through a stand of massive cryptomeria trees and the driver pulled to a stop beneath a porte cochere connected to a long, low sprawling house that appeared to be a blend of Japanese and European. The driver conducted Corwin to the door where another Japanese servant bowed him in and led him through a reception room to a study, asking him if he would be so kind as to wait. Mr. Swann would join him in a few minutes.

The room was large, with heavy beams, a wall full of books, nautical charts hanging against rich walnut paneling, a weathered figurehead from an old sailing ship standing in the corner. He remembered Swann's background, a grandfather with a ship works in Liverpool converting to wooden yachts in the early part of the century when the clippers had become relics. The residue of that financial empire was here, reflected in the furnishings.

Only a part of his mind was aware of the room, the orderly strains of a Bach fugue in the background; his legs were possessed by an almost uncontrollable trembling as if they might refuse to hold him. He had come close to dying out there; he could not dismiss the attempt to kill him.

He turned around as Swann appeared in the doorway, a lank apparition of a man in a rumpled suit, a cold questioning on his face, the most skeptical eyes Corwin had ever seen. "I can offer you whiskey but no tolerance," Swann said. "I don't have much tolerance or civility at this time of night so we might as well get down to it."

"I don't want your whiskey and I sure as hell didn't come here to defend myself."

"You will defend yourself," Swann said. He picked up a decanter and poured himself a cordial. "Unless you prove yourself to me, unless you can provide me with information I can't get for myself, I will turn you over to the Japanese police."

"I've had my bellyful of attacks tonight. Somebody fired on me at the stadium tonight. Somebody tried to kill me."

"Oh?" Swann sat down, the glass cradled in his hands. "Who knew you were going to be there?"

"Only you."

"Then you're accusing me."

"It could have been any one of a dozen people. We talked on the telephone. Do you have any idea how many ways there are to tap a telephone, to pick up signals? And your chauffeur. Can you guarantee he didn't pass the word?"

Swann reached out, picked up the telephone. He spoke in Japanese, delivering a cold and vicious reprimand to a government official in the Communications Ministry. His telephone had been tapped; eavesdroppers were at work and it was the duty of the Japanese government to protect his right to privacy. He put the telephone back on the cradle, then picked up the cordial glass again.

"It will do no good whatsoever," he said. "Even if the Japanese devoted full time to the problem, they couldn't make the lines secure. I learned to be skeptical in Admiralty Court, Mr. Corwin," he said in a brittle voice. "So you may consider me an adversary who's waiting to be convinced."

Corwin shook his head, poured himself a drink from the Scotch decanter. "How do I know you didn't put the man on the roof?"

"Because I would have nothing to gain by it. Who would gain by killing you?"

"Ives, the Red Watch."

"Why Ives?"

"He knows me. If I stay alive, I'll get him eventually." One of the toes on his right foot was paining him, distracting. He had stubbed it without knowing. "Hell, you've been covering the same ground as I have so I don't have to fill you in on the details. He's in a conspiracy with the Red Watch, that's the long and short of it." The gamble, yes, the laying out of information, all of it suspect under Swann's blinking disbelief. "I've been in the business a long time and I've never seen a setup as complete as this one. He's got documents with my name signed to them, and at the same time he's left things loose enough to allow for any slipups. It was his plan. It had to be, because he's the only person with power enough to bring it off. He caught me all right, he hooked me with solving the problem of Okata's death and used it to get me into the center of the problem."

"A poor performance," Swann said, critically. "You're dealing in generalities and your one fact is a mistake. If I were a Japanese prosecutor, I'd have you."

"What mistake?"

"Okata," Swann said.

"What about him?"

"Can you support Captain Forsythe's story? Did you call Singapore, check it out, verify a word of it? No, I'd have you cold right there. Okata's not dead."

Corwin closed his eyes, pinched the bridge of his nose, tired. He had not checked. "Are you sure?"

"Quite," Swann said. "The Japanese police checked that

out the moment they took your story. Singapore has never heard of Okata or a body fished out of the Straits. Okata was seen in Yokohama. If Ives is setting you up, he left a nice pitfall for you and you dropped into it. We'll move on. You accuse Ives. Back it up."

"He was the only one who could have coordinated it."

"Not true. You were in a position to do it."

"I had nothing to gain from it."

"The money."

"Bullshit. I had no pressing need for the money. And I'm competent enough that if I had done it, I wouldn't have left anything to incriminate myself." He paused, drinking. There was a touch of irony here. "Hell, that was his mistake."

"What?" Swann said.

"Trying to have me killed," Corwin said. "That's the one thing the Japanese would never buy. If there's an indestructible case against me, it would make no sense for someone to kill me." He smiled slightly. "There's a paradox for you, that I should have to allow myself to be killed in order to exonerate myself."

Swann lighted a cigarette, studying him through the smoke, but his face had changed slightly and Corwin could see that the point had not escaped him. "Why would Ives cooperate with the Red Watch?"

"Ives is in deep financial trouble. You know that as well as I do. There's nobody in the financial community who doesn't."

"Are you suggesting the Red Watch bought him?"

"No," Corwin said, thoughtfully. "He needs a minimum of ninety-five million to pull him out. They couldn't have raised a fraction of that. And if he intended to collect the insurance, he would have put on one hell of a display for you. And he's not diverting his own cargo."

"How do you know?"

"It's nowhere the amount he needs. And he wouldn't have involved the Red Watch for a scheme like that."

"How can you prove the *San Marin* didn't go down?"

"Did the Japanese make a laser analysis of the spill?"

"Bunkering fuel. Some gasoline."

"The newspaper pictures didn't show the gasoline."

"It was there."

"Show me any goddamned way the *San Marin* could have gone down with just enough of a leak to give you evidence and nothing more than that. If she were on the bottom, the chill of the current would be enough to congeal the black, but the gasoline would come streaming out like a banner. It's a fake."

"Not if the tanker split in the right place, athwartship."

"The odds are a thousand to one against that," Corwin said. "Hell, Forsythe was ready for a long voyage, fully provisioned, making a large point of having the loran fixed at a crucial time when he didn't need it for the Kobe run. He knew about the crew long before the roster was made up. Ives planned an absolutely marvelous fake and the captain went along with it all the way."

"Would you like another drink?"

"Yes."

Swann mixed it himself. "It might interest you to know that the Japanese maritime people are following the same line of thinking you are. Or so they informed me when I began to make inquiries. But unfortunately, you can't prove anything by logic." Swann handed him his glass. "Now, Ives isn't pressing for any immediate settlement. That in itself makes me slightly dubious, but it doesn't prove anything." He emptied his glass. "But suppose the *San Marin* did not go down. Suppose that she is on a long voyage. This is something the Japanese are considering. Then where is she headed? And for what reason? Do you have an idea there?"

"Yes," Corwin said. His attention was caught by a long harpoon mounted on the wall, solid, ugly, the point barbs like teeth.

"I understand your family was involved in whaling at one time."

"Indeed," Swann said.

"Did the whales ever shake loose once the harpoons were imbedded?"

"Rarely, I believe," Swann said. "I'm no expert. But the harpoons were designed to hold, after all."

"I'm on the side of the whales," Corwin said. "Unsuspecting, suddenly barbed, hooked, trapped. No sport there, no chance."

"It was never a sport," Swann said. "And there was never any mystique about it among the professionals. It was an industry, after all. You were about to tell me what you think the *San Marin* is up to."

"An attack," Corwin said.

"An attack?" Swann said, skeptically. "On what? Where."

"How the hell would I know?" He glanced up at the harpoon. "If a whaling ship went out armed with those, you'd have some idea what they intended. I don't need to tell you the *San Marin*'s potential. I'd give you odds that Okata himself is on board and running the operation. So you figure out where the Red Watch wants to make another grand gesture and that's where she's headed. One of the Arab countries, maybe. Can you imagine the kind of chain bang she'd make in a harbor full of tankers? Or maybe blackmail, who knows?" He realized that he no longer cared what they intended to do at this point; the plan had become a hypothesis, an abstraction with no reality behind it. If a group of radicals decided to blow themselves out of the water, then so be it. "Hell, I've talked enough," he said. "If I stay in Japan, I either end up dead or in the hands of the police.

I want passage out of the country for me and Forsythe's daughter."

"In return for what?"

"Ives can't hide what he's doing from me. I've worked for him too long."

"This is all very interesting, Mr. Corwin."

"Which means you're not buying."

"That's not my meaning at all," Swann said. He stood up, seemingly restless, his hands laced behind his back, turning away as if to study an ancient map of Europe on the wall. "I am a businessman, Mr. Corwin, and if I take a risk, it has to be for a very good reason." He reached out to touch the tiny spot of England with the pad of his index finger. "By helping you, I would be open to the charge of aiding and abetting a felon. At the same time, if there's a chance that what both you and the Japanese consider to be a possibility, then I can't very well turn my back on it."

Corwin said nothing.

"I'll be stopping in the States myself in a couple of weeks on my way to London. What I propose is this. I assume that you have a reasonably safe place to stay. You can't move around, of course, and you can't expose yourself in any way. But we can arrange a safe communications system. Use your brain, give me any leads you think are worth exploring and I will have them followed up. When I leave, I will take the both of you with me."

"Two weeks is a long time."

"Tankers don't move very fast. And I can't arrange it any sooner."

"I appreciate this," Corwin said.

"One further thing you should understand. If at any time in the next two weeks, sufficient evidence emerges to demonstrate that you are indeed guilty of murder and that you have manufactured this whole story, then I won't hesitate to turn you over to the police. Do you accept those terms?"

"Yes," Corwin said.

"Fine. It's very late and I have an early engagement in the morning. I'll have my chauffeur take you anyplace you want to go. And we'll be in touch."

"We'll be in touch," Corwin echoed.

PART

1

IVES HAD NEVER LIKED SAN FRANCISCO. IT BROUGHT OUT IN him a certain inferiority, an inner clumsiness that he suffered in no other city. It was as if this place bestowed on some men a snobbish grace, a sense of superiority. The executives here had an urbane look about them, a smoothness that was lacking in him. It was as if they had been born to the mannered language of business, operating with others of their kind on a level to which his money or his successes could never take him, and he felt much more comfortable in the wharf area where he could understand the men and their boats and the kind of life from which he had come.

Now, as he stood in front of the modernistic steel and concrete building that overlooked the fog-shrouded bay, he was apprehensive. His was the new money of the entrepreneur and he was about to be judged by the establishment, by the Ivy League men who represented the immense corporate power of inherited wealth, and he did not like the idea. He had parked his Maserati in the small executive lot at the rear of the building, knowing even as he did so that there was another even more exclusive garage beneath the sprawling building to which he did not have access and that Campbell's car would be there, parked next to a private elevator that would whisk him directly to the penthouse suite.

As he reached the glass door he saw an image of himself

and checked his appearance, smoothed his thinning hair, examined his suit, for in this negotiation with Campbell he could ill afford to appear rumpled or affected by jet lag. But he was betrayed by the hollows beneath his eyes, by the dullness that attention to too many details had exacted from him, by the long hours he had spent with Meg, the rehashing of promises he was not so sure he wanted to keep. She was a screwing machine and that was a fact, and she was expensive; he had seen many a man lose everything because he was hung up on a woman.

He checked his Rolex, the second hand moving in precise and measured ticks. Nine-fifty and twenty seconds and his appointment was for ten-fifteen, which meant that Campbell would not see him until ten-thirty at the earliest because that was the way Campbell demonstrated his power, by conforming other men's schedules to his own. Well, he could use the time.

He moved out of the chill of the bay wind and into the foyer where he paused, looking up at the elegant bronze plaque in the black marble of the wall. Association of Petroleum Carriers, Inc., Campbell's own empire, built not on the same combination of sweat and hard work and gambling that had marked Ives's own rise, but rather on Campbell's ability to organize, to bring together a variety of entrepreneurs and oil companies in a professed spirit of cooperation and mutual protection. Ives resented this manipulative ascendancy, for he was approaching bankruptcy through no fault of his own, through an unpredictable turn of events in the world economy, and it would be Campbell who would sort through the wreckage with uncalloused hands, selling off a piece here and a piece there and enriching himself in the process.

Ives approached the receptionist, a stunningly beautiful woman in a circular booth in the center of the lobby, a ravishing smile, freely dispensed, full of promises. He handed her his card, confirmed his appointment with Campbell, and requested any messages.

"If you'll take the escalator to the mezzanine, Mr. Ives, I'll have Linda bring your messages to you. Suite fourteen B. And welcome Stateside, sir."

Yes, welcome Stateside indeed, and he took the escalator, rising to the mezzanine, suite fourteen, definitely a hospitality suite, leather and expensive paneling and on the wall a gigantic painting of a new cryogenic tanker and in an alcove a more discreet painting of Campbell himself, posed with one hand resting in the pocket of his jacket, his thin face with its patrician nose turned as if he were peering off into the future, and behind him a seascape, placid waters, as if he had commanded the sea to be still and the waters had calmed to provide a tranquil setting for his portrait.

Ives sat down in a leather chair next to a telephone by the window and looked up as a girl approached him. Linda. The land of first names and she was a replica of the woman downstairs, fantastic, and she reminded him of Meg lying in bed, naked, displaying the same fantastic energy that Linda was putting out now on a different level, all the right moves, the right noises, and he would never know whether any of these women were acting or whether they were real.

Linda carried a silver tray with a teapot, his preference, of course, on file, and she proceeded to place the tray next to him, the smile unflagging. "I'm Linda, Mr. Ives," she said. "How are you today, sir? How long have you been in from Tokyo?"

He smiled automatically and picked up an envelope from the tray while she poured his tea. "If you need secretarial services, Mr. Ives, just touch three-six on the telephone and I'll be here. You are familiar with our Telex and communication facilities?"

"Yes, thank you."

He watched her depart, the perfect legs of a model, swinging hips, long free-flowing hair, blonde. California. He sorted through the envelopes, avoided the communication from his board of directors, opened the Telex from Jackson first, half expecting to find that Ito had risen from the sea, been hauled aboard a fishing boat, indestructible and bloody, and subsequently had confessed his duplicity and implicated Ives at the same time. But the Telex contained no surprises. The Japanese police were still looking for Corwin and unofficial opinion was trying to connect Corwin with the inspector who had disappeared.

He discarded the envelope, retaining the sheet for inclusion in a briefcase file, picked up his cup of tea. The fallibility of information, for they could have his beverage preference on file, but it represented the past, not the present, not this week, not today, and no preference remained constant, nor was any life process static. And at this moment, somewhere in the world, Corwin existed, lungs intaking air, expelling, heart pumping, blood flowing. He existed, and perhaps even now his mind was putting together the vagrant pieces of the puzzle and in a moment or two his hands could be reaching out for the telephone to call the authorities.

And Ito, in what process of dissolution was he now? Had there been a soul in that body, some quality of spirit that was now loosed and capable of touching him in some way? He did not think so. Meg would believe it of course because she was willing to believe in anything, Atlantis, Mu, est, Primal Scream, and she would interpret his troubled sleep as Ito's revenge. He, of course, would not. He believed in no afterlife, no survival of any parts except the random molecules and atoms, but life could be extinguished. He had been conditioned against killing, that was his trouble. By his act of killing he had violated that conditioning, ruptured some part of his psyche, and therefore he slept badly. But it would right itself eventually; the balance would be restored.

He opened the Telex from Wolfe who was making a routine report, a financial update with no sense of the drama that lay behind the figures. By his estimate, the *San Marin* was worth two to five million, the cargo three million seven, liability on the crew in varying estimates from three to five million, depending on whether the sinking was an act of God or the result of company error.

He was about to open the envelope from his Japanese partners when he saw Linda approaching. "Mr. Campbell will see you now," she said. "You do know how to reach his office?"

"Certainly."

He took the elevator to the top floor, no cramped offices here, vast expanses surrounded by glassed-in views of the bay and the city, deep carpets, rich velours, partitions that somehow provided privacy for Campbell without dissipating the sense of openness. Campbell's private secretary, another flawless woman, was at the elevator to lead him past a series of seascapes to an area where Campbell was holding court, standing straight as a reed against the background of a window wall framing the Golden Gate. He was meticulously dressed, groomed, the new American aristocracy. Ives saw he was not alone. There was another man sitting in a wing chair, a lean Latin face, no trace of mestizo, another expensively dressed aristocrat.

"Here you are," Campbell said, smiling. "I want you to meet Luis Galvez, George."

Galvez stood up, extending a hand and Ives recognized the relationship here. Campbell was treating Galvez with importance but not liking him at all and the dislike was imperceptible to Galvez because Galvez was a self-centered man. Campbell offered Galvez a refill and Ives a drink. "Luis is the new Mexican energy minister," Campbell said. "George here is Ives Shipping, Tokyo."

"I am familiar with your operation," Galvez said. He had that patina of the Mexican aristocracy, immensely wealthy, Ives was certain, with inherited lands, glossy women, a house at Cuernavaca, and that certainty of authority that stemmed from an unbroken breeding all the way back to Cortes. "I'm pleased to have the chance to meet with you personally. You would be receiving an official notification from me in another month or so, in any event."

"Perhaps Ives can change your mind," Campbell said with a smile, handing Galvez his glass.

"About what?" Ives said.

"We think it is imperative to implement a new policy in Mexico," Galvez said. "A new reform policy."

"Reform generally means restrictions."

"Precisely so." And he launched into an expository harangue that Ives only half heard, sitting down in a chair by the window, his eyes fixed on Galvez's face as he pretended to listen, for it made little difference to him what Mexico was going to do when his own problems were so pressing. He could not understand why Campbell had insisted on his stopping here in the first place or why he was being subjected to Galvez's earnest convictions. Apparently, Mexico was trying to join the big leagues with their proved oil reserves, immense fields, and Galvez was to be the change agent here. Mexico was going to put severe restrictions on all foreign tankers and Mexican industry connected with petroleum was going to squeeze out foreign influences which tended to dictate policy, and Ives found himself thinking of Meg, undecided as to whether to include her in his flight to Zurich. She did not withstand stress well nor could he expect her to fit in with a low profile. She hated pressure but she demanded excitement. He was strongly inclined to leave her in the States.

"What do you think?" Campbell was saying to him. He had not heard the question.

"It would take a lot of study," Ives said, evenly, knowing how to cover his inattention.

"There's nothing personal in this,"' Galvez said, pleasantly. "Mexico has been exploited long enough and it's time for us to take our place in the brotherhood of strong nations." He stirred slightly. His alarm watch had alerted him, soundlessly. He checked the time. "I'm sorry," he said. "But I'm supposed to meet Senator Vetter." The effusiveness of parting, handshakes, cordiality, and Campbell watched him go.

"A pompous son of a bitch," Campbell said, still smiling. "That happens when you get a polo player who decides to become a public servant. Give him five years in charge of his new oil fields and he could screw up the industry in the whole Western Hemisphere."

"Then he's the target," Ives said, bluntly.

"Primarily," Campbell said, sitting down. "He has a half-dozen assistants with him, all in line for his position, representing all the distinguished families. They all want to play oil."

"And with them out of the way, who moves into Galvez's slot?"

"A moderate, that's all we care," Campbell said. "Someone we can count on to preserve the status quo."

"The status quo," Ives said and a picture of Ito's face flashed into his mind, the image of that precise moment when the strength was gone and he turned loose and fell. Ives forced the image to disperse. "My whole fucking life is tied up in my company," he said. "Now, I've made a lot of mistakes and guessed wrong, but I can't believe there isn't some goddamned way to save the company."

"I would like to see that happen too, George," Campbell said. "But you know as well as I do that it's impossible."

Ives nodded mutely. Campbell was right, of course. He did not like the son of a bitch, but Campbell was a realist. Ives realized he had been caught up in wishful thinking for the past few weeks, continuing to fight the unions and push his staff as if by some miracle the company would be reprieved. And only at this moment did that last hope die. "Well," he said. "That's the end of it then. No use whipping a dead horse. I want to finish up here and be on my way. I'm flying to Switzerland tomorrow."

"There may be problems there," Campbell said, pensively. "About your getting away so soon. Have you read the Telex from your Japanese board yet?"

"No."

"Perhaps you should."

The suspicion was there in Ives's mind, suddenly bright. "Suppose you summarize it for me. You know what's in it, right?"

"Yes," Campbell said, dryly. "You've been caught in a bind, George. It's one of those unfortunate things. Now, their message to you is couched in honorific language, of course, but bluntly it reminds you that under Japanese law, your failure as director to disclose financial jeopardy within a very strict time limit is fraud. You can be prosecuted and held personally liable. They're asking you to return to Japan immediately."

"They would, yes," Ives said, drinking now, knowing there was more to come, his intuition correct. "You're telling me that this action on the part of these Japanese bastards affects our deal."

Campbell regarded him soberly. "I'm afraid so. It's a goddamned shame, George, but your funds in Zurich are apparently not as safe as we would like them to be. The whole Swiss banking system has deteriorated. The Japanese have a great deal of influence with the Swiss government and we don't see any way at this time that they're going to allow you to stay there."

"Don't give me this shit," Ives said. "You could have the funds transferred."

"We could," Campbell said. "And we will, at the proper time. You know the way things work, George."

Ives went cold. Ten years ago he would have knocked the man flat on his ass for what was happening here. But now he just went cold. "I'm not one of your goddamned employees, Campbell. I went into this because I believed it was important."

"No," Campbell said, flatly. "You cooperated because your ass was in a sling and we offered you a way to get clear and wind up personally solvent. You'd better get that straight and keep it in mind. You can't walk away." He laced his fingers together, thoughtfully. He wore a Florentined gold wedding band, and Ives could envision a wife, socially impeccable, who followed Campbell's orders with precision, power on two fronts. "We're going to need you here to handle some things. You were responsible for losing Corwin, after all."

"The hell I was," Ives said, flatly. "That was Ito's game."

"I'm not trying to lay any blame," Campbell said. His hand reached out for his glass, a gesture designed to illustrate that this was not an adversary position after all. This was simply business and any pressures he was exerting were business pressures. "We want you to be on hand following the incident."

"We?" Ives said. "Are you speaking for the group?"

"Yes. When it happens, you will be available to the media, imminently available, so that there will be not the slightest shred of suspicion that you are connected with it in any way. You will express surprise, shock, the proper indignation. And then, as a gesture of goodwill, my principals will see that your mess in Japan is cleaned up and that you are truly free and clear. This is just one of those things we have to face, George. Things get screwed up and we have to adjust to them."

"You have a limousine and a driver, correct?" Ives said, abruptly.

"Yes. What's the point?"

"And you live in the country and your driver picks you up every morning and brings you over the bridge by a fast and pleasant route."

"What are you getting at?"

"And he drives you into the basement and you have a private elevator straight up to the top," Ives said. "When you work late, you have an apartment here, a town house, and you live a totally insulated life. You simply make up your mind what you want to happen and you pick up the telephone and it happens. You don't have to get your hands dirty. You won't even see it when it happens." He finished his drink. "I began by financing one goddamned tugboat on the Mississippi River and I pulled myself up by my fingernails. I left my wife in the States when I went to Japan and I slept in a room in my dock building because I was determined to make that goddamned business work." He brought himself up short, realizing Campbell was just letting him ventilate and in the end it would make no difference. He finished the drink. "If I had a way to pull the rug out from under all of you and dump you on your collective asses, I would do it," he said.

"I know that," Campbell said. "But you won't. Because you're standing on the same rug."

Ives looked past him, through the window at a freighter pulling out under the bridge and shortly it would be on the trackless ocean. The anger was stillborn within him; at this point it was useless. Campbell could sit here with such untouchable confidence only because there were unassailable powers behind him who wanted something done.

They were backing him to the fullest and their leverage was such that Ives was certain to be moved. He could not go against them. This was the principle of international business, the alliances, the power groupings, and there was no individual alive who could buck the tide. You either went along or you were swept under.

"All right," he said, finally. "When you say I will be taken care of, what does that mean? I will want a million transferred here, the other four million left in Zurich. There's nothing wrong with that, is there?"

"It may take a little doing, but there's nothing wrong with it."

"Then I can count on your doing it."

"I'll put it in the works."

"You're in touch with the ship, correct? And Okata is aboard?"

"Yes."

"Where is the *San Marin*?"

"It's best you don't know that."

"The hell it is. There are too many things that can go wrong."

"Nothing can go wrong," Campbell said. "This isn't your concern anymore, George. Everything's under control."

"I killed Ito," Ives said, with a sudden urge to share it. "I shot him and I watched him fall. It had to be done and it was fairly easy to do. Why in the hell are you going to all this trouble to kill a few Mexican petroleum officials?"

"How it's done is really not your concern, George." There was a muted sound of a chime and he excused himself and opened a walnut box on the table that concealed a telephone.

"Good morning, Senator Vetter," he said, a great charm in his voice, all buddies together, both with coinciding interests despite the temporary difference in view. Ives stood up and wandered to the window, looking for the freighter that he had seen earlier, but the patchy fog had already obscured it. Campbell was laughing into the telephone, nothing forced about it, genuinely amused, as if he were able to compartmentalize and shut off all thoughts of Galvez and his cohorts. Ives envied that trait even if he disliked the man. Another few days and it would all be over and done with and perhaps he could find a good psychiatrist in the Los Angeles area and work through the melancholia that was beginning to cover him like a pall.

2

Corwin felt at times as if he were lost in a maze and would never get out. He lost track of the days and the passage of time was marked only by Faye's departure for her job and her return to the apartment with material sent to her by Swann in response to Corwin's queries, a cumbersome means of communication at best. And during this time, he could feel the Japanese police drawing closer to him in their painstaking search of the city. According to the information Faye gathered in the paper, the police were almost certain he was out of the country, but they would continue to comb the metropolitan area, house by house, apartment by apartment, until they were certain.

Day after day he shuffled through the mass of documents on the coffee table, a pile that grew larger with each new addition until it threatened to engulf him. He slept only fitfully, awakening once to find Faye crying uncontrollably, the grief over the death of her father finally catching up with her.

And everything he read, every new piece of material that came in only confirmed his belief that the terrorist plan for the *San Marin* was still operative. Repainted, renamed, with new registration papers, the *San Marin* would be unrecognizable, just another of thousands of tankers of the same class.

He found nothing to give them a hint of their intention.

Captain Forsythe was the key, of course, because the old man must have known what was happening all along and the problem was to penetrate his thoughts, to discover what he had kept locked away in his mind. He backtracked through the medical records, the doctor's reports, which were only now being uncovered, a cancer of the bowels that had kept the old man in excruciating pain except for the relief of drugs. Forsythe had known for at least two months that he was going to die because his condition was inoperable.

It was imperative that he stay on the *San Marin* to get it out of Tokyo Bay. And in his last conversations with both Corwin and his daughter, he had implied that here at the end of his life he was going to go out in one grand blaze of orderly significance.

Forsythe was no longer alive, Corwin was sure of that, for in all of the doctor's reports, in all of the examinations and projections, he had gone long past the estimated time of death as he sat in the harbor at Yokohama. So he would certainly be dead by now, dying in the midst of drug-induced euphoria perhaps, sewn into a weighted sack and dumped at sea. But where had he been headed? What impelled him? What was the greater plan?

It was on a Thursday early in September that Corwin's time ran out. He had been working on charts all afternoon, pursuing the course that the *San Marin* could have taken to reach the Arabian Gulf, working with a calculator and tidal charts to estimate possible positions where the *San Marin* might be when the door unlocked and Faye came in, her face pale, agitated. She gave him a kiss and then broke into tears. He took her in his arms and let her cry, convinced at first that she was distraught under the pressure of the last two weeks. But finally she was cried out and she pulled away from him, bringing herself under control and sat down on the divan, looking very frail, vulnerable, and scared.

"Okay," he said. "Tell me about it."

"We are going to have to get out of here," she said.

He took her hands in his. Her fingers were cold. "Start at the beginning."

"First things first," she said. "I need a drink. My God, that is a cliché, isn't it, darling, a terrible day at the office and I come home and tell you I need a drink. But I do."

"I'll get you one," he said. "But talk to me."

Things had gone badly all day, she began. She had received a letter that had upset her, a communication from a firm of lawyers in Trenton, New Jersey, concerning a trust her father had established for her. One of the conditions of that trust was that she would agree not to return to her house in San Pedro. She was sure that there had been some mistake because her father knew how much that house meant to her, but she had no chance to place a clarifying call to the States because two men from the metropolitan police came to her office.

They questioned her for two hours about her father, about her possible connections with ultraright organizations, about everything under the sun.

"Did they ask about me?" Corwin said.

"Only briefly," she said. "They had already talked to the staff. It had been reported to them that you had called me at the paper and I had told you to go to hell and hung up on you. They asked me if you had said anything when you were at the ship that could have indicated what you were going to do, where you were going, how you were going to leave the country. Anyway, I finally told them I had a headache and wasn't going to talk anymore and I went back to my desk."

But the worst was yet to come. She had left early and taken the train to the station and walked from there. And just a few minutes ago she had passed an apartment complex that catered to foreigners, just as this one did, and there were Japanese police cars all over the place, the metro's "Flying Squad." She asked a woman what was going on and was told that the police were searching all the foreign apartments.

"This one's next," Faye said. She finished the drink.

He looked around at the confusion in the apartment, the papers everywhere. "How many people in this building know I'm living here with you?"

"None of them know that it's you," she said. "About a half dozen know I'm living with someone and I've hinted it's a Japanese professor who's finishing a book. The rest don't give a damn because there's as much bed jumping in this place as there is in a Seattle whorehouse."

"Then we're getting out," he said. "I don't know where in the hell we're going, but first we're going to erase every indication that I was here at all."

"If you have some silly idea about our splitting up in the name of protecting me, you can forget it," she said.

"We're not splitting up," he said. "We're also not going to waste any time arguing. You take the bedroom. Put everything of mine you can find in a bag, every scrap. Don't miss anything."

He started gathering up the papers, all of the dossiers, the folders, the charts, and his eyes fell on the Forsythe material. Jesus, it was here, the one lead he had been looking for and it had almost gone past him without his notice. He went into the bedroom. Faye was in the bathroom, sorting out the shelves of the medicine cabinet, taking his razor and shaving cream off the shelf. "I want the letter from the law firm in Trenton," he said.

She looked at him quizzically. "It's in my purse, on the bed."

He found the envelope, scanned the typed lines until he found the phrases he was looking for. All here, fortuitous and it could mean nothing, but he suspected it meant everything, the answer for which he had been searching. He went back into the living room, dialed Swann's number, insisted on speaking with Swann, and ended up instead with a soft-spoken Englishman named Quinlan.

"I'm sorry, Mr. Corwin, but Lord Swann is hosting a dinner party tonight for some Japanese cabinet members. He won't be free until well after midnight."

"That's too late."

"He can't be disturbed."

"Then get a message to him. I know your telephone is tapped but it doesn't matter. Tell him I think I know where the *San Marin* is going. I want a call-back within ten minutes."

"I'll relay the message."

He went back into the bathroom. "Exactly where is your house in San Pedro? Is it on the harbor?"

"Yes," she said. "Overlooking the channel."

The telephone rang. He answered it in the living room. It was Swann. "I'm talking from a safe telephone, Mr. Corwin. What's on your mind?"

"How soon can your jet be ready to leave?"

"That question seems a bit premature. You told Quinlan you knew the target. What is it?"

"You don't get that until Faye and I are out of the country. You'll have to rig passports in other names for the both of us. And we'll leave tonight."

"That's out of the question," Swann said. "I don't see any quid pro quo here."

"There's a hell of a quid pro quo here," Corwin said. "You can be responsible for saving the United States a lot of embarrassment and you can have the gratitude of the Japanese government as well. I can offer you a ninety-percent chance of knowing exactly where the *San Marin* is headed, a general idea of what they're going to do and when they'll do it. Once you have the information, you can handle it in your own way. But I have to get back to Los Angeles before I can get the final piece."

"You're calling for an extreme act of faith on my part, Mr. Corwin. Why should I believe you?" Swann said in a dry voice. "I'm a practical man, first and foremost. I know your reputation, but I also know the extremes a man will go to when he's desperate."

"You're neither that helpless nor that innocent," Corwin said. "I have no illusions about getting off your hook just because I'm in the States. Assign a man to me, a whole goddamned team if that would make you feel any better. If you find out that I'm bluffing you, you can take any action you wish."

Swann cleared his throat. "I'm glad you have a clear picture of your jeopardy," he said. "At this stage of my life, Mr. Corwin, I'm capable of taking extreme measures."

"Then consider this an extreme measure," Corwin said. "I'm willing to lay my life on the line."

"The destination and a time frame," Swann said, thinking it over. "When do I get the information?"

"I'll give you the general area before we reach Los Angeles. I'll give you specifics within three days after we get there."

"It will be midnight before I can conclude this dinner," Swann said. "So my jet will be ready to leave Haneda by two o'clock in the morning. Can you make it on your own?"

"No, the police are gridding this area, block by block. They should reach here in the next hour or two." He paused, thinking, orienting himself. "This apartment is called the Sakura, in Yoyogi. I believe there's an alley behind it. I can't give you any address."

"My driver can find it. And I'll take care of the passports. I know what you look like, Mr. Corwin, but I need a description of the lady."

"Dark hair, long, around the shoulders. High cheekbones.

Very pretty with a kind of fragile air. About twenty-seven."

"I think we can come up with something suitable. What time do you have now?"

"Seven-fifty-two."

"Expect the car at eight-thirty. The alley in the rear."

He went back into the bedroom. "We'll be picked up in about forty minutes," he said. "So everything needs to be put back where it was."

"I'm ahead of you. It's been done."

"Fine. Do you know the people in the next apartment?"

"The Swains," she said. "He's a retired professor from the States and she teaches languages. Lovely people."

"All right," he said, improvising. "Go next door and tell them that you are expecting a package in the next couple of hours and you're afraid you'll miss the delivery. Ask them to accept the package for you if it comes before you get back. Tell them you'll be back about ten."

"You have a fine sense of fantasy," she said. "They'll have something to tell the police, right?"

"On the nose."

He went into the kitchen and opened two cans of soup, pouring them into a pan that he put on the stove. He turned the heat to its lowest setting. Then he put two soup bowls on the table with the proper silverware, napkins. The surface was everything. It must appear that they would be back at any minute. He put the papers he wanted to take with him in his attaché case, left the rest strewn around the apartment. He found a piece of paper and dashed off a note.

"Darling: Pick me up at the Meiji Memorial Gallery at 2100. Important. C."

He left the note on top of the papers on the coffee table. This was sufficient. He did not want to overdo it. He had seen enough of the Japanese police to know that they would accept this scene as he had laid it out, and their force would be split in two directions, one toward the Meiji Gallery, the other concentrated here. They would stake this place out, interrogate everyone in the complex, collect every scrap of evidence they could.

Faye was back in ten minutes, feeling easier now. She even managed a smile. "That's taken care of," she said. "Now where are we going?"

"The States."

"What can I take with me?"

"Nothing," he said. "Not even a toothbrush. What's across the alley in back of the apartment?"

"A high stone wall," she said. "Is that what you mean?"

"They're going to pick us up in the alley. How visible are we going to be?"

"Not very," she said. "None of the apartments overlook the alley. But there's a service gate, the only way out."

"A guard?"

"Yes," she said. "Usually."

"Shit," he said, frustrated. A matter of simple egress was going to be denied him. He could set up the illusion in the apartment, but he was going to have trouble getting past that goddamned guard. "What kind of business cards do you have in your purse?" he said.

"Pardon?"

"Those damned omnipresent cards with English on one side and Japanese on the other. Every time you turn around, somebody is handing you one. Do you have any of them?"

She extracted them from her purse. "Everything from dry cleaners to taxi services," she said. "What are you going to do with them?"

He sorted through them, found most of them useless, Japanese names, Japanese firms. Finally, he found one with what appeared to be a German name. M. ROBT, it said. COMMERCIAL PHOTOGRAPHER, INDUSTRIAL. He showed it to her. "Who's this?"

"He does occasional aerial photography for the paper,"

she said. "He's a red-haired German with a gift for taking a picture that makes the grimiest industrial plant look clean."

"It will have to do," he said. "Do you have a camera?"

"Not a good one," she said. She opened a drawer, took out an ancient thirty-five millimeter. "I don't have any film."

"I don't need it," he said. He checked his watch. It was eight-sixteen. "I want you to go out the front gate of the apartment. If you see anybody you know, you're cheerful but obviously in a hurry. You go down the street to the corner and then follow the lane to the alley."

"What are you going to do?"

"Bluff it through," he said. "I'll meet you in the alley in fifteen minutes."

He gave her time to clear the stairwell and then he picked up the briefcase and looped the camera strap around his neck and let himself out, closing the door behind him with a slight feeling of regret as he heard it lock. There was no going back now. He could hear sounds of people laughing from one of the apartments, a party, relaxed, drinking, and in the growing darkness the exterior lights in the garden were beginning to come on, bulbs inside of paper lanterns, and he went down the rear staircase, the briefcase in one hand, the camera in the other. He traversed a narrow walk and then he saw the gatehouse, the light glowing through a window, a middle-aged Japanese standing outside it, smoking a cigarette. He was wearing a uniform and Corwin wondered if he was armed, if he had been alerted by the police. The man was looking in his direction now, and Corwin felt the nerves twitching in his arms. He put the briefcase down and pulled up the camera, cocking it, pressing the shutter release, advancing the nonexistent film, framing the guard in the viewfinder, clicking away, advancing slowly as if to find a better angle, cocking the camera to one side and then another.

The guard threw down his cigarette, ground it out beneath his heel. No pushover here, a broad face, closely cropped hair, perhaps a former member of the Self-Defense Forces or the police.

"Hold very still," Corwin said abruptly, in Japanese and the guard stopped short while the shutter clicked. Then Corwin moved to a different angle, close to the man's face, the roof line of the guardhouse in the background. "Move a little to your left, please," Corwin said, and the man obeyed reflexively, a strained expression on his face as if he did not know how he should look in this photograph. He pressed the shutter release. The camera gave an obedient whirring click.

"What are you doing?" the guard said, in Japanese.

"You don't know?" Corwin said. "Of course, you don't know. How long have you been on duty?"

"An hour."

"You're very lucky," Corwin said with a smile. He handed the man the card and the guard moved into the light of the gatehouse to read it. "Lobt," he said. "Lobt."

"No, there is an R sound there," Corwin said, "Robt."

"Robt," the guard said.

"That's very good. A difficult name and an even worse profession. I'm taking pictures for an advertising brochure."

"There's not enough light for pictures."

"I'm using very fast film. Do you know photography?"

"No."

Corwin picked up his briefcase, edged closer to the gate, letting the camera hang while he extended his right hand with the thumb and forefinger simulating a viewfinder. "I'll need one more picture of you, a silhouette. If you'll stand in the doorway, with the light behind you."

"Is it necessary?"

"Yes. If you would be so kind."

And the guard moved, striking a pose in the doorway, and

Corwin could see the holster on his hip quite plainly now. "That looks very efficient." He lifted the camera, took a shot, edged through the gate. "One more from here." The camera clicked again.

He was in the alley. He could see the limousine down the alley at the point where the stone wall ended and a lane began. She would be there by now, in that car, waiting, and he felt as if it were miles away. "I think that should do it," he said. "Thank you for your cooperation." He started to move, but the guard's voice stopped him.

"Wait a minute."

He froze in his tracks, turned slowly, walked back to the guard, hoping that his fear would not show. "My name is Shinza," the guard said. "Do you think I could get a copy of the pictures?"

Corwin exhaled very slowly. "Certainly," he said. "I should be back the early part of the week. I can bring you copies then."

"I would appreciate it," the guard said.

Corwin walked down the alley toward the waiting limousine.

3

Ives sat up in bed, gasping for breath, his chest heaving. He rubbed his face with his hands, trying to dispel the dream, looking around him for the comforting signs of normalcy, and through the lightproof drape covering the window there was a faint glow of the lights of the city. Meg was beginning to stir beside him, that soft rounded form coming awake.

"What's the matter, darling?" she said in a sleepy voice.

"Nothing's the matter. Go back to sleep."

"Something's the matter. I can tell. Would you like an Alka Seltzer?"

"No, I don't want an Alka Seltzer. Go back to sleep."

But her hands were on him now, rubbing his stomach and then moving down to his penis as if this were the answer for everything, as if erection were the universal panacea and then she stirred, beginning to go down on him. "This is what my honey needs," she said. "This is what my darling wants."

"Goddamnit, Meg," he said and she stopped short, bewildered.

"What's the matter?"

"Nothing is the matter. I'm not asking you, I'm telling you. Turn over and go to sleep and leave me alone."

"If that's the way you want it," she said with a sigh and turned her back to him. He felt no desire to comfort her because she did not need comforting. She belonged to a different generation of women through which emotions seemed to flow unconnected, and she was totally unperceptive about him, as if all of his feelings were in a foreign language that she pretended to understand but did not.

The dream had gone sour, that was the long and short of it. He should have stayed with Phyllis, limited himself to a machine shop where he could think with his hands, because there was a beautiful consistency to brass and steel and if there was trouble with a machine you could always find it because its parts were solid, finite, and you could always improve a design. But he had chucked it all, everything solid, moving into the quicksand of international business, working his ass off and putting together a small empire and marrying a beautiful woman who was the envy of all the men around him, and he had created something immense only to find in the end that he did not control it at all, that he was not sharp enough to maneuver in the world of big money, that the beautiful woman was vacuous, that there was no one to talk to who was not in a trading situation. And that finally, he had become persuaded in his own mind to kill a man because it was necessary, expedient, and even that had not solved his problem.

He could not believe now that he had actually killed the man. He did not consider himself capable of murder and yet he had drifted into it. Meg stirred slightly, moving into deep sleep and leaving him stranded in wakefulness. More deaths in the future, at least seven of them, not by his hand, no, but he could stop them, save seven lives and perhaps there was a redeeming equation there, saving seven to atone for one.

He was sweating. It was too warm in the room. He went to the bathroom and turned on the light so he could find the thermostat and then he turned it down as far as it would go. He found Meg's plastic container of blue Valiums in the bathroom and he took two of them and went back to bed, his decision made, waiting for sleep.

2

CORWIN HAD ANTICIPATED A SENSE OF RELIEF AT LEAVING Japan, but there had been none, for Swann had decided at the last minute to make the flight himself and during the Hawaii leg of the flight, Swann had occupied the forward compartment of the plane with two other Englishmen in Bond Street suits, leaving Faye and Corwin alone in the smaller rear compartment.

It took little time to clear customs at Honolulu (no difficulties; the passports were barely examined; Corwin and Faye were included as a part of Lord Swann's staff). Two members of the staff departed. After a two-hour delay the jet had taken off again for Los Angeles, Corwin was feeling the pressure again, as if he were the only person who could put an end to what was happening. An hour out of Los Angeles, Swann asked him to come to the forward compartment for a drink, introducing him for the first time to Quinlan, a drab little man who shook hands firmly and then excused himself, leaving Corwin and Swann alone.

"I've demonstrated my good faith," Swann said. "Now, it's your turn. Where is the *San Marin* headed?"

"Los Angeles Harbor," Corwin said.

Swann looked at him skeptically, removing a cigarette from a box. "Los Angeles? Why? What would they possibly do there?"

"I'm not certain. But you put a tanker full of gasoline in

the hands of a group of terrorists, and you can be pretty god-damned sure there's going to be an incident."

Swann's cheeks pursed to draw the flame into the tobacco. "My trust level in you, Mr. Corwin, is about seventy percent."

"Do you consider that high or low?"

"Neither." The smoke was pouring out now. "This is by way of saying that Quinlan represents the other thirty percent. While you're in Los Angeles, he will be your constant companion, not obtrusive, just omnipresent."

"I don't object to that. But you tell him to keep out of my way."

"He may be of help to you."

"I don't need any."

"You can't be sure of that. I would like to know how you arrived at Los Angeles as the target."

"I won't tell you that," Corwin said. "What kind of instructions have you given to Quinlan?"

"He's to give you every freedom and watch you like a hawk. As long as it's evident that you're living up to your part of the bargain, he won't interfere."

"And if he thinks I'm not?"

"He will break one of your legs," Swann said dryly. "He's convinced that you're guilty, by the way, and he's done his best to talk me out of what he considers a foolish waste of time." He took an oversized wallet from an inside pocket, placed ten one-hundred-dollar bills on the small table, then added a thousand-dollar bill. "This will cover your initial expenses. I have a house at Palos Verdes, but I'm going to be staying at the Beverly Wilshire for a day or so. I'll expect a nightly report from you, whether you have any hard information or not. You will have a three-day limit. Do you have any questions?"

"No," Corwin said. He folded the bills, pocketed them. He went back to Faye who was looking down at the tiny specks of fishing boats. On the horizon lay the yellowish smog cloud of the landfall and the serrated ridge of mountains rising above the stratum of pollution. He felt a sense of ambivalence about Los Angeles, not the active dislike he felt toward Tokyo or New York, but an uneasiness as if this were a diffused city with no center to it, defined only by the shape of the smog that blanketed the basin and had spread inland to plague the valleys beyond San Bernardino, contained only by the barriers of the mountains.

"What's new?" she said, putting her hand in his.

"I'm about to get compulsive," he said.

"Meaning?"

"What do you think of that little man up there?" he said, referring to Quinlan who sat relaxed, legs slightly spread, feet planted firmly on the floor, casually turning the pages of a newspaper, every bit the picture of a retired British civil servant checking the daily stock prices.

"Mean," she said. "A real son of a bitch."

"Come on now," he said with a startled smile. "You can't know that."

"I can see his aura," she said. "He's mean, love, believe me."

He did not pursue it. The jet was moving toward the International Airport, into the landing pattern, running parallel with a 727 following the same track, so close he could see faces in the windows.

"A hundred-to-one shot," he said. "You remember the man at your paper who was making the odds?"

"Yes." She smiled. "We should have placed a bet."

The jet landed and all the arrangements had been made in advance at a private terminal, with Quinlan handling all the details, stowing the new luggage and clothes Corwin had bought in Honolulu into the rented car. There was a limousine waiting for Swann and he delayed his departure long enough to repeat his admonition about the nightly reports and then left. Quinlan established himself behind the wheel of the Buick after Corwin and Faye were in the backseat and then looked over his shoulder as if seeking instructions.

"Do you know Los Angeles?" Corwin said.

"Quite well."

"Then find a place where we can have a drink. There are some things we need to get settled before we start."

Quinlan found a sedate businessman's bar in the middle of a garish section of nude bars and X-rated motels, a dark cave of a place with a chill to it and candles burning in red glasses on the tables. "I come here once in a while when Swann has a brief stopover," Quinlan said. "It's one of the few quiet places around."

He followed the hostess to a booth with high leather partitions surrounding it. "It's gin and tonic for me," he said. "What's your pleasure, Miss Forsythe?"

"Nothing," Faye said. Quinlan looked to Corwin.

"Bourbon and water."

He said nothing until the drinks arrived. He lifted the glass slightly in Faye's direction, pulling his lips back from his teeth in a tight smile. In the light of the candle, one of his incisors glowed gray. Was it false, capped? Had it been knocked out? "Cheers," he said. "I'm a straightforward man and I'll get to the point. I believe you're faking it, Corwin. I can smell deception like a bloodhound because I'm trained for it. I believe that you sold out, knocked Jordan off and that you're a cool enough customer to cover it."

"I don't give a damn what you believe."

"You should," Quinlan said. "You should be very worried about what I believe. I've been instructed to give you room for a few days and I'll do that because Swann has a tendency to believe you can help avoid what might be a bloody incident here. But in the end I'll prove you're a fraud and see you handed back to the Japanese just as slickly as you were brought here."

Nonsense, of course, the continual challenge of assertive men, each with his own particular drives, Ives toward money, power; Swann toward a kind of international equilibrium; Quinlan toward the capturing instinct. Corwin could change none of them. But he was aware that he himself had changed, for he had passed the intellectual compulsion to sort out, to unravel, to understand. His priority now was survival and he had no doubt that the little man sitting across from him would do his best to jeopardize it.

Quinlan was fastidious. His fingers dampened by contact with the glass, he dried them on his napkin. Faye was right. Quinlan was indeed mean, lacking any quality of give in him, and as Quinlan had spelled out his intentions, he would make every effort to realize them.

But beyond the level of personal concern lay another area, somewhat abstract but nonetheless compelling. A group of men, a consortium, a number of individuals with Ives at the front had set out to accomplish an objective and in seeking to reach their goal had implicated Corwin. He had no doubt at all that the objective, if realized, would be a particularly bloody one, and he would feed Swann the information to prevent it, if he could, but deeper than that he found a certain cold-bloodedness in himself that had nothing to do with the saving of lives, a meanness to match that in the man who sat across from him.

Corwin finished his drink. He looked directly at Quinlan. "We're going to San Pedro," he said. "This is your game. How do you want to play it?"

"You run along," Quinlan said, pleasantly. "Keep in mind that I'm a professional, Mr. Corwin, with more angles than you ever dreamed of." He put the car keys on the table.

"I'm going to stay here and have another drink or two. Don't forget to check in. If Swann doesn't get his call, then that's my signal."

2

From the moment he saw the house, he knew that he was right, and the knowledge brought no comfort to him. The house was perched on the ridge that fronted the main channel of the harbor on the west, an older clapboard house built in the 1920s. The boards had been painted yellow and the small front yard contained an arched arbor of bougainvillea with an old porch swing suspended from it.

He parked in the driveway. Faye made no move to get out. She looked through the windshield with an expression of great sadness. "I always hoped he would retire here someday," she said. "But things never go like you plan them."

"Are the utilities turned on?" Corwin said.

"Yes," she said. "I have a retired man, a Mr. Parker, who sees after the place."

"I want you to go in and call the lawyers in New Jersey," he said. "I want you to find out exactly what conditions your father put on the trust fund for you."

She nodded. "You're not coming in?"

"No," he said. "I want to look around."

Faye went inside while he sat in the arbor, facing the channel, drowsy in the afternoon sunlight. There was a bank of yellow storage tanks to his left and directly across the boulevard from the house were parking lots flanking the main channel.

He watched the slow progress of a freighter up the channel, a tugboat at the bow, and he heard the loudspeaker from the mock fishing village named Ports of Call on the west bank blaring out a greeting. There was a seaplane taking off on the channel from north to south, lumbering along the water like a pelican until it finally rose from the water. A line of sailboats proceeded south, passing the freighter, sails unfurling to catch the wind as they passed the Coast Guard station at Reservation Point and tacked through the basin toward the opening in the breakwater and the open sea beyond.

The ocean was crowded with sailboats today, the white sails dotting the expanse of the Pacific he could see from here. He had always liked this harbor, the orderliness of it, a casual charm as if it existed only partially as a major commercial port and was primarily a recreation area in which the massive clifflike supertankers at anchor in San Pedro Bay to the southeast were simply attractions for the sight-seeing boats.

He began to doze, came awake as Faye emerged from the house and joined him in the swing. "I talked to a man named Harris," she said, perplexed. "I don't know what's going on, Charlie, and that's the truth."

"What did he say?"

"My father left me a half-million dollars, payable at the rate of fifty thousand dollars a year. But there are stipulations. I have to be in Trenton on the tenth of the month to sign the papers. If I'm not there on the tenth, it's possible I will have to forfeit a part of the money. He said my father's instructions were quite explicit. I will have to make plans to live someplace else. Let me have a cigarette, dear." He lighted one for her. "Why would he do that? I don't understand any of it."

He said nothing for a moment, no longer drowsy, staring down toward the channel. A containerized freighter sounded its horn as the loudspeaker wished it a happy voyage. "I understand it," he said, finally. "It sounded far-out but it's true. They covered all the bases, but they left an opening because there was no way they could avoid it. Your father was determined to protect you, no matter what, and they had to go along with it."

"What are you talking about?"

He looked down toward the tourist village, a pair of chartered buses pulling into the parking areas, disgorging dozens of senior citizens on holiday. And across the channel, in its permanent mooring, sat the old passenger ship from the Alaskan run, the *Princess Louise*, and he could see people on the decks. Behind it on the east bank were the batteries of massive oil storage tanks, glittering in the sunlight. "Madness," he said, aloud. "They'll end up killing thousands of people, thousands. And I don't even know why."

"You're frightening me."

"There's reason to be frightened," he said. "Your father wasn't erratic when he made those conditions to your trust. He had to protect you, to get you out of here on the tenth, because he knew an explosion is going to sweep this whole area and there won't be any house for you to come back to."

"Explosion?"

"They're going to sail that goddamned tanker right up this channel," Corwin said. "The goddamned tanker with all the force of a small atomic bomb stored in her and they're going to blow it up. Within the next five days."

3

Ives was assigned to an office in the building, temporarily, of course, because he would occupy it no longer than a week at the outside. It lay in a corner of the third floor with a bay view and a deep-blue pile carpet, a spacious office with a separate conference room he would never use, a wet bar stocked with a complete range of bottles and decanters, all untouched except for the Scotch. There was an engraved brass nameplate on the door and Linda was assigned as his secretary with her perfect smile and her perfect ass, everything so perfect he found it artificial and plastic. From the day he moved into the office, he felt uneasy, knowing that he was harboring a secret rebellion and looking for an out.

He sat behind the huge walnut desk and went through the press releases that Campbell had sent out through a dozen different sources, profiles of the American senators meeting with the Mexican delegates in San Francisco. The leader of the Senate delegation was Senator Vetter, of course, the sharp-eyed idealist who was out to break up the massive American oil companies, to force them to divest themselves of their interlocking sections, which the senator claimed were strangling the American consumer and piling up inordinate profits. The senator was attacked in none of the press releases; his battle was ignored. Instead, the emphasis was on the Mexican delegates, the new energy czars of a country just beginning to develop tremendous oil and gas reserves.

All of the press releases were laying the groundwork for what would happen, the eventual confrontation between the Japanese terrorists and the Mexicans. A number of stories had been leaked to the press concerning Mexican problems with the Red Watch, recent threats made against the Mexican delegates that protested the jailing of six Japanese terrorists in Mexico City, demanding their release. Those jailed terrorists were to play a key role in what would happen and people would remember the stories so that when the slaughter took place, it would seem logical, inevitable.

He wrestled with the problem of his own press conference to be held after the incident, and he wrote a dozen different statements and consigned them all to the shredder beneath his desk. He began again, writing as if in response to hypothetical questions asked by a hostile television investigator who pounced on any sort of falseness with a relentless ferocity.

Q: You don't expect us to believe, sir, that you didn't know one of your tankers was being taken by Japanese extremists?

A: As I mentioned in my statement, it was a carefully planned conspiracy, brought off by a man I trusted implicitly . . .

Q: . . . who deceived you so thoroughly, so completely, that until today you did not have the slightest shred of suspicion?

A:

No answer, blank, and he saw himself wordless in front of his accusers, sweating, face glistening wet in the lights, and he would be damned on the basis of any answer, no answer.

"Excuse me, Mr. Ives."

He looked up to see Linda standing by his desk, her sparkling teeth smiling down at him and his first instinct was to cover the words on the sheet of paper until he realized he had written nothing.

"What is it?" he said.

"Mr. Campbell would like you to come up, if you're free."

"Free," he said. "Yes."

He took the elevator up and from the moment he saw Campbell he was on guard. Something was terribly wrong. Campbell had a diffident look about him, a practiced non-concern that Ives recognized as a cover for minor disaster. And now there was a white-jacketed Oriental servant as well, a neutral third person to serve as a buffer against any emotional displays. "Scotch, right?" Campbell said. "Sit down. Take a load off your feet." He gave instructions to the houseboy, sat down himself.

The houseboy served the drinks from a silver tray and Ives noticed he had immaculate fingernails, perfectly manicured, the half-moon circles perfect, precise. "Let's not beat around the bush," Ives said to Campbell. "If there's trouble, let's take it head on."

"Let's call it a troublesome potential."

The houseboy was at the wet bar, running a cloth over silver that was already clean. "Get him out of here," Ives said, quietly.

"He doesn't speak any English."

"I don't give a damn. I want this private."

Campbell shrugged, spoke to the houseboy who departed with a bow.

"Now," Ives said. "What in the hell is going on?"

"Two items," Campbell said. "First, Ito."

"What about Ito?" Ives said, startled. "He wasn't found?"

"No," Campbell said. "But you know the Japanese. They found his car and they know he was picked up by an aircraft. They have one witness who identified the pilot as Caucasian."

Ives felt a sudden chill along his arms. "They will make the connection," he said. "And goddamned soon if they haven't already."

"We don't think so," Campbell said. "At least not for a long time."

"What in the hell do you mean by 'we'?" Ives said, illogically, full of a combination of fury and fear. "Where in the shit do you get this 'we' business? It's my ass on the line." He shook his head. The world was full of witnesses and loose ends, always a catch, a loophole, an exception to the rule.

"Item two," Campbell said. "Swann is in Los Angeles. He brought Corwin with him."

Ives shook his head in bewilderment, discomforted by the realization that his face was smiling when he did not feel amused in the slightest, as if his facial muscles were operating independently. He stood up, unable to sit any longer. "Where did you get that information? What's your source?"

"Swann himself. He called here," Campbell said. "He often calls our staff to do legal research for him." Swann had called a couple of times, as a matter of fact, Campbell went on, and they had a good working relationship based on respect. The roles were clearly defined: Swann, as a major maritime underwriter had the power, if he wished to use it, to harass independent operators, and Campbell, as head of the most powerful association of chartered petroleum carriers was in a position to make Swann's work difficult, if he chose. Therefore, one could call the relationship between them a stable détente in which frankness was the key ingredient.

Swann expressed his doubts about the sinking of the *San Marin* and was following a routine path, requesting the names of any new tankers in the modified T-2 category that Ives might have put into service, knowing, of course, that if Ives were making a switch, the *San Marin* would have to have a fresh registry and a new name. Campbell told him there were no new Ives registrations that the association had recorded and that it was unlikely there would be any since the Ives Company was in the process of dissolution. Then Swann revealed that he had taken the chance of bringing Corwin out of Japan, to Los Angeles, with the view that before he had gone with the Ives Company, Corwin had been one of the best maritime investigators in the business and that now, in order to prove his innocence, he was leaving no track unfollowed. Corwin was staying at a hotel on the water east of Long Beach and Swann had placed himself in the Beverly Wilshire.

"Corwin is following the lead of the payment to Forsythe's daughter," Campbell said.

"I warned you against that goddamned business," Ives said.

"The captain was a sentimental man," Campbell said. "He wouldn't have gone along otherwise. Corwin's gone further. He told Swann he believes the *San Marin*, under a new name, will come steaming into Los Angeles Harbor within the next few days and blow up."

Standing at the window, staring down at the water that seemed to be on fire from the sun, Ives felt a sense of relief, and only at that moment did he realize how much he had girded himself against the eventuality of the mass murders and the holocaust. "Well, there are always other ways," he said.

"Beg your pardon?"

"I never liked your goddamned plan in the first place."

"There seems to be a misunderstanding," Campbell said. "Nothing has changed."

"Everything has changed," Ives said. "They know what's going to happen. And Swann has a hell of a lot of high-level clout. He'll go to the authorities and the tanker will be stopped at sea."

The telephone chimed and Campbell picked it up, his whole tone shifting immediately and Ives knew he was talking to Senator Vetter, calling him Bob, bantering with him, intimate chatter. Ives felt very old, very heavy. Campbell finished the call and then wiped his hands with a fresh linen handkerchief, treating each finger individually, biting the corner of his lower lip with a dog tooth, obviously deep in thought. "You'll have to make it up with Galvez tonight," he said.

"Make up what?"

"He's under the opinion you are responsible for the anti-Mexican publicity."

"Nonsense."

"I agree. But it will help if you assure him that you have no grudges against either him or the Mexican government. I don't know how he got the idea in his head, but it wouldn't do to have this kind of thing floating around after the incident. He's a supercilious son of a bitch, extremely sensitive to slights. He mentioned this to Vetter and Vetter's afraid that he may blow this up to more than it is, just to score a point."

Ives said nothing. The larger question was still hanging. "You still intend to allow the attack to proceed? My God, an earthquake wouldn't move you."

"There's no need to change anything," Campbell said. "Swann's in a bind. He stuck his neck out when he brought Corwin out of Japan. And he can't go to the authorities on the strength of Corwin's guess about what's going to happen. He simply doesn't have the proof, nothing substantial enough to back him up. So if he goes to the authorities, he would have to admit his complicity in breaking the laws of two countries. No, he won't do anything without absolute proof and he won't get that."

After his conversation with Campbell, Ives spent no more than an hour in his office before he went back to the apartment that had been provided him and that he did not like. It was modern, Scandinavian, he supposed, too spare for his tastes. And Meg smiled at him from the exercycle, which was stretching her naked body, a rivulet of sweat glistening down between her breasts. She was enduring torture in the name of maintaining those proportions she considered vital, absolutely essential, for this was the sum of her life, the functioning of that body. He waved, smiled at her over the racket of the machine, thinking of Phyllis, wondering where she was, Buffalo, he believed, remembering a time when she had sailed through the phase of life in which Meg was stuck.

He holed up in the cramped den, studying the Mexican position papers and retaining none of the content, the passage of time marked only by the progressive stages of Meg's preparation, the sound of her successive showers, one boiling hot, the next icy cold, her singing through both of them, practicing (she still aspired to be a professional someday), then her appearance in a terry-cloth robe to offer him a drink (declined), and then the muted clank of jars from the dressing room, the subdued roar of the hair dryer as she worked on herself for the evening. By the time he had showered and put on formal clothes for the evening, she was at the mirror, examining the end result of her labors, the exquisite product, the body in a tight black evening gown that offered no restraints to flesh that needed none.

In the limousine, he avoided rehearsing the scene with Galvez, listened to Meg instead. She was expressing the hope that he could find a free week that they could spend at Pebble Beach; she so longed for the fashionable, for the name of the place above the experience itself. At the club, the uniformed doorman helped them from the car and through the heavy glass doors.

The cocktail party was a quiet one, a small orchestra, fashionable women, the men in clusters, and he had a drink with someone from the government, familiar face, a support statistician for the senators, chatted about Los Angeles while Meg bathed the man in a radiant abstract sexual smile. Ives located the Mexican delegation in a corner of the room, standing with drinks in hand. They reminded him of fat seals, all males, bunched up on a rock. He left Meg with the young statistician and wandered over toward the Mexican group and Galvez who greeted his approach with a cold stare.

"Can I buy you a drink, Señor Galvez?" Ives said.

"I have one, thank you," Galvez said. "But I could use some fresh air."

Ives led the way onto the flagstone terrace where the lights of the city were obscured by a refractive fog. "I believe something needs straightening out," Ives said, coming directly to the point. "I've heard you believe I have been issuing some sort of propaganda against you and your government."

"Yes, I believe that," Galvez said, flatly.

"On what basis?"

Galvez took a cigarette from a silver case, an unusual brand, oval shaped. An image of Ito and his English cigarettes flashed through Ives's mind. Unsettling. He forced his mind back to Galvez who was exhaling smoke into the damp air. "I am aware that you feel a proprietary interest in Japanese shipping," Galvez said. "I am also aware that you have a considerable amount to gain by appeasing the Japanese unions. That is not an unusual tactic. But I don't intend to allow either my government or myself to be vilified."

Ives felt the desire to laugh but he did not show it. "Hell, I'm not going to apologize to you," he said. "Because I don't have anything to apologize for."

Galvez shook his head slightly. "I've been told by unimpeachable sources that you are responsible."

"Your unimpeachable sources are mistaken," Ives said. "Personally, Galvez, I find you to be an overbearing son of a bitch, but that's my general feeling about most aristocrats in politics. But I'm free to tell you that face-to-face. I don't need to create stories in the press. That's not the way I do things."

Galvez froze for a moment; the ash from his cigarette tumbled, shattered, but he had been reached. "I appreciate your candor. Do you think the Americans could be putting out these stories?"

"Hell, no," Ives said. "You wouldn't have a whole group of American senators coming all the way to San Francisco for parties and talks and a coastal cruise if they didn't need what you have to offer. The hemisphere is going to hell in a handbasket. They want concessions from you and that means smooth talks. They wouldn't gain a damn thing by stirring up trouble between you and the Japanese."

Galvez began to pace, his heels clicking against the flag-stones and Ives realized he was wearing elevator shoes, cleverly built to increase his stature. He was wavering in what had been a solid belief, Ives could see it, and that crack in conviction gave Ives a sense of power, confirmed him, for it had been a long time since he felt persuasive enough to change anything. One piece of information could clinch it and he balanced the revelation in his mind, calculating its long-range effects, seeing if it would change anything down the line.

"I can give you proof of what I'm saying, but you have to agree to keep the information confidential."

Galvez paused, considering. "All right," he said.

"I wouldn't have one goddamned thing to gain by attacking you," Ives said. "My company is insolvent and will be dissolved within the next sixty days. It may go into reorganization and it may get enough transfusions to make it look healthy until it can be salvaged. But I don't have any business to push for."

The clincher, the startled expression on Galvez's face, unguarded belief. "Your corporation? May I ask why?"

"If you have a couple of free days sometime, I'll spell it out," Ives said. "Some of it was Japanese labor problems. They screwed me blind. But basically, it's the old trap. Skyrocketing prices for everything, all the big companies shifting around. And hell, let's face it, I guessed wrong. I was committed to supertankers when the trend went smaller. So I lost money and made the shift to smaller tankers and the trend reversed again. I've been in the business long enough to know there's no way to control it. If I had moved against the trend, I'd have one hell of a large operation. But I went with it and lost my ass." Only now did he realize he was carrying a drink. The ice had melted to slivers. He poured it out in a potted plant.

"A son of a bitch," Galvez said with a smile. "So that's what you believe I am?"

"*Sin duda,*" Ives said. "That's the right term, isn't it? Without a doubt. You're only a son of a bitch because you're so new to what you're doing that you think you understand it. I'll make a prediction, Galvez, and this is no goddamned guess. You hold to your dogmatic line, whatever it is, and sometime within the next couple of years, you'll have the shit kicked out of you. It won't be because you're either right or wrong but only because you'll be so predictable you can be had."

Galvez pursed his lips, thoughtfully. "Since your corporation's going under, what are your plans?"

"I don't have any."

"Then perhaps you would be interested in a proposition. What would you think of coming to Mexico as a member of my advisory staff? This is not a firm offer because I will have to talk with the president, but it would appear to be a good idea to have somebody around who's not easily intimidated." He was interrupted by the appearance of one of his aides at the French doors. Galvez dropped his cigarette, ground it out. "Perhaps we can talk in Los Angeles, later in the week."

Ives blinked, nodded, reality intruding with a chill, and he shook Galvez's hand and said something, not aware of his words, and then stayed behind on the terrace to collect himself, shivering, either from the damp fog or the realization of what he had done. For he had been so caught up in the conversation with Galvez that it had become real and he had forgotten why he was here, to soothe Galvez sufficiently to make sure he got aboard the cruise ship, and he had been so taken aback by the offer that he had forgotten that within a week, Galvez would no longer exist at all.

Ives shook violently, wrapped his arms around his chest, convulsively. The spasm existed only briefly, passed. He went inside, spotted Meg practicing on one of the senators, head tossed back, laughing, as if to display the firm underside of her chin, the line of her neck.

Ives carried another drink away from the bar, located Campbell talking to Vetter, made certain that Campbell saw him, and then stayed put until Campbell disengaged himself and came to join him. Campbell was obviously pleased, perhaps a little drunk. "You brought that off very well," Campbell said. "Galvez is in a very pleasant frame of mind. That makes Vetter happy and that makes me happy."

"Fine," Ives said. "I'm saying good-night."

He collected Meg and called for the car and on the way back to the apartment was aware of the way she settled in against him, comfortably, infinitely flexible, able to be wrenched away from the party with no resentments. Her hand was resting on his crotch; being in touch with sex seemed to make her happy. She was humming.

But his mind was dealing with the offer Galvez had made him, with the reversibility of the action Campbell was planning, with what it would take to wash out the plan without incurring the wrath of Campbell's principals. He was not sure he could do this, but with the Mexican government as a shelter, it might be possible. He had been foolish to think about the past, about Phyllis, about the destination to which another course might have taken him. He could do well in Mexico City, in a time of turmoil. He would install Meg in an apartment while he had a look at Mexico's oil transportation problem.

"I'm getting ready to make a very large gamble," he said. And then he saw her eyes, intent as if this time she would certainly understand what he was telling her because she had no grasp whatsoever of business. It existed to her only in a broad and general sense, an area that was his private preserve and totally beyond her grasp. "Would you like to live in Mexico City?"

"What part?"

"The Zona Rosa."

"I'd love it," she said.

He said nothing more and she took the cue from him and allowed the conversation to lapse. His course of action was becoming more clear to him all the time and in many ways Campbell was abetting it. For either Campbell was not as bright as he seemed to be or he had made the mistake of underestimating Ives, for Ives was fully aware of the pitfalls ahead of him which he could not avoid. The stories which in a larger sense laid the foundation for the Japanese attack incriminated him, made him responsible and would, in the end, bring him to trial in a federal court. The only way out now lay in Los Angeles and Corwin's investigation and Swann's power to change what would happen.

She sat relaxed against him. "What are we going to do tomorrow?" she said.

"I think we'll go out of town," he said. "I think we'll fly down to Los Angeles."

4

The harbor was sheltered and yet it was impossible to defend, Corwin decided, sweeping the outer basin with his binoculars from his position on the boat he had rented, a thirty-foot sloop with the canvas sails furled. He had killed the diesel and put out an anchor against the drift. He sat at the bow, feeling the rise and fall of the water beneath him while he studied the rock breakwater where the harbor opened into the sea-lanes. The breakwater was a long line of mounded boulders, a few fishermen perched on the rocks; beyond the entrance he saw a pilot boat at anchor, preparing to make way as a freighter became distinct through the glaring haze.

Corwin made a sweep of the channel to the north with his

glasses and consulted his charts again, his guides to the berths. The tanker would have to come this way, passing between the black ore piles and the supertanker dock to his left and the landscaped Coast Guard compound at Reservation Point on his right. There was something about the business that made no sense at all. Even under optimum conditions, the tanker would have to explode on the west side of the channel to affect the Forsythe house and to offer a threat sufficiently large for the captain to move his daughter away. But there was no target there, nothing of significance, no reason at all for that area to come under attack when the *San Marin* could cause much damage elsewhere.

He put the binoculars back in the leather case and climbed aft, past the cabin to where Faye lay on an air cushion, her body a pale white in contrast to the black bikini. The twin circles of her sunglass lenses were mirrored and he could see a double image of himself reflected in them. He could not tell whether she was awake or asleep until one hand moved vaguely. "What time is it?" she said.

"Four o'clock."

"I'm going to burn if I'm not careful," she said. "When I was a kid I used to lie on the beach with a radio. I'm a real sun freak." She sat up, drawing one knee up for balance, pouring wine from a Thermos into a glass. "Have a drink," she said. "You've been sitting there all afternoon looking for ghosts."

He took the glass. The wine was cold and as he sat down, feeling the sun hot against his bare back; he realized he was wound tight, so out of touch with himself he had not felt the sun during his time on the bow nor the cool breeze freshening from the southwest. She reached up and touched the furrow in his forehead. "You're worrying too much," she said. "You're going to lose your looks."

"I have a lot to worry about."

"Oh?"

"They've stymied me this time," he said.

"They?" she said with a gentle smile. "You're always talking about 'they' as if you're involved in some sort of grand game between we and they. Do you have the slightest idea who 'they' are?"

"Ives for one. And whoever's behind him."

She poured a glass of wine for herself. "But you don't even really know that there's a 'they' here."

"I don't need any clarifying examination."

"I think you do," she said, unfazed by his irritation. "Just listen to me, darling. What happened to you in Japan was quite real, I'll admit that. It was a hyped-up experience, dangerous, and even now you don't know what happened or why. But you've brought me over here and I look around and I don't see what you're seeing." She put her hand on his. "Just one question and I want you to think about it. What would anyone have to gain by blowing up a tanker here?"

"There could be a dozen reasons," he said. "It could be a gesture. It could be an extortion attempt. Maybe they're after a lot of money. It could be any one of those things but I don't believe it. I think they're making a specific move into this harbor for a specific reason."

"They," she said again, gently. She finished the wine and lay on her back again. He could see the sea gulls in her glasses, wheeling overhead.

"You make a good case," he said. "But I don't go along with it for a minute." He poured himself another glass of wine.

"Pride," she said in a lazy voice with no malice. "The invulnerability of the great American masculine pride. You're a damn good man, Charlie Brown, the best in the business, and if you can uncover a plot and prevent a holocaust it would certainly even out all the kicking around you had to take in Japan."

Perhaps she was right. There was sense here, in his desire to be at the center of things, the need to resolve something when few things in life ever came to the point of resolution. He left her on deck and went below to the cabin with its teak trim and walnut paneling. He felt the slight wake of the freighter passing in the distance. He spread his chart of the harbor on the small table and went through his calculations again, punching figures into a pocket calculator, trying to determine the force of the explosion assuming that the tanker was fully loaded with gasoline and that the Japanese had wired explosives for a maximum blast. He contrasted that figure with the potential force of the tanker if she was empty and full of fumes. Or she might have changed cargoes. There were too many variables here to even hope for accuracy, and it would take an engineer and a computer to come close. He did not abandon the project.

He used a compass and fixed the center at the Forsythe cottage, arcing lines across the channel, and even under the most volatile conditions he could not create an explosion that would be close to anything vital. He finished his glass of wine and lay down on the bunk. Shit, there were too many pieces of information missing for him to make any sense out of it and the doubt was there that it really made any sense at all. The *San Marin* could very well be at the bottom of the sea off Japan and he could be on a wild-goose chase.

She came down the companionway, the sun flooding in behind her, a golden creature carrying the Thermos. With a sigh, she poured the last of the wine into the glass and handed it to him. As he drank it, she reached behind her back and untied the halter, freeing her breasts, then she removed the bottom of her suit and sat down beside him and began to kiss him, without a word. Her skin was warm from the sun; her hair smelled of salt water and he pulled her down to him, his penis tumescent, freed by her hand, which positioned him between her legs and then rubbed him slowly back and forth until he moved her hand away and entered her slowly, fully. Neither moved; she was backed against the juncture of the bunk and hull, her eyes watching him. And without moving, he could feel her building, until with a shudder she pressed her hands against the hollow of his back and he began to move, pushing into her until he was at the point where he was totally committed and he felt her body go taut against him, a small cry escaping her as she contracted around him and he spent himself.

"No, don't move, please," she said, clinging to him. "I like to feel you inside me. God, you please me, Charlie Brown."

"Not half as much as you please me."

"Damn," she said, reluctantly. "You'll have to move after all. I'm getting a cramp in my leg."

He withdrew, gave her room and she sat up and began to massage the calf of her leg. "It's a big world, darling," she said. "There are all sorts of places I haven't been." She reached down and patted him on the stomach, playfully. "You've had a lot of women, right?"

"That depends on what you mean by 'had.'"

"Oh, come on, I don't mind."

"A lot of women, yes."

"What were they like?" She sat cross-legged on the bunk. "I want to know everything about you." She brushed the hair from her eyes. "Have all of your women been temporary?"

"Most," he said. "They've been bored, transient. The longest relationship lasted a year."

"And what happened?"

"I don't know. Nothing traumatic. One day she decided to move out, to go on her own for a while. The last I heard she had married a car dealer in Yonkers and had twins."

"And you weren't upset about that?"

"No."

"Do you consider me one of your temporaries?"

"No," he said. He reached out and pulled her down beside him. "It's an odd situation, babe. There's nothing I would like more than permanence with you and there's never been a time in my life when I've felt any more temporary. You may be right, you know. All of my logic may have led me into an absolute dead end. Everybody in this business is had at least once, and this may be my turn."

She settled in against him. "What would happen if we sailed this boat right through the breakwater and down the coast to Mexico?"

He laughed. "Grand theft for one thing. And even if we made it, even if by some miracle we weren't hauled back on charges of stealing the boat, or if the Mexicans didn't decide to hand me back to the Japanese, or Quinlan didn't find me, what would we do for a living?"

"I can take shorthand after a fashion, type a little."

"Do you speak Spanish?"

"Not a word."

Illogically, he found himself content at this moment, lying with her in a narrow bunk, the boat riding a light swell. The desire for permanence with her was quite real as if the rootlessness in him had come to an end and the ambition had burned itself out and he was ready to settle.

He heard a bullhorn outside, but he could not make out the words. He sat up, pulled on his pants, and padded up the companionway, barefoot. A few yards off the stern sat a small boat decorated with a red-and-white-striped canopy, empty of passengers, a young man in a yachtsman's hat at the helm, a bullhorn pointed in Corwin's direction. "Are you Mr. Corwin?" he said.

"Yes," Corwin yelled. "Come alongside."

The boat pulled up, rocking gently, skillfully handled, and the young man reached up to hand Corwin a bottle of champagne. "Your friend asked me to tell you that the sea out there is rough and that you're liable to break a leg if you leave the outer harbor."

"I see," Corwin said. "And where is my friend?"

The young man squinted through the light haze. "The cabin cruiser, off the Union Oil dock."

"Thank you." Corwin watched the taxi pull away. He picked up his binoculars and made a sweep of the dock area, locating the cabin cruiser. Quinlan was sitting on the deck, his feet propped up on the railing, still wearing his business suit despite the heat of the day.

"What is it?" Faye said, coming onto the deck, dressed in her bikini. He handed her the binoculars, indicated the direction. She took a moment to locate him. "It's Quinlan, isn't it?"

"He sent us a bottle of champagne."

"Making his presence known. Making sure we don't get carried away by our fantasies." He was suddenly tired, the euphoria of the moment fading to be replaced by irritation. He dropped the champagne overboard, the bottle slicing into the water with scarcely a splash, and then he went below, with Faye following him. He counted out the money from his wallet. Out of the two thousand, about half was left, and he would get back another hundred from the boat deposit and would have to pay that hundred for the motel. "Do you have any American credit cards that are still good?" he said.

"Yes," she said. "What do you have in mind?"

He put his hands on her shoulders. "Before I tell you, you're going to have to make a very hard decision, dear. I'd prefer that you get on an airplane and go to New Jersey and go along with what your father planned for you. That way, I would at least know you're safe."

"While you do what?"

"I've had enough," he said, quietly. "I intend to make

a run for it. I still have a notion that the roof is going to fall in someplace around here, but I know damn well I'm not going to be able to stop it."

"Quinlan's not going to let you go."

"Not if he can help it." He separated two hundred-dollar bills from the pile. "I want you to buy me a pistol," he said. "And a box of ammunition. I don't know a goddamned thing about California gun laws, but you've lived in San Pedro and you know your way around. If you can't get me one legally then buy one on the street, a Smith and Wesson, preferably, a thirty-eight. Can you manage that?"

"What do you know about pistols?" she said, concerned.

"Enough," he said. "You buy it for me, put it in a box, and send it by messenger to the motel. And then you take off. I have the address in New Jersey. I'll contact you there, once I'm away."

"No," she said, simply.

"I may not even have to use the pistol," he said. "Once I'm out of L.A., I'm in the clear. I'll let you know where I am and you can join me."

"No," she said again, sitting down on the edge of the bunk. "I don't think you could get past Quinlan. And if anything happened to you, I wouldn't even know about it. They would dump your body at sea and that would be the end of it. I'm not that romantic, darling. I don't believe in miracles. And that's what you're counting on."

"I don't want anything to happen to you."

"I don't want anything to happen to either one of us," she said. "So I'm staying."

"For the time being."

"That's good enough. I'll buy that."

"You'd better get dressed," he said. "Street clothes. There's a restaurant dock at the *Princess Louise*. I'll let you off there. If Quinlan's alone, he will have to follow me. If he's not, if you see any sign that you're being followed, you forget the pistol, have lunch at the *Princess Louise*, and go on back to the motel."

"All right," she said.

He went topside and pulled in the anchor before he went to the bridge and cranked the diesel into life. He began a long and leisurely circle as if he were angling close to the sea channel and the opening in the distant breakwater. It was important to him now to know the way Quinlan's mind worked, to test his reflexes and see how quick he was, whether he was methodical or impulsive. Quinlan was watching him, he was sure of that, because Swann was going to take no chance of losing him. Through the binoculars, he could see Quinlan's boat begin to move, not any great burst of speed, just idling. Corwin tested the diesel. It was sluggish and at full power he could get no more than fifteen knots. But there was a supertanker just preparing to enter the breakwater, tugs already in place, a huge ship a quarter of a mile long. From this distance, it looked like a massive iron cliff shearing up from the sea.

He lighted a cigarette and pulled the diesel down to a crawl, creeping in the general direction of the supertanker, training his glasses on Quinlan's cruiser, which also slowed. But Corwin could read Quinlan's mind now, sense his indecision, for Quinlan would be judging distances, guessing Corwin's intentions, and he would be clicking on his marine radio, checking weather conditions in case Corwin made a run for the open sea where the cruiser would be at a disadvantage. Quinlan would have to kick into a straight line to cut him off at the breakwater. Was he armed? Would he open fire at a close enough range? Would he run the risk of collision?

The supertanker was creeping north at a speed of no more than three knots. Corwin waited and then kicked the diesel open and angled across the bow of the supertanker, checking

Quinlan again. The cruiser seemed to leap forward and Quinlan was heading straight toward the opening of the breakwater, taking no chance that Corwin would use the blind cover of the supertanker to make a run for open water. Corwin crossed the bow of the supertanker that loomed above him and then, once he was on the starboard side, out of Quinlan's view, made a turn to port and headed up the main channel, reducing his speed against the chance of being stopped by the harbor patrol. Behind him, the supertanker was beginning a slow turn toward the Union Oil dock to the west and somewhere behind that massive barrier of steel, Quinlan's cruiser would be out of sight for a few minutes, plenty of time.

As Corwin approached the *Princess Louise,* he could see children on the promenade deck and there was a wedding reception in progress, the sound of Mexican music. A man at the rail lifted a glass in Corwin's direction as the sloop moved by. Faye came on deck, wearing a dress and a hat against the sun.

"Where's our friend?" she said.

"He won't be far behind." He eased the boat into the narrow docking area in front of the bow of the *Princess Louise* and helped her step to the wooden planking. "Think it over," he said. "If you don't show up, I'll understand."

"I'll be there."

He pushed into reverse, easing out from the dock and now he could see Quinlan's cruiser easing around the slight crook in the channel. Quinlan was not interested in running afoul of harbor regulations either, for the moment he came within view of Corwin's boat, he cut back to a slow crawl and maintained the same distance as Corwin went under the bridge and into the turning basin and headed east into the Cerritos Channel leading to the marina.

At the marina, he passed what seemed to be hundreds of boats of varying sizes, all neatly moored in slips, and by the time he reached the rental dock, he could no longer see any sign of Quinlan. But the son of a bitch had not lost sight of him; he could sense that. He checked in the boat and sat in a canvas chair on the dock for a long time, finishing a cigarette and a beer, hoping that Quinlan would show himself, but Quinlan did not. He watched the families trooping along the docks, young men scrubbing down the decks of the boats, tanned girls in shorts and halters, sun-bleached hair, and from somewhere the beat of a portable radio, the articulate glibness of a disc jockey, and he leaned back in his chair, closing his eyes, the beer comfortable in his stomach and the sun warm on his face. Southern California, yes, the sounds of normalcy, a peculiar American sanity, and his sense of urgency faded. Quinlan and what he represented was intrusive here, alien, and somehow what had happened to Corwin in Japan seemed impossible here.

He had been foolish to send Faye in search of a pistol, for none was needed here. He had allowed Swann to bluff him, to convince him of a greater sense of power than he actually had, for this was Corwin's country, for God's sake, and there was no way they could contain him here. He had proved Quinlan fallible, proved that he could be faked out and if he had done it once, he could do it again. At the proper moment, he would catch Quinlan off balance and get past him and that one small-time window would be all he needed. Because America was an immense country and they could not touch him here.

He dozed off, came awake, and decided to go back to the motel, certain that Quinlan would catch up. He wanted to make it easy for Quinlan to track him now. When he caught a taxi and instructed the driver to take him back to the motel, he found himself very much in touch with Quinlan's thoughts. Quinlan would be wondering about the girl, why Corwin had let her off, but that would be an idle curiosity because Corwin was his main objective. Quinlan would be feeling a sense of excitement at the tracking because this was his game as well as his business.

The motel was a sprawling three-story stucco establishment across the parkway from the manicured lawns of a public park and the white sands of the beach from the bay. Corwin went to his room on the second floor and ordered a bottle of bourbon sent up, then he sat down by the window and waited, patiently watching the boulevard until he saw a car pull into a metered space along the way, a green Plymouth from which no one emerged. That would be Quinlan, following an established procedure, and Corwin thought he saw the glint of the sun reflecting from binoculars trained in his direction. He pulled back the drapes to make himself plainly visible. It was important for him to fix his position in Quinlan's mind, to let Quinlan know he was in his room.

He poured himself a drink and waited. An hour passed and the green Plymouth did not move. Corwin saw the taxi pull up in front of the motel and Faye climbed out, carrying a sack of groceries, disappearing from his view as she passed beneath the portico and entered the building. He opened the door to let her in, taking the heavy grocery bag from her and setting it down on the table. She went to the window. "He's in a green Plymouth across the boulevard," she said. "Did you know that?"

"Yes."

She came back to the table and unpacked the paper bag, laying out cartons of cereal until she reached the bottom of the bag. She pulled out the pistol and laid it on the table as if she did not like the feel of it, placing a small box of cartridges beside it. "Is this what you want?" she said.

"I don't think we'll need it. I want you to call the lawyers in New Jersey," he said. "Someplace in the conversation, mention that you won't be able to be there by the tenth, that you're going to be stuck here a few days. You might mention that you intend to contest the conditions of the trust."

"Any particular reason?"

"Quinlan's bound to have the switchboard operator paid off. I want him to believe you're staying put."

She picked up the telephone, asking the operator to place a long-distance call for her. He positioned himself near the window, only half listening to Faye's conversation with her lawyer as he observed the green Plymouth. There was still no movement. Beyond the car and the green strip of park he saw sailboats on the water and what appeared to be a miniature island with freestanding colorful panels rising from it, and it took him a moment to realize that the island was a drilling rig and the panels a compromise against the eyesore of machinery spoiling the view. Illusion, compromise.

Faye finished her conversation. "They're very sympathetic," she said. "I'll eventually get the money. But my father was very insistent that they make every attempt to get me up there."

He said nothing. A teen-aged boy had left the motel and was crossing the boulevard toward the green Plymouth, stopping at the driver's window, reporting to Quinlan. A simple method. The plan was full-blown in Corwin's mind now. He left the window, planning a schedule. "We'll have to work this very closely," he said. "I want you to call room service and order an elaborate dinner sent up. Then I want you to go out of the motel the back way, with no one seeing you. There's a service station a block over. Use their phone and call a cab. When it arrives, you call here, this room number and ask for Gibson. I'll tell you it's a wrong number. When the food gets here and Quinlan's convinced we're settled in, I'll join you."

"Then we're leaving? What about our clothes?"

"The same as the last time. We take nothing. By the time Quinlan's tipped, he'll have no idea whether our departure is permanent or temporary." He reached out, took her hand. "This isn't a game," he said soberly. "And just because we leave doesn't mean that they stop looking. Six months from now, wherever we are, there could be a knock on the door. If there's no incident in the harbor, Swann won't rest until I'm returned to the Japanese authorities."

"So?"

"You can get the taxi for me and I can leave alone. That's an alternative."

"Don't be foolish," she said. "The credit cards are in my name, remember?" She kissed him briefly. "And six months is better than nothing." She picked up the telephone again and called room service, ordering steaks and wine. "No, there's no hurry," she said. "We'll be in for the evening." She put the telephone down. "They said half an hour."

"That will work out about right," he said.

Once the door had closed behind her, he felt very much alone, isolated. He wondered if the dinner order would be reported to Quinlan as well as the telephone calls. He wondered how long Quinlan would sit out there in that car, whether he was listening to the radio, and for a moment he felt a perverse empathy for that little man who would spend the rest of his life doing exactly what he was doing now, demonstrating an infinite patience while he ran Swann's errands. Swann, yes. Thinking of Swann reminded him that he would have to check in. It was somewhat early but he could not see that Swann would give any significance to the timing of the call.

He picked up the telephone, asked the hotel operator to get him the Beverly Wilshire and then asked for Swann's room.

"Swann here."

"This is Corwin."

"You're a little early this evening. Do you have anything for me?"

There was no need to lie now. He had a surfeit of facts and suppositions that he could feed to the ear on the other end of the line. He was amazed at his own glibness. He told Swann about the rough calculations of the extent of the blast, using the Forsythe house as the center for the projected circles.

"That's very interesting," Swann said. "I'll feed the figures into a computer. It may take a few hours to get the computer figures."

"I'll be here for the rest of the night."

Once the conversation was terminated, he prepared the room for the waiter. He found a dress in the closet, draped it onto a chair near the bathroom door. He turned the shower on full and left the bathroom, closing the door behind him. The sound of the shower was unmistakable. He checked the room again, putting the groceries back in the sack and the pistol and cartridges in his pocket.

The telephone rang. He picked it up. It was Faye. "May I speak to Mr. Gibson please?"

"I'm afraid you have the wrong number."

He severed the connection and poured himself another drink and sat down to wait. In a few minutes, there was a knock at the door and he opened it to admit the waiter, a young man in his twenties, pushing a serving cart. "Shall I serve at the table, sir?"

"Hold on a sec," Corwin said. He went to the bathroom, opened the door, and stuck his head inside. "Are you about ready for dinner, honey?" he said. He paused a moment as if listening and then closed the door and turned back to the waiter with an indulgent smile. "Just leave the food covered. I'll take care of it." He took the bill from the young man, removed enough money from his wallet to cover it and then added an extra five dollars.

The waiter left. There was a joy in deception, Corwin thought, a feeling that went far beyond the practical necessities of the moment and had nothing to do with life or death. He stood near the window, observing the car one last time, observing the final shuttle of the boy carrying the message to Quinlan. He was done here now. He turned off the shower in the bathroom, pulled the drapes, turned on the lights. He was about to leave the room when the telephone rang. He picked it up and immediately recognized the voice. Ives, yes. The old chill returned.

"Corwin, is that you?"

"What do you want, Ives?" Abrupt, cold. "How did you get this number?"

"What I have to say isn't easy for me. Is your line monitored?"

Immediately, Corwin thought of the operator at the switchboard, the informal relay of information to Quinlan. "I have no idea. Assume that it is. What in the hell do you want with me?"

"It's too late to apologize to you. But I think we can help each other at this point. You weren't the only one who was screwed in this deal."

His anger was alive but he controlled it. Ives had never been good at feigning any emotion and the fear in his voice was real. "What did you have in mind?"

"A meeting. Here. Tonight. I can guarantee you'll be cleared of all charges. This is as much to your benefit as it is to mine."

"You're a lying son of a bitch, Ives," he said. "You've set me up before. How do I know this isn't another one?"

"Arrange the meeting any way you want," Ives said. "But it has to be tonight."

Corwin fell silent, thinking, balancing. He could tell Ives to go to hell and follow his original plans and the odds were about even he could get away with it, but what he had told Faye was true. Two years from now a part of him would still be waiting for the knock on the door, the sudden hand on his shoulder. "I want an honest answer from you. Is the *San Marin* headed here?"

"Yes," Ives said.

"All right. There's a public pier at Huntington Beach. Do you know where it is?"

"Yes."

"It's about six now. I'll meet you there at ten o'clock. You walk out on the pier alone. I'll be watching you but you won't see me. But if there's the slightest indication that you've set up a trap, I'll kill you. Do you believe me, Ives?"

"I believe you."

"Ten o'clock."

He severed the connection, picked up the telephone book. He would have to throw Quinlan off the trail somehow to give him time for the meeting. He opened the telephone book at random, picked the name of Carlos B. Alvarez, a Long Beach address. He lifted the telephone and gave the number to the operator. The voice that answered was heavily accented.

"Carlos?" Corwin said.

"Yeah."

"Is your wife there? Can she hear you talking?"

"Yeah, sure. Who is this?"

"That's fine," Corwin said hurriedly. "Just listen to me and don't say anything. They've been in touch and I'm supposed to meet them. But I'm going to need your help because I think they're trying to set me up. I'll leave here at nine and be at your place by ten. We'll go from there."

Carlos said something in Spanish, then switched to English. "What in the hell are you calling me for? Who is this?"

"That's fine," Corwin said. "Tell your wife this is a wrong number." He put the telephone back on the cradle. That would throw Quinlan for a while, sidetrack him just enough and he could picture the confrontation between Quinlan and this man picked at random from a thick book.

He took one more look at the room, then closed the door and tested it to make sure it was locked. He was not observed as he went down the exit stairs of the west wing. He walked across an alley entrance to the hotel parking lot. Daylight was fading; already patches of fog were beginning to drift in from the bay. She was waiting in a taxi parked by the gas station and the question was on her face, almost as if she knew from the moment she saw him that there had been a change in plans.

He told the driver to drive north; it made no difference where. Then he sat back on the seat, close to her. He told her about the call from Ives, the confirmation that the *San Marin* was indeed coming here.

"And you believe him?" she said.

"Yes, I believe him," he said. "He knew where I was. If he wanted me dumped, he could have had the police move in before I knew what was happening. He's running scared."

"And what if he's setting you up again?"

"I have to be clever enough to see that he doesn't."

"There's that damned masculine pride again, that macho cleverness." She drew away from him silently, thoughtfully. "Is there any chance that my father is still alive, still aboard?"

"No," he said.

"I think he would have liked it better if he had gone down with the ship, fighting the storm all the way."

The driver looked over his shoulder. He was a middle-aged man with a harried face. "I'm sorry," he said. "But I need more specific directions than just north."

"Where are we now?" Corwin said.

"Paramount."

"This will do." He paid the driver and helped Faye onto the curb.

"If you don't mind my asking," she said. "Just what in the hell are we doing?"

"Dissembling," he said. "Killing time." He looked around to get his bearings. This town was indistinguishable from any others in the collection of towns that made up the metropolis, middle class, slightly seedier than some, traffic heavy on the street. They were in front of a church, beige stucco with a neon sign that proclaimed FIRST CHURCH OF THE REDEEMING LOVE. Down the street, past a row of stores he saw a café and he took her arm and began to walk. The fog was just beginning to move in here, no more than a wispy halo around the streetlights.

The restaurant was bright, cheerful, one of a chain, and as he slid into a booth he realized how tired he really was, the toll that the past couple of months had taken on him. He was suddenly resentful of the claims against him, toward Ives for calling, on the intrusion of reality. Sitting here now, going through the motions of ordering something to eat, he could see a long night ahead of him.

Faye picked at her food. "What's going to happen? Can you tell me that?"

"No," he said. "But whatever happens, it will be settled tonight."

"You guarantee it?"

"Yes," he said. "If he has specific information, I'll get in touch with the Coast Guard and they'll put an end to it. And Swann will be off my back as well."

"That sounds too good to be true."

"If it doesn't work that way, we simply follow our original plan and leave and take our chances."

"All right," she said accepting.

He ate hungrily and then checked his watch. It was now

a few minutes past eight o'clock and he was uncertain how long it would take him to get to Huntington Beach. He could be fairly sure that Quinlan would be on track again by now, having checked out the Mexican name, and he was sure to show up at the pier. Well, he would have to work that out when the time came.

He asked the cashier to call him a taxi, but by the time it arrived the fog was heavier and he was certain it would be very thick along the beach. He gave the driver his destination and then settled back, taking the pistol from his pocket, fitting the cartridges into the cylinder, keeping his hands low so the driver could not see what he was doing. Faye watched him in silence, then stared out of the window. He put the pistol back in his pocket.

Nearing the town of Huntington Beach, visibility was reduced to less than a block and the taxi slowed. Corwin told the driver to cruise past the pier and as it came in sight, he swore under his breath. The pier itself sat on massive concrete pilings and extended perhaps two hundred yards out into the ocean. It was wide enough to contain a beach patrol tower a quarter of the way down on the left and a couple of small eating places and bait shops.

He had made a mistake remembering it from the past, ten or twelve years ago when he had been here on an evening when it was all but deserted. It was not deserted now. The fog was so thick he could see no more than a third of the way down the pier and still he could see fishermen in the slight projection off the pier, and there was a crowd of people in the restaurant abutting the pier entrance to the left.

The cab stopped at a light; a stream of young people crossed the coast highway onto the pier from a row of head shops and the disco on the north side of the boulevard. Goddamn, there was no such thing as security here. Ives could stand in the open with the complete appearance of innocence and be surrounded by his men stationed in the restaurant or walking the pier loaded down with poles and bait buckets. But the meeting was set and he would have to make the best of it.

"What's your name?" he said to the driver.

"Mike Mullens, sir." The tone of respect, a man in his early twenties, long hair, and Corwin decided he would have to take the chance.

"How long are you on duty tonight?"

"I generally knock off about midnight."

"You still in school?"

"I go to UCI, yes, sir."

Corwin took a hundred-dollar bill from his pocket, folded it, and extended it across the back of the front seat. "I would like to hire you for the next couple of hours," he said. "It's nothing illegal or dangerous. A business matter."

Mullens took the hundred, examined it under the dash light. "What do you want me to do?"

"First, just swing around the block and pull into one of the metered spaces west of the pier."

"Yes, sir."

"My name is Corwin," Corwin said. "And this is my secretary. I'm an attorney and I'm supposed to meet one of my clients here. He's paranoid as hell." Suddenly, his imagination failed him. He could think of nothing plausible, no way to tie things together. "Anyway, I'm not sure whether he's going to show or not. Is the hundred enough to cover it?"

"Sure," Mullens said. "But I don't understand what it is that you want me to do."

"I'll tell you when the time comes."

He circled the block, pulled into a space along the boulevard. He killed the motor. "Would the radio disturb you, sir?"

"No," Corwin said. He offered a cigarette to Faye, lighted one for himself. The driver was listening to rock, settled back against the door, his fingers drumming on the dash. Corwin kept his eyes on the sidewalk in front of the pier. A group of kids had congregated around a couple playing guitars while a girl in a granny dress passed out pamphlets, tracts, beach preachers, yes, salvation in the fog. He could hear the faint vibration of the guitars above the radio. His hands were sweating.

"You're nervous," Faye said, sympathetically.

"Hell, yes, I'm nervous," he said. "There's always a god-damned gap between the plan and reality."

"Is there anything I can do?"

"No," he said.

A car pulled up to the curb in front of the restaurant and a man climbed out. He was sure it was Ives until a woman joined him and another couple left the car and they all went into the restaurant together. He checked his watch. Eight minutes after ten. Ives was late. Perhaps he would not come. Corwin would have to place a limit on this. If Ives was not here by ten-forty-five, he would assume that he was not coming. He finished one cigarette, lighted another. An old man was walking onto the pier, carrying a bait bucket, a heavy woman by his side, dressed in what appeared to be a housedress over a pair of coveralls. She was carrying the fishing poles. Ten-twenty-eight.

And then he saw the taxi pull to a halt in front of the pier and Ives got out, continuing to stand on the sidewalk after his taxi pulled away. He was dressed in a dark suit, plainly ill at ease in the presence of the beach evangelists. He pulled back his cuff to check his watch, then wandered down the pier into the fog.

"That's the man," Corwin said to Mullens. "His name is Ives. Now, drive on past the pier and park again." The taxi moved forward, slowly, with Corwin keeping his eyes on Ives who was now little more than a shape in the fog. The problem was Quinlan. Was he already here, established in a vantage point of his own, watching? The unpredictable element, yes, and Quinlan was bound to be around somewhere.

The taxi pulled to a stop. "All right," he said to Mullens. "I want you to walk back to Ives and tell him that Corwin will meet him at the second lifeguard tower on the beach east of the pier. Have you got that?"

"Right." Mullens left the taxi. Corwin put his hand on Faye's leg. "You stay here," he said. "I'll talk to Ives and then I'll come back here. If you see any signs of Quinlan, you hit the horn three times."

"I don't like this," she said.

"I don't either, but it will have to do."

He closed the door behind him and went down the flight of concrete steps to the beach, shivering involuntarily from the cold sea air. The fog was very heavy and he could see the glow of lights from the pier to his right, but the beach area itself was dark. He could not see the structure of the lifeguard station. He moved in the direction of the sound of the breakers hitting the beach and his shoes became bogged in the dry sand, so that walking was an effort. Sounds were distorted in the blackness. The bleating of a foghorn sounded very close at hand, the thumping of the guitars and the ragged hymn very far away.

He was about to think he had come too far when he saw the metal legs of the tower, the small elevated cubicle on stilts. The side panels were tightly closed. No one was on duty at this time of night. He checked the number painted on the side of the tower. The right place, yes, and to the west he could see the dim outline of the first lifeguard tower against the luminous glow of the pier. He took the pistol from his pocket again, reassured by the feel of it.

A ship was passing off the coast; he could make out the different timbre of its horn. He heard an odd moaning sound, almost catlike, a stirring off somewhere down the beach and with an odd feeling he realized that there was a couple fucking out there. It struck him as peculiar that the fog seemed less protective than straight darkness and he felt particularly vulnerable in it, as if at any moment a shape could materialize on any side of him and he could not cover all directions at once. The moans and muffled cries intensified and then ceased altogether. In a few minutes he could hear the couple talking as they slogged through the sand toward the coast highway, only the tone of the voices, none of the words. He lighted a cigarette, hoping that Ives, if he was coming at all, could fix on the beacon of the glowing coal. The sea continued to slap against the shore and then he heard Ives's voice, tentatively pushing through the fog. "Corwin?"

"Over here." He heard the sound of shoes in sand and he cocked his head as if to determine direction, looking around, and then Ives emerged from the fog to stand at the metal supports of the guard tower on the other side. Ives just looked at him a long moment and sat down on one of the cross supports, hauling out a silver flask from his jacket pocket, taking a long pull before he extended it in Corwin's direction. Corwin let the hand with the flask hang in space until Ives withdrew it and drank again before he put it away. He sighed, stared vaguely in the direction of the unseen breakers. "He was a son of a bitch," he said, his voice slightly slurred.

"Drunk," Corwin said with quiet incredulity. "You're drunk."

"Not drunk at all," Ives said. "Shit, Charlie, this is important. I had a goddamned good business on the Mississippi. Jesus, those diesel engines, powerful sons of bitches. But then I met Meg. She has a cunt like the inside of a clam, did you know that? Beautiful."

"I don't give a shit if she has the finest cunt in the Western Hemisphere," Corwin said, beyond irritation, boiling with anger. "I want to know what's going on."

"Ito was a son of a bitch," Ives said. He uncapped the flask again. "I killed him and when it happened, I didn't feel a goddamned thing. He was a Jap, after all, and I've had my bellyful of Orientals." He raised the flask to his lips and suddenly Corwin reached out and slapped the flask out of his hands with such force that Ives lost his balance and toppled backward in the sand. He just lay there a moment, his feet propped up on the metal crossbar. Corwin knelt down beside him.

"You either get to the point or I'll beat the shit out of you."

Ives sat up, leaning against the metal support, and the words began to come out of him in spurts of phrases, a goddamned looping whorl of thoughts from which Corwin had to extract the meaning and provide the continuity.

It seemed that a group of very powerful American oil companies were having trouble with the petroleum ministry of the new Mexican government. Ives did not fully understand the nature of this trouble except that Mexico was refusing to conform to the rules by which the game of international oil was played. Ives really didn't care to know all the details because he had been scrambling to save his own company. And six weeks ago, he had been contacted by a reputable middleman from the States who offered him a way out. The man was Campbell and the oil companies he represented were not the only parties with grievances against the Mexicans. The Japanese Red Watch currently had six men in a Mexico City prison and the Japanese terrorists were determined to force the Mexican government to release them.

"The terrorists wanted a tanker," Ives said. "They were going to use it to force the release of their comrades and Campbell saw a way to merge the interests of the oil companies and the terrorists. Hell, Campbell offered me a Swiss bank account, five million dollars, so when my company went under I would be left with something. And I had Forsythe commanding the *San Marin*, about to die. He was willing to go along for a half-million dollars, to ensure his daughter's future. So I agreed."

He stood up, making an uncoordinated effort to brush the sand off his suit. He stepped over the metal support, retrieved the flask, and carefully wiped the cap with a handkerchief.

"Why did you drag me into it?" Corwin said.

"No clear-cut decision," Ives said. He put the flask in his pocket. Someplace along the line, it was decided that a man was needed to take the blame and it had to be someone in the company. Corwin just happened to be the logical candidate for the spot. So a story was manufactured that Okata had been killed on the *San Marin*, just to get Corwin involved, and everything was manipulated to make it appear that Corwin had been bribed by the Red Watch. It was really not so difficult. With each countermove that Corwin made, a way was found to weave it into the fabric of the scenario. Jordan had been killed because he got wind of what was happening and they could pin Corwin with a specific felony. Inspector Ito had been bribed to delay the investigation, keep Corwin inoperative.

Corwin heard a faintly intrusive sound, a shuffling of feet, somebody humming. He froze, taking the pistol out of his pocket. He peered through the fog, saw a woman in a jogging suit and a bandanna tied around her head moving across the sand, earphones on her head connected by a wire to a metal detector on the end of a short rod that she passed over the surface of the sand. She paused, leaned down with a sieve, scooped something from the beach, and frowned at it before she threw it away and moved on. She had not even noticed that they were there.

Ives was looking at the pistol in Corwin's hand, bemused. "It's harder to kill a man than I thought it would be," Ives said. "I always thought you just shot a man and he died. But Ito didn't. Not right away."

Corwin was chilled. He put the pistol back in his pocket. "Why did you call me? Why are you here now?"

"They reneged on their deal. They're going to hold me here to take the fall if anything goes wrong. They hadn't counted on Swann digging into this business. So you and I need to get together on this. If it doesn't happen, they don't have any hold on me. I give you the information and you block the operation. They'll think it came from Swann."

"What do I get in return?"

"If the operation isn't carried out, Swann's company is off the hook. He's a powerful man. He'll take care of you."

"Specifics."

"What?"

"What is the operation? What's going to happen?"

"Jesus, I need a drink," Ives said, staring off into the fog. The Mexican petroleum chief and his subordinates were meeting with a group of senators in San Francisco and would wind up their talks with a cruise aboard the Mexican luxury liner, the *Culiacan*. They would come down the coast at a leisurely pace and have a look at the offshore drilling rigs out from Santa Barbara and new pollution control equipment, but Ives suspected they would do little business because the *Culiacan* was reputed to be a floating pleasure palace, amply supplied with whiskey and women. The only man who would end up sober was Senator Vetter who took his reputation as a watchdog so goddamn seriously that he would *really* be looking at the offshore rigs and pollution safeguards.

The *Culiacan* would come into Los Angeles the day after tomorrow, tying up at a dock on the west side of the turning basin, arriving in sufficient time for the Mexicans to get a full view of the Port of Los Angeles and the oil-handling facilities. There would be a formal dinner aboard and that evening, as the wives of the delegates came aboard, the Mexican ambassador would be there as well as other dignitaries, and a group of the Ballet Folklorico would entertain. There would be a formal ceremony of parting and the Americans would go ashore. At one o'clock in the morning, the *San Marin* would come through the breakwater. As the terrorists passed the fireboat station on the east side of the main channel, they would begin to pump gasoline onto the surface (all carefully planned, practiced in Tokyo Bay) relying on the outgoing tidal drift to carry the spill into position, allowing sufficient separation between the gasoline and the tanker to guarantee the tanker's safety, then touching it off in an inferno that would not only knock out the fireboats but involve the Union Oil tank battery on the east side of the channel.

At that moment, with the full attention of the authorities on the holocaust, men armed with automatic weapons would take over the tug and Okata would place the tanker next to the *Culiacan,* his men seizing the vessel and preventing any of the passengers from escaping. There were some estimates that the *Culiacan* could not be taken without a fight, but Okata would announce that the tanker was filled with gasoline and that charges of explosives had been placed throughout the ship, so that in effect, it was a gigantic floating bomb.

Ives shrugged. Corwin shook his head in disbelief that Ives could detail an impending disaster in such a flat and emotionless voice. "Once they have the *Culiacan,* the Japanese will demand the release of the members of the Red Watch held in Mexican prisons. They'll go through all the negotiation shit and the Japanese will let the women off the ship and the political prisoners will be released."

"What do the American oil companies have to do with any of this?" Corwin said. "They don't give a shit about political prisoners."

"No," Ives said. "That's all window dressing. The negotiations will go on for four or five hours. There will be various plans by American agencies to storm the tanker, to rescue the Mexicans, but they will all fail. Because there's absolutely nothing they can do. They can't open fire on the tanker because that would set it off. They might try snipers, but the Japanese will make it clear that at the first sign of any such action, they will detonate. Anyway, whether the Mexicans release the Japanese prisoners in Mexico City or not, it won't make any difference. In the end there will be an artificial crisis, and the Mexicans will all be wiped out. The Japanese will try to make it out of the harbor. If they can't, they will touch it off. Boom." He made a slight resonating sound with his lips again. "Boom."

Craziness, Corwin thought, wordless, an absolute compounding of insanity, illogical enough to be real. Something disturbed him that he could not locate. The guitars had ceased their thumping in the distance, but the slapping roar of the surf continued and the foghorn continued to bleat in the distance. He could picture the explosion in his mind, the wreckage it could cause, the people obliterated, and all for some economic principle that might or might not change. But now it was over, done with, and the incident would never take place. More negotiating ahead of him, a session with Swann to ensure that he would be cleared and then a practical way to handle this formerly powerful man who was leaning against one of the tower supports, sand clinging to his suit, a sodden look on his face.

Suddenly, Corwin heard a faint whispering noise from somewhere in the fog close at hand, the slight abrasion of a jacket sleeve against a cuff, the exhalation of breath. He did not raise his voice. "You're a prick, Quinlan," he said. "You don't even have enough sense to know when things are over."

Quinlan took shape in the fog, standing slightly at a distance, wary, a quizzical and humorless smile on his face.

"The dinner in the room didn't fool me," he said. "You did something similar in Tokyo and you should never repeat your patterns. The random Mexican, however, was somewhat classic. I hadn't run across that one before. But I'd suggest that you remember next time that a diversion has to be made in a definite direction, which yours lacked."

"There won't be a next time," Corwin said. "Is Swann still in Beverly Hills?"

"No," Quinlan said. "He's at the Palos Verdes house."

"Then that's where we'll go."

"I need a drink," Ives said. "And I want to call Meg."

Quinlan kept his eyes on Corwin. His face reflected a mild disappointment. "So you really do have things under control," he said. "And you won't be making a run for it after all."

"And you miss your game," Corwin said. "But you would have lost anyway, Quinlan. Because you're playing on my territory now."

Quinlan shrugged slightly and said nothing.

3

"ALL RIGHT, WE WILL COVER IT AGAIN," CORWIN SAID. "WHO was your contact? Who made the proposition?"

"Campbell," Ives said.

"And he claimed to speak for a consortium of oil companies?"

"Certainly."

"Which companies?"

"He didn't say."

"He must have given you some hint. Jesus Christ, you didn't undertake this whole goddamned thing on his word, not without some proof."

Ives rolled the ice in his glass, plainly beyond any discomfort, on one level drunk, on another sober, as if he could say whatever came to his mind without pushing to defend it. "He had the money," he said. "He had the plan. I assumed that the companies behind him were the big ones."

"Did you make the contact with the Japanese terrorists?"

"No, one of Campbell's men did that, I suppose."

"But you don't know who?"

"No."

"Who made the arrangements for Forsythe's payment?"

"Campbell, I suppose."

"What was the plan for the *San Marin*?"

"Exactly what they did, to make it appear she had gone down."

"What was their route across the Pacific?"

"I don't know."

"What name did they use for the change?"

"I don't know."

Corwin leaned back in the chair, lighted a cigarette, trying to sharpen his mind again after battering at Ives for what seemed like hours. Swann was standing by the fireplace, listening. Corwin checked his watch, yawning. Only two hours, not many, and gradually the line was being drawn between what he could know for certain and what he would never know. "Who killed Jordan?"

"Ito arranged that."

"And you have no idea who the man was?"

"I didn't want to know." He lowered the level in his glass. The moisture glistened on his upper lip. He glanced in Swann's direction. "I intend to be protected in all this," he said. "I won't be connected with it in any way."

"I don't know whether that's possible," Swann said.

"You'll make it possible," Ives said, without rancor. "I've saved a lot of lives and made it possible for you to save a lot of money. You owe me. All you have to do is tell Campbell you developed this information on your own. Hell, you take it any other direction and I deny everything." The glass was empty. He stood up. "Where's your toilet?"

"Through that archway to your right. The second door down the hallway."

Steady, yes, only a slight shuffling of his feet, a tendency to list as he went through the archway.

"I want the whole thing," Swann said. "I want the names of the companies behind this. I want the full reason why they would go to this extreme to kill off a few Mexican officials."

Corwin laughed slightly. "You're being naïve," he said. "I know this fucking business backward and forward. Why do you think they went through Campbell? If they wanted to make a nation disappear they could find a way to do it so slickly that nobody would ever miss it. If they have a private reason for this elaborate mayhem and they want to keep it private, you won't be able to break it open."

"I have more faith in the law than you do, perhaps. I don't believe there is any fact that's not uncoverable."

"Only by accident," Corwin said. "Maybe fifteen years from now, some little scandal will break open and accidentally reveal a piece of this one."

Swann was silent a moment. "Suppose I offered you a quarter of a million dollars to uncover that reason for me?"

"Is this a hypothetical situation?"

"No," Swann said. "It's a firm offer. It would be worth that much to me, to my company, to know the specifics of any corporate war between the Americans and the Mexicans."

Corwin finished his cigarette, snubbed it out. "I'd be stealing your money if I took that on."

"Then you're convinced it can't be done."

"Absolutely. Now, what have you done to get me off the hook?"

"I talked to some of my friends in Tokyo about an hour ago," Swann said. "I suggested to one of the ministers that you were simply caught in the middle of a rather substantial international situation and not responsible for any of it. They'll need a deposition from you, sooner or later."

"And what will you do about Campbell?"

"Remove him from power," Swann said. "The underwriters will let it be known, unofficially, of course, that insurance will be withdrawn from any tanker companies belonging to his organization. It won't take long for the word to get around."

As simple as that, yes, for a man with the right kind of power, and Swann had it. Well, he could keep it, Corwin thought, and he could go back to London and join the political battles and Corwin did not envy him. He could see freedom stretching ahead of him and there was an irony to his position now; powerful men had trapped him in the first place and now another powerful man was setting him free. He heard a telephone ringing and in a few moments one of Swann's aides came into the room, relaying the message to Swann in a hushed and confidential tone.

"I think we had better put this matter into official hands," Swann said. "I've learned that a Commander Shuman of the Coast Guard is in charge of harbor security. I'd prefer that you handle it, if you will."

"I'll go over there now, if you'll provide me a car."

"Certainly."

"Where's Miss Forsythe?"

"We put her in one of the guest rooms."

"Tell her I'll call her in the morning." He stood up, his legs stiff.

"One more thing," Swann said. "I want to apologize for Quinlan. He's not the most tactful man in the world, I'm afraid."

"Fortunately, he's your problem, not mine," Corwin said.

"Quite," Swann said.

2

It was only as he was driving into the Coast Guard station that he remembered the pistol in his pocket and he was tempted to hand the pistol to the guard who cleared his entrance and ask him to dispose of it. But he did not. He was directed down a palm-lined drive to a low white building with a red-tiled roof and a single light burning through the fog from a central window.

Shuman was a tall, hearty man in his early fifties, full of what appeared to be a boundless energy. He shook Corwin's hand and ushered him into an office with a large chart of the harbor area on the wall, then poured two cups of coffee from a pot. He placed one in front of Corwin and then sat down behind the desk. "I appreciate your coming down here at this hour," Shuman said. "I understand we have a high-level situation here and the port warden seems to think that there's some need for discretion until we can establish the facts."

"There are no facts," Corwin said. He tasted the coffee. Strong. Fine, he could use it. "No facts but some pretty certain possibilities." He sketched in the background, the faked disappearance of the *San Marin*, the projected attack on the Mexican liner.

Shuman blinked. "An attack? Here?"

"Yes," Corwin said.

"And they intend to bring leverage against the Mexican government?"

"Yes."

Shuman pulled a piece of paper out of the desk and began to write on it, talking at the same time. "I can't say this comes as a complete surprise," he said. There had been a good bit of concern about the protection of the harbor and the eventuality that sooner or later it would become the target for a major terrorist attack, simply because it was so vulnerable.

"What preventative measures have you taken?" Corwin said.

"We're beginning to shape up a general policy now," Shuman said. The pencil halted. He tapped the eraser against his teeth. "In this case there are a hell of a lot of things we can do. What's the name of the Mexican liner?"

"The *Culiacan*."

Shuman picked up the telephone, dialed, and from the conversation Corwin gathered he was talking to Coast Guard District Headquarters in San Francisco, inquiring about the *Culiacan*. He nodded, repeated his name, and then put the telephone down. "They'll check it out and call me back," he said. "Is the *San Marin* listed in the Federal Registry?"

"I don't think so," Corwin said. "She's been on the Mideast–Japan run for the past ten years."

"You don't have a hunch what name she would be carrying now?"

"No."

"Then I'll need a general description."

"I can provide you that. She's a modified T-two design, about sixty-five thousand tons, carrying in excess of two hundred thousand barrels. She was carrying Liberian registry. I imagine New York can give you a complete description."

"What approach do you think the *San Marin* will take?"

"You can't count on anything. It's possible they've changed the name to fit any similar vessel on the coastal run. She can be flying any colors. The crew that left Japan was totally Japanese, aside from Forsythe, but it's my bet he was buried at sea. But that's not to say they couldn't have stopped along the way to give the crew a different racial mix."

The telephone rang and Shuman picked it up, answered, and then began to write again. "All right," he said. "I want you to send a private communication to the master of the *Culiacan*. Tell him we have received word of a possible attack on his vessel from a tanker, sixty-five thousand tons, indeterminate, in the Port of Los Angeles. Advise him to return to San Francisco. In the meantime, assign him a cutter escort and send me a Teletype of the names of his passengers." Corwin sipped his coffee, listening, disturbed by something that he could not locate. Shuman put the telephone down. "They left San Francisco at eighteen hundred hours last night," he said.

"Why are they ahead of schedule?"

"Beats the hell out of me. We'll get a response from the Mexican captain shortly." He pressed the buzzer on his intercom. "I want the schedule of all ships due in from twelve hundred hours to twenty-four hundred hours tomorrow. I also want schedules for all traffic from San Diego to Alaska that will be passing our area in the same twelve-hour period."

"You're able to put up a pretty effective screen," Corwin said.

"The *San Marin* won't get through," Shuman said. "I can guarantee that. We'll board any possibles, alert the tug services, pilot boats, all coastal personnel." The telephone rang again and from his manner, Corwin could tell that he had an adversary on the line. "I understand that, Mr. Galvez," he was saying. "It is our policy to issue an advisory whenever a threat is received. We are not interfering in any way with your right of decision." He frowned slightly, tapping the pencil point against the blotter on his desk in a dull tattoo. "Yes, sir, we will provide a cutter escort, but we still must go on the record with an official advisory. Can you connect me with your captain, please?" He waited a moment. "Can you give me your course, Captain, and your ETA Los Angeles?" He jotted something on the notepad. "Yes, sir. Thank you. We'll keep you advised." He put the telephone back on the cradle. "You wouldn't believe the animosity of some of the foreign nationals. The Mexican official is accusing us of interfering with his national sovereignty. He says he will hold us personally responsible for any incident involving his ship."

"Can a cutter escort do the job?"

"Of course," Shuman said. "Jesus, the *Culiacan* is an antelope compared to an old tanker like the *San Marin*. Even without an escort, the *Culiacan* could run circles around her."

"There won't be an attack on the high seas," Corwin said. "It will have to be spectacular and that means inside the harbor. Now, I don't have any official capacity here, but I do have some strong recommendations. There are a hell of a lot of implications I can't tell you about, but the attack will have to come here to accomplish what they're after. If you establish your screen, they will back off. I'd advise you to play this as close to the chest as you can. No publicity.

And I wouldn't limit my security to the *Culiacan* as long as she's here. I'd give her an escort as long as she's in American waters."

A change came over Shuman. The pencil stopped its restless motion. His eyes had a steely glint to them. "These implications you mention," he said. "I don't need to remind you, Mr. Corwin, that there are at least a dozen laws dealing with any withholding of information in a case like this."

"It's not solid information."

"Solid or not, I'd better have it."

"I believe the Japanese are a front, that this attack is being financed by American oil companies."

Shuman blinked. "Oil companies?"

"Yes."

"That doesn't seem logical," Shuman said.

"It is not logical, but it is true," Corwin said. "They will have to make things look good. It will have to be a clearly obvious attack by Japanese terrorists, something the media can cover from the moment it starts. And if they managed to bring it off, there would never be a hint of suspicion that it was anything more than it appeared to be."

"I'm no expert in international affairs, Mr. Corwin," Shuman said. "I don't know what the oil companies are doing or not doing. I hear a lot of rumors but most of them are nonsense. I deal with the men who run the downstream oil business and I don't believe for a moment that any of them are capable of what you're suggesting. But if there's a group that's handling this kind of corporate warfare, then it's my job to find out about it. Do you know the potential for sabotage in a port like this?"

"Yes," Corwin said. "That's the reason I suggest you stop this one. If this attack doesn't work, it will be a long time before anybody else has a try at it."

"And all of this comes because of animosity between business interests here and in Mexico."

"I don't know. It's possible."

"I think we had better call in the FBI," Shuman said, thoughtfully.

"No," Corwin said. He yawned slightly. "I've been through the mill, Commander. If there was a chance in hell of unraveling this, I'd have a crack at it. But now, I've done all I can. I'll hang around until the *Culiacan* comes into port and they have their formal dinner and steam out again. And then I am going to get married and find a life that's no more complicated than it has to be."

Shuman sagged slightly, a shrug of resignation. There was a slight tap at the door and an orderly came in, deposited papers on the desk. Shuman glanced at them then slid them across the Corwin. There was a traffic schedule, the passenger list for the *Culiacan*, assorted compilations of statistics. "Do you want a Xerox of these?" Shuman said.

"Yes, please."

Shuman handed them back to the orderly and then stood up, refilling his coffee cup, a thoughtful concern on his face. "I have to send out our alerts," he said. He tasted the coffee, put the cup down. "Is there any chance this is a hoax, Mr. Corwin?" he said. "I've been here a long time and I've seen every trick in the book. This doesn't make any sense. If you're out to kill Mexican officials on board a ship, there are dozens of less complicated ways to do it. Why a gigantic operation like this one?"

"It's a good point," Corwin said, again on the verge of recognizing something that lay just beyond the periphery of his vision, something he should recognize but did not. There was a flimflam here, something that did not ring true, but he could not pinpoint it. The orderly brought back the Xeroxes and the commander handed him a set.

"Well, as you say, this is my problem now, not yours," Shuman said. "Stay in touch."

"Certainly," Corwin said. "May I use your telephone?"

Shuman punched an open line and put the telephone in

front of him. "I'll leave a clearance for you at the gate."

"Thank you." He waited until Shuman left the room and then he dialed the number on the card Swann had given him and left a message for Faye that he would be back at the motel. Only now did he notice that it was light outside the window. The sun had managed to come up and the fog was beginning to lift, both without his notice.

He took the lists with him and drove around the harbor, peaceful in the early morning light. He slowed down as he passed a dock entrance, a cluster of merchant seamen crossing the street, going back on duty. There were trucks unloading at a warehouse, but the traffic seemed light. He drove across the bridge to the other side of the channel and parked outside the diner. He found a table overlooking the water, ordered coffee from a cheerful waitress, and then unfolded the traffic list for the day. The computer had listed Active Vessels in Port, Vessels Sailed, and he skipped over these categories to Vessels Due to Arrive, a list that eliminated all ships other than tankers.

VESSEL	BERTH	FROM	OPERATOR
American Trader (Tk.)	39	Ozoi	Amer. Trad. and Prod.
Anco Duke (Br. Tk.)	163	Kobe	Panocean Arcotankers
Anco Sceptre (Br. Tk.)	163	Portland	Panocean Arcotankers
Anco Prudhoe Bay (Tk.)	LB-118	Drft Rv	Arco
Houston (Tk.)	Anc.	Anacartes	Trinidad
Narica (Gr. Tk.)	Anc.	Singapore	Shell Int.
Pecos (Tk.)	168	Martinez	Sabine Transp.
Porsanger (No. Tk.)	187	San Fran.	Odfiel-Westfel

No sense there, all reputable names, known companies, nothing either hidden or sinister, for the *San Marin*, or whatever name would be stenciled on the bow and stern, by now would have to be coming in under the aegis of one of the little-known foreign operators, probably flying Liberian colors. There was no way it could pass for any of the tankers on the list.

He put it aside, went down the official passenger list, eight members of the Mexican delegation, none of the names recognizable except for Luis Galvez; six United States senators, headed by Vetter, and a total of twenty-three aides, a normal complement of statisticians and experts in all phases of the oil business. The motive for the attack was bound to be there, right in front of him, centered in whatever agreement Vetter and Galvez were going to formulate. For the life of him, he could not think of a single issue between the United States and Mexico that would require such extreme action. But he had never believed in the basic sanity of either governments or large corporations and he had long since learned that there was no correlation between size and either brightness or logic.

After breakfast he called Shuman and was informed that the *Culiacan* was slightly ahead of schedule and that Coast Guard planes had cleared an area fifty miles out from its course. "Everything's negative," Shuman said.

"I think she will come in from the west," Corwin said. "Straight toward L.A."

"We have an operative air grid working the area," Shuman said. "We're working outward in an overlap to four hundred fifty nautical miles. That still leaves a hundred thousand square miles to cover."

"It'll narrow down," Corwin said. "What ETA are you calculating?"

"The *Culiacan* is due in at twenty hundred hours with a departure at oh two hundred. So we're calculating an ETA of eleven hundred to twelve hundred hours for the *San Marin*. But we have to locate by nineteen hundred. We have a fog forecast for tonight."

"I'm willing to bet money you'll pick her up at the Channel Islands."

He paid the bill and walked along the channel. The first of the seaplane flights to Catalina was taking off for the day, the plane gaining speed on the water. He saw a small harbor patrol boat making its rounds. A Greek freighter was moving slowly down the channel toward the open water. He was overlooking something and he knew it, some piece that just didn't fit. To hell with it. He had done all that he could do.

He went back to the motel, shaved, and took a shower. He emerged from the bathroom to find Faye turning down one corner of the spread, humming to herself. She smiled at him, fluffed up the two pillows at the head.

"You look cheerful this morning," he said. "Radiant."

"And you look like the wrath of god. You worked all night, right? I think you had better sack in for a few hours."

"I will," he said. "But I've made a decision and I want to talk it over."

The bed yielded to her weight and he sat down beside her. "All right," she said. "Talk."

He told her everything that had happened in his meeting with the Coast Guard. "I've carried it as far as I can," he said. "So we're leaving here today. I'm going to sleep for a while and I want you to buy a used car and drive to Palm Springs. Take a room at the Desert Inn."

"While you do what?" she said.

"I don't want anyone to see us leaving town together. I'll catch a bus late this afternoon." He was getting drowsy now. "We're going to take some time off, just the two of us."

He settled into bed and she leaned over and kissed him, her hair falling over his face. "I'm very pleased, to say the least."

"What time is it?"

"About nine-thirty."

"I'll call you at the Desert Inn before I catch the bus. You can pick me up."

"Will do," she said.

Once she was gone, he approached sleep and found that he could not turn off his mind. The images continued to flood in and he could see the sudden flash of fire in the lower part of Tokyo Bay, the exploding fishing boats. He plumped up the pillows, turned over to face away from the light. He forced his mind to think of the desert and gradually drifted into an uneasy sleep.

3

"Do you think we ought to take this to the Harbor Security Commission?" Shuman said.

O'Brien pursed his lips thoughtfully, tapped the ash off his cigar. He was a balding man in his late forties and his surface good nature covered a cold and rational mind. Shuman found comfort in his skepticism. O'Brien had been with the FBI for twenty-five years. He had seen everything at least once.

"It may come to that," O'Brien said. "The captain of the *Culiacan* is causing a general stink, Commander. He relayed a message to our office protesting the presence of your cutter. I relayed the situation to Senator Vetter, tried to calm him down, but he wants to know what's going on. We can't specify without involving the Japanese."

"I'll take care of it," Shuman said. He beckoned to an aide. "Contact the captain of the cutter. Have him stand off ten miles to starboard." The aide departed. "The *Culiacan* will keep him on radar but we'll cut down the visibility."

"Is it possible you could have missed the tanker?" O'Brien said.

"The odds are a hundred to one against that."

"We've covered the dock area on the west side of the

channel where the *Culiacan* will be berthed. It's clean as a whistle." O'Brien shrugged. "If there was anything going on in this harbor, I'd know about it. There are lots of rumors going around but nothing else. What's the latest time that this phantom ship could make the schedule, providing it could get past you?"

"About nineteen hundred," Shuman said. "They would have to try to take advantage of the fog. But we didn't miss them, O'Brien. That tanker isn't out there."

"Do you have a location on Corwin?"

"No. He checks with me off and on."

"When he gets in touch again, find out where he is and I'll have him picked up. We don't want any more publicity than we already have." He stood up. "I suggest we hold off on any big meetings, maintain security, and sweat it through. I'll give you a call."

"Do that," Shuman said. It was only after O'Brien had gone that Shuman remembered Corwin's story about the oil conspiracy. He was pleased he had not mentioned it to O'Brien. There was no sense accelerating what was happening into more than it was.

He went back to work.

4

Corwin came awake abruptly. He had been dreaming. He could remember none of the details except that it had to do with ships and in the middle of it he had realized how they were going to bring it off, the piece of information that had slipped his mind. The answer was there, right in front of him, needing only documentation. He lighted a cigarette, thinking, then he dressed and sat down with the papers Shuman had given him and there they were, a half-dozen possibilities. These people had been goddamned clever, all the way down the line. He picked up the telephone and dialed Shuman's number.

"I want to speak to Commander Shuman," he said.

"May I ask who is calling, sir?"

"Charles Corwin."

There was the slightest of pauses on the line, just enough to make him aware that something was wrong, an excitation in the man's voice that had not been there before. "He's gone home, sir. This is CPO Lattimer. He asked me to get an address from you, a telephone number."

Corwin severed the connection. The commander had gone home and the CPO had said it all. They did not believe him and this was a part of it too. Shuman had talked with the FBI and the order had gone out to pick him up. Clever, he thought, the whole thing excellently planned. He checked his watch. Two-thirty in the afternoon and he was tempted to say the hell with it and allow the plan to be carried out. But he knew and that made the difference. He knew and he would have to pass that knowledge along.

The pistol was a bulky weight in his pocket. He put it in the bureau drawer. He would build his case completely and present it to Swann and Swann could damn well do the following up this time.

He went downstairs and found the car Swann had loaned him. He drove down the coast highway until he found a marina where he bought a navigation chart of Los Angeles and a tide table. He took the time to consult both, to make certain he was correct, and then he drove to Palos Verdes, turning down the tree-lined drive that led to Swann's house, which was cantilevered on the edge of a bluff overlooking the ocean. Swann's aide admitted him into the living room. "He's on the telephone at the moment, sir," the aide said. "May I offer you a drink?"

"Yes," Corwin said. "Bourbon and water."

He unrolled the chart on a table by the window overlooking the ocean. He weighted the corners to keep the chart unrolled and then sat down in a leather chair, checking the names on the list. The bourbon was strong, relaxing. He looked up as Swann came down the two steps from the study, a rather solemn expression on his face. "Ah, Corwin," he said. "I'm glad you dropped by. I have some rather discomforting news for you." He accepted a drink from his aide, sat down across from Corwin. "The FBI is out to pick you up." He studied Corwin a moment. "You don't seem too concerned."

"It's predictable," Corwin said. "I've done what they wanted me to and it's time to remove me."

"I don't understand."

"I won't be prosecuted by anybody," Corwin said. "I've located the *San Marin*."

"Are you serious?" Swann was sitting very still now, his glass poised in midair, his eyes quizzical.

"Never more serious," Corwin said.

"Do you mind if I have Ives sit in?"

"Not at all," Corwin said.

Swann lifted the telephone and shortly Ives came into the room from the corridor. His face was slightly puffy; his skin was pallid. When he shook hands with Corwin, his fingers were cold. He looked to Swann. "Do you have any word for me yet?"

"Mr. Corwin thinks he has resolved the matter," Swann said. "Anytime you're ready."

"They have been goddamned clever," Corwin said, looking down at the chart. "The element that bothered me from the beginning of all this was the Mexicans. We made the a priori assumption that all of this was designed as an attack on the Mexican officials and that put us on a false track from the beginning. The Japanese terrorists are everywhere, God knows, highly mobile, absolute fanatics. So if I was out to eliminate the Mexican energy minister and his council, using Japanese terrorists as a means of attack and covering myself in the process, I would have it done in Mexico City, not in my own backyard. Mexico is so goddamned chaotic and disorganized that the terrorists could send a crew into Mexico City and wipe out Galvez and his staff a dozen different ways and no one would ever question the fact that the Japanese were acting on their own."

Swann cleared his throat, interrupting. "I'm going to play the devil's advocate with you, Mr. Corwin. It seems to me that an attack here would be even more convincing proof that no oil company had anything to do with it. This is the major western terminal for the United States and the whole distribution system could be disrupted."

"That supports my argument," Corwin said. "The potential loss here is an enormous one, a loss to be avoided at all costs. If they were just after the Mexicans, they wouldn't need all this elaborate preparation. And Forsythe would never have gone along with such a plan. He wanted his life to count for something. I talked with him aboard ship, remember? He was full of cryptic self-importance. Could he get worked up over a Japanese cause? Never. He didn't like Orientals and said as much. Could he have felt that it was a grand and glorious thing to rid the world of a few Mexican politicians? Impossible. He spent most of his life in the Far East and as far as I know didn't give a damn about the Mexicans one way or another."

"Aren't Forsythe's motives a little beside the point?" Swann said. "Who knows how a dying man reasons? You can't predicate any theory on that."

"It's a central point," Corwin said. "And it goddamn well fits all the facts. He was a licensed pilot for Tokyo Bay and he was master of the *San Marin*, so he could get the ship out of there without any hassle and they were willing to pay him enough to make financial provisions for his daughter. But the provisions included another item as well. He knew damn well he would never live long enough to reach Los Angeles, so he tried to protect Faye by seeing that she was out of town on the date of the explosion. And that gives us precise information." He picked up a pen, blocked in the approximate location of the house west of the channel. "He would know in advance the magnitude of the explosion, a hell of a large one by any standards. But look at the location of the *Culiacan* docking area, up here in the turning basin."

He drew an X at the dock. "It would take a good-sized hydrogen bomb to affect the house down here from an explosion in the turning basin and we're not dealing with hydrogen bombs. A supertanker exploded down here at the Union Oil dock and the concussion broke windows for miles around, but the off-ship damage was limited to the dock area itself, no exploding oil batteries, nothing. So if the explosion is to have a chance of endangering the house, it would have to take place here."

He put a circle in the channel. "The assumption then would be that the attack would be made on the *Culiacan* as she weighed anchor and started down the channel and the *San Marin* would have to time it so carefully that she came through the breakwater, managed to get tug service, and proceed up the channel at precisely the same time, cutting over to ram the *Culiacan*, at approximately this point."

Abruptly, Ives stood up and crossed to the sideboard where he poured himself a drink. "Hell, you're way off base," he said. "They've worked out a scenario, Charlie. I've seen it. They intended to hit the *Culiacan* at the dock. There were to be negotiations to substantiate the cover story. Shit, that's the way it was."

"They wouldn't need substantiation now," Corwin said.

"I don't see your point."

"They put sufficient pressure on you to force you out with the story."

Ives sat down heavily, his drink in his hand. "Hell, they couldn't count on that."

"It was a pretty good bet. If they had paid you your money, you'd be out of the country by now. But they put you in a bind and to save your own ass, you had to blow the whistle. They would have found another way to get the word out if you hadn't done it, but you did. And the authorities bought it. My God, there are planes all over the coast looking for that goddamned tanker, and the story will have leaked all over the city. They are prepared to believe that the Japs are coming."

Swann said nothing for a moment but the skepticism was clear on his face. "As far as the Coast Guard is concerned, they haven't turned up anything. There isn't any ship. And the time is past when it could meet the intricate kind of maneuvering schedule you're talking about. So if you're accurate, there has to be another plan."

"Precisely," Corwin said. "And I'll get to that in a minute. But we have to go back and reexamine the target, why they would go to all this trouble. I believe that whoever planned this is not after the Mexicans at all. They're after the American senators."

"Bullshit," Ives said. "The American Petroleum Institute controls the Senate."

"Do they?" Corwin said. "Maybe in the past but no more. Vetter's out for the divestiture of American oil companies. He announced that a long time back and nobody took him seriously. But, by God, he's getting support all the time. Vetter's the idealist, the noncompromiser, one of a kind, a prime mover, and a pain in the ass. One man challenged General Motors and shook up a whole damn country. Vetter will do the same thing with the oil companies."

"I don't think they would set this up to kill one man," Ives said. His voice was thickening again. Corwin doubted if he had eaten all day.

"It would be well worth it," Corwin said. "Vetter's whole team will be wiped out along with him. It will be a long time, if ever, before anyone reaches Vetter's position again. At least five years, probably never." He looked to Swann. "Do you agree?"

"I don't know that much about American politics," Swann said. "But I can see your point."

"Now the timing fits," Corwin said. "I've already served my purpose. I've cried wolf and everybody's been all stirred up and they've discovered that everything I said was nonsense. So by the time the attack does come, they won't be expecting it at all, and yet my warnings will be used to explain the motives after the fact. They plan to hit the *Culiacan* as she comes into the harbor, while the Americans are still aboard. The Japanese terrorists may go through the motions of making demands on the Mexican government, but I can guarantee you that not one person is going to get off the *Culiacan* alive."

"Bullshit," Ives said again, beginning to drift off into a world of his own now. "Do you know how long I worked to put my goddamned company together?" He drank from his glass, nodded toward Swann. "None of this has anything to do with me. I want transportation to Puerto Vallarta. I have friends there. Meg likes the place."

Swann ignored him. "How do they plan to do this?" he said to Corwin.

"They gave us a clue in Tokyo Bay," Corwin said, remembering the fire in the fishing village, the sheets of flames on the water, objectively, the event itself removed from him now, as if it had not really happened to him at all. "The *San Marin* was working with the incoming tide, releasing the gasoline as they went, counting on the current to carry the spill away from them." He picked up the tidal chart for Los Angeles Harbor. "The *Culiacan* will be coming in with an incoming current. There's no way the *San Marin* could attack from behind. No, they will have to attack *down* the channel, from the turning basin, releasing their spill, which will catch the fireboats at the station on the east side of the channel, creating enough confusion that they will have access to the *Culiacan* bow on. Jesus, a beautiful plan."

Swann was entranced. "Are you saying that the *San Marin* is already in port?"

"Exactly," Corwin said. "She probably came in yesterday, the day before."

"Under what name?"

Corwin removed the Coast Guard report on ship movements from his pocket, smoothed it out on the table. "You can take your pick. There are six modified T-two style tankers at berth. You can eliminate the *Arco Prairie*, she's unmistakable. You can also eliminate the *Lompoc* because she's too small and she's on the coastal run anyway. My choice would be either the *Showa Maru* or the *Persevera*. They're both Liberian and both are listed in from South American ports. Neither is operated by a company I'm familiar with. There's one outside possibility, the *Sansibar II*, Panamanian registry." He was suddenly tired from the effort of words, of making sense. He lighted a cigarette, Swann's face was white, as if he had been struck a physical blow. Anger? Perhaps.

"I want the names of the American companies involved," he said. "I'm still willing to pay a quarter of a million for that information."

"You put a large staff of investigators and lawyers on it and in a year you might crack it," Corwin said. "It will cost you a couple of million dollars before you're through. And even then the trial would lead you to no more than a couple of middle managers in each of the companies who would take the responsibility while the corporate heads went untouched."

"May I have your list?" Swann said. "I'll call the Coast Guard base commander personally."

Corwin gave it to him. Swann went back into his study and Ives sat down again, carrying a bottle with him this time. "I should never have gotten involved with Campbell," he said, ruefully. "It's like a rabbit asking a wolf for help. I'm sorry as hell about this, Charlie." He poured the glass halfway full, held the amber liquid up to the light. "But nothing can be done about that now. Hell, it was just one of those goddamned coincidences."

Ah, Jesus, Corwin thought with a sudden sagging of the spirit, one coincidence too many and he had not seen it until this minute, one tree he had not seen for the forest of details that engulfed him. He felt a tightening of his stomach, close to nausea. He did not deal with it directly, could not, for whatever he did now, whatever move he made would have to be a careful one, for he was quite alone, paired with a drunk who sat ruminating on his wife's sexual prowess, the precisely controlled vagina with which Meg could pick up a quarter from a table—Ives had seen her do it—sexual talk flowing from him while Corwin considered the alternatives that faced him.

Perhaps it was his imagination, but he could not bring himself to test the situation, not yet, and he poured himself a drink and sat looking out the window. This section of the house was cantilevered over the bluff, a two-hundred-foot fall to the rocks below. The talk of Meg continued, that marvelous ass of hers, as if it were in some way a stable reference point to which Ives was fixed, a walking sexual fantasy in the flesh. Corwin walked to the front door, looked out the diamond-paned windows at the long lane with its line of poplar trees winding up a hill. Almost idly, he touched the latch. He was not surprised when it did not yield. No, Swann would have considered that. If things went wrong, if there was a need to contain, he would take this minor precaution.

Just as casually, he turned to examine the room. He wondered if he was being observed. He could see no trace of a camera, no vantage point. A pleasant, luxurious room in Swann's temporary quarters, nautical here as the house in Japan had been, a seascape above the fireplace, a translucent painted wave, backlighted by the sun, a case full of scrimshaw. Even if they were observing him, they could not read his mind. Perhaps the room was bugged, monitored, in case he reflected any verbal doubts in conversation with Ives.

The telephone lay on a carved table, attractive, but he could not pick it up, for another ear would be on the line and the moment he tried to call, the game, the pretense would be ended. He could not even call Faye, but he was comforted by the thought that she was free.

"What do you think?" Ives said.

"About what?"

"What would you do if you were me, Charlie? Would you give up all your freedoms for a piece of ass like that? I think I'll go to Rio after all. I like the climate."

Corwin was aware of time passing, an interval sufficient for Swann to have pretended to make his call. How many minutes were left? "I like Rio," he said, for the sake of any electronic ears. "But I'm thinking about the east coast myself. Maine."

"Too cold," Ives said, eyes glazed. "Rocky goddamned coasts."

"Where's the toilet?" Corwin said.

"Down the corridor. First door on the left."

Corwin put down his drink. Nothing suspicious about bodily functions, nothing to alarm them in pissing, and he went into the corridor. At the far end he saw double doors, a bedroom perhaps, and it might even have a sliding glass door opening onto a sun terrace, but he could not risk it. He went into the bathroom, closed the door behind him, locked it, a temporary respite. There was a massive sunken marble tub with gold fittings in an alcove and velvet drapes held apart by ornamental sash cords. The window was ample, a single metal casement with a crack, no shade, for privacy was assured with nothing but a view of the open sea beyond the window.

The screen attached from the inside and he unfastened and removed it, propping it against the wall, grasping the crank, which at first refused to turn. But he pressed against the window with the palm of his hand and gave another turn on the crank. Gradually, reluctantly, the window began to open, creaking slightly from disuse.

He opened it to a ninety-degree angle and it caught the wind, a light sea breeze, and he leaned through the opening, momentarily dizzy, for below him was the sheer cliff and the foam of breakers against the rocks at the base. Over to his right, perhaps a hundred feet away, there was a promontory that jutted beyond the site on which the house was built and a lessening of the sheer drop, outcroppings of rock and at the foot of the promontory a suggestion of a small dock area. He could see nothing more than the triangular corner of decking there, but it implied that there was a way down to that dock beyond the promontory, a very steep and narrow stepway perhaps, the possibility of an automatic incline lift up to a neighboring house.

He took the sash cords from the drapes and tied them together and found himself with no more than a twelve-foot length. He had no idea whether it would hold his weight. He would have to assume that it would. He knotted the end of the cord around the lower hinge frame in the window and then knotted the cord at three-foot lengths. Dizzy again, he leaned against the wall, his heart pounding, an acrid metallic taste in his mouth.

Insanity, yes, for once he was out that window and down that cord, he would never have enough strength to pull himself back to the window again. And he would be gambling that one of the steel cantilevered beams that supported the base of the house and angled off to the cliff would be within reach, that he would somehow be able to swing himself to it, hold onto it. Impossible. If he was a conditioned athlete, he might take the chance, risk it, but he was not.

And perhaps Swann would be open to a proposition, a deal, a bargain, for he was apparently a rational man, extremely intelligent. And then he remembered Jordan, dead, and the casualties at the fishing village and he could picture the eventual slaughter on the *Culiacan*. And above all, he could see the disintegration of Ives who had been a strong son of a bitch and was now reduced to a drunk in the parlor, counting on the powers larger than himself to save him rather than destroy him.

He had no choice. He lowered the cord and then eased himself over the sill and committed his weight to it, hanging free, the pain intense in his hands against the first knot, the fright so heavy within him that he was paralyzed. He forced his mind to a different level, away from the pain and the fear, concentrating on the cord itself. Alive so far and the cord was holding and he tried to wind a leg around the cord, could not, and he worked his way down to the second knot. He was beginning to swing slightly, a pendulum effect, and he could not rest for fear that his fingers would betray him, refuse to function.

He moved down again and from here he could see a steel beam joined to a girder traversing the width of the house, and the girder slanted down at a forty-five-degree angle toward the stone face of the cliff. Too far, yes, a yard away from him, three lousy goddamned feet, and his arms were at the point of refusing to hold him. He pushed against the side of the house with his feet, trying to accelerate the swinging motion, back and forth, again and again until he was close enough to the girder that by releasing his grip with his left hand, there was a chance he could throw his arm across it.

But in that moment he knew that the strength of his right hand clutching the cord would not hold him and if he tried he would be committed to the ultimate gamble. He came close to the girder, could not bring himself to do it, swung away again, and then as his weight brought him back to the girder, he made a sudden grab for it, his left arm going across it, hanging on, releasing the cord in blind panic, scrambling to embrace the girder, to wrap his legs around it. Slowly, with the last strength he had, he pulled himself atop it, holding on, his full weight resting on the steel. Alive, lungs pumping air; he closed his eyes a moment, easing the vertigo. He rested his cheek against the cold steel and then he opened his eyes, looking downward toward the cliff. How far this time? Seventy feet perhaps? He could do it. As long as he lay against the steel and inched his way, he could not fall.

He began, working his way toward the junction of steel and rock. The girder was abrasive, rusty, shredding his shirt and the front of his jacket. His flesh was expendable. He was alive. A pair of birds sat in front of him, eyeing him warily as he made his way downward. They flapped away as he came too close. He continued to move downward. The wind moaned underneath the house; he could hear the sea crashing against the rocks far below them and imagined he could feel the spray. An inch at a time.

And finally he came to the junction with the bluff and he inched around to sit with his back against the rock, and there was an exuberant welling of the spirit within him and he laughed aloud. Jesus, both hands were bleeding, shredded raw, and his chest was mottled with blood where the rough iron had grated away the cloth. There was no part of him free from pain and he did not try to move away from it. By God, his body had not failed him, no, he had called on the resources of sinews and tendons and muscles, exhausting himself in the process and he had done it.

He closed his eyes again, resting, then he studied the face of the cliff, a chiseled ledge traversing the face of the bluff carved into the rock when the construction company set the braces. Gradually, he pulled himself onto his feet, pausing long enough for his pounding heart to subside, and then he moved out onto the ledge, hands flattened against the rock wall, feet facing outward. He moved laterally and fell into the rhythm of the waves pounding the rocks. One foot at a time. Out over the ocean he saw a man in a hang glider, resplendent blues and reds, soaring back toward one of the cliffs, and farther out still, the distant glint of sun on water and white triangular sails and on the horizon the bank of fog that loomed like low gray hills. He had never felt more alive than he did in this instant.

He reached the edge of the construction ledge, began to pick his way down the side of the promontory. There was a dock there; he could see half of it as he drew closer, pilings supporting a sun deck, the stern of a sailboat, and up the slope from it a power tram that led to another house. He would sail around Point Fermin and into the harbor, directly to the Coast Guard station, not dealing with Shuman this time but going directly to the port warden who would have no choice but to hear him out and then follow up. He scrambled down the last few feet, reached the wooden planking of the dock. There was no chain binding the sailboat to the dock, only mooring lines neatly looped around the davits. He looked back up toward Swann's house, no direct view from here. He could not be seen. He was in the clear.

He took a cigarette from his pocket, lighted it, drawing the smoke deep into his lungs. His fingers fumbled with the nylon mooring line, painful, stiff, leaving a smear of blood. He heard a noise, a snuffling intake of breath.

"God, you look awful," a voice said.

He turned, slowly. Quinlan was sitting on the stone steps of the boarding platform for the incline lift. His legs were slightly askew and he held a pistol in his hand, rather loosely, as if it were very heavy and he had been holding it for a long time. He squinted against the sun. "I didn't think you'd make it and that's the truth of it. You really bloodied yourself up, didn't you? Quite a feat, if you ask me. I'd hate to have to try that myself and I think I'm in better shape than you are. But you can console yourself with one thought, Mr. Corwin, the getting back up will be much easier than the coming down." He stood up and pressed the button on a pole. There was a whir of machinery and the wedge-shaped lift began to descend the steep incline. "I don't expect any trouble from you, Mr. Corwin, because it seems to me a man who has risked so much wouldn't want to make it easy for himself to be killed. So we will go back quietly. I'm sure Mr. Swann will want to have a drink with you."

Corwin said nothing.

5

"Not too tight," Swann said to his aide who was wrapping gauze around the palms of Corwin's hands. "We don't want to cut off the circulation." He stood at the bar, pouring from a bottle. "There's not a man on my staff who doesn't admire what you did," he said to Corwin. "The sheer boldness of it is overwhelming." He extended the glass toward Corwin.

"Ice," Corwin said.

"Pardon me," Swann said. "I do keep forgetting." He picked up silver tongs, dropped ice into the glass. "Water?"

"No." Corwin accepted the glass with his free hand. Swann went to the corner of his massive study desk and if he was feeling the slightest sense of pressure, Corwin could not detect it. He was reminded of the men he had known who represented absolute power, regarding victories as a matter of course. And Swann was one of these, standing thoughtful now, a curious expression on his face, the fingers of his right hand touching a button on his vest.

"I'm curious," Swann said. "What brought you to the point of realization?"

"The fact that Ives knew where to reach me," Corwin said. "He wouldn't have known unless you told Campbell and you wouldn't have any reason to give Campbell my address unless it was necessary for Ives to feed me the information."

"I should have foreseen that, I suppose," Swann said.

Corwin shook his head. "None of this makes any sense," he said. "Sending me to alert the Coast Guard, for instance. That was taking an unnecessary chance. Why didn't you have me killed back in Japan?"

"That was a mistake on my part, perhaps," Swann said. "But when I met you in Japan I was impressed by both your efficiency and your sense of bluff, Mr. Corwin. It occurred to me that eventually you might become a part of my organization." His voice was quiet, persuasive. "And in the interim, you became my litmus paper, so to speak. If anyone could break my scenario, it was you."

"Scenario?" Corwin said, filled with a sudden cold rage. "You sat down and deliberately planned this whole thing. Jordan's murder, my death, the whole fucking thing as a scenario?"

"Yes," Swann said, evenly. "It has really worked quite well, I believe. The question is now, who else knows what you know?"

Corwin's anger soured. He could feel a muscle trembling in his leg, variable pains throughout his body. He had used himself up, depleted his resources. "Nobody," he said.

"Not even Miss Forsythe?"

"No," Corwin said. "I came directly here."

Swann removed a cigarette from a packet, took his time lighting it. "What would it take to buy your silence, Mr. Corwin?"

"Buy my silence?" Corwin said, startled.

"Certainly," Swann said. "I don't relish violence, Mr. Corwin, and if at all possible, I avoid it. I can well afford to pay you half a million dollars and have Mr. Quinlan remain with you and Miss Forsythe at the motel until the incident is over and then set you free."

Corwin leaned back in the chair and found himself wanting to believe what Swann was saying. Swann was unruffled, rolling his left arm slightly, nudging the cuff away from the thin gold watch, as if he were checking the time against a plane to be caught rather than a holocaust in the harbor. And Corwin remembered Jordan dead, the glazed eyes, and he knew that Swann was doing no more than making conversation, the socialized process, making certain that Corwin had not passed the word before he gave the order to have him killed, not here, no, away from the house.

"I have an account at Citibank in New York," Corwin said. "I would like to have the money deposited there."

Swann nodded, his lips pursed around the filtered end of the cigarette, eyes obscured by the smoke. Corwin could detect no feeling in the man, none. Just as well, for he had been granted more time and he would find a way to use it.

"Done, then," Swann said. "Quinlan will drive you to your motel."

4

SWANN WAS ON EDGE.

The others would be waiting in their boardrooms in the United States or at their homes in Europe and the Mideast. He would not contact them direct (the plan called for no communication), but they would know when it happened, and that knowledge would be satisfaction enough for him. He would be invited to the Bohemian Grove again next year, that exclusive businessmen's camp on the West Coast to which the shapers of international commerce came to drink freely and talk without inhibition, and around a roaring fire in the secluded lodge, they would conduct a postmortem of this operation.

He had developed the plan there, the bold stroke that had to come from a member of the old school like himself. For boldness was lacking in the new breed of businessmen, the corporate myrmidons springing out of the major business schools in the world, and in the new lexicon reason was paramount, and a dangerous man like Vetter was a target for manipulation, for negotiation. But the "old boys" of the business world knew better, for no empire had been erected on the foundation of talk without action.

And one night at the Bohemian Grove, Swann had presented his plan to a few petroleum executives on his level, men who could understand the necessity to eradicate the single greatest threat to world petroleum that had appeared in a half century, a solution to be effected by force, skillfully applied, a final and complete solution. They had been with him from that night, working with him to eradicate any weaknesses in the plan, routing the necessary monies through Hong Kong so they could not be traced. And Swann had reserved the final power to himself, the option to cancel the plan at any time right up to the final moment of commitment.

But he would not cancel. Everything was working perfectly and within another twenty-four hours it would be behind him, and when he went back to London, he would find that the public shares in British Petroleum were waiting for him to pick up from a dozen different sources, all legitimate, so that in the end he would have personal control of the non-government shares.

He sat down at his desk and for a final time thumbed through the computer projections. The telephone rang and he pressed the scrambler button and Campbell's voice came through, professionally buoyant. He neither liked Campbell nor the idea of men like Campbell, smoothly obstreperous, eternally pushing for something, but he tolerated him because his hunger kept him efficient.

"I thought I would call you for an update," Campbell said. "The *Culiacan* has just passed checkpoint one. She's making better headway than we expected, so we'll have to update about thirty-two minutes. I've already signaled our captain to make the necessary adjustments. By our estimates here, the *Culiacan* will pass through the breakwater in exactly one hour and fifty-three minutes."

"All right," Swann said, irritated. Campbell was merely calling to have his efforts recognized in the sure knowledge that somewhere down the line his efficiency in the matter would give him leverage.

"We have a complication," Campbell said. "Since we're not

able to control the exact angle of impact, the tanker may explode on contact. In that event, the scenario will have to be cut short."

"It makes no difference in the long run, now does it?" Swann said curtly. "We won't have any further communications. Thank you for your efforts." He severed the connection. There was a buzz on the intercom. It was his aide.

"Everything is ready, sir."

"We'll leave in about thirty minutes." He carried the computer projection to the cold fireplace and stood it on end, so that the accordion folds were open. Then he drenched them with lighter fluid, and standing at a distance, tossed a lighted match into the fireplace. The paper exploded into flames.

He sat down at his desk and took a cigarette from a wooden box. He was trying to cut down on his smoking but he felt the need for one now. He inhaled the smoke into his lungs, felt the almost immediate exhilarating dizziness. He walked over to the fireplace and with the poker stirred the ashes of the print-out, reducing the larger pieces into powder so that no human skill could ever reconstruct the disintegrated papers. Then he went back to the desk and picked up the telephone, dialed the mobile operator and gave her the number for the Mercedes. Quinlan answered immediately. "Yes, sir," he said.

"You are to answer as if I am requesting routine information," he said. "You are in full control of the car. That's right, isn't it?"

"Yes, sir. We're on Atlantic Boulevard."

"Allow Corwin to change his clothing. Then dispose of him. I will leave the details to you, but I would suggest a suicide. You mustn't be longer than an hour. When you have done it, come back here and pick me up. Can you manage that, Quinlan?"

"Yes, sir. I will."

Swann put the telephone back on the table. He snubbed

out the partially smoked cigarette. He had no further need for it. He would have nothing further to do except to wait.

2

From the moment Quinlan answered the telephone in the car, Corwin was aware the call concerned him and that the prognosis was not a pleasant one. The tone of Quinlan's voice had changed almost imperceptibly and he proceeded to frown and suck air between his teeth, replacing the telephone on the hook with too much studied indifference, leaning forward slightly as if to peer around a slow-moving truck that blocked his lane of traffic.

"What did he want?" Corwin said.

"Just a routine check."

No, it did not have the right sound to it. Plausible enough, yes, the message sufficient, nothing designed to alarm him, but he knew that the order had been passed for his death.

No violence here, not in the middle of traffic on the boulevard with a truck ahead of them and a small red sports car jammed up behind. Would it happen in the privacy of the motel room? Possible. Quinlan was a methodical man and Corwin would have to move ahead of him, keeping him off balance.

For the pistol was still there in the drawer of the bureau in the motel room, still there, waiting for him, and once he had it, he could deal with Quinlan. He had never been a violent man, but if it came to it, he could kill Quinlan without a twitch of conscience, and for a moment he felt the same sense of exultation he had experienced on reaching the end of the girder, as if the rules that had constricted him for a lifetime, the set of beliefs and values and all the rational judgments, had been suspended and he was free to anticipate the satisfaction of another man's death.

He reached over and picked up the telephone with his bandaged hand and caught Quinlan by surprise. He was pleased with Quinlan's discomfort, the dilemma of allowing Corwin to communicate with anyone and being unable to do anything about it without making a premature move. Corwin gave the mobile operator the motel number and then asked to be connected with room service.

"This is Mr. Corwin in room three twelve," he said. "I'm on my way there now and I want a bottle of seven-year-old bourbon sent to my room, plenty of ice cubes. Put together a tray of sandwiches. There's a ten-dollar tip in it for you if you get moving right away."

"Yes, sir."

He put the telephone back on the hook. Guarantees now, no foul play here, the mobile operator would have a record of the call, the motel secure, the presence of a third party. He was pleased that Faye was out of it, safe. He could play the chances here. He glanced at Quinlan. Ah, you son of a bitch, he thought, move your thinking ahead another square. I've wrested a half hour from you now. That's going to run you short.

"A ten-dollar tip?" Quinlan said.

"Why not?" Corwin said. "Your boss is making me a rich man. Turn right at the next corner." Quinlan made the turn into a busy street, aging residences, stucco.

"All that money," Quinlan said. "I would change places with you. To be turned loose in Africa with a fortune in my hands, that would be the life. I would go to Nairobi. Civilized conversation. Fine climate. You might want to consider Nairobi."

Corwin saw the motel through the windshield. "Here we are," he said. "I don't want to be seen in this condition. Drive around to the rear parking entrance."

"Surely." Quinlan turned down an alley, parked near the rear entrance. "About time," he said. "I have to piss."

Corwin shrugged. A young woman was crossing the parking lot, wearing brief shorts, high-heeled shoes. He waited until she climbed into a Jaguar and drove off and then he got out of the car and went up to the motel, climbing the stairs with Quinlan following. When he reached the third-floor hallway, he was relieved to find it empty. The time was close at hand and he began to tense, his body hurting, the anticipation keen and quick in his mind. He unlocked the door to his room, deliberately not looking at the bureau where the pistol was hidden for fear that Quinlan would read his mind and know what he was thinking.

Quinlan moved to the bathroom, leaving the door open, urinating into the stool, but his eyes did not leave Corwin for a moment. "A great relief to have the pressure off the kidneys," he said. He came out of the bathroom, zipping his fly. There was a new and strange expression on his face, a suppressed exhilaration. "Where's your bird?" he said.

"Out of town," Corwin said.

"Is that right?" Quinlan said with a smile. "I'm a strong believer in the ladies myself. A good romp in the sack but nothing permanent. Fair exchange is no robbery, I always say." Almost casually he took the pistol from beneath his coat. There was no urgency to the motion whatsoever.

"What in the hell are you doing?" Corwin said.

"Come on, come on," Quinlan said softly. "I'm a great believer in many things, Mr. Corwin, but I'm deceived by very little. That's my profession, you might say, not being deceived." He glanced out the window, down toward the pool, a tangential dart of the eyes. "You weren't fooled and I knew it instantly." The smile turned rueful. "A ten-dollar tip for sandwiches. Not logical. Ten dollars for protection while you're here. That's logical."

"You've misjudged. Room service can be here anytime."

"Your mistake this time." Quinlan smiled at a space next to the door and Corwin saw the goddamned serving cart, the bottle of bourbon, the ice, the tray of sandwiches. "Splendid service, I'd call that. A flash of a waiter. But it blows your protection."

"Now you're being foolish," Corwin said. "You won't kill me here."

"Oh, I will," Quinlan said, a pleasant lilt to his voice. "And I will be wanting you to clean yourself up first. You're a bloody mess, if you don't mind my saying so. You had better change your trousers and put on a fresh shirt."

"They'll hear the gunshot."

"They?" Quinlan chided gently. "They? Quantify that for me, if you will. A few children in the pool downstairs, most of the guests not settled in yet at this hour. And what could they hear? A single loud crack, and not so loud at that. And if somebody hears, they won't know what it is. And if they did know it was a gunshot, how many would take any action at all upon that recognition? And were they to report a gunshot from somewhere indeterminate, upstairs, downstairs, what would there be for management to do?" He waved the pistol slightly. "I'm running out of time, I'm afraid. So if you will be good enough to change your clothes, you can at least draw breath that much longer. If you don't cooperate, then I will kill you sooner and take my chances."

Corwin was strangely cold, numb. He began to fumble with the buttons on his shirt. He could picture the pistol in the drawer, trace its dimensions in his mind. It was waiting for him, an inanimate ally, but he would never reach it because even if he managed to lay his hand on it, he would have no chance to use it. For Quinlan was too keenly aware, his responses razor honed and the time differential was too great. Because Corwin would have to lift the pistol and Quinlan had only to apply the slightest pressure to the trigger and Corwin would die where he stood.

His shirt was loose. He removed it, his shoulders aching

with the exertion. Delay. Stall. Talk, yes. Words. "They'll know damn well you brought me here," he said.

"A very natural act," Quinlan said. "I work for his lordship and so do you. I brought you back here and you changed your clothes. People rarely commit suicide without some thought as to how they will appear to the person who finds them, and then you went into the bathroom, more suicides occur in the bathroom, tiled surfaces, easier to clean up, I suppose, thoughtful to the very end, most people are. And I'm sure the police will find some way to tie you in with the dreadful incident in the bay, killing yourself from a sense of guilt, who knows? But we will be on our way to London by then."

Corwin took off his trousers, laying them across the bed. He must try for the pistol in the drawer, take the chance, find a way to allow himself time for that. "Ah, too much killing," he said with a sigh. "And what did you do with Ives?"

"Aboard ship. Drunk. The end for him, one way or another and he will never know it."

Corwin unfolded fresh trousers from the hanger, dropped them, picked them up, laid them across a chair. His hands were hurting. His fingers were stiff. He could not count on them to respond quickly enough.

"You must get on with it. You do have a clean shirt," Quinlan said.

"In the drawer."

"Get it."

Corwin moved toward the bureau, slowly. He was certain that whatever he did now would make no difference. He paused, resting his fingertips on the top of the bureau, not even real wood, Formica, the appearance of walnut. Quinlan was restless. He moved to the window to take another look at the pool and then he came closer to Corwin. "I told you to get on with it," he said. "If I can't have things the way I want, then I'll take them the way they are."

Corwin opened the drawer. His shirt lay atop the pistol, only an ellipse of the grip visible, rough matte finish, and he picked up the shirt with his left hand and the pistol with his right. And at that moment, at the instant when he was sure to be discovered, there was a knock on the door and Quinlan flicked his eyes toward it, reflexively, and in that moment, with the eruption of an insane rage, Corwin picked up the pistol and swung it with all his force, blindly, and the metal caught Quinlan in the middle of his face, across the narrow bridge of his nose, smashing cartilage. Quinlan fell back, stunned, the blood spurting from the wound in his face, the pistol falling to the carpet. He lay sprawled at the foot of the bed and Corwin knew that he could beat him to death, expending the rage stored up for weeks, pounding his face into a shapeless mass with no sense of remorse.

The knock sounded on the door again. "Just a minute," Corwin said, getting his breath, calming. One thing at a time now, the appearance of normalcy, for the tanker still sat in the harbor, time passing, and he would not allow that tanker to move. Priorities, yes. He put on his robe, retrieved Quinlan's pistol, put both weapons in the pocket of the robe, opened the door a crack. A middle-aged man in ill-fitting uniform stood there. "Room service," he said. "Were the sandwiches satisfactory, Mr. Corwin?"

"Yes," Corwin said. "Very nice. Hold on." He closed the door and found his wallet, extracting a twenty-dollar bill. He opened the door again, gave the money to the man, signed the bill.

"If there's anything you need, Mr. Corwin, just ask for Harry Hill. I'd appreciate it if you would ask for me by name. Harry Hill."

"I'll remember, thank you." Corwin closed the door, slipped the night chain into place, removed the pistol from his pocket as he approached Quinlan who had struggled to a sitting position. He pulled a handkerchief from his pocket and pressed it against his misshapen nose. His eyes were not quite in focus. Corwin knelt beside him, pulled back the hammer on the pistol, jabbed the muzzle into the soft flesh of his throat. "You mother-fucking son of a bitch," Corwin said, quietly. "Can you understand what I'm saying?"

"Yes," Quinlan said.

"We're changing things around. You're going to do exactly what I tell you to do or I'll blow the top of your fucking head off. Do you understand me?" He jammed the muzzle into the flesh with greater force.

"Yes."

"You are going to call Swann, tell him that everything here is taken care of and you're on the way back."

"My nose is broken."

"I don't care if you choke on your own blood," Corwin said. "Make the call."

Quinlan nodded slightly. "I can manage it," he said. The handkerchief was soaked through now. The blood was pouring down the front of his shirt. "It was nothing personal," he said. "I don't know anything about you one way or the other."

"It is highly personal with me," Corwin said. "Get on your feet."

Slowly, Quinlan struggled to get up, placing an arm on the foot of the bed, pulling himself to a crouch, then to his feet. Corwin knew he would have no more trouble with him for the moment, for Quinlan was quite mortal, afraid of dying. His eyes reflected the fear. He sat on the edge of the bed, his fingers assessing the damage to his face, probing the misalignment of his nose.

"Place the call," Corwin said.

Quinlan picked up the telephone, placed the call with the operator. "This is Quinlan," he said. "The matter has been handled, sir. I will be starting back directly." He paused, listening. "Yes, sir, quite satisfactory." He replaced the telephone on the cradle and then just sat, waiting, quite obviously resigned to his own impending death.

3

Shuman peered at the radar screen. He had never accustomed himself to the sweeping bar of light, the revelation of the white phosphorescent blips. The motion made him slightly dizzy. He could see the ships at anchorage in the outer harbor, a large blip outside the breakwater, the smaller blips of tugs and the pilot boats. "And that will be the *Kitsu Maru*," he said, almost to himself. "She's containerized. Not our baby. Get me the six-mile range."

"Yes, sir," the operator said. The screen diminished, the coast shrinking, a dozen more blips appearing in the waters off the coast, all smaller craft, sailboats, and power cruisers.

"You should be picking up the *Culiacan* in the next half hour or so. Let me know the second she comes within the six-mile range."

Shuman went back to his office through the back door only to be confronted with a neat and sizable stack of telephone messages, all checked URGENT/IMMEDIATE REPLY REQUESTED. For the moment, he ignored them. He took two aspirins from a bottle in his desk, washed them down with lukewarm coffee. He knew in advance that the headache would persist until the *Culiacan* was into port and safely out again.

He was turning up the heat under the coffee when Lattimer came in, closing the door behind him. He stopped short when he saw Shuman. "I didn't know you were here, sir."

"I just got in. What do you have?"

"A half-dozen reporters, a couple television crews. The minicams have camped."

"What else?"

"A dozen more rumors," Lattimer said in a harried voice, not without humor. "Jesus, sir, we've had everything this afternoon from the sighting of a submarine in the Cerritos Channel to a fisherman who claims a minefield has been laid off Terminal Island."

"A perfect atmosphere for the nuthatches," Shuman said. "What did you do with the messages?"

"Forwarded them to harbor police and the FBI."

The telephone rang. Lattimer picked it up, then covered the mouthpiece. "It's Corwin," he said.

"Shit," Shuman said, wearily. "All right, I'll talk to him." He reached out for the telephone. "What can I do for you, Mr. Corwin?"

"You've been looking in the wrong direction," Corwin said. "The *San Marin* is already in port. She'll make the attack downchannel when the *Culiacan* comes in."

"Can you give me the *San Marin*'s new name?"

"Check the tankers in the same class as the *San Marin*. There are six of them. I think you can eliminate all except three, the *Showa Maru,* the *Persevera* and the *Sansibar II.*"

Dutifully, Shuman jotted down the names. "All right," he said.

"You can expect the whole crew to be armed and dangerous," Corwin said.

"We have everything under control, Mr. Corwin."

"Then you will take action."

"We'll take any necessary action to protect the port, Mr. Corwin." There was a click on the line. Corwin had hung up. Shuman leaned back in his chair, lacing his hands behind his head. "The secret of surviving is to separate the hard facts from the rumors and then act only on the facts." He shrugged, then picked up the telephone and called O'Brien. "I just had another urgent communiqué from Corwin," he said. "He advises that the *San Marin* is not approaching from seaward but is already in the port under another identity."

"Planning to do what?"

"She'll steam out and ram the *Culiacan* midchannel."

"That's a new approach," O'Brien said. "I haven't heard that one before."

"He gave me three names, the *Showa Maru*, the *Persevera*, and the *Sansibar II*."

"Hold on." Shuman could hear him riffling through a pile of papers. Shuman could detect a certain apathy in him. O'Brien was older, perhaps close to retirement. He had chased many a wild goose in his time. "It's been one of those days," O'Brien said. "Let's see, yes, I have the reports here. We had agents at every berth in the port today. Nothing out of the ordinary on any of the three ships you mention."

Another light blinked on the telephone. Shuman motioned for Lattimer to get it. "Hold on a second," he said to O'Brien.

"We have the *Culiacan* ten miles out," Lattimer said.

"We have the *Culiacan* on an approach," Shuman said. "You going to take any action?"

O'Brien chuckled. "Beyond our jurisdiction, friend. You can always put out some emergency boarding parties."

"Go to hell, O'Brien."

Shuman terminated the call. Lattimer was lighting a cigarette. "It's an incredible world, Lattimer," he said. "Positively incredible."

"Yes, sir."

"Hypothetical question, Lattimer. You know the situation, right?"

"I think I have a pretty good idea," Lattimer said.

"All right. Then tactically speaking, how would you handle it?"

"You already gave me the answer to that one," Lattimer said. "If I remember the regulations, sir, we are required to take specific actions to specific situations and I don't see any specific situation here. We have negative reports from air and surface search teams. We've had another call from Corwin that we have to classify as a totally unconfirmed suspicion." He sucked on the cigarette, expelled the smoke in short bursts. "We don't have any hard information. The FBI doesn't have any. The harbor police don't have any. Nobody has any. So we have nothing that could justify an interference with commerce."

Shuman smiled. "I think you have a pretty good grasp of it," he said. "And what would you say to the press?"

"A categorical denial that anything's going on except a bunch of rumors, nothing to warrant anything more than normal precautions for visiting dignitaries," Lattimer said. "I'd make them comfortable, serve them coffee and doughnuts."

"Very good," Shuman said. "So let's get all this behind us. Ask them to come in."

4

He stopped the car down the lane of poplars from the house and made his approach from the south wing, climbing along a rocky area toward the garage that had been erected on the solid footing of the bluff. It was almost sunset; the sun was touching the rim of the sea. Swann would be waiting somewhere near the entrance foyer to the house; he would have to count on that, on the vastness of the house to cover the noise he was bound to make in entering it. He followed a footpath behind the garage, bound on the seaward side by a cast-iron railing on the edge of the bluff itself. Full circle, yes, and from here he could see the steel beam he had climbed down to reach the cliff and now he was back again and it seemed that the events of the afternoon had happened weeks ago, except his hands hurt; his body ached.

He reached the service door into the house, saw his face reflected in the glass of the small panes backed by a drawn shade. Gaunt, drawn. Through the grinder and not done yet. He removed the pistol from his pocket, tapped it gingerly against the glass pane closest to the doorknob. A single diagonal crack crystallized in the glass like a frozen lightning bolt and he tapped it again. This time the pane split in two, a quarter of it falling inward, not breaking, no noise, and he put his hand through the hole, avoiding the jagged splinters of glass until his fingers could reach the knob. He fumbled with the lock lever attached to the knob, pulled it up.

He went into a utility room off the pantry, carpeted, then followed a short hallway into the kitchen, moving very quickly now, easing open another door into the dining room. The house was silent, air-conditioner turned off. He could hear the faint and distant roar of the sea. At first he thought that Swann had escaped him, frightened off perhaps by the tenor of Quinlan's voice on the telephone. Then he stopped short as he heard a slight scraping noise from the foyer and he eased himself into the living room. Swann was standing in the foyer, looking through the tall and narrow pane that flanked the massive door. His briefcase rested on the tiled floor beside him.

"He's not coming," Corwin said.

Swann jumped slightly, recovered instantly when he saw him. "Where is Quinlan?"

"Not dead, no," Corwin said. "Tied up in my motel room."

"I see," Swann said.

Corwin approached him, nudged the briefcase with his foot. "What are you carrying?"

"Papers," Swann said. "They have nothing to do with this business, I assure you."

"I believe you," Corwin said. "I want you to open the door, Swann, and walk out. Leave the briefcase behind. The car is parked beyond the curve in the drive."

Swann opened the door, walked out into the fresh evening air. They walked to the car in silence and Corwin waited for Swann to get in before he slid beneath the wheel. He started the engine, turned the car around. Swann sat with his hands in his lap.

"Which ship is the *San Marin?* Where is she docked?"

Swann shook his head. "I won't tell you."

Corwin yanked the steering wheel toward the curb, brought the car to a stop. He kept the pistol below the level of the seat, aimed it toward Swann's chest. "You son of a bitch," he said, vehemently. "I don't want anything to do with your goddamned tanker and I would like nothing more than to have you refuse to tell me so I could put a bullet through your chest and end it all right here."

Swann's face was very pale. "The *Persevera.* Dock one eighty-one."

Corwin eased the car away from the curb, caught in a visceral trembling so violent he found it hard to breathe. No pretenses here, none at all, for he was frightened at the thought of the tanker and he had willed Swann to refuse, knowing he would have shot him to conceal the knowledge from himself so that he would have to do nothing more. "How large a force does Okata have?"

"Twenty-seven Japanese," Swann said, his voice stronger now. "They are a well-trained, well-disciplined, highly motivated group. They're armed with M-11 automatic rifles and Uzi submachine guns. I will have absolutely no influence over them whatsoever at this point. Do you mind if I smoke?" He took a cigarette from a box, lighted it.

Corwin said nothing, concentrating on the road, aware of Swann sitting beside him, exuding an air of quiet self-confidence, and suddenly Corwin knew what he was going to do. His fear had subsided into numbness. There was an oily smear of something viscous on the steering wheel and it took him a moment to realize that his right hand was bleeding again, the bandage soaked through. He eased the car around the headland curve and saw the port below him, peaceful, wisps of fog beginning to ease in from the open ocean, sailboats coming in through the breakwater.

"You're in an untenable position, Mr. Corwin," Swann said.

"We'll see." He drove up over the bridge and looked down at the harbor. The whole area was full of sailboats. The dock shifts were changing and the streets were heavy with traffic.

Swann studied the glowing coal of his cigarette. "One million dollars," he said. "I can make one telephone call and have a million dollars in your hands within the hour."

"I have no doubt," Corwin said. He whipped the car into one of the streets approaching the docks. "This is a big money game. You could raise twice that." He was driving down a wide street, the dock lying behind a battery of small storage tanks. He saw the water from here, a catamaran with slack sails running on auxiliary power, a bronzed woman stretched out on the afterdeck as if to catch the last rays of the sun, a man in a yachting cap at the wheel, pipe clenched between his teeth, and beyond them a sight-seeing boat loaded with passengers.

He drove around the tanks. Ahead of him lay the gate and beyond the low building the single stack of the *San Marin*, the strip repainted now, a white colophon decorating it. Corwin slowed the car to a stop before they came within scrutiny of the gatekeeper.

"Give this some thought, Mr. Corwin," Swann said quietly.

"I've given it plenty of thought," Corwin said. "When we reach the gate you are to identify yourself fully. You represent the marine underwriter and you wish to talk to the captain directly."

"He will know that something's awry," Swann said. "The Japanese have a strong sense for protocol. A man in my position simply wouldn't do this."

"Then you're going to have to be very convincing," Corwin said.

He shifted into gear again and approached the gate. Swann composed himself instantly, whatever discomfort he had been feeling carefully tucked away, out of sight, now that he had a specific job to do. Corwin stopped at the heavy chain that drooped between two metal posts, blocking access to the dock. He held the pistol in his left hand under his jacket as the uniformed guard approached, a heavyset man in middle age, passive face, eyes partially screened by lightly colored glasses.

Corwin lowered his window and said nothing as Swann leaned across him, displaying his credentials in an oversized wallet. "It's necessary that I see Captain Okata," he said with authority. "We're having a problem with port clearance in Caracas."

The guard examined the credentials, handed them back. "Park at the side of the building, please. I'll have to clear you with the bridge." He lowered the chain and Corwin pulled through, occupying one of the spaces heading into the building. And there she was, the *San Marin*, renamed the *Persevera* now, rising like a black cliff against the heavy wooden planks of the dock. He could hear the chatter of the bullhorn from the bridgewing, in Japanese, and he could see the figure of a man in a turtleneck sweater and a captain's hat far above him. They were preparing to make way and the tugs were already moving into position, diesel engines roaring. They had not yet cast off the mooring lines; the gangway was still in place. Time, always the pressure of time, and up there on the bridge Okata would be feeling it, too. If they were preparing to move, the *Culiacan* would be close to entering the breakwater, the two ships moving into the channel at the same time from opposite ends.

The guard emerged from the building. "The captain would like to speak to you on the phone," he said to Swann.

"Certainly," Swann said. As he approached the building, Corwin was close behind him, his hand touching the pistol in his pocket. The effect was not lost on Swann. Inside the office, he picked up the telephone and began to speak in Japanese while Corwin listened, his eyes on the dockmaster, an older man with no hair at all who stood with his hands on his hips, surveying the ship. Swann was delivering a good performance on the telephone, just the right touch of imperious authority. Swann listened a moment, then replaced the telephone on the cradle. "We have permission to board."

On the dock, the gate guard was talking to the dockmaster. Corwin touched Swann on the arm. "You had better make no mistakes," he said. "If you try to cross me, I'll kill you with the first shot and blow up the tanker with the next."

Swann shrugged. Swann would take no chances here. Once Corwin was on board, he could be contained.

They were approaching the dockmaster now and Swann shook hands with him and then introduced Corwin by another name and the dockmaster expressed sympathy over Corwin's bandaged hands.

Small talk, smiles, good humor, and Corwin's eyes continued to take in the tanker, the men at the bow, high above him, silhouettes, and his eyes looked for the Plimsoll mark to see how heavily she was loaded, three quarters. And what was she carrying in those deep tanks that ran like caves behind the thick black steel plates of her hull? Enough, sufficient, whatever it was, calculated for its explosive effect. He moved toward the gangway, one of the newer ones, self-leveling treads, and he followed Swann up to the deck, everything perfectly normal, Japanese sailors, all middle twenties, two standing by a mooring line, one talking, the other laughing, the deck immaculate in its coating of red preservative, marred only by a trickle of water that ran across the deck from the hissing steam of a loose valve beneath the elevated catwalk that crossed between the bridge and the aft housing of the engineers quarters.

The ship was alive. He could feel the vibration of the electroturbine engines in the boiler rooms, humming through the plates of the deck. The Baker flag was flying amidships, red, dangerous cargo, and another Japanese sailor was standing next to the chalkboard hung from the railing with the name *Persevera* chalked in and the sailing time and the destination, Venezuela, and the sailor was chatting in Japanese on the deck phone, at the same time probing a back tooth with the nail of a little finger.

No apparent tension, and Corwin followed Swann up the catwalk to the bridge, to the wheelhouse where Okata was standing, watching the pilot on the starboard bridgewing who was bellowing through the bullhorn down at the tug, jocular good humor. Corwin recognized Okata immediately, not only from the posters that had decorated the meeting hall in Chiba but from Japanese movies he had seen and forgotten; he was a handsome man in the style of Oriental movie actors, lean, lithe, wearing a uniform of sorts, black, and goddamn it, Corwin could detect no signs of tension in the man at all.

When Swann introduced Corwin, Okata gave him a pleasant smile and a half bow, then shook his hand firmly and disengaged only as the first mate called attention to the radar and Okata moved to the side of the wheelhouse to discuss the radar picture with him, a delay, yes, the time was not yet quite right. Okata moved into the open air of the bridgewing to check the position of the tugs.

"It's still not too late, Mr. Corwin," Swann said quietly.

"We stay," Corwin said.

Okata exchanged remarks with the pilot on the bridge-wing and then returned to the wheelhouse to lead Corwin and Swann to his quarters. Jesus, it was no wonder Okata had been able to fool any authorities who had come onto his tanker in the past three days, for he was fully professional, affable, no signs of the radical in him, and his quarters were freshly painted. On the wall there was a photograph of a smiling Japanese woman and a small round-faced girl by her side, both squinting into the sunlight as the picture was snapped.

Once the door was closed, Corwin drew the pistol from his pocket. The smile did not fade from Okata's face and his only expression of surprise was a quizzical glint in his eyes. "Ah," he said. "Always surprises, correct? And Mr. Swann is not here because he wants to be." He glanced at Swann for confirmation. "I am correct, yes? You wouldn't have come here otherwise." He peered through the port-hole, in constant motion, checking a smaller chart mounted on the wall of his cabin, monitoring the time while an entirely separate part of his mind dealt with the matter at hand. He smiled at Corwin again. "I think you realize, Mr. Corwin, that if you were to shoot me, if there was any gun-shot at all, my men would explode the ship immediately." The darting mind, quick flashes, and Corwin had a sudden insight into the man.

"I want you safely out of this port with as little loss of life as possible. But as it stands, you won't make it."

"I think there is a very good chance," Okata said.

"None," Corwin said. "If the American delegation is killed, you're totally without protection."

"We have considered the risks," Okata said.

"Not a risk, a certainty," Corwin said. "You've heard all the rumors in the past twenty-four hours. You're fully aware of what the government officials expect to happen here. Swann never intended you to steam out of this harbor. He even allowed Captain Forsythe to move his daughter away from the explosion as a part of the deal."

"This is preposterous," Swann said. "Absolute nonsense."

"Is it?" Okata said.

"We had an agreement in Tokyo and I expect you to honor it."

Okata looked to Corwin as if for rebuttal. The opportunity was here and Corwin could feel it. He shifted the pistol in his hand, aware that Okata had a bemused and half-expectant expression on his face. Swann was oddly attentive. The weight of the pistol hurt his hand. He turned it around, grasped it by the barrel and then extended it to Okata who took it and examined it as if he had been given a gift.

"Now," Corwin said, nothing to lose anymore. "You have a free choice. I have been in touch with the Coast Guard and they know me personally. When this operation is under way, they'll realize I was telling the truth all along. At this point, I don't give a damn about your operation. But when you're finished with it, I think I can get you and this goddamned tanker out of the harbor." He told Okata what he had in mind, Okata listening quietly, absorbing, continually turning the pistol over in his hands, clicking the cylinder open, snapping it shut again.

"It won't work, I assure you," Swann said. "You will allow me to leave this ship immediately and you will proceed with the original plan. Otherwise, I can guarantee you that no port in the world will be open to you."

"You are a powerful man, correct?" Okata said. "So the question is, how would you bring this about, being on this ship, under my control? The question is, how could you do it, *ne*?"

Swann said nothing.

"I don't think you could do it," Okata said. "That would involve a miracle, correct? I don't think you are powerful enough to cause miracles." He turned to Corwin. "So the question is with you, Mr. Corwin. How do I know that I can trust you?"

"You have the tanker, the firepower, the men. I gave you the pistol. What in the hell could I do to stop you?"

"But the question is why?" Okata said, rubbing his temple with the tip of his finger. "What do you want?"

"I have been involved in a situation that was meant to destroy me," Corwin said. "You know the details. Swann stays aboard. If the tanker goes up, he goes with it."

"Revenge, correct? Is that all you want?"

"I want you out of this port with as few fatalities as possible," Corwin said. "That will be enough."

"Then we are agreed," Okata said.

"Yes," Corwin said. "We are agreed."

5

Shuman sat with the telephone pressed against his ear, Senator Vetter on the other end of the line, and he could picture Vetter sitting in a stateroom aboard the ship, a distinguished frown on his face. "I don't have to tell you, Commander, this business has me worried. The Mexican government has informed Señor Galvez of the terrorist threat," Vetter was saying. The words continued to flow out of the receiver and Shuman could picture them stacking up in a corner of his own head like falling leaves. A rehash. The Red Watch business. Okata.

Okata.

"There's nothing to any of it, Senator."

"We've seen pictures of the police outside the docking area on television," Vetter said.

"They're strictly security precautions, sir. Nothing more. What is the *Culiacan's* position now?"

"I think we're close to the breakwater. Can you keep the security precautions low profile? And how about advising the media to back off for a while?"

"I can give you an affirmative on the first, a negative on the second. Shit, if I issue another denial, that will just add fuel to the fire." *Should I have said "shit" to a senator?* "I would suggest, sir, that we leave things as they are. Once you're safely docked and there's no incident, they'll lose interest."

"I hope to God that's the case." He ended the conversation.

Okata. The name flashed into his mind again, not the sound of it, but the impression of print. He had seen it recently. Foolishness, for the name Okata was as common in Japan as Smith was in the United States. And then it struck him and he fumbled among the papers on the desk for the notes he had made earlier, the names of the tankers Corwin had given him. He found it, looked to Lattimer. "Get me the names of the masters of the *Showa Maru*, the *Persevera*, and the *Sansibar II*."

Lattimer opened a filing case, sliding out a metal drawer, thumbing through a folder, everything in its place, compulsively filed, the thousands of names, facts, and statistics, and he hoped that the one he wanted would not be there, that this was all an illusion. Lattimer lifted the manila folder and thumbed through the sheets. "Mishuye on the

Showa Maru, Abe on the *Persevera,* Randolph on the *Sansibar II.*"

He knew and with a sense of dread extended his hand and Lattimer placed the papers in it, and there it was, on the *Persevera,* written in the Japanese style, the names reversed, Okata Abe, master of the *Persevera.* His hands were sweating; his armpits staining the uniform. Not fast enough now, no way to be fast enough, and Corwin had been right and the nuthatches were the bearers of truth this time. Already in the channel, both of the ships, and now would come the game of unraveling, of blocking the inevitable. He picked up the telephone.

6

Corwin stood on the starboard bridgewing, watching, doing nothing more than that, for he had made his bargain and it was the best that he could do. And he looked at Okata, standing with his hands on the railing, perfectly calm, staring down at the tugs, which were taking up slack now, the tanker beginning to move, and in the wheelhouse the Irish pilot, Macmahan, was that his name? A florid-faced red-haired man who did this for a living, dozens of ships a week, technical problems, knowing the water of the channel as intimately as he knew his wife's body, placidly relaying orders to the Japanese mate at the helm who carried them out. From here, Corwin could only half hear the instructions, the course settings relayed through the mate to the engine room, and all the while Okata stood as if the end of the world was not approaching. He wondered what was going through Okata's mind now, whether he was playing a role, how he could rationalize the insanity of what was happening here. And he had joined in it now, for the first time fully, playing the role of adjudicator and trading in effect for fewer deaths instead of many, because he could not stop them.

The tanker was moving, slowly, inertia overcome, and suddenly he remembered the captain's cabin as it had been in Yokohama and as it was now, totally different, repainted, different furnishings, all traces of Forsythe obliterated. "What happened to Forsythe?" he said to Okata.

"He died," Okata said simply.

"Died."

"He was sleeping when he died. A very sick man, *ne?*"

"Buried?"

"At sea." Okata did not take his eyes off the tug.

"And Ives?"

Okata shrugged. "Still alive. Drunk."

He saw the catamaran, still in the turning basin, scarcely moving, and the woman was sitting up, taking off her sunglasses, taking the bandanna off her hair, blonde, beautiful, and the man was lighting his pipe. Corwin felt like yelling to them, to tell them to get the hell out of here, but he was on shaky ground here, no footing at all, and at all costs he must be reasonable when there was not one ounce of reason left within him.

"There's no need for the spill," he said, almost absently. "A lot of innocent lives."

Okata said nothing.

"It's to your advantage to make this as simple as possible," Corwin said. "This is a goddamn tricky channel. What do you intend to do with the pilot?" Okata was still silent, hands resting lightly on the railing, and suddenly Corwin realized that there was within this man the image of the Kamikaze pilot he had played in the films and he was standing here as if he expected the protection of the divine wind to guide him, to somehow carry through his plans, the superimposition of the metaphysical. Corwin could not allow that. "I want your permission to talk to the pilot," he said, politely. "I want your agreement that he be allowed to come alongside the *Culiacan* if he can be persuaded to do it."

"Do you know the pilot?" Okata said.

"No."

"And you think you can persuade him?"

"Yes."

Okata shrugged again, assent. And Corwin moved into the wheelhouse where the pilot was standing with his hands laced behind his back, peering through the tinted window. He was a natty man with slightly blotched skin and an air of routine authority. He ignored Corwin. "All ahead slow," he said to the Japanese helmsman and the signal was relayed to the engine room, the tanker trembling.

"My name is Corwin. Does that mean anything to you?"

"I don't have time to talk to you."

To shortcut, to communicate without explanation. "You must have heard the rumors floating around the port all day, Macmahan. They're true and you're right in the middle of it."

The hands unfolded from behind the pilot's back. "What?"

"This is the *San Marin*, renamed the *Persevera*, and right now the *Culiacan* will be coming up the channel. The captain intends to ram her."

"Get off my bridge, Mr. Corwin."

"You can't afford to ignore this. Look around, goddamnit. Open your eyes. The ship's under the control of Japanese terrorists who won't hesitate to blow your fucking head off if it suits them."

"Half-rudder," the pilot said, but the command was not as firm now. "All ahead slow." Corwin could see the muscles working in his jaw. "I'm listening," he said, quietly. "But I don't believe you." He nodded toward the turning basin and Corwin saw the Coast Guard cutter standing off. "I've been a pilot in this port for seventeen years. The Coast Guard wouldn't allow something like this to happen."

"If it's true, how could they stop it?" Corwin said. "They're not going to open fire on this tanker and take everything out within a mile radius. And they sure as hell can't board."

"I just don't believe it." He looked toward Okata who came into the wheelhouse from the bridgewing. "It's my duty to inform you, Captain, that this man is making very serious accusations against you."

"Oh?" Okata said.

"I'm going to have to ask you to get him off the bridge." He looked to the helmsman. "One-four-two," he said.

"You are a working man, correct?" Okata said to the pilot. "And you would also have a family, I suppose?"

"What's going on here?" the pilot said. "You have the right to officially take back command of your ship, Captain. Now, you either do that or you let me go about my work."

The tanker was turning slowly, almost pivoting amidships, and it seemed to Corwin as if the tanker were fixed and the channel were revolving around it. The pilot wore a puzzled expression on his face at Okata's silence. Okata was watching the Coast Guard cutter, which had begun to move, angling toward their bow, and Corwin could hear the garbled words from the bullhorn, instructions to the catamaran and the sailboat to clear the area. Shit, too late. Shuman had finally believed and taken action and now it was too late. The pilot shook his head slowly, wonderingly, and the cutter's movements were not lost on him. He did not repeat his statement to Okata. "It's true then," he said finally, to no one in particular.

"The question is one of navigation," Okata said. "We will be intercepting the *Culiacan* downchannel."

"What do you want from me?"

"You are a skilled working man. I want you to bring this tanker alongside the *Culiacan* and allow us to board."

"It's impossible," the pilot said. "Nobody's going to be able to meet a moving ship like the *Culiacan* head on without a hell of a lot of damage both ways." He frowned. The sailboat was running alongside the tanker now, ignoring the Coast Guard warning, and Corwin could see children on the deck, waving.

"I don't think it will be so difficult," Okata said. "We have no desire to harm you in any way. So I think you will want to try to do what I suggest."

A slight exhalation escaped the pilot. "You're serious, then."

"Yes."

"It's a difficult maneuver," he said, his voice light as if there were no force of breath behind it and now Corwin realized he had grasped the full implications and moved into the nightmare. But he managed himself very well, a practical man, and he rubbed his chin and gave a course correction to the helmsman to bring the tanker straight down the channel, doing his job. The tugs were dropping away. "I need to know the full situation, Captain Okata."

"The *Culiacan* will be stationary," Okata said. "She will be anchored and you will have no interference. At the moment we are releasing one thousand barrels of gasoline a minute. In three minutes we will ignite them."

"Jesus," the pilot said, under his breath. Off to port, the catamaran was in trouble. The engine had stalled out and the man in the yachting cap had opened the engine hatch at the stern while the woman in the bikini sat watching him. No sense of danger. An inconvenience.

"The ship is fully wired with explosives," Okata said. "All of my men are heavily armed and we are willing to take extreme measures." The cutter was picking up speed now, lights flashing, sirens blaring, moving to a position off the bow.

"I don't know," the pilot said. "I've never been in a position like this."

"We will all work together. You will place us alongside the *Culiacan* and Mr. Corwin will serve as negotiator. You will want to cooperate, correct?"

"I'll try it."

Corwin could see an officer with a bullhorn on the cutter bridge and the words boomed across the water, hollow, sepulchral. "Ahoy, *Persevera*. You will shut down your discharge pumps immediately and prepare to be boarded. You will heave to immediately."

"I suggest you make an answer, Captain," the pilot said, but he was really not there at all now because he had moved away to some safe place in his mind and he was simply going through the motions. Okata looked to the helmsman, spoke in Japanese and the telegraph rang as he signaled the engine room and the tanker increased its speed. The bullhorn was still clamoring and the sirens were wailing in the far distance.

"You will continue down the channel," Okata said. "I do not believe they will risk explosion."

"Yes, sir," the pilot said. "But I'm going to have to have full power. I need the steerage."

"Full power, yes," Okata said. "All the power you need."

7

"They're what?" Shuman said, hearing the words through the telephone but somehow making no sense of them, something within him turning icy cold, and there flashed through his mind a dozen different memos on terrorism and countless simulations conducted at the base and in institutes all over the country, and his first thought was that none of them applied, the simulations did not match the reality. The inconceivable had happened and no one had made any real preparations for it.

"Hold on." He covered the mouthpiece, yelled at Lattimer. "Get me a helicopter, open board communications." Lattimer moved. "Tell the cutter not to fire under any circumstances." He slammed down the telephone and ran outside, fretting because minutes were passing and he had not caught on soon enough and he could see the channel traffic from here, congested, with fog coming in and visibility was bound to deteriorate at a time when he needed to see most clearly. He heard the chopping sound of the helicopter; it seemed to take forever to land and he urged it to settle for God's sake. When it was finally down he ran to the open door, swinging aboard as it lifted off. The pilot's name was Green, normally a jokester, a throwback to the old flyboy syndrome, but Green was sober now. "What in the hell's going on, Commander?" he said.

"Insanity," Shuman said. "Give me five hundred feet. Head for the turning basin."

"Aye, aye, sir."

But as he lifted above the channel, the alternatives that had begun to form in his mind evaporated, for the sleek *Culiacan* was already in the channel and there was no room for her to undertake a turn within the limited confines of the channel. And even above the noise of the helicopter he could hear the loudspeakers from Ports of Call blaring out "La Cucaracha." The innocence of isolation, they could not see the impending disaster, but he could, like model ships on a tactics board, and downchannel came the tanker, creeping under the wide sweep of the bridge. The tugs had pulled away, trying to get distance, and the cutter was standing off the tanker's bow, ineffective, Jesus, useless, no force there because the water around the tanker was opalescent, a spreading stain, rainbow-colored in spots where the light reflected from it, and shit, the tanker was indeed spilling, at least a thousand gallons a minute. There was a catamaran surrounded by it—did the man at the engine hatch know, did he realize what was about to happen to him?—and the stain was creeping alongside the cutter. Sweet Jesus, it could flash at any moment. He could not fault the captain of the cutter for courage, but he could fault him for stupidity. He put on his headphones and plugged into the open band emergency frequency.

"Blue One, this is Skyhawk," he said. "Can you read me?"

"Affirmative, Skyhawk. This is Blue One."

"Tell your captain to get his ass out of there. Move ahead of the tanker, at least a hundred meters."

"We have a vessel dead in the water, sir."

Split-second decision, no thought. "Leave it there. Move ahead."

To hell with the agreed-upon codes, extraneous baggage now, the jargon that emerged from multiple rational meetings. "Harbor police," he said. "Are you monitoring?"

"We're on," a man said. "We have our bird over to your right."

There it was. He could see it, north of Terminal Island, above the channel there, hovering over a congestion of small boats, a harbor patrol boat trying to keep them back, and this they had not taken into account in their planning sessions, the curiosity factor, and there were perhaps a hundred sightseers in those small boats, come to witness what could be their own incineration. He had to sit on his anger, squelch it, because he needed all his resources now. The spill was spreading erratically, pushed by the tidal currents, approaching the dock inlets to the north, beginning a slow counter-movement to the south along the edge of the channel. He drew a deep breath. "Get the fireboats out of the channel berths," he said. "And alert all the dock fire teams that we have a low flash point spill."

"Right," harbor police said. "We're doing that now."

Yes, they were beginning, and he could see a crew at one dock putting the heavy hose into operation, the stream of water trying to force the edge of the spill away from a pier, to keep it contained. And then, incredibly, he spotted the sailboat astern of the tanker, right in the middle of the spill, and through his binoculars he saw a man taking pictures of the tanker while three children stood at the rail. Goddamn illogic, oblivious to everything, they were just sitting there. He tapped Green on the shoulder, pointed down at the sailboat, and was about to plug into the bullhorn when he saw the flash astern of the tanker and the gasoline spill began to burn, a visible shock wave moving erratically across the surface of the harbor, and quite suddenly he saw the man drop his camera and start herding the children toward the cabin, and then, almost immediately, the sailboat burst into flame and almost at the same moment the fuel tanks on the catamaran exploded, sending debris flying, and he saw a man and a woman thrown into the burning water. No chance, none, the movement of bodies through the air, disappearance in the flames.

Priorities. Green banked away to the west, standing off, the heat rising in the helicopter cabin, and the open line was cluttered with confused noises, a high level of background chatter of commands and expletives and he felt a sudden angry desire for order. "Harbor police," Shuman said, a command. "Keep this channel clear. We're going to have tidal drift up the East Basin Channel, so get those goddamned sightseers out of there. Move them up into the East Basin extension and clear the Cerritos Channel for fireboats. And get the LAPD to block off traffic on the Vincent Bridge. If the tanker blows now, the bridge will go with it." In control now, the pulse of anger clearing the brain, leaving him the observer who no longer identified with people burning to death, with pain. The observer in command. The cold logistics.

"Blue One, what's the tanker's condition now?"

"They've shut down their spill pumps. The crew is armed. We don't have good visibility."

"What kind of firepower do they have?"

"Automatic weapons. They appear to have M-11's, submachine guns."

"Don't assume anything."

The cutter captain's voice broke in. "They've cleared the bridge. Request permission to disable her before she reaches the curve."

"Denied. Control, are you in?"

"Affirmative."

"Get me a rough calculation of the devastation radius if she blows."

"We're working on it. Stand by." And then a recital of the facts that were not facts, only conjecture delivered with the forceful certainty of facts, a fifteen-hundred-yard radius if the tanks were all detonated at the same instant, problems of a different sort if there was a partial explosion followed by a spill and burning, the inevitable creation of a powerful holocaust with winds sucked into the vacuum created by the blaze to reach a hundred miles an hour, violent updraft, a rain of oil over the southern part of Los Angeles.

"The captain of the *Culiacan* is requesting that we clear slip two ninety-two and allow him to disembark passengers."

"Denied," Shuman said. "We would have to clear out a crane ship. She's not even under steam. No time."

Thoughts racing now, the coursing of a tremendous frustration through him, for there were no outs, and his only concern now was to keep those goddamned fanatics from touching off the tanker, nothing more than that. He could see cars jamming up the boulevard fringing the west side of the channel, streets hopelessly snarled, and from here on in, if the tanker went up, thousands of people would go with it.

"The captain of the *Culiacan* requests permission to increase his speed and try to make a run past the tanker."

"Jesus Christ. Tell the son of a bitch that the whole turning basin is on fire. We have a slip drift down the channel on his side." He used his binoculars, dozens of fires now, a sample, only a touch of what they could expect if the *Persevera* went up. The whole of the turning basin was in flames now. And Green was taking evasive action, automatically, no request for permission, rising to a thousand feet with the heat chasing them, burning the fog away from the water. The sailboat was totally in flames, engulfed. No survivors. And Shuman knew that the responsibility was squarely on his shoulders now, no simulations, no games with subsequent evaluations. Real terrorists. A real tanker. The initiative was his.

He switched to the emergency frequency. *"Persevera,* this is the United States Coast Guard. Do you read me?"

A Japanese voice, good English. "This is Captain Okata."

"This is Commander Shuman, Captain. I won't take the time to list the violations you've already committed. You've created one hell of a bad situation. I want to know exactly what you're after."

"Relay the order to the *Culiacan* to stand to," Okata said. "She is not permitted to put any passengers ashore. If such an action is attempted, then we will detonate."

His skin prickled; an easy approach was required, a conciliatory tone. Sweet reason, no urgency, no panic. "We're going to cooperate with you any way we can, Captain. But your request is going to take some time. The *Culiacan* is carrying first-rank foreign dignitaries as well as members of the United States Congress."

"The *Culiacan* will stand to and anchor. We will board from the port side."

"I'm partially aware of what you hope to accomplish, Captain. It would help if you could make your demands specific at this time."

"The *Culiacan* will anchor. No resistance. Correct?"

"We'll do our best, Captain. Stand by and I'll get back to you."

Shuman flipped back to the open channel. "Did you get that, harbor police?"

"Affirmative."

"Get O'Brien. We're going to need an end run in the shore area but no action. Not even a hint of it. Make that clear to him."

"We're working together on this."

"Fine. I don't want this blown to hell because somebody gets overeager."

"This is Control," a voice broke in. "We're going to request a hold, Commander. We have a special team of negotiators who are training in this field. But we're going to have to have time."

"Where are they?"

"At a seminar in Dallas."

Shuman laughed. "Texas? Good God, we're not going to have the time to get them here. Tell the *Culiacan* to heave to and shut down."

"You're going to need the admiral's approval on that. We have a special protocol we have to follow with officials on this level."

Shuman felt the explosion before he saw it and he looked around as a ball of smoke rolled upward from a lighter ship in the Southwest Slip. "I'm aware of the protocol," he said, his voice slightly shrill in his own ears. "I am going to assume that I have the admiral's approval until I am informed otherwise. Now, get me the captain of the *Culiacan* on this frequency immediately."

In a moment the *Culiacan* had been switched over and

Shuman was speaking to the captain who gave his name as Gomez. Shuman informed him of the situation. "I'm going to have to ask you to heave to and anchor, Captain Gomez," he said. "Have your crew stand by to receive lines from the *Persevera*. This is going to be a tricky maneuver, skin to skin. I don't want any accidents."

"We have been relying on the protection of your government," Gomez said. "I am responsible for the safety of this ship."

"And I am responsible for the safety of this port, Captain. It's a goddamned unfortunate situation but it exists. If you don't drop anchor, if you insist on the integrity of your national rights, then the tanker is going to ram you and there's not a damn thing you can do to prevent it."

Static. The captain was considering. "We will comply, but we will also file a protest."

Shuman switched to the emergency channel. "*Persevera*, this is the Coast Guard. We suggest that you use a tug for your approach."

"No tugs," came the answer. "Is the *Culiacan* complying?"

Shuman checked with his binoculars. The *Culiacan* had stopped dead in the channel, immediately abreast of an oil dock on the east side of the channel. "She's complied, but you can see that for yourself. It's a complicated maneuver you're about to make, Captain. Can we give you assistance of any sort?"

"No. One further requirement. No one will board the *Culiacan* from your side."

"All right. Then at least permit me to board, alone, unarmed."

"No." The final word, end. The *Persevera* was no longer transmitting.

"What position do you want?" Green said.

"Further downchannel. But not close enough that the bastard's going to interpret us as any kind of threat."

Green nodded, kept the helicopter crawling. The sun was gone now; the harbor was still bright as day. There was another fire off to the east, a dock burning in one of the slips off the East Basin Channel. Shuman accepted, concentrating on the tanker, shutting out the devastation on the periphery of the turning basin, identifying with whoever was navigating the tanker. Was the pilot still on board? Which one, Jesus, it would take experience, a man who could cope with a paradox, for he had to have greater thrust for steerage and at the same time constant deceleration. Shuman could see the churn of water at the stern as the turbine engines reversed, the screw coming to rest, spinning in the opposite direction, the sluggish hulk of the tanker continuing forward of its own momentum, rudder hard over to port while the bow responded only slightly. Play your goddamned current, he urged silently, and the tanker seemed to drift, very slowly, an island, not a vessel, transversely, lateral movement as if she were slipping sideways, and at first it appeared she would overshoot the *Culiacan*, which seemed almost fragile in comparison, but the reversed propeller was grabbing now, taking hold, slowing the forward progress and he could see the Japanese crewmen, in the flickering light of the fire, gathering at the port side, throwing the messenger lines, a good sign, for Okata did not mean to ram the Mexican ship.

Shuman found his breath suspended, waiting, the tanker sitting lower in the water than the *Culiacan*. The Mexican winches were reeling in the hawsers from the *Persevera*, a ten-foot gap, slowly narrowing, and Okata was releasing his anchor, chain rattling, precisely at the right moment with the forward motion of the ship insufficient to break the chain. The two ships came together lightly and Okata's men swarmed up onto the deck of the *Culiacan* to secure the lines to make her fast.

Shuman found himself sweating. A fantastic piece of seamanship that he himself could never have done as well.

"They're joined," he said into the transmitter. "Now, nobody is to do one goddamned thing. There will be no further radio communication on this channel." He took off his earphones. "Cross over," he said to Green. "Keep at least a hundred yards between you and the tanker. I don't want to spook them."

"Aye, aye, sir."

He saw the fires off to his left, brighter now in the gathering darkness, the giant arching streams of water from the fireboats glinting like solid silver. A perverse beauty. There was a parking lot north of the oil dock and it was half full of cars, the eternal curious coming to see what was happening. "Do you have enough room to land?" he said.

"I think so. Yes, sir."

"All right, then. Set her down."

5

AH, IT WAS ALL WRONG, BACKWARD, CORWIN THOUGHT, AFTER the *Culiacan* had been boarded, for he was still alive and beginning to feel grateful to Okata because Okata had not had him killed. Madness, this gratitude of his, for the respite from dying was only a temporary one. Jesus, anything could touch off this floating bomb and there was no way to calculate the odds that he would be alive an hour from now.

He stood at the side of the wheelhouse, watching Okata as he took off his captain's hat and replaced it with a white headband bearing the red insignia of a rising sun at the right temple. Serene confidence, unhurried. He gave orders to his men in a staccato Japanese, then in English thanked the pilot for his efforts and sent him to one of the quartering rooms on the deck below. Everything precise and polite, unreal.

The harbor was ablaze and Corwin could hear the dull and distant explosions and the wail of sirens and for the moment he did not care, for he was alive, still breathing, perfectly willing to do what he was told in exchange for that privilege. Okata sent one of his men to bring Swann to the bridge, and when Swann came through the door, Corwin could see his fatigue, his strain. He was unaccustomed to this kind of stress and he stood just inside the door, lips slightly pursed, knowing that he occupied an untenable position. Okata studied him, gauging, saying nothing until he asked an aide to bring him a bottle of whiskey and then he put out three glasses and poured each of them half full. One was placed on the protruding edge of the shelf in front of the flag rack, but Swann did not touch it.

Okata drained his glass, put it down. "The time has come for an honest dealing," he said.

"I don't think that's possible," Swann said, coolly. "We had an agreement and you have abrogated it."

"You meant for all of us to die here," Okata said, matter-of-factly. "So whatever agreement you made was designed for your own benefit. That doesn't please me." His voice was rational, but Corwin could feel the tension in it. Okata was quite capable of a sudden shift of mood and the hand that held the whiskey glass was perfectly capable of grabbing up a knife and slitting Swann's throat. One death would lead to many. The bloodbath would begin. That had to be avoided at all cost.

"I know you intended to have the Americans killed and the tanker blown," Corwin said to Swann. "Now, if you've made any specific arrangements to bring that about, I think the captain is offering you a chance to rectify them."

"That is correct," Okata said, filling his whiskey glass again.

Swann had a bemused expression on his face. "You're over-estimating your own countrymen," he said to Corwin. "It wasn't necessary to make any specific provisions. It really makes no difference what the captain does at this point. They're not going to allow this ship out of the harbor."

Swann's composure was back, Corwin realized, that unshakable aura of confidence. "If we go, you go," he said.

Swann shrugged. "In any case, I get what I want," he said to Corwin. "I'm as prepared to die as you are, perhaps more so, considering our ages and the circumstances." He looked to Okata. "But if you deviate from our agreed plan, you're courting disaster. One of your reasons for agreement was to force the Mexican government to release the six members of the Red Watch they're holding. I wonder if you're willing to write them off. If anything happens to me, Captain, you've lost it all. I assure you."

Okata blinked, as if considering, and Corwin could see the whole thing going down the drain, his own credibility destroyed, nothing ending here, no, Swann's plan temporarily neutralized. Okata's face was passive, no emotion at all, and then quite suddenly his hand lashed out, slapping Swann's cheek with such force that Swann was momentarily stunned, his head snapping back, the color draining from his face while Okata launched into a harangue in Japanese, pouring out an angry invective while he pulled a pistol and held it within an inch of Swann's face. Swann was a liar, a disgrace, a traitor, an opportunist, but he was wrong about a disaster here because Okata was under the protection of the Divine Wind.

"If you kill him, he wins," Corwin said, quietly, and Okata's harangue stopped abruptly. The pistol was still leveled at the point between Swann's eyes. "One gunshot from this ship and there won't be any chance of negotiation. He's not telling the truth now any more than he did in the beginning. He's bluffing."

Slowly, the pistol lowered. Okata nodded slowly, under control again. The pistol returned to the holster. Swann stood perfectly still as if he were frozen in a static position. "You are correct," Okata said, finally. "I will kill him later but this is not the time for it." He took a deep breath. "You will relay our demands to the Mexican delegation," he said to Corwin. "We want the immediate release of our six comrades in Mexico City and we also want ten million dollars,

American, as reparation. The Mexicans are highly unpredictable, correct? So it is possible they will turn the prisoners loose to satisfy our demands and then kill them before they leave the city. So we have established a communications center in Cuernavaca. Only when the prisoners reach that point will we take any action here."

"How much time are you talking about?"

"Ordinarily, four hours. But considering the slowness of the Mexicans, eight hours."

"Then you agree to my plan," Corwin said.

Okata nodded, walking around the dimly lighted wheelhouse, ignoring Swann, dictating what Corwin was to say to the Mexican officials. Both they and the Americans would be taken aboard the tanker as hostages. Okata would steam down the west coast of Mexico. Corwin was to arrange a trade for the Mexican prisoners in the waters off Acapulco, in full sight of the media, a humiliation for all the forces of oppression. Leaving Acapulco, he would retain the American congressmen as hostages until he reached a port that he would not announce in advance.

"They will want some guarantees," Corwin said. "Something to demonstrate your good faith. I think you should release the crew of the *Culiacan*."

"I don't have to demonstrate anything," Okata said. "Will American television be covering what we are doing here now?"

"Yes," Corwin said, numb. He could hear louder explosions now, a battery of storage tanks somewhere west of the turning basin.

"I will wish to make a statement at a later time."

"Yes," Corwin said.

"You must impress on them that none of us are afraid to die," Okata said, finally. He turned and gave an order in Japanese to his aide. Corwin was to be taken to the *Culiacan*.

The words were flat, direct, but the implication was clear. Corwin was a prisoner, not a guest. One wrong action and the guard would not hesitate to kill him. And Corwin was aware, as he left the wheelhouse, that Swann's hand was reaching for the glass of whiskey, and that he drank it in a single downing, silent.

2

As Shuman approached the oil dock, he was stopped by a cordon of policemen, and when he was asked for identification, he swept past them, paying no attention, trailed by Green. He went into the small building that housed the dock office to see that the FBI had already arrived, their communications systems set up, O'Brien hunched over a worktable, examining some papers.

"They're carrying a half load of gasoline," he said to Shuman. "Benzine in their midships tanks. They know what they're doing."

He was interrupted by a man from the communications desk. "We have a signal from the *Persevera*, sir, in Japanese."

"Where's Yomuri?" O'Brien said. "Get Yomuri." But Yomuri was already coming through the door, a tall Nisei with close-cropped hair. He sat down, put on the earphones, picked up the microphone. He clicked a ball-point pen and began to scribble notes on a small pad, pausing occasionally to ask a question in Japanese, grunting his understanding as he began to write again. Finally, he removed the headset.

"What's the bottom line?" O'Brien said, impatiently.

"They want the Mexican government to release the six political prisoners, the Japanese terrorists captured last year in Mexico City. If they don't get that, they blow both ships sky-high."

"What time limit?"

"Immediate contact with the Mexican government, an official authorized to deal. They want an agreement in principle within the hour. They also want an unspecified amount of money, American."

"What else?"

"That's it for now. Okata wants the Mexican official to call on frequency one fifty-six point seven MHz. No passed-on messages, nothing secondhand."

"That's about what I expected," O'Brien said. He began to relay orders to his men and Shuman was amazed at how well prepared he was, for there was a man from the State Department standing by on an open line and the Mexican ambassador had already been alerted.

"Where do you have your marksmen posted?" Shuman said.

"On the tops of the oil storage tanks."

"We have to find a way to get men aboard the *Culiacan*," Shuman said, absently, thinking it through, forcing the calmness. No precipitate action. One random spark could set the tanker off.

A man from communications signaled O'Brien. "Problems," he said. "We have a report from the Mexican consulate. There are only four terrorists alive in Mexico City. The other two were killed last week in an escape attempt."

O'Brien looked to Shuman. "Do you think Okata's going to buy four?"

"No," Shuman said, suddenly chilled.

"Then we have to keep him from knowing," O'Brien said. He looked to the man at the desk. "Tell the Mexican officials to put a lid on this." He turned to Shuman again. "We can't keep that kind of information down for very long. Sooner or later, the media's going to run with it."

"Then we have to take out Okata before that happens," Shuman said. "We have to give it our best try."

3

All of the passengers and crew members of the *Culiacan* had been gathered in the *Culiacan's* dining room, most of them sitting at tables, some of the crew members squatting against the wall, beneath an immense mural of Popocatepetl and Ixtacihuatl covering one wall. Apt, Corwin thought as he came into the room, the portrait of a volcano, and there were three Japanese gunmen standing in almost rigid positions, muzzles of automatic weapons extended to cover the room, and the music system was playing a lively song from Vera Cruz, and yet as Corwin was ushered in there was not a stir of movement and he could feel the fear in the room. Conditioned, yes, too many films of terrorists, stories of erratic slaughters, and so they all sat at their tables like mannequins as if their practiced stillness could keep them alive.

Corwin was halted by the aide at least twenty feet from the group. "I want to speak to Senator Vetter and the head of the Mexican delegation."

Vetter stood up, rather stiffly, recognizable by his mane of hair, broad shoulders, appearing older in the flesh than he did on television, and a Mexican stood up as well, a smaller man of patrician bearing and they both looked at the Japanese gunmen as if anticipating resistance, then moved forward. Corwin looked to the Japanese gunman. "I wish to speak to them in private," he said in Japanese. "Away from the group."

The Japanese nodded toward an extension of the dining room where a folding wall had been drawn part way to provide a separate card-playing area. There were still cards on the tables, abandoned bridge hands given up when the *Culiacan* was seized. "I suggest you sit down," Corwin said to the two of them.

"Would you identify yourself, please?" Vetter said.

"My name is Corwin. I'm as much a prisoner as you are, but I've been appointed spokesman to relay their demands."

"I do not cooperate with people at gunpoint," Galvez said.

"We all cooperate with people at gunpoint," Corwin said.

"I suggest that we listen to their demands, Señor Galvez," Vetter said, ameliorating, looking toward the young Japanese with the automatic weapon held across the crook of his arm. "Does he speak English?" he said to Corwin. "Is he a part of this discussion?"

"You can assume that he understands every word we will say," Corwin said. "Not that it makes a goddamned bit of difference at this point." He sat down. Vetter took the place across from him. Galvez glared at the Japanese and then sat down. "I'll give you only the pertinent facts," Corwin said. "There are two plans operative here, but it seems that one overrides the other." He told Vetter about the conspiracy against him and the subsequent change of plans by the Japanese, and as he talked he could not even be sure that Vetter was believing him, for there was an expression of concern on Vetter's face, a practiced nodding of the head that was precisely correct, and it could be interpreted as a practiced political mannerism or as a real understanding, but in the end it made no difference. Vetter could either accept or reject the truth, but nothing would be changed by it.

Finally, Corwin took out the folded sheets containing the names of the prisoners in the Mexican jails, handed one to each man. "These are the men they wish to have released. He wants the exchange of hostages to be made off Acapulco. He also wants ten million dollars, American. He's already made the demands to your government."

Galvez looked up from the list with a skeptical eye. "Do you know what these men did?"

"That's beside the point."

"I will not recommend that a single one of them be released."

"I'd consider the cost before I decided to take a hard line," Corwin said. He had gone through the progression from despair to bravery to cooperation and now he was seized by a realistic numbness. He had neither the will nor the energy to drag Galvez past his resistance. "I don't think it makes a damn bit of difference whether you recommend or not, in the long run. You either cooperate or they'll kill everybody in this ship."

"Everybody?" Vetter said.

"Everybody."

"It's against my personal beliefs," Galvez said.

"Then I suggest you demonstrate those beliefs here and now," Corwin said. He looked toward the Japanese. "He appears to be perfectly at ease and if you asked him a question you would undoubtedly get a polite answer. But he's strung-out, you can count on that, tighter than a drum, and he's looking for a chance to release it. So challenge him here and he'll kill you where there's no chance of anybody else getting hurt."

"Nobody wants that," Vetter said, again the mediator. "In my experience, there's no problem that's not negotiable. Do you have a cigarette, Mr. Corwin?"

Vetter took the pack from Corwin and distributed the cigarettes himself, offering a light to Galvez and then lighting his own, perfectly timed. Corwin no longer cared whether he was sincere or not because Vetter's sense of the appropriate was going to be invaluable here and Galvez was already calming. Corwin could see the fright beneath the belligerent exterior and Vetter could see it as well. "This may not be the place for it, Mr. Corwin, but I want to know about the conspiracy against me. I don't want to believe it, so I am going to take some convincing."

"It's a new ball game, Senator," Corwin said. "The old rules don't apply anymore. Do you know an Englishman named Swann?"

Vetter frowned. "Lord Swann? Yes, I've met him."

"How about a man with the Petroleum Carriers, Campbell?"

"In San Francisco?"

"Yes."

"I know him."

"There may be a dozen of them you don't know. But they know you."

"And they really think they can change the energy policy of the country by killing me?"

"No, they can keep you from bringing about any changes. And it would work, wouldn't it, Senator?"

Vetter displayed a thoughtful frown. "I suppose it might," he said. He inhaled the cigarette. "If Señor Galvez and myself are the key figures here, the main hostages, then there's no point to holding the rest of these people. Do you think he might agree to release them?"

"I don't know," Corwin said. "I'll suggest it. I'm going to need your full cooperation, Senator, your willingness to relay a message to the government stating that you've been well treated and asking that the tanker be allowed to steam out of the port with no interference from the American armed forces."

"I'll be glad to do that," he said.

"At the same time, see if you can get the media people to cooperate in carrying Okata's message. I think it will reduce the steam in him."

"Certainly," Vetter said. "If there's to be a money payment, I can also arrange that, if it's to be paid here, in the interest of saving time."

"I'll see." He looked to Galvez. "I will need the same guarantee from you, Mr. Galvez, concerning the political prisoners."

"They are not political prisoners," Galvez said. "They killed two dozen people."

"Will you agree to make the request? That's all I'm asking."

Galvez tapped the cigarette with the tip of his index finger. The ashes showered onto the table. "I'll make the request," he said, finally. "At the same time I will tell you that I hope they refuse."

"I'll pass on the willingness," Corwin said.

He stood up and the Japanese motioned with the rifle that Galvez and Vetter should join the others. As Corwin went out onto the deck, the feeling of unreality persisted. He could hear the strains of a mariachi band floating through the air behind him and ahead of him he could see the flames up the channel reflected in the water of the swimming pool on the foredeck. The distant smoke was so dense he could not see the extent of the burning area, and he allowed his mind to drift away from this moment, picturing Faye in Palm Springs, by the side of a swimming pool in the darkness, insulated from what was happening here.

And in that moment, with the realization that there was nothing he could do to insulate himself from dying, he felt something relax within him and no longer really gave a damn what happened to himself or any of the others. He would anchor to something different, something uncomplicated, set himself a goal. The ship, this old woman of a ship, ready for the scrap heap in another couple of years, he would make the tanker his problem and he would get her out of this channel before he was through.

There was an acrid stench in the air as he boarded the tanker, smoke, a thousand substances burning, metals melting, and he wondered if he himself would emit a particular stench if he were vaporized. He went to the bridge where Okata was perched on a stool, peering through a pair of binoculars at the fire back to the north. Corwin was no longer intimidated; the gratitude had evaporated. He found the bottle and poured himself a drink, comforted by the semi-darkness of the wheelhouse. He sat down in the captain's chair and put his feet up.

"What are you doing?" Okata said, and Corwin could see that Okata was finally discomfited, on guard. He rejoiced in the power to bring him to that point.

"They've agreed to your terms, Admiral," Corwin said with a smile. "They will both send messages to their governments and the senator will use his influence to get you on American television where you can exercise your ego, although at the moment I don't see how he's going to bring that about. And I imagine that unless somebody fucks up, you'll be able to sail out of here without a lot of difficulty." He raised the glass in Okata's direction. *"Compai,"* he said, He sipped it. Strong. His stomach burned.

"What's the matter with you?" Okata said. *"Baka, ne?* Or drunk."

"Neither drunk nor crazy."

"Then what are you doing?"

"Listen, Okata, everybody's trying to pressure everybody else into something and suddenly I don't give a shit. I win if I can get this tanker out of the harbor without its blowing up."

Okata was very disconcerted now. He lifted a skeletal carbine. "I am in command here. You can't even protect yourself."

"True."

"We do not depend on you in any way."

"Of course not."

"Then what do you want? I don't have to bargain with you."

"I'm not suggesting any bargains," Corwin said. "Sooner or later, somebody will get you, probably in some minor goddamned incident, nothing major, a man plinking you through the back of the head while you're eating dinner or fucking and feeling perfectly safe. That's not my concern.

As for myself, I may die in the next few minutes or I may live to be an old man and die of a heart attack, but that's no more important than how or when you die." He put the glass down. "I think you're erratic as hell and I know the men ashore are just as erratic, and the men you're proposing to take hostage are unpredictable too. At any minute, any one of a dozen people could make one misstep and the whole thing would be over. But I think I can get the ship out of the harbor because I'm not tied up in the bullshit on either side."

Now he could see that Okata was intrigued, his Japanese mind searching for ways of making use of this new attitude, and he put the carbine back against the bulkhead. "All right," he said, making a decision. "If you aid in getting the ship out of the harbor, I will put you ashore when we make the exchange at Acapulco."

"That's neither here nor there," Corwin said. "I don't intend to explain it any more than I already have. But I will get the tanker out of the harbor. You have Ives on board?"

"Yes."

"Have him brought up here. But first, how many of your men on the *Culiacan* speak fluent English?"

"Three of them."

"Have one of them get Vetter and Galvez to the *Culiacan's* radio room. Allow both of them to speak to the authorities ashore. They'll probably play this the way they've agreed to play it, but it wouldn't make a hell of a lot of difference in the long run. They could plead with their governments not to honor your demands and the governments would pay anyway. It's far easier for a government to give in to rescue brave men. And then I want to see Ives."

Okata nodded, gave instructions to an aide standing guard in the doorway. Then he picked up the binoculars and trained them on the fires.

In a few minutes, Ives came through the door, bewildered,

a stubble of beard on his face, ashen, eyes blinking, suit rumpled. He stared at Corwin as if he could not believe Corwin were really here.

"Well, George," Corwin said. "You look like you've been sandbagged."

"What's going on?" Ives said, no fire left in him. He saw the whiskey bottle, looked to Okata for permission, and poured himself a drink. "Are you with them now?" he said to Corwin.

"Would it make any difference?" Corwin said. He watched Ives consume the glass of Suntory. "I feel sorry for you, Ives. You're a poor hungry son of a bitch who bit off more than he can chew and you're choking on it."

Ives wiped his mouth. "What do you want with me?"

"That depends on the Admiral here," Corwin said. He looked to Okata. "I suggest you send him ashore."

"For what reason?"

"Strategy," Corwin said. "If I'm right, there are a group of hawks who want nothing more than to blow you out of the water despite any bargains. You release one man and it will give support to the doves who are pushing for a compromise."

"Ah," Okata said with a smile. "So your price is revenge, correct? Because he can inform them of the true nature of the conspiracy, vindicate you."

"Mr. Ives here is a drunk," Corwin said. "He has no proof of anything. I suggest sending him because he was an important man and he's totally useless to you. If you want to pick one of the Americans or Mexicans instead, then go ahead."

Okata studied Ives a moment and then nodded. "He will be allowed to go ashore. He will carry the message that we will honor any bargain we make. And he will not be escorted ashore."

"Whatever conditions you want," Corwin said. "But he's

in no condition to relay any messages. I want radio communication myself. I'll explain it to them."

"There will be a man with you who speaks English."

Corwin smiled slightly. "I'm beyond threats now, Admiral. So have me monitored. If you don't like what I say, have me shot." He stood up.

Ives appeared to be bewildered. "I'm to be sent ashore," he said. "I'm to be turned loose."

"You're a gesture, George, a rather pathetic one, but you should give us all an extra hour or two of time, so you do count for something."

Ives nodded. "I will want to call my wife. She'll be worried sick about me."

4

The operator looked up from the switchboard. "The *Culiacan* is lowering a boat. Okata says this is a gesture of goodwill."

O'Brien nodded, went outside, grabbed a pair of binoculars from one of his men. Forms, shapes, and his eyes refused to pick up the details lost in the shadows, but a boat was being lowered with what appeared to be a solitary man in it. "Get a light on him," O'Brien said, and a powerful beam of light shot across the water and speared the boat as the man started the motor.

Shuman came down the dock, peering out toward the boat. "Can you make him out?"

"Caucasian male, late fifties, early sixties. Business suit," O'Brien said, his voice even. "How are your boys doing?"

"We're going to need an hour," Shuman said. "We have a special team we can put in the water from slip two twenty-one. But I don't think we're going to get the time."

"Oh?"

"The story about the two terrorists dead in Mexico City is out," Shuman said. "I have public information contacting the media, but they don't have a pooled operation here. Shit, they could break the news anytime."

"True," O'Brien said. And for the first time he was truly aware of the media coverage and the recognition that the image of the man in the boat making his way toward the oil dock had been picked up by a dozen cameras, and even now television researchers would be seeking to identify him.

The boat came alongside the dock and a half-dozen men helped the man from the boat, and he stood unsteadily in front of O'Brien and Shuman, one hand placed flat across his chest as if to make certain his heart was still beating. The man reeked of alcohol. "My God, I thought they were going to kill me."

"I am Special Agent O'Brien, Federal Bureau of Investigation, and this is Commander Shuman of the Coast Guard. Who are you?"

"Ives. George Ives," the man said, and Shuman placed him immediately, Ives, the shipbuilder, the conspirator in Corwin's account, once a powerful man but now frightened, disheveled, more than a little drunk. He fumbled with a cigarette, which Shuman lighted for him, trying to phrase the one key question in the jumble of questions that could be asked, for time was running out. O'Brien was filling the vacuum, coaxing Ives into an account, debriefing him, one piece of information at a time. The number of Japanese on the *Persevera*: twenty-five as nearly as Ives could judge; the number of explosive devices: none, as far as Ives could determine.

"None?" Shuman said. "They announced themselves that the ship was wired."

"They don't need explosives," Ives said. "The fucking ship is a bomb. They could fire into a hatch and set it off." He sucked on the cigarette. "Corwin wants time. He persuaded

Okata to dump me ashore to show that he's reasonable, that he'll honor any bargain he makes."

The key question was there suddenly, in Shuman's mind. "How flexible is Okata?" he said. "Is he willing to compromise on his demands?"

"He's a crazy bastard," Ives said. "I need to call my wife."

"You didn't answer my question," Shuman said. "Will he compromise? Will he take less than he asks?"

Ives shook his head slowly, deliberately. "He's a crazy man," he said. "And you better give him exactly what he asks for. Because if you don't, he's going to blow this part of the harbor into little pieces. Very little pieces."

5

The guard signaled Corwin, a wave of the hand, and he went into the wheelhouse. He was directed to the radio room where the Japanese radio operator was having trouble translating the message he was receiving from English into Japanese.

"I'll take over," Corwin said, in Japanese, and the young man grimaced at him and yielded, reluctantly, and Corwin sat down. "Would you repeat the message, please?" he said, and then began to take notes, jotting down the information on a pad. It was the Mexican consul in Los Angeles and he was preparing to go on television, but he was not sure that there was a television set aboard the *Persevera* so he was relaying the text of his speech in advance.

The Mexican government was fully ready to cooperate and agreed to the release of the Japanese being held in Mexico City. The exchange would take place off Acapulco where the money would be paid and the Mexican government would provide refueling for the *Persevera* at that time. The Mexican government was asking for the release of some of the nonessential crew members and the secretaries and aides to both delegations. "If your captain wishes reassurance on any of these points, or if he wishes to discuss them with me personally, I will be available on this frequency," the consul said. "We are acting in good faith for the benefit of all concerned."

Corwin signed off and leaned back in the chair, contemplating the scribbled notes, and the idea seemed to be in his mind all at once, full grown. He added a few words to his notes and then offered them to the radio operator who simply glanced at them, waved them away, and resumed his place at the headphones. Corwin took his time, looking out the companionway at the sweep of the ship bathed in the work lights, the catwalk running to the engineers' section, the whole solid, substantial.

He went to the captain's quarters, trailed by his guard. Okata was watching a color television set, pictures of the flames in the upper harbor, live coverage of the two ships from one of the helicopters standing off to the west, and he almost laughed aloud at the ridiculousness of the situation, in which Okata, at the center of this shit storm was peering intently at the screen as if to see what he himself would do. There was a commentary from Washington now, an interview with an official on the background and treatment of terrorism, and there was a congressional committee and a negotiating team on the way to California. Filler, yes, a pause to move away from the saturation coverage of fires and incipient violence that was taking too long to happen, and they were instinctively trying to work what was happening into a comprehensible drama, to give it form.

Okata was feeling the strain. He stood up, fidgeting, pulling a clip out of an automatic weapon, flicking the thin edge of a protruding spring with his thumbnail. He put the clip back into place.

"I just talked to the Mexican consul," Corwin said.

"So?" Okata said, sharply. "Why did you talk to the Mexican consul? How? My radio operator is responsible for such communications. Why did he allow this?"

"The consul has a heavy Mexican accent. Your man couldn't understand what he was saying."

"Are you telling me how to do things?" Okata said, with mounting irritation. "I make the decisions. I say what to do and what not to do. I am getting tired of waiting."

"You're a realistic man, Admiral," Corwin said, sitting down. "He's going to come on television in a few minutes to give you his message face-to-face. But there are other things he told me that were to be delivered to you personally and alone. First, they'll meet your conditions for the exchange of hostages. They'll also provide refueling and a safe passage through Mexican waters."

"I don't leave them any choice."

"Don't fool yourself," Corwin said. "Hell, the Americans are not that simplistic. There's a large group of them that's angry because Americans are being held hostage in a dispute that doesn't involve the United States as far as they know, especially when they're not too happy with the current Mexican government anyway." The words were coming easier now, the great verbal drift, and he allowed himself the luxury of silence, poking around among the bottles in the liquor cabinet, aware that Okata was growing more restive by the moment, the television set droning on in the background with, ironically, an oil company commercial, as if bringing the incident full circle, disassociation by association. He found another bottle of Suntory, slit the seal with his thumbnail. "The American government doesn't give a shit about you except that you're a current threat to physical property."

"What are you suggesting?"

Corwin filled his glass. "The Mexican consul made a suggestion, not in exact language of course. But he left a door open. If you release all the Americans here, then the situation will be between you and Mexico, a clear-cut diversion, no way to misinterpret what you're doing. The Americans will have to let you sail out of here with Mexican hostages because the Mexican government will demand it. You can trade for your men at Acapulco and still keep enough hostages to guarantee your safe passage."

He sipped the Suntory. It was tasteless now. He was aware that he was rewriting the present, reshaping the moment, but it was important that Okata should be left an opening, a way out of the situation in which he would appear to triumph.

And a peculiar thing happened, for Okata's fretfulness passed and he became thoughtful, sitting in a chair with the carbine across his lap, beginning to speak in Japanese. Corwin sat and listened and it seemed that Okata was trying to justify himself, like a character in a traditional Japanese drama, and he said he should have taken the tanker himself, captured it by superior strength so there would be no *on* involved, no spirit of obligation. In the end the power structures of the world would collapse upon themselves. He had bargained with Swann to kill the Americans. Now he felt that obligation had been discharged by Swann's treachery.

Corwin lifted his glass. "To your revolution, Admiral."

"You? Revolution?"

"Hell, yes. What do you think I'm doing here? In my own way, I'm a dyed-in-the-wool revolutionary. They're trying to take over by killing some enemies who I happen to believe are worthwhile people. I mean to change things. So I begin by preserving this ship." He forced himself away from his own interior. His hands were hurting. The gauze around the palm of his right hand was irritating the flesh.

"If I choose to let the Americans go, I want more money from the Mexican government."

"How much?"

"Another million dollars."

Corwin shrugged. Okata was converted; Corwin had won and yet the victory seemed to wash past him like a low wave that he perceived but did not feel and now he would have to move into action, to implement the new course before something happened to change the situation. "They will pay the money."

"You make the arrangements. Eleven million dollars."

Corwin nodded. Reluctantly, he put the cap back on the bottle, put it back into the cabinet. He went back to the radio room, trailed by his guard. In Japanese he told the operator to tune to the emergency frequency and get the consul on the line. The operator did as he was told and then moved out of the chair as if he instinctively knew that Corwin had the authority now.

"This is Corwin," he said. "I've been authorized by Captain Okata to serve as an intermediary here. Is that agreeable with you?"

"Yes," the consul said.

"I will rely on your discretion in what I'm about to say," Corwin said. "This is a highly delicate and volatile situation, but I don't have to tell you that."

"I understand."

"Captain Okata is willing to release all the Americans aboard the *Culiacan*. All of the arrangements will be made from this end and they will be put ashore at the oil dock. The Mexican nationals will be taken aboard the *Persevera* once the Americans are released. Captain Okata wants a payment of eleven million dollars."

"The money is no problem."

"Captain Okata will need the services of a tug that will be manned by a minimum crew. I want to remind the American authorities that any attempt to use the tug as a carrier for troops or agents will result in an absolute disaster. Is that clear?"

"Perfectly. But I won't need to inform the Americans. They are monitoring this channel."

"I'm aware of that. But I want your government to insist on this."

There was no immediate response and Corwin could hear the voices in the background discussing, arguing. "I'm not certain that I can guarantee American cooperation on my level."

"You don't seem to understand," Corwin said. "There's no time for protocol on this."

"I understand. We'll do our best. When will the Americans be released?"

"Within a half hour. The American pilot will be retained on board and allowed to leave on the tug after the *Persevera* clears the breakwater."

There was some confusion on the consul's end of the line and Corwin could feel the hesitation there. "You do understand that I will have to confer with my government before all this is absolute."

"Goddamnit," Corwin said. "I'm telling you the way things are going to be. You drag your feet now and you'll screw it up. You don't have any choice but to accept, unconditionally." He terminated the conversation.

He went back to the captain's quarters and from the moment he entered the room, he could see that Okata had gone through another shift in mood. For he was preening himself in front of a mirror, adjusting the white band about his head until he was satisfied with it, and his hair had been perfectly combed, a raven's wing black. There was a hard set to his face.

Jesus, Corwin thought, they were going to make it impossible in the end, the bureaucrats on one hand who would delay and stall, seeking consensus, and this actor-revolutionary on the other who might decide to change his mind at a moment's notice. "The Mexican government has agreed through their consul," Corwin said, calmly. "I think we had better have a direct communication with the American authorities now so we have no misunderstandings there."

"Denied," Okata said. He turned slightly to see himself from a different angle. "It would prove the stupidity of a capitalist society if they fire on their own people. It would demonstrate their bad faith."

Gestures again, Corwin thought, demonstrations to prove that Okata's enemies were wrong, even at the cost of his own life. He said nothing. This was no time to argue.

Okata picked up the telephone and gave orders in Japanese to a man aboard the *Culiacan*. The Americans were to be separated from the Japanese and television sets would be provided for all the hostages to hear the remarks of the Mexican consul. He put the telephone back on the cradle.

"I am ready to go," he said. His eyes were cold.

6

SHUMAN WAS STUDYING THE *Culiacan* THROUGH THE BINOCU-lars, the line trailing into the water from the davit that had lowered the boat carrying Ives. Access, yes, his men could use that line, and in his cockiness, Okata had been careless, making a number of mistakes, not consolidating his operation, not moving his hostages aboard the tanker immediately. And he could see one of the Japanese at the bow of the *Culiacan*, fully exposed, leaning against the railing with his carbine, one of Okata's lookouts certainly, and another man was posted amidships, in shadow, profiled. Just possible, Shuman thought, just possible his men could bring it off.

O'Brien came out of the dock house to join him. "What's your schedule?" he said, and from his tone of voice, Shuman knew that there was another complication. "We're committed," Shuman said. "Our men are in the water. They'll be boarding in approximately three minutes."

"We've just received another signal from the *Persevera*," O'Brien said. "They say they will agree to release all the Americans."

"Shit," Shuman said, abruptly.

"You can't abort the attack?" O'Brien said, quietly.

Shuman shook his head. "No." He forced himself to breathe. He opened his mouth and with conscious effort sucked in air. "Are they telling the truth?" he said. "Are they really intending to release the Americans?"

"We couldn't count on it," O'Brien said. "Even if we weren't committed. We've discussed this kind of thing. The studies on terrorism are filled with this strategy. They dangle all sorts of false hopes to gain time when they have no intention of carrying through. We're doing the right thing, the only thing we can do."

"Yes," Shuman said, gratefully. "The only thing we can do."

2

Perfect staging, Corwin thought, and when Okata entered the dining room there was a sense of form established here, with the Mexicans sitting at the tables, awaiting an explanation, and the Americans standing near the polished bar, Vetter slightly in front of the rest of his men. And three color television sets had been brought into the dining room and set up facing the hostages, the sound turned down, different channels, one showing the fire consuming an old wooden dock, fireboats pumping, and another displaying a helicopter-shot of the two ships locked together and the third showing an old film of a swaggering Okata in black and white during a demonstration in Tokyo. But there was nothing swaggering about Okata now, and the moment he came into the presence of the hostages, his manner became congenial and he smiled as if he were welcoming them to a social event.

"Good evening," Okata said to the Mexicans with a pleasant bow. He smiled to Vetter. "I hope that you have not been too uncomfortable. The Red Watch is not a merciless organization. You have heard that we are merciless, correct? But the question is what we are doing in the world and that is to make it better. We are not unaware of human feelings."

The ham, Corwin thought, the actor who could not resist

a final scene with a captive audience, and he would have an opportunity to exercise his theatrical and political rhetoric here. "If you are frightened, that is an appropriate feeling and I would take to heart the warning you have experienced here." Corwin tuned him out, making his decision now. He would go ashore with the Americans. He had done all he could. What he had begun in Tokyo was now almost finished. He rubbed his palms together lightly, impatiently, waiting for Okata to be finished. "This time we are dealing with the Republic of Mexico and as you will soon hear, they have agreed to release our comrades in Mexico City from political imprisonment and to pay indemnity for their wrongness of attitude. In this agreement, to show the good will of the Red Watch, we will release all American citizens."

There was a stir of protest in the group of Mexicans, no more than that, and among the Americans a feeling that Corwin could not identify at first, no instant jubilation, and then he saw Vetter's face, that noble truculence. Christ, Vetter was going to make another one of his heroic gestures, but he did not get the chance. For the face of the Mexican consul appeared on one of the television screens, a round face with a moustache and hair swept straight back from a sparse crown. He was sitting behind a desk with the flag of Mexico mounted behind him and he was visibly distressed, uncomfortable with his role, reading from a prepared statement.

"I have been authorized by my government to make the following announcement . . ." All of them watching now, the mesmerizing effect of a face on a tube, stating in a heavily accented English the agreement that had been made, and Corwin was watching Vetter's face as he listened. The time for gestures had passed. Vetter would accept the reprieve without protest. "In releasing the six prisoners in Mexico City, we demonstrate our belief that, in this regrettable situation, the preservation of human lives is of paramount importance."

The perfect tone, noninflammatory, and yet Okata was frowning furiously and he was not looking at the Mexican consul at all but at the picture on one of the other sets, not the face of the Mexican consul but black-and-white photographs of the faces of Japanese men, and Okata ordered the sound turned down on the set carrying the consul's remarks and turned up the volume on the second set himself. "And according to reliable sources," the voice was saying, "the deaths of the two Japanese prisoners in Mexico City last week were caused by an attack on a guard . . ."

Gone now, in the flicker of an eyelid, blown all to hell, an incredible blunder someplace and at first Okata stood where he was, frozen until the impact of what he was hearing struck him. Now was the time for Corwin to move, to say something, but he could not move, for he saw the terrible look on Okata's face. With a hoarse yell, Okata grabbed the machine gun from one of his men and sprayed all three television sets, the tubes exploding in a shower of sparks; he turned toward the Mexican delegation, the weapon still firing and just as Galvez was in the act of standing, the bullets exploded a line across his chest as if he were erupting and he fell backward, collapsing his chair.

Corwin saw the shadows through the small windows on the starboard side, realized the Americans had boarded, and two Americans in wet suits burst through the door, firing submachine guns. Gone, hopeless, too late, and Corwin was on the floor without knowing he had fallen, scrambling away, the room thick with screaming, running people, the acrid smell of cordite, more firing, and one of the Japanese fell sprawling near him, half of his face torn away. Boarded, yes, and in an impossible situation the Americans had decided to act and he saw one of them fall to a half crouch, fishlike in his wet suit, firing, yelling something, and Corwin grabbed the automatic weapon that had fallen from the hands of the Japanese and scrambled behind the bar.

Broken bottles. The smell of alcohol. Were the terrorists retreating? He could not tell, but quite suddenly the firing stopped and he looked around the side of the bar, dazed, bodies sprawled on the floor, blood, a hand outstretched, men runing toward the starboard deck. He stood up, waiting, cautious, and then he went through the door and into the open air, gasping, sick to his stomach. He could see people going over the side into the black water far below and hear the sound of a bullhorn from the oil dock, words he could not understand.

He moved forward on the starboard side, staying in the shadows. There was gunfire on the port side of the ship. The Japanese had retreated and there was a small fire on the deck of the *Culiacan* and he expected at any moment to see the flash from the exploding tanker, which would be the last thing he would ever see, and he would never hear the sound.

Incredibly, it did not come. As he rounded the corner near the swimming pool, he saw the Americans in position on the far side of the deck, holding their fire. The Japanese had retreated down onto the deck of the *Persevera*. Ah, Okata, you canny son of a bitch, Corwin thought, you fucking nontraditional Japanese, you're not going to incinerate yourself. No, he was certain Okata was going to make a run for it, pragmatist to the end, and the Americans were not going to try to stop him from here.

Corwin could hear the engines throbbing in the *Persevera*, revving up, lines cast off, the hull of the tanker groaning against the hull of the *Culiacan* for an interminable moment before the screw caught the water and the *Persevera* began to pull away. The tanker crawled, yawed back to bump the *Culiacan*, then began to make headway, pushing out into the channel.

It was then the thought occurred to him, the wild possibility, and he ran up the companionway, ascending to the bridge, flights of stairs, and when he reached the wheelhouse, he was out of breath, dizzy, his heart pounding. Deserted. Everybody long gone. He went out onto the port bridgewing, staring toward the tanker that was by now retreating into the wispy fog. Not retreating, no, not heading down the channel, but instead angling toward a battery of oil tanks on the downstream starboard side of the channel. Okata was playing his role now, the Kamikaze pilot to the end, knowing that if he reached open water the Americans would not let him go.

His lungs were hurting; the sweat was pouring out of his scalp. He propped the automatic weapon on the railing, his eyes straining against the flickering reflection of the flames on the tanker, looking for shapes on the bridge, for Okata. If he could bring Okata down, perhaps Okata's men would not be so anxious to immolate themselves. Perhaps the plan existed only in Okata's mind.

Corwin thought he saw Okata on the bridgewing of the tanker, standing outside the wheelhouse for better visibility, calling orders to his helmsman, but he could not be sure; a shadow softer than a field of shadows, the form blending with the darkened door to the wheelhouse. He drew a deep breath, held it, and his finger tightened against the trigger. The automatic rifle bucked, fired a stream of bullets into the darkness, and when his vision cleared he could no longer see the man on the bridgewing.

The tanker veered slightly, course corrected to carry it down the channel. Corwin saw a man scrambling down the catwalk and knew where he was going. He centered him, led him, squeezing off burst after burst, but the man did not stop. He disappeared behind the catwalk and Corwin could not see him but knew what he was doing, turning the valves, the deck beginning to glisten with gasoline as if it were bleeding. And then Corwin saw the stuttering burst of fire from a carbine, little stabs of light, the sound muted by the distance, delayed, and suddenly the fire began to run along the deck, a flashing sheet of flames.

The flames leaped up amidship, burning away the fog, and the first explosion occurred in one of the deck pipes and the catwalk seemed to peel away from the tanker, intact, flinging itself high into the air, noiselessly, and then came the sound, like the explosion of a giant cannon, followed by an intense and blinding light as the center tanks of the *Persevera* went up in a fireball that flashed into the sky, rocketing hundreds of feet straight up, so bright that Corwin was temporarily blinded, and then he was knocked off his feet by the force of the concussion and the *Culiacan* rocked wildly and the plates of the tanker's hull were shredded and flew outward. Corwin lay on the deck, hearing the glass shatter in the wheelhouse windows, the ship trembling beneath him.

Another explosion, pure white light, concussion and the stern section of the tanker was thrown away at a crazy angle and flipped over on its side, the propeller turning in the night air, the foresection still incredibly intact, afloat, covered with fire as if the metal itself were burning, the foretanks spilling, covering the water with burning gasoline, great coils of boiling black smoke, and then there was a submerged explosion in the bow, a hissing of steam and another rupture of the deck plates, like the opening of a metal coffin and the bridge was twisted off the hull and thrown a hundred yards into the harbor, sinking immediately. No more explosions, only the roar of the fire, steam from the burning sea, and Corwin stood up, shakily, numbed, his skin feeling the uncomfortable heat of the fire, even from this distance.

Over, finished. The tanker had cleared the point before it exploded and the flaming gasoline was in the open harbor, and there were no peripheral fires, no wind, and with the ebbing tide the flames would be carried toward the break-water. He dropped the automatic rifle overboard, the black water swallowing it without a sound.

And at that moment the realization hit him and he stopped short, leaning against the rail, blinking at the burning gasoline.

All dead, and that included Swann who had stayed aboard the tanker.

3

"Eight Mexican nationals dead," Corwin said. "Five of them energy officials. Sixteen wounded Mexicans. Two of the attack team dead. All of the Japanese." He peered through the windshield, looking for his turnoff. "And Swann." He looked over at Faye, then touched the solid flesh of her leg, needing contact.

Vetter would be waiting for him, at a spot Corwin had stipulated, the deserted Union Oil dock where Vetter would be alone, without the presence of media, the stenographers, the conditions of a formal meeting. But now, in the bright morning sunshine, he was not so sure he wanted to go through with it.

Faye's hand covered his. "It's almost too much," she said. "Right, Charlie Brown?"

"Almost too much," he said. "What do you say we turn around right now and head for the desert?"

"And leave the senator in the lurch?"

"Right in the goddamned lurch."

"Bad idea," she said. "For you, I mean. You need to finish this, for yourself."

"Hell, there's nothing that can finish it."

"I suspect there is." She looked out the window and he knew she was seeing her house, up there on the rise. She smiled slightly. "The explosion broke the windows, nothing more. But I won't be living in it again." She shook her head, wonderingly. "What's going to happen now? Will they ever straighten it out?"

"No," he said.

"You're being unusually pessimistic."

"Realistic," he said, remembering the face of the FBI agent as he took Corwin's statement with the lack of curiosity that implied disbelief. "Swann's dead, yet still Campbell has confessed to the whole thing, the plot against the Mexicans, putting the terrorists on the tanker. Nobody can get past him even if they want to dig deeper." He laughed aloud. "The absolute craziness of it."

"You're in a rare mood."

"Compounded insanity impresses me that way. Why didn't they make a direct attack on Vetter? Because they're all infected with a sense of dramatic power, with scenarios and computer projections, everything designed to obscure the real reason behind anything. Everybody's all caught up in the complexity of grand schemes."

They were passing an official building now where workmen were removing slabs of plywood from the shattered windows, preparing to reglaze them. He turned left, drove down toward the dock, which sat by itself at the end of a sandy spit of land, no buildings other than a small office next to the chain link fence, the automated hose-handling arms hanging stiff and inactive.

Off to the left, he could see the man-made mountain of powdered black iron ore extending in a ridge to the north, waiting to be shipped. The senator's black Mercedes was parked next to the gate.

He stopped the car, leaned over and kissed her.

"What was that for?" she said.

"A demonstration that I take nothing for granted," he said. "This shouldn't take very long."

There was a strong breeze blowing in off the water and

out in the harbor the cranes were at work clearing the channel, grappling for the remains of the *Persevera*. The senator climbed out of his Mercedes, in his shirt sleeves, his arms tanned and muscular, his fine brown hair tousled in the wind. Corwin could read his signals. The senator was going to play this one informal and relaxed, but he wanted something.

They exchanged greetings and Corwin followed the senator to the gate and out onto the concrete dock, which stretched a quarter of a mile along the spit of land. "I'm glad to have this opportunity to talk to you, Mr. Corwin," the senator said. "We've all been through a hell of an ordeal and it's good to have it resolved."

"The incident's over but nothing is resolved," Corwin said.

"I think it is. Campbell has confessed to the whole thing, an unfortunate and terrible business. We shall have some fence mending to do with the Mexican government."

"And Swann?" Corwin said sharply. "How do you explain him away?"

"He's dead, after all," Vetter said. "The story is going around that he discovered what was happening and tried to stop it and died in the process."

Corwin looked off into the harbor, the reflection of the sun on the water so bright it hurt his eyes. He could see divers in wet suits working off the crane barges, looking like human seals. "It's all bullshit, Senator, and I think you know it. I was there. I was Swann's intended victim."

"If you can give me one shred of proof, one bit of hard evidence to support what you're saying, then I'll give you my personal guarantee that nothing will be swept under the rug," Vetter said.

"What do you really want from me?" Corwin said.

"I read the statement you made against Swann. Unless you have objective proof, I want you to withdraw it. If you make a charge against the oil industry that you can't support, then it inhibits my investigation and puts everything on a different level. It's entirely possible that the government and the oil industry can effect a compromise concerning divestiture, pricing, all the issues. There are a great many petroleum executives who are true patriots, Mr. Corwin. To link them in the public mind with any terrorist attack would split any possibility of meaningful compromise." Vetter was silent a moment. "And even if what you say is true, Swann's dead. And what he was doing is over."

"Is it?" Corwin said with a tight smile. "You're right. Swann's dead and that means Campbell could have implicated him, told the truth. But he didn't. Swann may be gone, but the others who were in on the plan will pay Campbell well to accept the blame and the responsibility. So just because Swann's gone doesn't mean they'll give up."

"I'll take that chance."

Corwin looked off at the mountainous ridge of iron ore. "There's your paradox," he said.

"I don't follow you."

"When the companies first began to pile the ore there, nobody had any objections. It seemed a good idea because no one was hurt by it. But pretty soon somebody discovered the wind was picking up dust from that ore and polluting the atmosphere. So the companies said fine, no problem, and they began to wet it down to keep it from blowing. And then, to everybody's horror, it was discovered that the weight of that wet-down ridge was so immense that the ground beneath it was steadily sinking. The ore should never have been put there in the first place, but now there's such a massive pile of it that there's no practical way to move it. So everybody either has to breathe the contaminated air or watch the land sink."

"If that's a metaphor for the oil companies, I don't see it," Vetter said. "They're seeking an honest solution to the problem as I am. We just have a different view."

"Shit," Corwin said with a humorless laugh, realizing that he had begun in the position Vetter now occupied, the rational man seeking reasonable conclusions. "They're as immovable as that pile of ore. They're not willing to compromise. The whole plot was conceived to destroy you, Senator, to wipe you off the face of the earth. You're an honest man, I believe that and the country believes it and that makes you one hell of a threat to them."

If Vetter was shaken, he did not show it. "If you believe in what I'm doing, you won't compromise it."

A clear-cut course and Corwin could see it now. "If I do nothing, then in a few months, when everything dies down, they'll try again, something a good deal more simple, I would guess. You'll be hit by a truck or die of a heart attack, nothing that will cause the slightest suspicion, but they'll be behind it." He shook his head. "I intend to release the whole thing to the papers, the whole goddamned plot. Now, it may be that nobody will believe it and nothing will come of it and within six months most of it will be forgotten. But if anything happens to you, Senator, or to me, then that will give final credence to the story and there will be enough investigative reporters crawling over the whole operation to blow it wide open."

"I can't stop you," Vetter said. "But I think you will be doing the wrong thing. You don't have any evidence."

"I'll find it," Corwin said. "They left holes, you know. Okata was berthed here for three days. The company that did business with him had to know what he was here for. That will do as a start."

"Perhaps," Vetter said. He smiled slightly. "I'm not in any position to fault you for sticking to your convictions, am I?"

Corwin suddenly felt very free, as if a heavy load had been lifted from him and very soon this would be behind him and he would be crossing the desert with Faye, with absolutely no idea where he was going but with an absolute conviction about what he was going to do. He extended his hand to the senator. "You're a good man, Vetter. Keep your guard up."

He turned and walked back to the car.

"Well," Faye said. "Finished?"

"For the time being," he said. And at that moment, far out in the harbor, he saw the cranes lifting the wreckage of the bridge from the water, the sunlight reflecting off the twisted steel, the windows like vacant eyes, and in some way it struck him as perfectly appropriate, a sign, beautiful in its own way. And he started the car and with no great speed turned around and began to drive away.